Made in the USA
Monee, IL
29 March 2022

The Know-it-all's Guide to Life

How to climb Mount Everest, cure hiccups, live to 100, and dozens of other practical, unusual, or just plain fantastical things

By
John T. Walbaum

CAREER
PRESS

THE CAREER PRESS, INC.
Franklin Lakes, NJ

THE KNOW-IT-ALL'S GUIDE TO LIFE
EDITED AND TYPESET BY NICOLE DEFELICE
Cover design by Cheryl Cohan Finbow
Printed in the U.S.A. by Book-mart Press

To order this title, please call toll-free 1-800-CAREER-1 (NJ and Canada: 201-848-0310) to order using VISA or MasterCard, or for further information on books from Career Press.

The Career Press, Inc., 3 Tice Road, PO Box 687,
Franklin Lakes, NJ 07417
www.careerpress.com

Library of Congress Cataloging-in-Publication Data

Walbaum, John T.
    The know-it-all's guide to life : how to climb Mount Everest, cure hiccups, live to 100, and dozens of other practical, unusual, or just plain fantastical things / by John T. Walbaum.
        p. cm.
    Includes bibliographical references and index.
    ISBN 1-56414-673-1 (paper)
    1. Life skills—Handbooks, manuals, etc. 2. Self-help techniques. I. Title: How to climb Mount Everest, cure hiccups, live to 100, and dozens of other practical, unusual, or just plain fantastical things. II. Title.

    HQ2037 .W35 2003
    646.7—dc21

                                                        2002041250

Dedication

For my wife, Margot. Without her constant love and support, this book would not have been written.

Acknowledgments

I am indebted to many people for their assistance in preparing this book. In no particular order, I would like to thank Gordon Janow with Alpine Ascents International on climbing Mount Everest; Kyle Steckel with Military Adventures and Greg Claxtom of Incredible Adventures on flying MiGs; Paul Turner on being a movie extra; Jim Carlson on jury selection; Amir Aczel of Bentley College on income tax audits; Anita Walbaum and Ed McClure for IQ Tests and Questions; Claudia Bourne Farrell with the Federal Trade Commission on identity theft; Evan Cattanach of Schieffelin & Sommerset and Richard Paterson, master blender at The Dalmore, on single malt whisky; Dave Hughes on curing hiccups; Dr. Jack M. Gwaltney at the University of Virginia School of Medicine on avoiding the common cold, and Mark Johnson on Allocating Your Assets.

I would also like to thank Gary Webb and Bob Soukup for reviewing the first draft and, despite their better judgment, foolishly encouraging me in this endeavor. And thanks, of course, to all the people at Career Press, especially Mike Lewis, who saw value in my manuscript. There are surely others I should mention and I regret their omission.

Contents

Introduction

Like millions of other Americans, I treat bookstores as my private library. When I want to know something, I pull a how-to book off the shelf, skim it, furiously take mental notes, and then return it to the shelves for the next consumer to rough up. It's no wonder bookselling is a tough business.

Well, who wants to spend $30 on a book just to look up how to cut crown molding (upside-down and backwards) by the way? Don't get me wrong. I love those old Time-Life guides with illustrations of people wearing bell-bottom pants installing their own ceiling tile. Step-by-step books are great for hobbyists and weekend carpenters. But let's face it, most "instructional" books are overloaded with arcane details just so the authors can show how smart they are.

Then there are books that purport to offer the "secret" to something (losing weight, curing wrinkles, growing hair, etc.). The trouble is, you might read one book only to find another one pushing a completely different theory. Take a stroll through your local library and you'll see that the half-life of each new miracle cure is about six months. Who has time to keep up with all this stuff? You need the straight scoop and nothing but. Life's too short, after all, to waste time plowing through books written by fast-buck doctors, talk-show hosts turned authors, and former vice presidents.

So to make your life simpler, I've written the *Know-it-all's Guide to Life*, a wry, wisenheimer's look at approximately 90 subjects, ranging from the practical (how to stop solicitors) to the fantastical (how to travel to space). Although it's lighthearted, the material presented is serious. Each chapter is a distillation of the best advice available on a given topic. I've done the research so you won't have to. Besides my personal experience,

I've read dozens of books, hundreds of articles, and interviewed numerous experts to assemble this guide.

The topics have not been selected scientifically. You will find chapters on health, sports, careers, finance, food, travel, and politics, among others. Some chapters will prove useful to you, others will not. But I think you will find most of them entertaining.

A handful of serial how-to books boldly proclaim their target market to be readers who identify themselves as dummies, idiots, or fools. Not this book. The target audience for *The Know-it-all's Guide to Life* is smart people with a high degree of intellectual curiosity. If you are a news hound, trivia buff, do-it-yourselfer, or all-purpose aficionado, this book is for you.

So flip through a few of the chapters, and I'm sure you will find that this is one book you can't afford to put back on the shelf.

—John Walbum
www.johnwalbum.com

How to travel to space

Hey, if a codger like former Senator John Glenn can go up, why not you? Well just about anybody in good physical shape will be able to go soon—anybody that is, with $100,000 in spare cash. Although NASA has not yet bought into the concept of consumer space travel, private American companies (and possibly the Russians soon after) expect to offer suborbital flights for amateur astronauts sometime between 2003 and 2005.

Space Adventures of Alexandria, Virginia is offering seven-day packages culminating with a two-and-a-half-hour flight into space. The tickets, which cost $98,000 and require a hefty deposit, are reported to be selling rapidly.

During the trip, amateur astronauts will feel the pull of multiple G-forces on takeoff and reentry, and be able to clearly see the curvature of the Earth, though not that great blue marble as seen from the moon. The space trip will feature a two-minute-and-30-second period of weightlessness, during which tourists will do aerial backflips on videotape...that is, if the trip ever takes place. Space Adventures has not quite worked out the details of how they are going to get there. It is working with several rocket makers that are competing to develop the best design. Stay tuned for more developments.

If a ride in space costing $600 per minute seems a little ridiculous to you, just wait a few years. Robert Bigelow, who is president and owner of the Budget Suites of America motel chain, believes in the future of space travel. He has committed $500 million towards the construction a 100-passenger, half-mile-long luxury cruise ship that will orbit the moon (presumably at a lower cost). British entrepreneur and balloonist Richard Branson—a man with a nose for opportunity as well as publicity—wants to get into the act with Virgin Galactic(!) Airways. Former astronauts, like Buzz Aldrin, are also pushing to take the masses to space. There is even a course taught, at the Rochester Institute of Technology, called "Space Tourism Development," to train the next generation in space hospitality management.

Perhaps the real future is in space vacations. A joint study by NASA and the Space Tourism Association estimates space travel and tourism could be a $10- to $20-billion market. Bigelow Aerospace, also owned by Robert Bigelow, is exploring the construction of space hotels that would be partially assembled on Earth and carried into space for final assembly.

But don't pack your bags yet; the cost to put things in space is still prohibitive. NASA's space shuttle costs work out to about $10,000 per pound to put satellites into orbit, and rockets aren't much cheaper. Bigelow Aerospace believes launch costs need to fall to $550 per pound before space hotels become a reality. A California company, Space Island Group, thinks it has the solution: a space station built from used external fuel tanks left in orbit by space shuttles.

If big space hotels are not cost effective, how about a little orbiting bed and breakfast? MirCorp, a Netherlands-based company that attempted to salvage the Mir space station, hopes to launch a tiny space station in 2004 for tourists. The space bungalow, to be called Mini Station 1, will hold only three visitors at a time. Bring your own Tang.

On the other hand, if you have $20 million, you can now reserve a seat aboard the Soyuz rocket, like tycoons Dennis Tito and Mark Shuttleworth, who lodged at the orbiting International Space Station. All you have to do is learn to speak Russian and spend six months training at the Gagarin Cosmonaut Training Center in Star City, Russia. Space Adventures, which also offers rides in Russian military aircraft, (see "How to fly a jet fighter without joining the armed services") is brokering the trips. The latest would-be visitor to the Space Station is Lance Bass, a 23-year-old rock star with the band *NSYNC, who, after failing to come up with the money last September, was bounced from his seat and replaced with a cargo container. No other takers as of this writing.

Even if space hotels do not become a reality in your lifetime, don't be too chagrined. Space cabins are not exactly the Ritz-Carlton—or even a Budget motel, for that matter. Simple activities like using the toilet, bathing, and eating are a chore in space. Although the food is no longer served in squeezable tubes, as it was on the early Apollo missions, it has more calories than flavor (think TV dinners). Weightless sleep is reported to be heavenly, but 70 percent of astronauts experience space motion sickness (symptoms include nausea, vomiting, and headaches) in response to microgravity. The body's reaction to weightlessness also means strenuous daily exercise is required to keep muscles from atrophying.

Microbes thrive in the closed environment of a space cabin, making staph infections and other illnesses common. It's expected space visitors would be given a complete physical exam and quarantined prior to takeoff to reduce the risk of infecting other travelers. Even with filtration systems aboard, a crowded cabin can stink to high heavens from stale air and body odors. Another appetizing thought: Scientists expect longer space trips will mandate "closed systems," meaning that all water aboard the space-craft—including human waste—will be purified and reused.

Furthermore, as the Challenger shuttle disaster made clear, the odds of a fatal catastrophe in a space trip are enormous. They are estimated by NASA to be about 100–1, or 70 times higher than the average chance of dying in an automobile accident this year.

If you don't have the money or live long enough to see the price come down, there is one more way to get to space. For just $5,300, Celestis Inc., of Houston, Texas, will launch a portion of your cremated remains into low-Earth orbit. If you were truly destined for the moon, for $12,500 Celestis will deliver your ashes to the Sea of Tranquility aboard NASA's Lunar Prospector satellite.

How to join Mensa

If you are the only one on your block who understands Heisenberg's Uncertainty Principle, can't find anyone to play chess with, or are tired of meeting people who think the Socratic Method is a new way to lose weight, Mensa may be for you.

Mensa, founded in 1946, is the world's largest organization for the super-intelligent, with over 100,000 members in 1,000 countries (43,000 in the United States). Members include a huge range of ages, occupations, and educations, making it less of a club and more of a gathering of smart people. Local chapters (180 in the United States) meet at least once a month. Mensa emphasizes that it is not just a bunch of dorks, but a highly social group with lots of "fun" activities, like playing killer Trivial Pursuit, watching Monty Python flicks, and discussing the existence of God. Of course many Mensans join simply to meet intelligent people of the other sex. (Some chapters are said to be pretty wild in this regard. One gathering featured a 100-foot-long, anatomically correct balloon...*of a brain*.) Though Mensans would prefer a combination of smarts, wit, and charm, even if you have the social skills of a houseplant, you can still join. The only criteria for membership is intelligence.

For entry into Mensa, you must score in the 98th percentile (roughly an IQ of 132) on an administered intelligence test. Mensa accepts most IQ tests, including the widely used Stanford Binet test, as proof of your genius. If you have taken college or graduate school exams, Mensa can convert LSAT, GMAT, GRE, pre-1994 SAT scores, and dozens of other standardized tests. Your results must be sent directly to Mensa by the testing service or certified and sent by the school where it was administered. Mensa requires a $25 fee to process submitted test results.

If you have not been tested, Mensa will test you for a fee of $30. The test consists of two parts. The first part, which lasts about 15 minutes, is a hodgepodge of 50 math and word questions. The second part, which lasts a little over an hour, has seven sections that test a wide range of cognitive and mathematical skills as well as memory. Mensa exams are arranged and offered on a periodic basis though local chapters. If you want some practice answering tricky questions, you can sign up for the home test ($18 fee) at the Mensa Website or by contacting the national office.

Curious how you might do on the test? Try these five questions.

1. John, David, Sam, and Jim work for Acme Hardware. They have worked for one, five, eight, and 10 years. Their ages range from 24 to 50. The oldest has not worked the longest. The youngest has worked 5 years. John is 14 years younger than Jim. Jim is twice as old as Sam. How old is each employee, and how long has each worked?

2. What four letter word can be added to the front of each of these words to make new words?
LINE   BORN   BOARD   LESS

3. What one other word can be formed using all the letters in TOASTER?

4. What is the next number in this sequence: 2 5 7 12 19 31?

5. Dog is to bird as spider is to: snake   squirrel   worm   raccoon

Answers: (1) John is 36 years old and has worked for 10 years; David is 25 years old and has worked for one year; Sam is 24 years old and has worked for five years; Jim is 50 years old and has worked for eight years. (2) BASE; (3) ROTATES; (4) 50; (5) raccoon.

For more mind-benders, take the "Mensa Workout" at *www.mensa.org. workout.html.*

For more information, write to American Mensa, 1229 Corporate Drive West, Arlington, Texas 76006-6103, call (800) 66-MENSA, or go to *www.us.mensa.org.* Annual membership dues are $49, which gets you a monthly newsletter you can leave lying around so everyone will see it.

If you are a super-achiever and resent being lumped in with the mortals below the top two percent, there are three extra-brainy groups to try, the Top One Percent Society, the Triple Nine Society (99.9th percentile), and the ultra-haughty Prometheus Society (99.997th percentile). Better brush up on your quantum mechanics.

How to try your own case

It is said that someone who decides to serve as his own attorney has a fool for a client. Unfortunately for most sorry *pro se* litigants, the judges tend to agree. Although many judges are sympathetic to self-representation, litigants who cannot follow basic civil procedure are doing themselves more harm than good. In fact, judges can turn downright hostile to the hordes of would-be Melvin Bellis who clog up their courtrooms with unnecessary delays. Self-litigants may sometimes win, but frankly, the system is rigged against them. So what do you do if you have a burning desire to sue someone and limited means?

First off, read up. You will quickly discover that the law is not alchemy. You can learn plenty by reading statutes and case law (see *Represent Yourself in Court*, published by Nolo Press) and by studying the rules of civil procedure and the rules of the court that will hear your case. With enough research, it is quite possible to bring or defend a lawsuit without legal representation.

However, no matter how strong your arguments, if you present them badly, you will probably lose. As an amateur, you are bound to make a major mistake somewhere. The opposing attorney certainly won't point it out, and don't expect the judge to bail you out either; judges are bound by a code of ethics requiring them to be impartial. As they say, ignorance of the law is no excuse—and neither is incompetence. The solution is to hire a legal coach to help you.

Legal coaches are trial lawyers who offer partial representation to clients on an hourly basis. Coaches can help you prepare pleadings, subpoena witnesses, present testimony, file motions, etc. They can also make suggestions as to where you can find information that will considerably shorten the time you spend doing research. Most importantly, legal coaches help you navigate that Minotaur's maze known as the American legal system. Why put in all that work only to have your case dismissed because you missed a filing deadline?

Although not all civil litigators are wild about doing hourly work (no chance to earn part of a juicy settlement), there are some who will take it on. If you can't find a good local attorney, for $144 per year you can join the Legal Club of America, which maintains lists of available legal coaches. Whoever you select, make sure you have an agreement that spells out what services you expect your attorney to provide for you. Be chary with your coach's time. Most attorneys bill in tenths of an hour. Even at their full hourly rates, though, you should save a bundle over full representation.

If you cannot find a lawyer to serve as your coach, consider hiring a paralegal. Paralegals are state-licensed legal professionals who assist attorneys in some of their more mundane tasks. Paralegals are not lawyers and cannot offer legal advice, but can help you prepare documents and locate information. Like lawyers, paralegals charge by the hour, though at a much lower rate.

Even with a coach you can still get run over by the wheels of justice. Small claims court is the best venue for *pro se* litigants because the amounts are smaller and the judges are used to people representing themselves. Never attempt to serve as your own counsel in a criminal case or where big dollars are at stake. And remember Cicero's advice: "If all else fails, abuse the plaintiff."

How to decode Wall Street

In the wake of all the bad press about Wall Street equity research analysts, you should know that all research is not bad and some is even quite good. Yet it is of no value if you don't know how to interpret it. Lawmakers and regulators in Washington are proposing new regulations that would, among other things, require analysts to explain their stock rating systems so ordinary investors could understand them. Until such proposals are adopted, here is a compact guide to translate what the analyst is saying.

Analyst's Rating	What It Means
"Strong Buy"	Buy
"Buy"	Buy
"Accumulate"	Hold
"Hold"	Sell
"Reduce"	Sell
"Sell"	What are you, nuts?

The Analyst Says	The Analyst Means
The stock is valued at a reasonable 35 times next year's earnings.	The company's current-year earnings prospects stink.
Due to the recent run-up in the stock price, we are cutting our rating to "accumulate."	Sell now before the really dumb investors figure it out, too.
We think the company deserves its premiumvaluation due to its strong market positionand superior management.	The stock is overvalued and we can't come up with any other way to manage it.
In the long-run, we look for significant price appreciation potential for these shares.	In the short run, you will be lucky if you don't lose your keister.
Based upon our discounted cash flow we believe the stock is worth $54 a share.	Based upon any reasonable comparison of price to earnings the value cannot be justified.
Note: The analyst owns shares of this company's stock.	The analyst works for one of the firms that believes in putting its money where its mouth is.
Note: Our firm acted as a managing underwriter of a public offering of securities for this company.	This is a "deal stock." We will defend it until it has one foot on a banana peel and the other in Chapter 11. Disregard our exuberance.

How to hire a contractor

Okay, you have gotten at least five recommendations, checked references, and prepared a short list of three contractors to do your remodeling. How do you herd these cats into your living room to give you their best shot at pricing out your dream kitchen?

As with all negotiations, the best position is one of strength. First, get your financing in place if you need it. (Strangely, contractors like working for people who can pay.) Then hire architects and have plans drawn up, if necessary, before sitting down with the contractors. Bone up by reading home improvement books and magazines and doing research on the Internet. Next, meet with each contractor at your home and explain, thoughtfully and in detail, what you are trying to accomplish. Share any architects' plans or drawings you have. Try to give the contractor the sense that you will be a dream customer: calm, rational, pleasant, and resolute. Don't waffle or seem tentative; if the contractor thinks you are a flake, he isn't going to give you his best bid. After thanking the contractor for his time, gently mention that you are getting "a couple of other bids" and you look forward to hearing his thoughts. The contractor is on notice there is competition and may not like it. Tough.

Once you have met with everyone on the short list, establish a reasonable deadline (two weeks is good) for receiving a written bid from each contractor. Chuck out firms that are unresponsive (it will only get worse after the work starts). After you receive the bids, walk through them with the contractors so you understand what they entail. Take copious notes of your conversations. Make certain you write down any promises, guarantees, and representations ("This floor will *definitely* support a swimming pool").

Small jobs are usually priced on a *time-and-materials*, or *cost-plus*, basis. Time is billed by the hour and materials are charged at cost plus a mark-up. Large remodelings or additions are typically bid on a *fixed-price* basis, although in a hot market, some contractors may refuse to give you a fixed-price bid. Nonetheless, if your project will last more than a few days, you should ask for one, because it puts the risk of poor estimating on the contractor, not on you.

As a rule of thumb, the more parties involved, the more important it is to have a fixed price. If you are dealing with a single specialty contractor, such as a painter or plasterer, hourly rates will do. With a general contractor and multiple subs, there are too many opportunities for featherbedding.

Regardless of the type of bid, it should feature a line-by-line breakdown of the components of the job, including labor, materials, and time to complete. Another thing: *Estimates* are not bids, which are firm prices unless otherwise indicated. If a contractor can only give you an estimate, cross him off the list.

In a competitive situation, bidders should come in at the lower end of their price range—exactly what you want—to try to win the business. Even if the pricing on each of the bids is acceptable, they can probably do better. If you like one of the contractors but not his bid, don't try to browbeat him into lowering his price (unless he is desperate it won't work—and if he is desperate he probably isn't any good). Instead, calmly explain that his bid is too high, ask him to sharpen his pencil and try again. The worst that can happen is he refuses. In the end you may decide he is worth the extra money anyhow.

Time-and-materials bids

With a time-and-materials bid, you need to pay attention to both the hourly rate and the estimated time to complete. Sixty dollars an hour for a carpenter sounds high, doesn't it? Well, it covers overhead, insurance, idle time, profit, and spiffy new tools. In the end, the hourly rate is not all that important—time to complete is the key. If the contractor knows what he is doing, he should be able to deliver on his estimate. If not, you eat the extra expense. The best way to limit your exposure is to specify a maximum allowable charge, known as a cap.

Unlike hourly rates, mark-ups on materials and finished goods are pure profit to the contractor. Mark-ups vary considerably, from 20 percent to 70 percent. For finished goods, such as appliances, you can lower your costs by purchasing them yourself and arranging for delivery. On raw materials, however, mark-ups are part of how contractors make a living. You have the right not to be gouged, but don't try to play materials supplier. It will create more problems than it's worth.

Fixed-price bids

Fixed-price bids are firm prices for the completion of the job. You agree to pay and the contractor agrees to assume the risk of cost overruns. Because cost control is so important, there is a moral hazard in fixed-price deals: cutting corners on materials. Only unscrupulous contractors would deliberately substitute inferior quality materials in a job (unethical *and* illegal). More commonly, contractors will push certain products over those you selected. Sometimes their choices actually *are* better or more cost-effective to install. Other times, contractors are merely trying to fatten their profits through a better deal from a particular vendor. If the logic sounds fishy, ask the other contractors what they think. Remember, you are the one who will have to live with it; be adamant if you feel strongly about a specific material or product.

In fixed-price arrangements, "change orders" (where clients change their minds about something midstream), are the bane of contractors. They cost time and money and often lead to finger-pointing about who is to blame for the inevitable delays. Even small changes can be expensive. When a change order crops up, put it in writing as an amendment to the contract that is dated and signed by both parties. The amendment should describe the change and—this is important—how much extra it will cost.

Completion time

If the projected completion date seems too distant, but the cost seems right, be careful you aren't being two-timed. Some contractors juggle multiple jobs at once, doing two days here, three days there, to avoid turning down work. If you need your project finished by a certain date, be insistent. Make the other customers wait. Also be wary of plodders who do high-quality work, but at a turtle's pace, which, on a time-and-materials basis, can cause you severe coronary stress. One way to ensure your project finishes on time is to insert a clause in the contract providing monetary incentives for early completion and penalties for lateness, although many contractors will balk at such provisions.

Deposits

For small projects, you should not have to pay anything up front unless materials have to be specially ordered. If a significant amount of materials must be procured ahead of time, you should arrange to pay the supplier directly. On larger projects, a deposit of between 10 percent and 25 percent is sometimes demanded. (If a design-and-build firm is involved, you will probably forfeit your deposit if you cancel after plans are produced.) Needless to say, if the general contractor you hire is insolvent, you may never see your deposit again. Check the firm out before cutting a check.

Payment terms

Contractors want to get paid as work is completed. Ask for milestones rather than weekly payments. *Never let the contractor get ahead of you in payments.* If the contractor goes belly-up and skips town, chances are it will be the day after he cashes your check. In addition, once you pay, you lose your leverage. Final payment is normally due upon completion, but you should demand a holdback of 10 percent to 20 percent to ensure all dangling ends are tied up. For a major addition, you may even want to stipulate that an independent home inspector will review the work prior to final payment.

Selecting a bid

Try not to make a decision based upon price alone. Rather than hunger for work, very low bids frequently result from incomplete understanding between the homeowner and the contractor. Or worse, lowballers can try to win the business and jack up the cost with "extras" later. Really high bids, in contrast, sometimes indicate the contractor has more attractive work on his plate. If one bid is more than 20 percent above or below the others, there is a good likelihood the contractor is missing something or simply not interested. Experience indicates the middle bid usually turns out best.

The contract

Contracts should contain everything you can think of, especially any verbal guarantees made by the contractor. The contract can be drawn up by your attorney, you can use a standardized form, or for small projects, simply amend the contractor's bid. Besides estimated labor hours, contracts should incorporate a detailed breakdown of products and materials to be used. If you have a product or material preference, write it into the contract. The more detail, such as product model numbers, the better, but also include acceptable substitutes in the contract (be specific; avoid saying "Brand X *or equivalent*"). If you require a specific grade of material, put it down. Make sure you get credit for unused or returned materials (you may not want 24 extra feet of crown molding lying around). The contract should also stipulate that the job site will be left clean (no piles of sawdust or dirty rags) at the end of each day.

State in the contract that the final payment will not be made until you receive final waivers of mechanics' liens from all subcontractors, verifying they have been paid in full by the general contractor and have no claim against you as the homeowner. All reputable contractors stand behind their work. Get a guarantee that covers defects in workmanship at no additional charge for at least a year after completion. You may also insert a binding arbitration clause, specifying that any disputes will be resolved by an independent arbitrator. (This option is far cheaper and easier than suing your contractor.)

Have a lawyer look over the contract before you sign it. A few hundred dollars in legal fees could save you a bunch later on. By federal law, unless the contract is signed at the contractor's office, you can cancel within three days of signing it. So if you have second thoughts (or your lawyer does) you can still back out.

Make sure the contractor is bonded and carries workers' compensation, property, and liability insurance. Also keep in mind Murphy's Law and set aside an extra 10 percent of the project cost for unexpected overruns.

How to get rid of the budget surplus

If there ever is another budget surplus, we don't need to go around declaring a "peace dividend" or disingenuously urging "Save Social Security first!" There are four easy ways to get rid of the money.

Padlock it

The so-called Social Security lockbox was supposed to keep Congressional hands out of the old folks' cookie jar. Unfortunately, it was a toothless accounting gimmick that changed nothing. The current pay-as-you-go system only works as long as the working outnumber the retired, which will (still) cease to be the case in about 25 years. A sensible sinking-fund mechanism to build up the Social Security Trust Fund would be both more honest and more fiscally responsible.

Return it

Guess what? Americans still hate paying taxes. The problem is that after 20 years of declining tax rates, slightly over half of the voting public does not owe any income tax. And without popular support, passage of further serious tax reductions will be difficult. As former Senate Majority Leader Russell Long said, "Don't tax you. Don't tax me. Tax that fellow behind the tree."

Save it

Forget about annual budget accounting. The American balance sheet still shows some $3.6 trillion in outstanding public debt. By paying it down, the United States makes the dollar more valuable overseas and helps keep interest rates low. Besides, there is less available for Congress to monkey around with.

Spend it

There is no end to the creative solutions devised by politicians to reduce the money in the Treasury: Vidalia onion research, shrimp aquaculture studies, the National Center for Peanut Competitiveness, construction of a Dr. Seuss memorial, etc. In a virtuosic display of pork-barrel spending, in 1981, the Department of the Army spent $6,000 to prepare a 17-page manual on how to buy Worcestershire sauce. You can just imagine the possibilities.

There is no doubt our bureaucrats will continue to do their part, too. As former U.S. Rep. L. A. ("Skip") Bafalis once said, "If you put a bureaucrat in the desert and hand him $1,000 with orders to spend it, he would—even if he had to buy sand."

Some might say a more effective strategy would be to send Congress to the desert instead.

How to take the cure

Suffering from a chronic case of the gout? Irregularity? Bad case of athlete's foot? When in distress, do as the Romans did and take the waters of Europe. As bathing enthusiast and noted fiddler Emperor Nero said, *"Sanitas per aquas"* (Health through water). Mineral baths are claimed to cure a plethora of afflictions, including rheumatism, arthritis, leprosy, itching, ulcers—even venereal disease.

Heck, even if the cure doesn't take, lolling around in hot water is a good way to take your mind off of work. Sure, some mineral waters smell like rotten eggs, and not everyone enjoys going around half-naked with a bunch of pasty-skinned strangers. Still, most mineral spas are so well staffed with pamperers that it would be hard to leave feeling worse than when you arrived. Unlike the United States, in Europe you won't find many free weights, aerobics classes, or wally-ball. Europeans go to the spa to get soft, not firm up.

Here are some of the better European spa possibilities:

England

Since Roman times, people have been immersing themselves in Bath's thermal waters in hopes of salutary outcomes. Bath's springs produce a constant flow of 300,000 gallons per day at a temperature of 116 degrees. The water, which can be sampled in the famed Pump Room, contains calcium, chloride, hydrogen carbonate, and 40 other minerals, and is said to have magical curative properties.

The Romans constructed Bath in 43 A.D. as a place where Legionnaires could come to get a little rest from guarding the frontiers. Bath got to be such fun that dictates from Rome were periodically issued to stop partying all the time. Bath was rediscovered in 1690 after centuries of disuse, and experienced its greatest period under master of ceremonies Beau Nash, from 1705 until 1760. During the Victorian era, novelists Charles Dickens, William Makepeace Thackeray, and Jane Austen all took Bath's waters. Bath served as a convalescent facility for British soldiers after the Second World War. During the latter half of the 20th century, the baths fell into decline and were closed in 1978 for health reasons.

Public baths are slated for reopening in February 2003, when Bath will regain its status as England's premier spot to take the waters. Sadly for purists, the reopening of the bathhouses brings with it the chi-chi trappings of modernity in the form of (ahem...) a five-story stone and glass spa smack in the middle of the old Roman baths. Well, even if the spa doesn't measure up, Bath is a perfectly preserved 18th-century city loaded with historical sightseeing. Regular trains run to and from London's Paddington Station.

Ireland

If you are looking for a completely different experience, try Killcullen's Seaweed Baths in Enniscrone, a seaside town on the northwestern coast of Ireland. Still run by the Killcullen family (now into the fifth generation since its founding in 1912), the bizarre baths feature a combination steam-and-dunk in a tub filled with oily black seaweed. Some visitors praise the kelp oil for its salubrious benefits, others find it an Edwardian horror chamber.

France

Some may chuckle about the idea of France as a center of bathing, since the French have always seemed rather too fond of their natural smells. (Napoleon once wrote home to his wife Josephine from the front, "Will be home in three days. Don't wash.") Not to worry. France actually has several excellent spas, particularly those specializing in hosing you down with seawater, so-called thalassotherapy.

During the French Revolution, long before its soft water was put into the ubiquitous pink and blue bottles, Evian was known as the water to drink if you were suffering from kidney stones. Evian sits on beautiful Lake Geneva, and has been a popular destination for wealthy and famous Europeans since the turn of the 20th century. Evian has two topflight hotel/spas, the Splendide Hotel and the Royal Parc Evian.

If seawater is what you seek, Biarritz has plenty. Located on the Bay of Biscay, near the Spanish border, Biarritz has been packing in highbrow tourists since Napoleon III's wife, Princess Eugenie, built a summer palace there in 1854 (now the Hotel du Palais). Check in to the reasonably priced Hotel Atlanthal, where the resident Atlanthal Institute of Thalassotherapy will wield the power of seawater in ways you never thought of to cure a host of maladies. Pristine beaches, golf, and gambling provide respites from the cures. Surfers can "hang 10" in the Bay's waves, considered some of the baddest rollers in Europe.

Germany

The most bath-crazy people in the world have to be the Germans. There are 347 mineral-water spas in Germany. The people believe so strongly in taking *der Kuren* that there was a huge uproar when the German National Health Service announced it was cutting the benefit from one month at a spa every three years, to just two weeks every four years.

Next to Bath, Baden-Baden (Baths-Baths) is probably the most famous spa town in the world, and why shouldn't it be—the Romans founded it, too. Located in the foothills of the northern part of the Black Forest, Baden-Baden has been the summer playground and place of rejuvenation for rich Europeans since the late 19th century. If you get bored with the waters, there are distractions galore, including nearby vineyards, first-rate food, a racetrack, and an opulent casino dating to 1820. If pure luxury is your goal, stay at Brenner's Park Hotel, a 100-year-old, world-renowned resort nestled in the forest about 20 miles away.

For the real Roman experience, visit the Friedrichsbad Roman-Irish Bath, a bathing complex constructed in 1877 on top of the original Roman baths. Friedrichsbad consists of a warren of bathing rooms decorated in elaborate faux-Roman detail, with marble, statues, frescoes, and hand-painted tiles. Friedrichsbad employs the original Roman method of taking the waters. Bathers first acclimate themselves to the water in the *tepidarium,* then hop into the steaming *caldarium* to get the circulation going, and finally, take a bracing dip in the icy *frigidarium* to seal the pores. Friedrichsbad also adheres to the oldest Roman bathing custom of all— no clothes.

In Pottenstein, Bavaria you can do a little spelunking while you bathe. Asthmatics find relief by sitting in the *Teufelshohle* (Devil's Cave), a limestone cavern strewn with stalagmites, stalactites, and water dripping overhead. Sufferers lie on beach chairs wrapped up in blankets and breathe in the moist air (open for cures only during the winter). Villagers swear by it.

Tucked between the Taunus Mountains to the north and the Rhine River to the south, Wiesbaden was known as an idyll of salubrity even before the Romans set up shop there in 12 B.C. Stay at the regal Hotel Nassauer Hof, which was built in 1819, burned to the ground during World War II, and rebuilt in 1968. The hotel sits over an ancient Roman spring that feeds its own thermal swimming pool. After soaking in the waters, try your luck at one of the oldest casinos in the world (established in 1771), where Fyodor Dostoevsky was inspired to write *The Gambler,* after losing all his money at the tables.

Switzerland

Next to the Germans, the Swiss take the prize for bathing. Switzerland's numerous ancient mineral springs, and its reputation as the leader in experimental medical treatments *almost* leave one comfortable with the idea of a Swiss mineral-water enema.

On the southern shore of Lake Neufchatel, Yverdon-Les-Bains is less than an hour's drive from Geneva. Stay at the Grand Hotel Des Bains, a modern hotel wrapped inside an exterior built in the 18th and 19th centuries. Besides its own pool, the Grand Hotel features covered access to the Centre Thermal, the main thermal pool in town.

Known to the Romans as *Aquae Helveticae*, Baden is a medieval city just 15 miles from cosmopolitan Zurich. Besides a little sightseeing, there isn't much to do in Baden besides soak in the mineral-rich water, and that's the whole point. Try the year-round outdoor thermal pool near the banks of the Limmat River, which runs through town. Regular trains to and from Zurich.

One of the few major springs in Europe *not* discovered by the Romans is Bad Ragaz, which was found in the 13th century. Situated in the foothills of the Swiss Alps, the year-round resort is approximately 55 miles from Zurich. At the bathhouses of the Tamina-Therme, the mineral waters flow in at a constant 98 degrees. The spa is fed by a spring that pours through the Tamina gorge, the setting for the story of Heidi, whose crippled friend Clara was said to be cured by the waters. You will find top-notch accommodations and dining at the stately Hotel Quellenhof.

Italy

Ever since Emperor Augustus was famously cured of a liver ailment after taking in the cold waters at a bath believed to be in Chiusi, the Italians have been nutty about water. There are hundreds of thermal baths in Italy, made possible by the constant bubbling and coursing of volcanic magma below underground springs. Water cures are considered a legitimate form of medical treatment in Italy. As with other countries in Europe, the state pays for therapeutic spa vacations—most of the visitors are Italians.

Roman statesman Agrippa built the first free public bathhouses in Rome in 25 B.C. (Unluckily, lead was the only material available to make pressure-withstanding pipes, and may have caused widespread poisoning of the Roman population.) At its peak around 100 A.D., Rome had 926 public baths fed by 750 million liters of mineral water per day. The vast, extravagant ruins of the emperor's Baths of Caracalla, Diocletian, and

Trajan can all be seen today, although none have been restored to use. Ironically, if you want the real spa experience, you cannot really find it in Rome, you have to go to the country.

In Tuscany, mid-way between Pisa and Florence, lies Montecatini, a resort town once popular with famous Italian composers Leoncavallo, Puccini, Rossini, and Verdi. A true tourist destination, there are over 200 hotels and five major spas in Montecatini. The Renaissance-style Terme Tettucio is best known and offers a complete array of treatments, including thermal baths, inhalation therapy, mudpacks (a local specialty), and massages. Those with internal afflictions can try three types of water, strong (purgative); medium (laxative); and weak (just salty). For a diversion, explore the neighboring medieval hilltop village, Montecatini Alto, reachable by cable car; or see Michelangelo's *David* at the Galleria dell'Accademia in Florence, only 25 miles away.

For a Dantean experience, visit the Grotta Giusti, five minutes away from Montecatini. There are three underwater caves, fed by a bubbling subterranean river, that get progressively hotter and are appropriately named Paradise, Purgatory, and Hell. Air temperatures up to 93 degrees and 100 percent humidity are supposed to detoxify a person—if you survive. Visitors from Houston should feel right at home.

Not just a bottled water, San Pellegrino is a lush, Lombardian retreat. Roman-era springs feed the 19th-century bathhouse and the famous bottling plant, where carbonation is added. Sample as much of the uncarbonated stuff as you want at the pump room above the cure center.

In the heart of Tuscany, the Saturnia volcano warms miles of the acrid, rotten-eggy Saturnia River and its pools and waterfalls. The water, which flows at constant 98.6 degrees, attracts swimmers and bathers year-round. At night, *fare il bagno nudo e nella voga!* If changing clothes in the car isn't your thing, stay at the full-service spa Terme Di Saturnia, conveniently located between Rome and Florence.

How to gain a firm grasp of the obvious

In 1997, the National Highway Transportation Safety Administration convened a blue-ribbon panel that included highway safety experts, sleep disorder specialists, and medical researchers to determine how to prevent accidents caused by people falling asleep behind the wheel.

The panel's conclusion? Don't drive if you are sleepy, and if you start to feel drowsy, pull over and take a nap.

How to get a good night's sleep

"Sleep is the only medication that gives ease."

—Sophocles

"Up sluggard, there'll be time enough for sleeping in the grave."

—Benjamin Franklin

Over half of American adults regularly have trouble falling asleep. Millions more are presumably tired enough to go to sleep, but choose to stay up for a variety of reasons (work, family, Three Stooges reruns). Between those who can't fall asleep and those who willfully decide they have better things to do, America is a land of zombies during waking hours.

Sleep researchers confirm the ideal amount of sleep is what your mother always told you: about eight hours per night. According to a National Sleep Foundation survey, the average American is short an hour of sleep, getting just six hours and 54 minutes per night. And it's getting worse: One-third of respondents said they got less sleep than they did five years ago. It is now the norm in many professions to regularly put in 12- to 18-hour days and get fewer than five hours of sleep per night. Ask a first-year investment banker at Morgan Stanley.

Sleep deficits catch up with you eventually. One out of five Americans reported feeling so sleepy during the day that it interfered with their activities. Exhaustion can be dangerous too. Sleep researchers have found that staying awake for 18 hours is equivalent to 0.08 blood alcohol content (the legal driving limit in many states). And those young physicians working 36-hour shifts? You don't want to know.

During sleep, your brain's nerve cells recharge themselves, according to the latest theory by the National Institute on Aging. If you regularly stay up into the wee small hours of the morning, consider that the latest research partially attributes obesity, diabetes, infections, and colds to a lack of sleep. Getting up in years is no excuse either: Researchers believe older people need just as much sleep as everybody else—eight hours.

Sleep consists of four stages: light sleep, true sleep, deep sleep, and rapid-eye movement (REM) sleep. One round-trip through the four stages takes from 90 minutes to two hours. A full night's sleep consists of four complete cycles. If your sleep is interrupted after stage two you will feel tired the next day. For this reason, naps should either be less than 45 minutes or a full two hours, to avoid disrupting the deep and REM sleep stages.

If you get eight hours but still seem fatigued, you may have sleep apnea. Some 14 percent of adults have the syndrome, which involves the cessation of breathing for a few seconds during sleep, and is caused by the tongue or other tissue blocking the throat. Intense log-sawing interrupted by spooky quiet is sleep apnea's signature. You can identify it readily: Ask your spouse. If you (or your spouse) just can't take it any more, a nasal mask worn to bed can give relief. Dropping a few pounds might help too; overweight people, especially males, are likely candidates for sleep apnea. Extreme cases may require surgery. See a sleep disorders clinic for your options.

Exercising regularly will improve the quality of your rest—so much so that if you take an hour to exercise every day you are likely to gain it back in increased productivity. Don't work out late at night, though, which can actually be a deterrent to sleep. Exercise releases hormones and elevates the body's temperature, signaling it's not time to go bed yet. The body requires about five hours to return to normal so you can nod off.

Caffeine stays in the bloodstream for up to 12 hours in some people. Limit coffee in the afternoon if you are having trouble falling asleep. Or switch to tea, which has about one-third the caffeine of coffee, for an afternoon lift. And chocolate hounds beware: Cocoa is loaded with a compound similar to caffeine called theobromine. Avoid chocolate cake and hot cocoa for dessert unless you are on your way to a late movie. Various medications also can keep you awake, including cold remedies containing pseudoephedrine, thyroid and ulcer medications, bronchodilators, and beta blockers.

The body's Sandman is the pineal gland, which releases the hormone melatonin. Research suggests elderly people with insomnia benefit from a very small dose of melatonin taken before going to bed, although younger people get no value from it and potentially some harm.

On the whole, sleeping pills are bad news. They put you under but leave you with a wicked headache in the morning. Hypnotics, barbiturates, and antidepressants all work to varying degrees, but have pernicious side-effects, including addiction. Even newer prescription sleep aids like zolpidem (Ambien) and zaleplon (Sonata) can have noticeable aftereffects.

Everyone knows alcohol makes you drowsy. A short one before bed probably won't hurt. But consuming larger quantities of alcohol will disrupt your sleep cycle, making you fatigued the next day—even if you sleep off your hangover until noon.

A glass of milk before bedtime might help. Milk contains L-tryptophan, which is claimed to assist in sleep by producing seratonin, a natural hormone similar to melatonin. Aspirin and other analgesics before bed have no side effects and may provide more restful sleep. Kava, catnip, valerian, and other strange herbs are also marketed as sleep aids. Do they work? Who knows. But the FDA wants nothing to do with this stuff.

Perhaps the best way to fall asleep is the natural way. Think quiet thoughts. Put on some soft music. Repeatedly clench and unclench your muscles. If you are not dozing within half an hour, get up and read a book until you feel drowsy. Deal out solitaire hands. Watch the Weather Channel. Have a midnight snack. If nothing does the trick, try napping the next day after lunch when your body energy naturally drops. A 20-minute nap is equivalent to drinking two cups of coffee and the effect lasts four hours.

How to become a movie star

Many famous actors and actresses got their starts as extras, including Bruce Willis, Dustin Hoffman, Bette Midler, Gary Cooper, Sharon Stone, and John Wayne. Extra work can be exhausting, time-consuming, and the pay stinks. On the other hand, extras get to rub shoulders with the stars, see a movie made from the inside, and, well, there is always that chance they will be discovered.

Virtually every movie requires scads of extras. Generally speaking, there are two ways of getting hired as an extra: through a casting call on location, or through a talent agency. Notices of upcoming filming sessions and extra requirements can be found in local newspapers, in trade publications, and on a number of Websites.

Talent agency members have more opportunities to work. To register with one you need identification and proof that you are licensed to work in the United States. Agencies will take a photograph of you that is digitized and maintained in their database. You also must fill out a form for their database that includes vital statistics, any special talents you may have (juggling, turning your eyelids inside out, etc.), as well as information about your wardrobe (formal wear, hospital scrubs, etc.). The largest extras talent agency in the world is Central Casting in Burbank, California.

Once registered with an agency, you will have access to its posted casting opportunities with that agency. Interested candidates may respond to postings either by telephoning or e-mailing the casting agent, who will pull up your image on a computer and decide whether you look the part. If you are chosen, you will be booked for the job and told where to go, when to arrive and what to wear. The process for on-location auditions is essentially the same, except you will probably wait in line. Besides your "look," the most important hiring factor is availability. Movies incur enormous fixed production costs and cannot afford downtime waiting for extras to show up. Because turnover is so high among extras, if you want to work, the odds of eventually getting hired are good.

Now the bad news: The pay for extras is awful; $46 per day is the industry standard rate. Overtime rates can be up to double that, but you still make less than the average waitress, with tips. You can boost your pay by joining the actors' union, the Screen Actors Guild. For extras, joining the Guild is a cumbersome process. If a union extra fails to show for a part and you are chosen as the replacement, you may receive a SAG voucher for working a full day. If you collect three vouchers, you may apply for membership in the Guild ($1,200 membership fee). Union extras earn a minimum of $100 per day and $596 per picture, plus future residuals and benefits. The main reason for joining the Guild is to further your career as a serious actor, because you gain access to talent agents (who are generally barred from working with nonunion actors) and union parts.

Although extras are usually well fed, there are few other perks. Autograph seeking and photography on the set are verboten. Bothering the principal actors is also frowned upon. There is generally a lot of time on the set spent waiting around. Extras are expected to be patient and remain until the shooting is finished.

Life as an extra is not all drudgery and boredom, though. During the filming of the remake of *Planet of the Apes*, star Mark Wahlberg had a close call in a scene where extras in ape suits were supposed to throw fireballs at him and miss. The extras, however, had their own ideas. "Later, I found out that the extras had this bet going," he said, "Whoever hit me with fire got $100." On the 10th take, Wahlberg got hit twice and his clothes ignited.

If you do get a shot at stardom, keep in mind Spencer Tracy's advice for aspiring actors: "Know your lines and don't bump into the furniture."

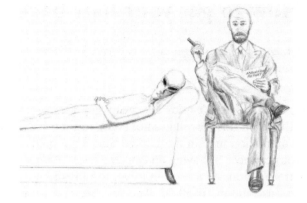

How to launch a new career

If you are languishing in a dead-end job, the victim of a corporate downsizing, or simply tired of playing golf five days a week, we have just the tonic.

For only $395 you can take a correspondence course that will certify you to become a professional past-life therapist. In this exciting occupation, you will help patients under hypnosis "regress" to their prior lives, and can experience the thrill of suddenly having Errol Flynn or Joan of Arc sitting on your couch. The bucks are good, too. The company suggests you charge from $65 to $125 for a 90-minute session of past-life therapy, which works out to $130,000 to $250,000 per year if you can find enough paying clients besides Shirley MacLaine. There ought to be a big market: A recent Harris Poll found that 23 percent of Americans believe in reincarnation.

If you live in rural New Mexico, Nevada or another area where UFO sightings are common (like near an Air Force base), you may also want to consider enrolling in the companion Certified E.T. Abduction Counselor home study course for $195. Among other things, you will learn how to distinguish between "star-children" and people who have *actually* been abducted. That skill alone should make the course worthwhile.

Contact Dr. Carole Carbone, International Association of Past Life Therapists at 31500 Grape Street #3-210 Lake Elsinore, CA 92532 (*www.pastlives.net*) for more information.

How to get your hair back

"A 100-percent optimist is a man who believes the thinning out of his hair is only a temporary matter."

—*Louisville Times*

If you are a male over 30, odds are pretty good that some of the hair you found in the drain this morning is not going to grow back. Yep. *Gone!* An estimated 40 million men in the United States are bald or losing their hair. While your chances of having an extreme case of *alopecia androgenesis* (male pattern baldness) are one in five, the likelihood of a receding hairline or serious thinning is 50-50. And just because your mother's father kept his hair does not make you safe. Research has shown male pattern baldness is inherited from *both* sides of the family.

Baldness can lead to depression, loss of self-confidence and the constant wearing of hats. The problems may not be all psychological either. One German study even found that bald men were significantly less likely to be hired for a job. Whether you are already follicly challenged or just curious about the future attractions of middle age, there are some things you should know about your scalp.

The causes

Scientists believe heredity accounts for over 90 percent of naturally occurring baldness. American researchers have identified genes they believe are responsible for certain types of hair loss, although a gene therapy cure for baldness is years, if not decades, away. Besides genetics, illness, stress, and poor health can all accelerate hair loss.

How it happens

About 15 percent of scalp follicles are dormant at any time. In most people, dormant follicles return to growing normal hair after a few months. In balding individuals, testosterone—a male hormone that controls hair growth—is converted into dihydrotestosterone (DHT), causing certain follicles to shrink and produce only fine, short hair called vellus—or no hair at all.

As countless men have discovered, male pattern baldness normally starts with a receding hairline and follows with a thin spot on the crown of the head. Your hairline recedes to meet the top of your scalp and, *voila!*...one day you look in the mirror and Telly Savalas is looking back.

The options

What to do about it is the question. You face a fish stew of choices, from the merely ridiculous to the grotesque. The quackery quotient runs high in cures for baldness, with any number of strange remedies, like undergoing electrical stimulation, hypnosis, and drinking essential oils. Sadly, the "accepted" products—expensive drugs, transplants, weaves, and wigs—are not much better. After looking over the menu, you may decide your head doesn't look so bad after all.

Drugs

Baldness has stymied physicians since Cleopatra's day, when a potion of animal parts, fats, and other ingredients was rubbed into Egyptian scalps to encourage hair to grow. Hair restoration is a $1.5 billion market that proves tempting for the unscrupulous. The Federal Trade Commission has investigated hundreds of false claims made by mountebanks hawking the latest scalp fertilizers, including special shampoos, tonics, and exotic herbal extracts.

Perhaps so many bogus products are on the market because the two FDA-approved offerings are pretty lame. The older of the two, minoxidil, has been around since 1988. It is available over the counter as Rogaine in both 2-percent and 5-percent "extra-strength" formulations. Rogaine is applied to the scalp twice a day and a month's supply costs about $25. Side effects, like itchy scalp, are minimal. Stories have circulated that minoxidil causes hair to grow in places where it is not wanted, but that rarely happens. Unfortunately, minoxidil does not necessarily grow hair where it *is* wanted either. If your hair is long gone, chances are minoxidil won't help.

Finasteride, on the market since 1997, is something of an improvement over minoxidil. In extensive clinical trials, finasteride—sold by prescription as Propecia—was proven effective at regrowing hair in a majority of men under age 40. (Propecia's maker, Merck & Co., is currently testing it on men over 40.) The drug works by blocking enzymes that turn testosterone into DHT. Propecia is taken one tablet a day and costs about $50 per month. Compared with Rogaine, its side effects are less common but more serious, including enlarged prostates and temporary sexual dysfunction in men.

While finasteride appears to be somewhat better than minoxidil against a receding hairline, it is not effective at combatting "chrome dome." For this reason, some dermatologists recommend using both treatments for maximum impact. Even so, do not expect dramatic results. With either drug it can take up to six months to see improvement and as long as two years for your hair to reach peak fullness. Furthermore, the benefits of each product only last as long as you keep using it, creating the Hobson's choice of financing a never-ending $25- to $75-per-month habit or watching your hair fall out again.

If neither one works for you, sit tight. GlaxoSmithKline is working on getting its prostate drug dutasteride (brand name: Avodart) approved as a hair loss remedy. Dutasteride works like finasteride by blocking the DHT conversion that causes hair loss, but initial reports indicate it is much more potent. If the trials pan out, it could be approved as a treatment for baldness as early as 2003.

Also on the horizon is a process called angiogenesis—used to encourage blood vessel growth in cancer patients—that researchers at Massachusetts General Hospital have discovered also causes thick hair to grow in laboratory mice. In a potential boon for hairless mice everywhere, the process is now being tested on a mouse with pattern baldness and looks promising...

Hair replacement surgery

If you have the money and the inclination, surgical hair transplants can give you your frontal hair back. Transplants deservedly got a lot of bad press after they first came out in the 1980s, when cheap operations left patients' hairlines looking like plugs of sod that didn't take. Today's transplants are much improved. By using more but smaller grafts, clumping is eliminated. The surgery is relatively simple and thousands of hair replacement operations are performed each year with no complications.

During the surgery, grafts containing from one to eight hairs each are taken from a donor area on the back of the head and stitched into a slit or hole on the front of the scalp. Typically the procedure—done without anesthesia—takes two to four hours, during which a surgeon transplants up to 1,000 hairs (a square inch of coverage requires about 175 hairs). Two or more sessions are usually necessary and some pain and swelling is involved. The cost varies from $5,000 to $20,000 for a complete treatment. Do not plan on sporting your new look right away: Transplanted hairs fall out and can take up to six months to grow back.

In a related technique called a "flap," a larger row of hair is partially cut away from a donor area and, leaving the end attached, is pulled into a sparse area. Although this method is faster than the grafting method and the hair does not fall out, it is trickier for surgeon to do properly and requires a real specialist.

Another surgical means of minimizing a bald spot is called "scalp reduction," usually done in concert with grafts or flaps. Although it sounds like something Cherokees practiced on western settlers, scalp reduction is actually the removal of hairless skin on the top of the skull, like a face-lift for the scalp. The more extra skin on your noggin the better.

Hairpieces and toupees

If all this talk of stitching on the top of your head makes you queasy, there is always that embarrassing personal appliance—the hairpiece. For most people, when a hairpiece comes to mind, it is a really bad rug—the kind where the hair is darker than the eyebrows and seems to levitate off the wearer's forehead. Various 1970s game show hosts come to mind and, of course, Burt Reynolds. But fake hair has come a long way recently and the newest models are not that bad.

These days artificial hair comes in a lot of varieties: extensions, weaves, wefts, hairpieces, toupees, cranial prostheses, and naturally, wigs. Some are made with human hair, some artificial, and some both. Human hair is more comfortable but can fade in sunlight (Italian hair is claimed to be the best), whereas synthetic hair is more durable but less natural looking. Both types of hair can be blended or dyed to produce an exact color match to your own hair. Newer lace hairpieces are so hard to spot you can even comb your hair straight back.

Small hairpieces can be woven into or fused with existing hair. Larger ones have to be either taped or clipped on and taken off at night, or in a more permanent form, attached with waterproof glue and worn constantly for weeks. There are also painful (and potentially hazardous) procedures where hairpieces are sutured or tied to skin grafts to keep them in place. Hairpieces cost from $1,000 to $2,000 for good custom-made jobs (about $300 to $500 for one off the rack).

Before you wear it, your furry friend must be trimmed by your barber to look natural. It also has to be shampooed regularly to keep it from smelling and replaced periodically (depending upon the type, as often as every three months). Some touperies offer leased hairpieces you can trade in every six months so you are always wearing low-mileage hair.

The Hair Club for Men, the largest chain of hair replacement salons in the United States, offers a one-stop solution. Hair Club salons can not only fit you for a woven hairpiece, but also give you a haircut and a quick styling every month. Contact Sy Sperling at (800) 424-7258 or at *www.hairclub.com*.

Hair-in-a-can

If you have a hot date and need a full head of hair fast, try Toppik, the successor to spray-on-hair. You shake Toppik, made of tiny protein fibers, into your hair like bacon bits. The fibers cling to your hair with static electricity until you shampoo, or at least they're supposed to. A one-month supply of Toppik costs $19.95 (*www.toppik.com*). It comes in eight colors and according to the company is "totally undetectable." Let's hope your date thinks so, too.

The comb-over

Who says you can't do a lot with a little? For centuries the lowly comb has been used by balding men to accomplish the impossible task of creating a hairline when there is only forehead. The comb-over offers multiple options depending upon the state of your pate: front-to-back, back-to-front, and the wraparound, which covers the real estate from one ear to the other. To do the comb-over, let your side and back hair grow out, artfully comb it around, then stick it in place with a little hairspray. Don't laugh—it works for Rudy Gulliani.

Other solutions

Some balding guys start wearing hats to avoid facing up to reality. Others grow beards or mustaches to compensate on the bottom for what has been lost on top. But why bother when being bald is so fashionable right now? Get a buzz cut from your barber or shave your hair off yourself. You will save money on shampoo, never have to worry about a bad hair day and best of all, you can comb your hair with a towel.

How to eat an artichoke

Beats us why someone would decide to eat a giant green thistle with leaves like a stegosaurus's back (maybe there was once a famine in the Mediterranean). Although the leaves often taste like strained peas on cardboard, the artichoke's heart is pretty tasty and worth the considerable amount of effort to get to it. Whether you are crazy about artichokes or not, they present an important test of your Epicurean aptitude. Eat the artichoke properly and your social standing will remain intact, no matter how low it may, in fact, be.

To begin, pull off the outside leaves of the artichoke with your fingers. Dip the leaves in butter (if provided) and eat them by raking the succulent meat between your teeth, then discard. If the artichoke has been properly prepared, it will have the fuzzy thing, called a choke, removed. If not, dig it out with a spoon. What remains is the heart, which looks suspiciously like what you get in the jar at the supermarket. Quarter it with a knife and eat the pieces with a fork.

Gastronomicists advise that you should always drink a dry, acidic wine with artichokes, as they clash with anything sweet or fruity. With lighter fish or chicken, try a pinot grigio or sauvignon blanc. For salmon, duck, or pork, dry German Rieslings and some pinot noirs work. With red meat or pasta with marinara sauce, try Italian reds like Barbera or Barolo.

How to buy a used car

Most people would rather get stuck in an elevator with a band of Hare Krishnas than negotiate with a used-car salesman. The aversion is so bad that some people will buy just about anything with four wheels so they will be left alone.

It is almost a rite of passage into adult life to be stuck with a lemon. Worse, the crummy car can be a cruel reminder of your impecunity, dragging behind it an unwelcome tailpipe belching repair bills for years to come. But there's no law that says you have to put your mechanic's kids through college every time you buy a used car. Why not buy a good car in the first place, so you won't be stranded at 1 a.m. on a Sunday in Tuba City, Arizona.

Research

You can determine the appropriate make and model for your needs by visiting dealer showrooms, reading Consumer Reports, and doing research online at *www.edmunds.com*. Good pricing information can be found in the Kelley Blue Book, sold in bookstores and available online at *www.kbb.com*. For information about safety features, recalls, and crash test results, see the National Highway Traffic Safety Administration Website, *www.nhtsa.dot.gov*, or phone (888) 327-4236. Never buy a car on the spot unless you have investigated it first. In this Internet age, anybody can find out what a vehicle is worth. The chance that you have found a dumb seller who doesn't appreciate the value of a car is low.

The first thing to do is to check out the car with a database search. Autocheck and Carfax each maintain enormous databases that contain vehicle histories (1.7 billion and 900 million vehicles, respectively) gathered from a variety of sources. By keying in the vehicle identification number (VIN), which is found in the corner of the dashboard on the driver's side, consumers can research vehicles for a modest fee. The report will indicate whether the car was damaged in a fire or flood, previously totaled, repurchased under a state lemon law, or failed an emissions test. According to Carfax, approximately 10 percent of the vehicles it checks out have some kind of problem with their histories.

One of the biggest potential problems detected through a database search is title "cleansing," which involves a distributor purchasing a car from an insurance company that has been classified "Flood Damaged" or "Salvage" and totaled. These special categories of titles exist in some states so that purchasers of the car can sell it for parts. Instead of taking them apart, however, shady operators will spruce up the cars and resell them in another state. The old title is replaced and no one is the wiser. The National Association of Independent Insurers estimates that 40 percent of all totaled cars end up back on the highways. Many of them have rusted parts and are dangerous to drive.

A tip-off to these shenanigans is a title chain that shows a migration from coastal or plains states that have had a lot of flooding to states that don't recognize such titles. Flood titles are the bigger problem. Four states issue flood titles: North Carolina, New Jersey, Virginia, and New York. (Florida discontinued flood titles in 2000, and now issues "Certificates of Destruction.") Flood damage can usually be detected by peeling back part of the carpet and looking for rust, or by a mildewy smell in the upholstery.

Another potential area of concern that a database search will illuminate is odometer fraud. Analysts estimate that 8 percent of cars have had their odometer rolled back, stripping an average of over 20,000 miles off the clock. Looking at the chain of titles and mileage, you will be able to tell if odometer fraud is likely (the database report will highlight it as well). A single report costs $14.95 from either Autocheck.com, (205) 414-2727, *www.autocheck.com*; or Carfax, *www.carfax.com*. Both firms also offer flat rates for 60 days' unlimited usage if you plan on doing a lot of shopping around.

Test drive

Be sure to spend enough time in the driver's seat to feel comfortable. The car should hold its line on the road and not veer to one side if you take your hands off the wheel. The steering wheel should not shimmy or vibrate at highway speeds; cornering should be sure and even. Noises during cornering are usually associated with the steering components or bad wheel bearings. Squealing sounds are often loose belts but sometimes indicative of a more serious problem. Punch the accelerator and brake pedal hard to test responsiveness. Persistent clicking sounds under heavy acceleration could mean the lifters or rods are worn, and only a matter of time before an engine overhaul. Don't forget to look under the car for leaks after you drive it.

Even if a vehicle handles well and comes up clean on a database search it could turn out to be citrus. A close physical and mechanical inspection is a must. A good local garage should be able to do the job for under $100. Some AAA Motor Clubs offer standardized pre-purchase inspection services for a modest fee. Ask your mechanic to prepare an estimate for any repairs that may be required. Be sure to ask the owner for the car's maintenance records. Here are the major areas to check out:

Engine

The first indicator of engine problems is blue or oily smoke coming from the exhaust. (Be sure to let the car warm up before looking at the tailpipe; all cars emit a whitish vapor when they are cold.) Ask your mechanic to do a compression test, which will evaluate the output from each cylinder and tell you whether the rings and pistons are worn. This test is very important because repairs to the cylinders, even comparatively minor ones, are expensive due to the time required to open up the engine.

Brakes

Although you can test the brakes for sponginess and squeaking noises during braking, only a close inspection will tell you for certain if the disc pads or drums are worn.

Transmission

The transmission can be evaluated during your test drive. If it slips or the car fails to engage when accelerating, it may be bad. Gears on a manual transmission should engage smoothly; if not, the clutch pads may be shot.

Electrical system

Your mechanic should test the electrical system with a diagnostic machine that will indicate if there is a problem with the starter, alternator, or battery. When you test drive the car, look closely at the dashboard to make sure no warning lights stay on. Airbags are particularly costly to repair.

Engine cooling system

If the engine is *completely cold*, take a look at the cooling system by unscrewing the radiator cap and siphoning off a little fluid with an anti-freeze tester. Coolant should be translucent yellow or green; if it's murky or dirty, chances are the radiator has some corrosion. Your mechanic can check out the cooling system by pressure testing the radiator to spot any leaks that could leave you stranded later.

Intake and exhaust

Sensors in the engine and exhaust system have a finite life and should be checked by your mechanic. The majority of states have mandatory emissions tests; bad sensors, catalytic converters, and loose tail pipes will have to be fixed before you take the car to be tested.

Frame and suspension

The suspension system, frame, and front wheel bearings should all be examined to ensure that the car is safe to drive. Examine the exterior carefully for signs of accident damage. Look for imperfections in the finish indicating it has been repainted. Also look inside the trunk and make sure the color matches the body. Another way to locate bodywork is with a magnet, which won't work in areas that have been patched with epoxy resin (*a.k.a.* Bondo). If the doors, trunk, or hood do not open and close smoothly, there is a good chance the car was previously wrecked. Never look over a car in the rain—water can hide surface imperfections.

Manufacturers' certified pre-owned programs provide a margin of comfort. Vehicles in these programs generally have lower mileage, are in better shape, and have been given a thorough going-over by the dealer before being offered for sale. Pre-owned certifications typically feature extended factory warranties as well. You pay for the added assurance, though; certified used cars cost from $500 to $1,200 more on average. Another good source for used cars is rental car companies. There is a reason why the national rental car firms always have new cars: Cars in their fleets are sold when they accumulate too many miles. Although rental cars can be abused, they are generally well-maintained and have complete service records. They often have time left on their manufacturers' warranties as well.

Although dealers give you a place to complain if you have a problem with the car, private sellers are significantly cheaper. Unlike the old days when dealers only sold trade-ins and you could occasionally find a bargain, today most cars in the used lots have been purchased at auctions. Buying from an individual can be dicey though. Some seemingly private sellers are really dealers of waxed-up jalopies who sell cars for cash and disappear without a trace. Be extremely wary if a private seller doesn't seem to know much about the car or wants to meet somewhere other than his residence. Also avoid buying from what are known as "curbstoners." These are unsavory operators who set up in vacant lots to merchandise used cars. Sometimes curbstoners use confederates who pretend to be private owners.

When it comes to price, car buying is an American blood sport: Haggle like the dickens! Arm yourself with blue book pricing data and copies of Hemmings Motor News to offer comparable data points. If you are buying from a dealer, be sure to write down any oral promises the salesperson makes.

State lemon laws, by the way, only apply to cars under warranty. If you buy an old hunk of junk you are probably stuck with it. Go to the video store and rent the 1980 classic *Used Cars*, starring Kurt Russell. At least you will be able to laugh about it.

How to select an ear of corn

Don't be a ninny and strip the husk off each ear. What do you expect to find in there? Worms?

The keys to good corn are size and weight, measures you can take without shucking it. If the ear feels thin and looks scrawny, put it back. Get a nice thick ear with no flat sides. If you have doubts, peel one ear's husk back a few inches and check the kernels. They should be decent sized and uniform, undented, and without gaps. The color is not necessarily important to flavor, although "supersweet" corn is almost always golden yellow. And a few brown kernels at the end won't hurt you. Corn should be freshly picked, which means there will be moisture in the silks and the husk. Fresh corn will keep two weeks or more in the refrigerator in a plastic bag.

How to get a patent

Have you ever had an idea for an invention that would revolutionize the world, but no clue what to do with it? Well, for once, the federal government can help the little guy. If your invention qualifies, you can receive a utility patent from the U.S. Patent and Trademark Office (PTO) that will protect you from infringement by others for 20 years. During which time, presumably, you can market your new device and make a bloody fortune.

The Criteria

In the eyes of the PTO, patentable inventions must be: (1) *useful*, (2) *novel,* and (3) *nonobvious*. Utility patents (the most common) are issued for new processes, machines, simple products, combinations of things, and new uses for old inventions. Mere *ideas*, no matter how earthshaking, are not patentable; you must explain exactly how something can be made and used to get a patent. Sorry, philosophers.

- *Usefulness:* Patent law says a candidate for a utility patent must be useful in some way, although the bar is pretty low. After all, the PTO has issued patents for a motorized ice cream cone, a flatulence deodorizer, and even a Santa Claus detector. Is it any wonder people lose faith in government?
- *Novelty:* Since 1790, the United States government has issued over 6.5 million utility patents. No matter how novel your idea may seem to you, somebody else probably has beaten you to it. Yet the way the law reads, novelty is a relatively easy requirement to satisfy. Any physical difference, no matter how trivial, meets the novelty test—even adding a doohickey onto somebody else's design.
- *Nonobviousness:* Much harder to prove than usefulness and novelty is nonobviousness. In order for an invention to be nonobvious (read: clever), a hypothetical average inventor with perfect knowledge of the pre-existing technology would not find it an obvious invention. Your creation has to yield results that are either (1) new or (2) could not have been predicted. Hence, a cosmetic or minor functional difference, while satisfying novelty, won't cut the nonobvious mustard.

The standards for a patent seem straightforward enough, but, as always, the devil lurks in the details. Follow these 10 rules to make sure you don't get tripped up:

Rule No. 1: Be prepared to prove paternity.

In the United States, the first person to create something gets credit for it. Experts recommend keeping detailed notes in a lab notebook that are dated, signed, and witnessed by someone who understands the technology. Careful records will enable you to prove later that you are the proud father. You never know, there may be some other guy fooling around in his garage with the same thing.

Rule No. 2: Don't create on company time.

Most engineers and R&D professionals give up ownership rights of anything they invent for their employer. In some cases, even inventions made on your own time may belong to the company (check your employment contract or employee handbook).

Rule No. 3: Do your homework.

Existing patents, even expired ones, and relevant technical literature, together known as *prior art*, may reveal that your invention is not new or nonobvious. You can research patents using the government's online patent archives (*www.uspto.gov*), which date back to 1790. For more thorough searches, visit the PTO in Arlington, Virginia or one of the Patent and Trademark Depository Libraries located across the country. Better yet, hire someone (see Rule No. 4).

Rule No. 4: Hire a professional to help.

Although you can do your own preliminary research, and even file a provisional (patent pending) application yourself, preparing a patent application is a job for an expert. Hire a registered patent attorney or patent agent to assist you. Full patentability searches can cost up to $1,000, and professionally prepared patent applications can exceed $10,000, but do you want to be known as a tinkerer or an *inventor*?

Rule No. 5: Assess the market first.

Many inventors are great at making things, but lousy at estimating their market appeal. If your invention won't sell, there is no reason to go through the hassle and expense of obtaining a patent. Filing a provisional application (cost: $80) gives you a year of protection to test-market your invention before you have to file a full-blown patent application. Use the one-year grace period to contact potential corporate partners and venture capitalists who can give you a reality check, help you develop the product further, or provide funding. Watch out for invention promoters (see Rule No. 8).

Rule No. 6: Loose lips sink patents.

If patent examiners determine your invention has been in the public domain for more than one year, your application will be rejected. For example, 3M had one of its patents invalidated because the company had given samples of a product to thousands of workers for their personal use. You could be on thin ice if you disclose your invention at a trade conference. Publishing your findings in a scientific journal is tantamount to running down to the patent office and tearing your application into tiny pieces.

Rule No. 7: Licensing is often better than manufacturing.

Developing and manufacturing an invention often requires a tremendous investment in engineering, testing, prototyping, and tooling. And while you futz around trying to produce your gizmo, the 20-year clock on your patent continues to run. If your invention is really good, somebody should be willing to license it from you. The royalties you earn may be less than the potential profits from selling the product, but 15 percent of something is better than 100 percent of nothing.

Rule No. 8: Watch out for invention promoters.

Slick promoters typically advertise on late night TV and radio with 800-numbers. For a couple hundred bucks, the firm will "evaluate" your invention. Invariably, the promoter is thrilled and thinks your whirligig has enormous market potential. The catch is you have to send them a few thousand dollars in retainer fees before they do spit. According to the Federal Trade Commission, the actual success rate of many of these firms is less than 1 percent. Ask for references and check them out with the Better Business Bureau or at *www.inventorfraud.com* before you send money. Some invention promoters *are* legit, just not many.

Rule No. 9: Defending a patent is expensive.

A patent gives you the right to sue others for infringement, which unfortunately is a darn expensive right to exercise. Patent lawyers don't work cheap; you would be hard pressed to find one willing to clear his throat for less than $300. Make sure you budget for legal fees. If you can't afford to sue infringers, you may as well have a patent on sunlight.

Rule No. 10: Misery loves company.

If you are struggling with your invention, there are hundreds of not-for-profit inventors' groups around the country. These groups provide a forum for exchanging information, evaluating one another's inventions, and lamenting how hard it is to be a misunderstood genius. See *www.patentcafe.com* for a listing of inventors' groups by state.

To apply for a patent, you need to file an application containing a discussion of the current state of the art, a detailed description and drawings of your invention, and at least one claim as to why it is unique, along with $370, to the U.S. Patent & Trademark Office, Washington, D.C. 20231, (800) 786-9199. See the agency's Website for more particulars.

The PTO's examining division will conduct a search to determine whether your invention is, in fact, novel and nonobvious. Be patient, it may take up to two years. The PTO's response, called an office action, will detail the examiner's objections to your application (examiners very rarely allow a patent on the first pass). Objections can range from failure to show novelty to nitpicky omissions in the application. You must respond by filing an amendment to your application that addresses each of the examiner's concerns. In some cases, you will have to narrow your claims to satisfy the examiner. Within six months, the examiner will respond with a second office action. If the patent gods shine on you and the examiner allows your claims, you will be asked to send in another $640 and your patent will arrive in the mail soon thereafter. Maintenance fees have to be paid at 3 1/2 years, 7 1/2 years, and 11 1/2 years from the date of issuance to keep the patent valid.

If, after amending your application, the examiner remains unconvinced and rejects your claims, you can try pleading, begging—even logic. If none of that gets you anywhere, you can appeal to the Board of Appeals and Patent Interferences, the Court of Appeals for the Federal Circuit and, ultimately, the Supreme Court.

And if the Supreme Court turns you down? Well, you can always go back to your basement and create something else. Ever thought about hair-in-a-can?

How to become a day trader

Now that Internet stocks have died their pitiful and well-deserved deaths, it is only natural to expect day trading would not survive. After all, day traders piled on when stocks like Yahoo! and Amazon.com were going to the moon, so one would expect them to be casualties when technology stocks collapsed in the spring of 2000. But day trading remains—with fewer but wiser participants. Like fleas, day traders leapt from the dying carcasses of the dot-coms to ride on the backs of other stocks.

A little history is required to understand how what is essentially an adult video game became a legitimate business. Day trading, or the intraday trading of stocks for short-term profit, first became practical in January 1997, when NASDAQ allowed individuals to display their best bids and offers. This type of information, called *Level III*, is the core requirement for *direct-access trading* (DAT). At the same time, commission rates, which had previously eaten up all the profit on small trades, dropped to where it became possible for little guys to trade with the big guys on more or less even footing. A raging bull market, particularly in technology stocks, caused droves of people to get day trading fever. Meanwhile, a constant stream of articles in the popular press proclaimed how students, housewives, and laid-off executives made a fortune from day trading.

There are an estimated 5,000 to 7,500 hardcore day traders and as many as 50,000 occasional day traders in the U.S. Many trade from their homes. Others trade from trading rooms set up for the purpose at brokerage firms. Some even sneak a few trades at work. Day trading is premised on the fact that investors frequently overreact to the news of the day. Overreactions create opportunities for traders, who can get in after good news has been overbought or bad news has been oversold. The main thrust of day trading is simple: create short-term profits by guessing correctly which way a stock will move, and aggressively act to truncate losses when you guess wrong.

Think of it this way. In a perfectly neutral market, stocks have an even chance of going either up or down. If a stock moves the wrong way, the day trader reverses the trade immediately and takes a small loss. If it moves the right way, the day trader lets it run but takes a profit at the first sign of weakness. Over time, good (or lucky) traders' wins more than offset their loses. Entry and exit from a position can occur within minutes. The average day trader makes 29 trades, or almost 15 roundtrips per day. Speed is in. Fundamentals and prosaic information like the company's market position are out the window.

A report issued in 2000 by the Senate Permanent Subcommittee on Investigations said 77 percent of all day traders lose money. Nevertheless, there is no question that some of the other 23 percent make pots full. If you are unemotional, disciplined, have a high tolerance for risk, and possess $50,000 to $100,000 in capital, you too can be a day trader.

The first thing a new trader should do is take a training course (offered by brokers and others) to get a general feel for trading and the markets. After that comes the most important part—spending time on a simulator. You can purchase or rent the simulation software from your broker or various other vendors. Be sure the simulator you choose uses live quotes so you can test your trading acumen in real time. Spend as much time as you need on the simulator. It is a very inexpensive way to make mistakes.

The next step is to open a brokerage account with a direct-access trading firm, of which there are dozens. These firms offer volume commission discounts, rapid executions and confirmations, real-time account information, and sophisticated trading software. In addition, good direct-access brokers offer trading facilities, ongoing support, and training programs. (Note: There is a significant difference between DAT firms and regular online brokers, like Charles Schwab and E*TRADE, that do not allow regular customers to post orders directly to the markets.

Day trading through an online broker is like taking a taxicab around the Daytona International Speedway. However, most online brokerage firms have acquired DAT firms so they can offer services to day traders.)

A DAT account is similar to a conventional brokerage account, except it allows you to trade directly into the market and features lower margin requirements for intra-day positions and a volume-based commission structure. Day trading commissions range from $9 to $25 per trade, with an average of around $16. Fixed costs for trading software and exchange access vary, but typically run from $200 to $400 per month.

Direct-access brokers are subject to the same SEC and NASD regulations as the Wall Street houses and discount brokers. They are required to ask questions about your trading intentions, annual income, net worth, and experience. How you answer them determines how much margin they will extend to you. (If you have meager means, you may only be able to trade on a cash-settlement basis—severely limiting the amounts you can trade; you may as well trade pet rocks for a living.) The NASD requires day traders to maintain a minimum of $25,000 in equity in their account in order to trade. Your broker will enforce this rule once you commence day trading.

You have to choose whether to trade at home or at the brokerage firm's facility. One advantage to trading with others is the opportunity to share information and trading strategies, (which may not be all that helpful because most of those guys are losing money—remember the old bumper sticker: "Don't follow me. I'm lost too!"). If you elect to trade at home, you will need a modem, high-speed Internet connection, and two phone lines in case one goes down. Your broker will set you up with trading software, analytical tools, and a live quote feed for a monthly fee.

Before putting your capital on the line, you should decide on a strategy, establish your own trading boundaries, and stick to them religiously. For example, true day traders never hold positions overnight. Another particularly common mistake rookies make is attempting to recoup losses by swinging for the fences. Others rationalize holding on to losing positions or chase stock upward before buying it. Capital preservation is critical. Experts recommend never risking more than 5 percent of your capital at any time. Successful day traders know their break-even points and have mental "stop-losses" in place. (Automatic stops are impractical for day trading).

Still interested? Here are some generic strategies employed by day traders:

- *Scalping* is the practice of skimming profits from tiny movements in price. Scalpers make dozens of trades a day. This strategy requires patience and quick reflexes. Research shows day traders who hold stocks more than two minutes are likely to lose money.
- *Momentum* trading is riding a stock up or down in the wake of a news event or major buying by an institution. This strategy is difficult to perfect since professional investors are usually sellers into good news and vice-versa. Getting on the wrong end of a stock at both ends (buying high and selling low) is known as being "whipsawed," which actually hurts more than you would think.
- *One stock* is the strategy of following just one stock that you know inside and out. This is an interesting approach because you will develop a better feeling for the Wall Street market-makers who are moving the stock, potentially allowing you an edge in reading the market.
- *Shadowing* is following large market-makers and institutional traders in hopes of riding their coattails into serious dough. Shadowing is very tricky because firms that place trades large enough to move a stock are also smart enough to disguise their intentions.
- *Opportunists* range all over the market looking for stocks that are not tracking with news on their peers or trading relative to their company's performance. This strategy requires self-control. An inexperienced trader can go from opportunistic to unfocused in a hurry.

Day trading is not for everybody. There is immense financial risk to people who are undisciplined. Still, how else can you make several hundred thousand dollars a year sitting in front of a computer in your underwear? And despite the negative press, not everybody loses. In a 1999 study by the DAT broker Momentum Securities Management, 58 percent of rookie day traders lost money during their first three months trading, but 65 percent made money after five months.

How to protect yourself without buying a gun

There are any number of possible self-defense weapons scattered around the average house: baseball bats, golf clubs, fireplace tools, kitchen knives, and less deadly implements like scissors, knitting needles, and broom handles. But whereas you can sleep with a Louisville Slugger by your bed, carrying a meat cleaver to the grocery store is liable to get you arrested.

You could carry a gun, but firearms aren't legal to carry in many areas—and dangerous in the wrong hands, too. What you need is a safe, discrete weapon that packs a wallop. Some options are listed below.

Pepper spray

This pocket thug repellent is cheap, effective, and easy to carry (there is even a model disguised as a fountain pen). Pepper spray is delivered via a pressurized canister of a liquid laced with red pepper that is sprayed into an attacker's face to cause temporary blindness and choking. It is designed to be used from 10 to 12 feet away. Although pepper spray has been shown to be effective 90 percent of the time, its effectiveness drops to 75 percent if the attacker is crazed or on drugs. ($10 to $25 at Pepper Spray, Inc., (866) 274-6366.)

Ultra-power flashlight

Marketed as the Security Blanket AL22, this baby produces 110,000 lumens, which is roughly 1,000 times brighter than a normal flashlight. The Security Blanket AL22 resembles a large flashlight, but weighs under two pounds and runs on a 9-volt battery. Shining the light into an attacker's face produces temporary blindness to give you time to run away or kick the menace you-know-where. ($500 at Electromax International, (281) 531-7437, *www.electromax.com*).

Stun guns

Talon, Stun Master, and Z-Force each make units about the size of a walkie-talkie that pack up to 250,000 volts of stun power. Stun guns are used by touching the assailant for three to five seconds, causing temporary disorientation and loss of balance by disrupting signals from the brain to the muscles. Most models feature safety switches to prevent zapping yourself. The main disadvantage to stun guns is that they must be used at arm's length from the attacker. In addition, they are not legal in all areas. ($25 to $40 at Personal Arms.com, (201) 641-1442.)

Roman knuckles

Brass knuckles have proven effective in fistfights since Roman times. They're easy to use, long-lasting, and fit in your back pocket. However, because real brass knuckles are not legal in many areas, they are often sold as "paperweights" (wink, wink). Other (legal) models are available in light-weight aluminum or hardened plastic. One size fits all ($10 to $20 at *www.selfdefenseproducts.com*).

Uncomfortable with offensive weapons? Play defense with this spy gear:

Shocking briefcase

If you carry lots of cash or deal in diamonds, there is a product on the market worthy of James Bond's eccentric armorer, "Q." The "shocker" briefcase can be set to not only shock a would-be robber with 40,000 volts, but also pierce his eardrums with a 104-decibel siren. The features can be triggered by a remote control from up to 100 yards away. Runs on re-chargeable batteries. ($500 at Electromax International.)

Ballistic raincoat

Those who spend a lot of time in the line of fire (Secret Service agents, inner-city schoolteachers) may want to consider getting the rain- and bulletproof macintosh. This trench coat makes a great companion piece to the shocking briefcase and looks good with a Burberry scarf. Available in tan, blue, or black. ($2,395 at the Counter Spy Shop, *www.ebm-online.com/djm.*)

Ballistic clipboard

The essential modern accessory for any office is the bulletproof clipboard, which improves productivity by allowing you to keep taking notes even during a hail of gunfire. Stops bullets up to .45-caliber. ($49.95 at Master of Concealment, (800) 601-8273, *www.masterofconcealment.com.*)

Anti-kidnapping system

Executive kidnappings are on the rise, especially in Mexico, South America, and Russia. For the ultimate in security, you can purchase an anti-kidnapping system that uses Doppler technology to locate signals from a micro-transmitter so small it can be hidden on your person. Indispensable for doing business in Colombia. ($2,250 at Spy Stuff, (800) 996-6023, *www.spystuff.com.*)

How to cure hiccups

Hiccups have bedeviled people since the first caveman shoved too big a hunk of woolly mammoth into his gullet. *Singultus*, as it is medically known, results from an irritation of the diaphragm, usually caused by indigestion. Phrenic nerve fibers discharge in response, resulting in the spasmodic, painful contractions of the diaphragm. Air is sucked in, then the windpipe abruptly closes (Hic!). Hiccups have no beneficial purpose, though they do argue for taking smaller bites and chewing your food slowly.

For hundreds of years, hiccups cures have been pretty much the same (hold a sugar cube or glob of peanut butter in your mouth, drink water through a handkerchief, stand on your head, breathe through a paper bag, munch on a wedge of lime, etc.), Thomas Assmar, of Jewett City, Connecticut, invented a supposedly miraculous hiccup-curing machine that sufferers would stand on while drinking water and be tossed up and down 92 times a minute. It is claimed that everybody who tried it was cured—over 100 people in all—but the machine has been lost since Assmar died in 1978.

Except for Assmar's inventions, for hundreds of years hiccups cures have been pretty much the same (hold a sugar cube or glob of peanut butter in your mouth, drink water through a handkerchief, stand on your head, breathe through a paper bag, munch on a wedge of lime, etc.) But if you suffer from frequent attacks of the hiccups, you have probably tried all of these remedies and found them wanting. Fortunately, medical science has weighed in on the problem.

Instead of a folk remedy, try the Hughes/Green hiccups cure, invented by former hiccups sufferer Dave Hughes, of Redwood Valley, California: (1) Pour a tall glass of water. (2) While holding your breath and pinching your nose closed, repeatedly take sips of water until you feel like you are drowning, then stop. (3) Inhale deeply and breathe normally. The hiccups should be cured. Hughes believes this technique works by depriving the spasmodic muscles of oxygen, causing them to stop the hiccuping reflex.

For more stubborn cases, try icing down the nerve fibers that are responsible. It turns out the ideal places to interrupt the hiccups are the sides of the neck. To stop the hiccups, use the method developed by S. Gregory Hipskind, M.D., of Bellingham, Washington. Find your Adam's apple (for women, this point is about 2 inches directly below the chin). Move back until you are above your clavicle (the big protruding bone at the base of your neck). You should be just behind the sternocleidomastoid muscles, well back of and below your carotid arteries. Apply ice cubes to each side until the hiccuping stops.

In really serious cases, your doctor can give you a shot of nefopam, an anti-shivering medication that is highly effective, or baclofen, a muscle relaxant. If those injections don't work, nimodipine, a calcium channel blocker that inhibits muscle contractions, has been shown to cure even the most intractable cases of the hiccups.

If all else fails, consider the last-resort, successful cure of the former hiccup world-record holder, Jack O'Leary of Los Angeles, who hiccuped an estimated 100 million times during an eight-year bout: a prayer to St. Jude, the patron saint of lost causes.

How to dodge speeding tickets

In the eyes of Americans, speed limits have joined the long list of laws that don't apply to them, like jaywalking, spitting on the sidewalk, and paying nanny taxes. Travel times are quoted in terms of speeding or not speeding. Going above the posted limit is not viewed as lawbreaking, but rather, a prudent timesaving approach to driving.

Of course, the police departments around the country have a different viewpoint. Most police officers actually take their duties of enforcing the traffic laws seriously. Every day in the United States, there are tens of thousands of speeding tickets written (100,000 by one estimate) with millions of dollars of penalties to motorists (not to mention higher insurance premiums for repeat offenders). For many municipalities, ticket writing is an important source of revenue, and state police departments often have quotas to keep troopers on their toes. Radar guns can be notoriously inaccurate to boot, and you may be ticketed even if you aren't the one speeding. To minimize your chances of getting a ticket, there are a number of tactics that can be employed.

Radar works by bouncing radio waves at a specific frequency off of a subject, which are returned at a different frequency. An algorithm calculates the speed of the subject based upon the change in frequency. Radar beams spread out over distance and are consequently less accurate the farther away the subject is. Regular radar has an operating range of about 2,000 feet, while laser radar is theoretically effective up to a mile. However, both radar systems' effective ranges are closer to 600 to 800 feet due to police department guidelines, requiring the officer to first obtain a visual speed estimate. Radar can be used in both stationary and moving vehicles.

Laser radar, or "Lidar," has been around for over a decade, but is still used by only 10 percent of police cars due to its high cost. Instead of radio waves, Lidar uses a beam of light that is bounced off the subject. Lidar is more of a threat to speeders than regular radar for two reasons. First, its longer range is deadly at night when coupled with the "instant-on" feature, which makes its radar signature harder to detect in advance. Second, it uses a very narrow beam of light that does not diffuse like radar, thus reducing errors caused by interference from neighboring vehicles. Lidar can only be used from stationary police cars and must be mounted on the outside of the vehicle.

Radar detectors

Currently lawful throughout the United States except for Virginia and Washington, D.C., radar detectors are your best insurance policy against a ticket (Virginia, in fact, equips troopers with a radar detector sensing device called VG-2.). Any good quality radar detector is effective against conventional radar. Using it regularly will enable you to distinguish between false alarms and a speed trap.

If the police in your area use Lidar or you are traveling cross-country, consider investing in a Lidar detector to improve your chances. You still must be cautious, though. Even the best models are no defense against the instant-on feature employed by police to foil detector users. On a highway with light traffic, particularly at night, the speeder is highly vulnerable to Lidar. Laser detectors should always be mounted on the dashboard, never on the rearview mirror or the windshield, where the height differential from the Lidar signal is greatest. Leading radar and Lidar detector manufacturers include Passport/Escort, Uniden, BEL, Valentine, Whistler, and Cobra.

Stealth helps

In order for Lidar to work properly, it must be aimed either at the front or the back of the target car. Some experts suggest reducing the effective range of the Lidar unit by lowering the reflectivity of your vehicle. It is easy to get carried away with this, taping over taillights and doing other unsafe things, but keep in mind that police usually aim at your front license plate. If your state does not require a front plate, take it off. (Tests show aftermarket license plate covers marketed as "radar absorbers" are of no value.) There are, however, other targets on the front of the car, particularly the grill and headlights that will return a signal. The more aerodynamic the car, the fewer the angles that will reflect back, (exactly the excuse you need to go out and buy that Lamborghini Murcielago!).

Jam 'em

While active transmissions of jamming signals are illegal in this country, passive jamming is legal in most states and effective against regular radar. (States that ban passive jammers include California, Minnesota, Nebraska, Oklahoma, Virginia, and Washington, D.C.) Jammers are the size of a radar detector and mount the same way. Standard radar jammers work by adding some FM "noise" to the radar signal and sending it back to the radar gun, which then cannot recognize the signal. The radar unit's readout will sit there waiting for feedback and not record any speed. Use jammers with caution, though; they only provide five to 10 seconds of protection. For this reason, always use a jammer in concert with a detector; a passive jammer should give you plenty of lead-time to reduce your speed after your detector goes off. Laser jammers also are available, although most models are too weak to be effective. One exception is the

Lidatek Laser Echo, which uses a powerful anti-Lidar laser. All Lidar jammers must be mounted at the front license plate to work well. Jammers are not cheap ($250 and up for good ones), but worth it if you want extra peace of mind.

Keep a sharp eye out

Police hide along highways on median strips, behind billboards, atop on-ramps, in rest areas, around curves, and on the other side of hills. They also operate in tag teams. After passing one squad car, you may accelerate just in time to see another one waiting up ahead. Brake lights coming on in fast-moving traffic and helpful headlight blinking from oncoming traffic are the best clues of Smokey nearby. You can also check for speed trap information by location at the Website *www.speedtrap.org*. Unfortunately, the information it contains is volunteered by your fellow motorists and may be spotty or out of date.

As for Bears in the air, signs that read "SPEED CHECKED BY AIR-CRAFT SURVEILLANCE" are 95 percent baloney. Police departments have almost totally abandoned air surveillance because it costs far more to operate an airplane plus several ground units to chase down violators. Keep your eyes on the road—where the police are.

Drive when the bears are sleeping

A simpler idea for avoiding the cops is to change your travel habits. There are fewer police on the road on Saturdays and holidays. Also, announcements about speeding crackdowns before major holidays are usually just bunk. Police officers get time off to spend time with their families, too.

Find the tolerance level

Big cities with more traffic have fewer on-duty police per car. Police know the ratios and will adjust their ticket issuance accordingly. The math works in reverse in rural areas, especially certain parishes of Louisiana and towns in New England. Also, do not speed through construction and school zones. Besides being dangerous, fines may be higher in these areas, and they are popular locations for speed traps.

Stay to the right

Cars on the right are less frequently targeted because they are usually going slower. In addition, radar aimed at the right-hand lane from the median strip, where troopers often sit, results in a slightly lower reading than your actual speed due to the angle. Plus, driving near semis can shield your car from conventional radar guns.

Use citizen's band

Not seen in most cars since the days of *Smokey and the Bandit*, the citizen's band radio is still one of the best ways to learn where the Fuzz is. If you wince at being seen by your neighbors sporting one of those whippy aerials on your car, don't worry. The newer radios have antennas that are practically unnoticeable. Plus, a CB will look right at home in your '76 Camaro alongside the eight-track tape deck. Just as a refresher, a *convoy* is a series of speeding vehicles; *double-nickel* is the hated speed limit in many areas; *putting the hammer down* is accelerating when there are no cops around. Copy that, good buddy?

Spike your brakes

If you suddenly come upon a squad car on the roadside that appears to be running radar, hit your brakes. He may have his gun pointed at a car in front of yours and give you just enough time to slow down and avoid a ticket. Be careful breaking in heavy traffic.

Be nice if you get caught

If you see a police car behind you with his lights on, safely pull over and slowly come to a stop. Roll down the window and sit there while the officer runs your license plate. Do not jump out of your car—they *hate* that. When the officer approaches, be polite but don't be patronizing. Take off your sunglasses and try not to look threatening. Remember, until disproved to the officer's satisfaction, you are potentially a dangerous felon fleeing from the law.

Don't act as if you are planning to fight a ticket in court (even if you are). The number one reason tickets are dismissed is poor memory on the part of the cop. If you act belligerently, he's more likely to remember you. Excuses generally do not work and may prompt the officer to ticket you just for spite. Instead, admit that you were speeding (if you were) and act sincerely sorry. You may just get off with a warning.

On rare occasions, however, the smart-ass remark works. Gene Mason, in his book *Save Your License! A Drivers Survival Guide*, tells the story of two women stopped by a Colorado State patrolman for speeding. "He walked over to their car, and the attractive young driver frivolously asked, 'Did you stop us to sell us tickets to the Policeman's Ball?' His immediate, unthinking answer was 'Ladies, state patrolmen don't have balls.' After a few seconds of speechless embarrassment, he turned abruptly, returned to his patrol car and peeled rubber into the night." You should only be so lucky.

You can win in court

If you get a ticket despite all your charm and are confident (or bull-headed) enough to go to court, you need to start building your case immediately. Take notes on the day, time, location, weather conditions, and other nearby traffic. Strong memory is very important in court, but you have the edge. The officer who stopped you has to remember details about dozens of tickets—you only have to remember one. Here are five defenses you can use to win your case.

- *Defense No. 1: The law you were charged with breaking does not apply.* Proving the law is inapplicable or ambiguous in a speeding case is very difficult. The police probably know the speed limit zones better than you, so you are unlikely to prevail. (You may think you have found the Holy Grail if the ordinance on the ticket has a numerical error, but most judges will overlook it.) If you were unfairly cited, go back and take photographs of speed limit signs and the area where you were supposedly speeding to use as evidence in court. Bring along your tape measure; sometimes signs are planted too far from the road or at an improper height, making them difficult to see. Check your state's signage regulations.

- *Defense No. 2: The officer did not use the radar gun properly.* While the officer may in fact be incompetent, the court presumes he knows what he is doing. If you truly believe he is a nincompoop, contact the police department and request information about the officer's training on the radar gun in question. Also contact the manufacturer and find out what the recommended training is for the unit. While you are at it, get information about the unit's usable range and factors that may limit its accuracy, such as multiple cars, wind, or snow. Armed with this information, you can cross-examine the officer on technical details about the operation of the radar gun and hope he stumbles.

- *Defense No. 3: The radar gun was broken or produced a faulty reading.* Request the police department's maintenance records on the officer's radar gun (these can be subpoenaed if necessary), including the date of the last calibration. Recent repairs may cast doubt on the unit's accuracy. You can also contact the manufacturer to obtain their recommended maintenance schedule for comparison. Blowing objects, such as leaves and raindrops, can also interfere with a radar gun's accuracy. You may have a case for dismissal if you got a ticket during a heavy storm.

- *Defense No. 4: You were mistakenly cited*. It was that red car that zoomed by. Didn't you see it, officer? Mistaken identity is hard to prove, but if plausibly shown, it warrants a dismissal. Make careful notes about other traffic on the road at the time. Also, scour your ticket for signs that it was partially filled out ahead of time (wrong date, time, etc.). One or more such errors and an aggrieved air in front of the judge could just get you off.

- *Defense No. 5: The officer fails to show*. Officer absences generally mean immediate dismissal because there is no one to testify for the prosecution. Policemen typically have a specific day during the month when they will be in court and write that date on the ticket. To improve the likelihood he will not show, call the clerk's office and request a change of the trial date. If you happen to be the only ticket on the officer's docket that day, he is less likely to bother.

How to photograph an active volcano

No, we're not talking about jumping out of the bushes to get a shot of Sean Penn before he puts a finger in your eye. We are talking about a *real* volcano, with magma gushing out at 2,200 degrees Fahrenheit.

There are active volcanoes all over the world, but some of the easiest to approach are in the Volcanoes National Park in Hawaii, including Mauna Ulu, Pu'u O'o, Halemaumau, Mauna Loa, and the world's most active volcano, Kilauea. Park rangers can give information as to which roads are open and what areas are safe. (Tip: Islanders make offerings of gin to Pele, the Goddess of Fire, and perhaps you should too—before you get too close.)

A high-quality, single-lens reflex camera and a variety of lenses are essential for photographing volcanoes. If you are on foot, 24mm to 85mm fixed-focal length lenses or a zoom lens equivalent will suffice. (Always have a protective filter mounted on your lens to protect against damage from volcanic ash and spray.) During the early morning and evening hours when the light is low, it is essential to use a tripod. Make sure yours is sturdy and has metal spikes on the end instead of rubber feet, which can't take the heat. A backpack will work better than a camera bag because it distributes the weight more evenly and will help you keep your balance on the uneven landscape.

Wear a helmet, long clothing, heavy boots, and carry a sturdy poncho. You should also wear a respirator with a filter for volcanic fumes. Guides with four-wheel drive vehicles can be hired to get you closer to the eruption sites. The intense heat will tell you when you are reaching the danger zone. When the bottoms of your hiking boots start to melt you are close enough. Check with the National Park Service rangers for information about which areas are safe to visit.

If a volcano is actively erupting, a safer and more effective way to photograph it is from the air. Both airplanes and helicopters are readily available for rent. In either case, make sure the doors come off (photographing through Plexiglas will yield distorted images). Helicopters are roomier, can fly slower, and hover in the wind, but are less stable and noisier. Light planes are smoother, but cannot fly slower than about 60 knots without stalling and need to stay above 1,000 feet. Whichever aircraft you choose, ask around and make sure you get a good pilot.

In the air, you will need longer focal-length lenses, from 35mm to 135mm, in order to avoid getting the plane's wings or the helicopter's skids and rotors in your pictures. With longer lenses and the vibration caused by the aircraft, you will need to use higher shutter speeds and a tripod.

The extraordinary luminosity of molten lava makes it an interesting subject for photography at dawn or dusk. During the day, photograph the myriad lava "ropes," swirls, and other patterns that the cooled lava creates. Black-and-white film and strong backlighting will best render the textural gradations of this monochromatic subject. From the air in low light, set your focus to infinity and open the aperture all the way. Fast color film will allow you to use higher shutter speeds with longer lenses. With a tripod on the ground, you can create more interesting effects using time exposures. Use a variety of f-stops to "bracket" the exposure and manually expose the film for 10 to 30 seconds to capture a stream of flowing lava. Polarizing filters work well with color film. Try yellow or red filters with black-and-white film.

If you decide to shoot lava flowing into the ocean—an incredibly photogenic sight—keep your distance. The steam spray it sends up contains sulfuric and hydrochloric acids, which can do serious damage to your equipment, not to mention your skin.

How to drive like Richard Petty

Enroll in his driving school, of course. In Petty's school and others like it, students learn the fundamentals of handling a race car, like heel-and-toe shifting, double-clutching, braking, cornering, and drafting. In instructor-led sessions, students drive modified stock cars through slalom courses, on slippery "skid pads," and around closed racetrack ovals at speeds up to 160 miles per hour. Participants learn vehicle dynamics, like weight transfer, understeer, and oversteer, through classroom lessons and demonstrations.

Besides a valid driver's license, all you need is the ability to drive a manual transmission—though quick reflexes and ice water in your veins also help. Students are allowed to proceed at their own pace. Squirrelly drivers are quickly isolated by the instructors and kept in the slow lane so they stay out of trouble.

Tuition runs from about $500 to $1,000 per day. Many schools offer one-, two- and three-day driving courses. At BMW's school, tuition is free with the purchase of an M5 (list price: $70,400). Schools may also require you to take out insurance coverage on their automobiles in case you crash. At the Porsche school, which features modified 911s, insurance carries a $10,000 damage deductible, although you can lower it to $2,000 for an additional $100 per day.

There are numerous driving schools, which run the gamut from road-skills clinics to hard-core racetrack driving sessions. Prominent graduates of the largest and best-known school, Skip Barber Racing School, include racing champions Michael Andretti and Jeff Gordon, and racing aficionado Paul Newman.

If you are a jaded adventurer, for whom going 160 miles per hour just isn't enough of a thrill, see "How to fly a jet fighter without joining the armed services."

How to go public

For the vast majority of private companies, going public is impossible if they are too small, are not growing fast enough, lack a good use of proceeds, have weak management, or in a crummy industry. Even for those that can, going public may be ill-advised. It takes real skill for a CEO to convert from running a private company to operating in the public markets, which feature such delights as Securities and Exchange Commission (SEC) reporting requirements, pesky shareholders, and your salary blasted all over the world on the Internet. But for a select few companies, going public is the answer. It is the cheapest way to raise large amounts of capital, bring notoriety to the company, and facilitate stock-based incentive plans. Before you phone Goldman Sachs, though, you should know what's involved.

The requirements

The bar for going public is moved all the time without fanfare. During the peak of the dot-com insanity in 1999, a handful of Ph.D.s with a novel idea and a short business plan—"three guys and 12 pages"—could raise venture capital and go public in six months. Those days are over as burned investors now insist on higher-quality companies with real businesses, profits, presidents older than 25, and CFOs who don't sport orange hair and hi-tops at annual meetings.

A high-caliber management team is paramount, especially in a young company. Experience dealing with public markets is a valuable plus. The chief financial officer is the second-most important member of the team during the Initial Public Offering (IPO). The CFO, who will field most investor inquiries after you are public, should be articulate and have SEC reporting experience. Underwriters often suggest beefing up with additional management talent prior to the IPO. It also helps if managers have significant skin in the game in the form of stock ownership. The IPO process is so arduous that you may want to offer a bonus to key employees if the company completes the offering.

The company should be growing rapidly and therefore have a bonafide use of the proceeds from the IPO. Ideally, the company will have already raised venture capital and/or tapped out its credit at the bank. Investors hate putting money into a company that won't use it to make more money. Plant expansions, working capital, and new product development are the best uses. Repaying high-cost debt is okay. Redeeming shareholders or otherwise sending money out of the company is a no-no. Insiders should never try to sell more than 20 percent of their holdings in an IPO. Insider-selling sends a very bad signal and makes investors wonder, "If the future is so great, how come you're selling stock so cheaply?"

The good part about analyzing an IPO is that unless you are *sui generis*, you can use the financial and valuation metrics of the public firms in your industry to precisely benchmark your company's performance. The bad part is that while your company may be chugging along, if the stocks of the comparable companies are sucking wind, you probably can't go public. Hopefully the comparable stocks will be closer to their 52-week highs than their lows.

Wall Street goes hot and cold on concepts with maddening frequency. Fads, such as conglomerates, consolidation plays, and the infamous dot-coms, caught fire and were quickly stamped out by fickle investors. Even solid industries, such as health care, energy, technology, and transportation, suffer from investor whimsy. In fact, sometimes only companies in the right industry *sector* can sneak through a narrow IPO window. For example, healthcare overall may be down, but medical device makers may be hot. Ask the underwriters if you have any doubts about investor sentiment toward your industry sector.

The National Association of Securities Dealers requires at least three independent directors on your board, but more is even better. Also, try not to have more than two board members with the same last name. Furthermore, byzantine ownership structures set up to minimize taxes, high salaries, non-working relatives on the payroll, sweetheart leases, related-party deals, company-owned airplanes, and condos will all have to go.

The SEC generally requires three years of audited financial statements to go public. While accountants can audit prior years if your records are good, the process is expensive and time-consuming. If your numbers were audited by a regional or local firm, they will have to be re-audited by a national firm before any reputable underwriter will take you public.

The company's size is a tricky requirement to estimate. Since the first biotechnology offering by Amgen in 1983, revenues and profits have been viewed subjectively. This subjectivity devolved into lunacy during the Internet stock craze, when firms with meager revenues and no ideas about how to become profitable were going public. Investors have sobered up since then and are much less tolerant of tiny companies that have limited track records.

Perhaps the only way to get a good gauge on what is acceptable is to look at your projected *market capitalization* (stock price times shares outstanding post-offering). The bare minimum market cap for an institutional-quality IPO is $150 million. For example, if the forward price-to-earnings ratio for firms in your industry is 15, you need to have projected earnings of at least $10 million (15 x $10 million = $150 million) to go public. Although there are underwriters that will take smaller firms public, you probably would be better off staying private than going public with a small market cap and limited institutional interest in the stock.

The players

There are numerous parties involved in an IPO. The process cannot start until all the parties are assembled. These include the company's management team, the company's attorneys, the underwriters, the underwriters' attorneys, the company's accountants, and occasionally bankers or other advisers.

After the company, the most important parties to the transaction are the underwriters, also called investment bankers. There are 40 or so quality underwriters in the United States. The top firms, like Merrill Lynch, Lehman Brothers, and Morgan Stanley tend to concentrate on the largest companies, but make exceptions for smaller, rapidly growing companies. There is a small middle tier that includes technology boutiques, such as SG Cowen and Thomas Weisel Partners, and a larger group of smaller regional firms, like McDonald & Co. and Robert W. Baird.

You should first identify a number of qualified underwriters to interview. Your legal advisers and accountants can make recommendations. Also, you can research who has done other IPOs in your industry by looking at *www.ipo.com* and reviewing public filings at the Securities and Exchange Commission's Website, *www.sec.gov*. Before interviewing investment banks, be sure to provide them with a business plan containing a detailed forecast for at least the next two years, as well as three years of historical financial statements.

The two types of underwriters in a public offering are managers and syndicate members. The managers are the ones you will be working with day in and day out for (depending how it goes), four to six months. The syndicate is largely immaterial to most transactions and will be selected by the lead underwriter later. For an IPO, you should always have at least two managers. Multiple managers give you more horsepower, aftermarket research and trading support. A good rule of thumb is one manager for each $25 million in gross proceeds.

The managers are directed by the *lead manager*, who is selected by the company. The lead spot is highly coveted because it counts towards industry "league tables" (the scoreboard for investment banking) and because there is serious money involved. The difference between lead manager and comanager on a typical $50 million deal with two firms is about $500,000 in fees.

Investment banks will bring a team of bankers and a "pitch book" containing promotional materials on their firm, analysis of the company, its valuation in the public market, how the offering will be positioned, and timing. Three things will become obvious: (1) whether the investment bank has done its homework (if not, maybe they have more important things to work on—a bad sign); (2) whether the firm has a decent track record in your industry (most statistics are slanted through creative manipulation); and (3) whether the underwriter is enthused about your company or just going through the motions. (Do they have a plane to catch in two hours?) The highest-caliber investment bankers will be distinguished by how artfully they can sidestep a question.

The one key person you will not meet is the research analyst, who will cover your company after it goes public. Although research analysts are no longer allowed to participate in pitches, the lead manager's analyst is the single-most important person on the deal team, and can be the difference between $50 million in net proceeds and $500,000 down a rat hole. The analyst markets the deal to the firm's sales force as well as to institutional investors. Analysts prepare quarterly financial models that become the "numbers" the company must hit in the future. Because analysts are so valuable, a number of rating systems have been developed to help exploit them, including the *Institutional Investor* All-Star list and the *Wall Street Journal*'s All-Star survey. Ask for references from institutional investors and copies of research reports.

It is extremely important to choose underwriters you like and in whom you have confidence. After you have selected two or three managing underwriters, you will have to choose the lead manager. This Solomon-like assignment is highly unpleasant. The underwriters will wail and moan like little kids, complaining that if they don't get the lead their children will have to go to public school, etc. Stick to your guns and keep in mind they are paid many hundreds of thousands of dollars per year. Pity is wasted on these guys.

If you haven't figured it out by now, undertaking an IPO is extremely expensive. The company will spend at least $500,000 for legal, accounting, printing, travel, and other costs. The underwriters get paid by receiving a *gross spread*, or commission, on the amount of stock sold. For all but enormous IPOs, this amount is 7 percent.

Provided you have a qualified corporate securities attorney and a Big Four accountant, your team is complete. If not, you need to hire them. Make sure your attorney has worked on numerous IPOs before and is current on the SEC's vagaries. If company counsel is inadequate, the transaction will quickly bog down and costs will balloon.

The process

Every offering is different, but each has three main components: (1) due diligence and drafting, (2) registration, and (3) the offering itself, also known as the *roadshow*. If everything goes smoothly, the whole thing could be done in about four months. But if you hit numerous snags, it could take six months or more to complete.

The due diligence and drafting stage has two goals: educating the underwriters about every nuance of the company and preparing the *registration statement*, called an *S-1*, that will be filed with the SEC. *Due diligence* is the term for the legal responsibility of the underwriters to exercise care in their examination of the company, and in theory protect the poor shareholders from buying dreck. The underwriters will ask a grueling series of questions over several days. They will interview members of management and conduct background checks. Get all the skeletons out of the closet right away. Surprises are costly.

The drafting of the S-1 is done en masse by the "working group," which can consist of 12 or more people. This impossibly cumbersome process helps ensure that nothing falls through the cracks, and allows everyone to put in their nickel's worth. (You'll swear some of these guys are paid by the word.) The registration statement must contain specific information in a form set out by the SEC, and can run from 75 up to several hundred pages in length and take six or more weeks to draft.

The registration phase is the period after you have filed the S-1 and before the SEC exhausts its commentary on your filing. The SEC reviews the documents and sends out comments about 30 days later. With luck, you will have all the comments resolved to the SEC's satisfaction within another two weeks. This phase of the transaction can be maddening because it is the only one controlled by an outside party. The S-1 will be refiled several times until the SEC is satisfied.

If the underwriters feel market conditions are receptive, the roadshow will begin right away. Thousands of copies of the prospectus (the guts of an S-1) will be printed and delivered to prospective investors. The prospectus tells investors how many shares you are offering and the preliminary price range. Other than the prospectus, all selling done by the underwriters' sales forces and the company on the roadshow is *oral* (statements must be consistent with information filed with the SEC).

Institutions (mostly mutual funds) typically purchase 70 to 80 percent of an IPO and individual investors purchase the rest. The lead manager will arrange a jam-packed roadshow schedule to maximize the company's exposure to important institutional investors, such as Fidelity, Putnam, and T. Rowe Price. Generally roadshows last for 10 to 14 days, cover 12 to 15 cities, and include as many as 100 meetings with institutional investors. Roadshows are a logistical challenge, especially when there are many other IPOs going on. Underwriters frequently agree to split the cost of leasing a corporate jet for the roadshow with the company—definitely the way to travel if you can afford it.

Roadshow presentations are made by two or three key members of management to institutional investors in "one-on-ones." Presentations are made using either slide shows or "flip-books," depending upon the size of the audience. Roadshow travel is grueling, and you have to repeat the same stupid, 35-minute presentation over and over. But it's the way deals are done; most institutions will not buy stock on an IPO if they have not met management.

Towards the end of the roadshow, the order book will start to build. Institutions give "indications of interest" that are non-binding but serious expressions of demand. On the last day of the roadshow, the underwriters and the company negotiate the IPO price based upon the order book. (If there is no book, you should plan on being private for a while.) The underwriters want the price to go up strongly in the aftermarket (it's good advertising for the next deal). However, if the price skyrockets on the first day of trading, the company sold stock too cheaply. The stock should go up a little bit (10 percent to 15 percent), but not be flat and certainly not down.

An IPO that falls below its offering price is known as a broken deal. Companies with broken deals usually cannot raise public equity in the future (one of the primary reasons to go through all this in the first place). Broken deals also attract the vermin of Wall Street—attorneys who run shareholder lawsuit factories. They file dubious lawsuits that are nonetheless costly to defend and sometimes extract large settlements. So leave a little money on the table for investors. Just don't leave a lot.

How to live like a king for a day

Balfour Castle is available for rent. Located on Scotland's Isle of Shapinsay, Orkney, Balfour is claimed to be the northernmost castle in the world. The grounds are about as isolated as you can imagine, sitting on a 70-acre estate bounded by 10 miles of private coastline and two uninhabited islands. People are significantly outnumbered by puffins, arctic terns, and grey seals. The only access to Balfour is by ferry.

Formerly the home of the Balfour clan, the last family member, David Hubert Ligonier Balfour, died in 1961 with no heirs. It was acquired by the current proprietors, the Zawadski family, shortly after his death. The Victorian castle, built in 1848, has 52 rooms, including eight bedrooms. Roaring fires abound to dry out visitors damp from trekking around the island. Meals prepared at the castle are sumptuous and decidedly un-Scottish— no haggis, and plenty of fresh-caught seafood, as well as chicken and vegetables raised on the castle's farm. The family rents out the sleeping quarters, as well as the conservatory, drawing room, library, and dining room for parties. Prices are reasonable, and parties as small as eight can be accommodated, at £100 ($160) per person, including a three-course dinner and breakfast. To get to Balfour, fly into Kirkwall airport and take the ferry from Mainland Orkney to Shapinsay. To make reservations, telephone the Zawadskis at 011-44-1-856-711-282 (*www.balfourcastle.co.uk*).

If you are looking for something a bit more grand, for...say, the wedding of the century... Skibo Castle, located in the Scottish Highlands near Dornoch, is the ticket. Formerly the summer retreat of United States Steel founder and Scottish-born industrialist Andrew Carnegie, Skibo was recently the improbable site of Madonna's marriage to Guy Ritchie. Its grounds encompass 7,500 beautifully landscaped rolling acres tumbling down from the castle to the Dornoch Firth. The castle has 200 rooms, including 20 available for overnight accommodations, a 7,000-book library, a marble swimming pool, and a gymnasium. Outdoor activities feature golf (three courses), grouse and deer hunting, fly fishing, riding, sailing, tennis, falconry, and more.

The castle and grounds are operated as part of the Carnegie Club, a private country club with over 500 members. Room rates start at around £600 ($900) per night. Besides the price, there is one hitch: you are only allowed to use Skibo as a guest once in your lifetime. If you wish to come back, you have to join the club at the rate of £3,000 ($4,500) per year. To get there, fly your Lear jet into Inverness Airport and have your driver take you to Skibo, about an hour away. For more information, contact the Carnegie Club at 011-44-1-862-894-600, *www.carnegieclub.co.uk.*

How to avoid an audit

In the past, few pieces of mail were dreaded more than the "OFFICE AUDIT NOTICE" sent out by the Internal Revenue Service to announce their "proctological" exam of a poor taxpayer.

Well, times have changed. Stung by widely publicized 1997 Senate hearings where taxpayers testified to its deliberate meanness, the IRS has been busy trying to look considerate and avuncular. Its Website drips with helpful hints to maximize your deductions. Even its notoriously unpleasant field agents now want to be liked. Still, if you peel back the honey-roasted shell, inside you'll find the same old cockroach whose sole mission in life is to collect money.

Fortunately for the vulnerable taxpayer, the actual odds of being audited have never been lower. After the injustices done to taxpayers were aired, Congress slashed the IRS budget, forcing it to make do with 15 percent fewer examiners. At the same time, using computer programs to test for mismatched information has supplanted the more labor-intensive, but effective, random review method. As a result, face-to-face audits have fallen significantly. Even taxpayers earning over $100,000—traditionally a target-rich group—have about a 1-in-150 chance of being audited face-to-face, down from 1-in-9 in 1989. Yet if the odds of being audited have dropped, those selected have been screened more carefully and 80 percent of them will owe more money.

Know your enemy

The IRS initially screens returns using computers that compare filed amounts with data submitted by employers and financial institutions. Besides matching data, the computers use top-secret benchmarking and other techniques to determine if you are likely to be a cheat. (The IRS targets dozens of occupations for special treatment, including trial lawyers, musicians, taxi drivers, waiters, and car dealers.) After all the numbers are crunched, the computers spit out a number for each return called a "discriminate information function" (DIF) score. Filers with high DIF scores are flagged for further examination. Thus you can substantially lessen your chance of being selected by simply avoiding the computer tripwires.

Incomplete returns or those with math errors are kicked out and typically handled through a "mail audit," which is generally painless if you have required information in your files. The more serious "office audit" is the one that puts the fear of God in the taxpayer. Office audits generally occur at a local IRS office and take one day or less, but on average you will be $9,500 poorer when it's over. (The field audit, where revenue agents show up at your office and grill you for hours is seldom used for W-2 filers.) To keep from winding up in the unpleasant circumstance of having an IRS agent probing every aspect of your financial life, there are some steps you can take. Here are a few expert suggestions:

Be circumspect if you are self-employed

For some reason, the IRS views the self-employed as particularly susceptible to moral hazard. Self-employed people are two to 15 times more likely to be called for an audit than company employees. Unsurprisingly, Schedule C, which details self-employment income and expenses, receives a lot of scrutiny. High deductions relative to income are the first tip-off. Professor Amir Aczel, a mathematics professor at Bentley College, calculated that if Schedule C deductions are at least 63 percent of your Schedule C income, you will be singled out for examination. Every expense line item must be thoroughly documented, particularly those in the "miscellaneous" category. Failing to pay estimated self-employment taxes is a big red flag. Don't try to stretch your hobbies into businesses either. The IRS takes a dim view of activities that do not generate profits three years out of five. Some tax practitioners even suggest self-employed professionals incorporate as S-corporations, which are rarely audited. Partnerships are audited even less frequently.

Watch out for the home office deduction

This deduction, on Form 8829, is taken by millions of taxpayers and is becoming more popular due to the boom in telecommuting. Beware the common trap of claiming the deduction if you already have an employer-provided place to work. Some people also lose the deduction by failing to calculate the prorated amount of housing costs based upon the amount of space used for work.

Form counts

Type or very neatly print everything and make sure all the attachments are complete. Using a software tax return package, such as Intuit's Turbotax, is even better. Put N/A in place of a blank line. And double-check your math.

Provide backup

Be sure to include documentation for unusually large deductions that would catch an examiner's attention. If you need to provide an explanation for a deduction, use the IRS Form 8275.

File an amended return

If your recent return has a problem, don't wait. File an amended return and send in a check with a letter explaining your error. In all likelihood, you will be treated with leniency. If, however, you realize that a return you filed a couple of years ago has serious errors, sit tight until three years have passed, then file the amended return. That way the statute of limitations on your original return will have run out and you can only be audited on the amended one.

Stay married and don't fool around

The IRS is known to pay for tips on tax cheats. The best sources are former spouses and ex-lovers.

Fess up

If you made a really big boo-boo and want to come clean, you can make an anonymous *proffer* to the government through your attorney. The proffer describes your circumstances and seeks assurance from the government that you will not be prosecuted if you make full restitution. Hey, it's better than going to jail.

If you do get audited, tax attorneys advise you to answer questions truthfully and succinctly and to shut up. Examiners are trained to create pregnant pauses in the hope you will start talking about that limited partnership in the Cayman Islands. Even better, according to the tax pros, is to let your adviser handle it without you. If you cannot afford an attorney or tax accountant, consider hiring an "enrolled agent." They are federally licensed to represent taxpayers before the IRS and are typically less expensive than traditional counsel (contact the National Association of Enrolled Agents at 800-424-4339).

Don't fear the examiner, though. He doesn't really have any power of enforcement and his findings are subject to appeal.

How to climb Mount Everest

The Nepalis call it *Sagarmatha* (Mountain Goddess). Tibetans call it *Chomolungma* (Goddess Mother of the World). Some climbers call it the "Big E." Sir Edmund Hillary called it a bastard. Whatever it is called, Mount Everest has fascinated men since it was discovered during the Great Trigonometrical Survey of India in 1852. Although it resisted climbing for 100 years, so many ascents have since been made that even people with minimal climbing experience can reach the summit through the well-trammelled South Col route.

In fact, although it has several tough sections, extreme altitude, and fierce winds, Everest is no longer viewed as especially challenging by expert climbers. Out of the 14 peaks in the world 8,000 meters or higher, 12 are considered harder to climb. But, at 29,035 feet, Everest still must be paid considerable respect. In 1996, the danger of novices climbing on the mountain was seared into the worldwide conscience when 11 people from three guided expeditions died after a ferocious snowstorm suddenly struck and pinned climbers down near the summit.

Yet people are unfazed. If anything, the tragedy drew more people to the mountain than before. At least 17 commercial guides now offer Everest expeditions for amateur climbers. It is estimated that 1,300 people have summited and 168 have died trying. Everest has been climbed by people ranging from age 16 to 64. Even a blind man has summited. It is said that, besides a modicum of physical fitness, you only need three things to summit Everest: good guides, good weather, and supplementary oxygen.

Mt. Everest straddles Nepal and China, and both countries issue permits to climbers. Because of the summer monsoon season, expeditions are only feasible during the April–June and September–November periods. One disadvantage of going in the spring is that the weather is more unpredictable and can be stormy at higher altitudes. There is also likely to be more traffic on the mountain. Still, because the days are warmer and longer, the vast majority of expeditions are undertaken in the spring.

The going rates for a fully guided summit bid are from $40,000 to $75,000 per person, excluding air travel to and from Kathmandu, Nepal. There are numerous other costs to be factored in, including personal gear, medical checkups, pre-trip immunizations, extra food, and insurance coverage. Group climbing gear is included in the price and comprises such things as ropes, tents, climbing hardware, oxygen, and camp stoves. Also included are climbing permits, the wages of the porters, climbing *Sherpas* (born climbers who provide essential support to every expedition), all your meals, and hotel stays on the trips in and out. You will need a visa to travel to Nepal. Generally there is a nonrefundable deposit required at the time you sign up. Due to the uncertainties and costs, trip cancellation insurance is strongly advised.

Personal climbing gear is typically not included in the price (add another $5,000 or so). Guides will offer specific advice on what to buy. Among the things you will need are down-filled outerwear, climbing boots and overboots, crampons, a climbing axe, mitts/gloves, glacier glasses, and a headlamp. Zinc oxide and a brimmed hat are essential to help prevent sunburn, which is particularly acute at altitude. There are also various prescription antibiotics that climbers can take to ward off intestinal bugs from local food, such as Cipro and Bactrim. Additionally, you should consider rescue insurance (as ominous as that sounds) to cover an emergency helicopter rescue, which can cost over $5,000. Besides money, you must devote a significant amount of time to an Everest expedition. Including travel, you will spend over 75 days away from home.

When evaluating the expedition, look for firms with guides who have all summited Everest before. In addition, a client-to-guide ratio of 2:1 or less, and a high climbing Sherpa-to-client ratio (1:1 is good) are the marks of a solid expedition. Although climbing Sherpas do not necessarily summit, they are strong climbers at high altitudes and can assist clients—especially those in trouble—in getting up and down the mountain. They also carry heavier loads, ferry oxygen up to higher camps, set up the tents each day, and help prepare meals. All quality expeditions have a camp physician who is trained in high-altitude medicine.

After the 1996 tragedy, there was a lot of criticism about novices on Everest. Nonetheless, guides still rely upon gut feeling rather than climbing experience in deciding whether a climber is suitable for an Everest attempt. The range of skill levels and occupations among Everest expeditions is very wide. In addition, although a rarity in the past, some parties now have almost the same number of women as men. Most guides reserve the right to take someone off the mountain who is climbing poorly or who is judged to be a safety risk to the other climbers.

There are many obvious physical risks to be concerned about, like falling off the side of the mountain or into a deep crevasse. In adverse weather conditions, frostbite also becomes a real possibility. But the most persistently serious danger climbers on Everest face is altitude sickness. High-altitude pulmonary edema (fluid in the lungs) and cerebral edema (swelling of the brain) are both life-threatening; either illness is fatal if allowed to progress untreated. In both cases, the most effective treatment is immediate descent to a lower altitude.

Minor altitude sickness (hypoxia) hits everyone at some point early on. Strong lungs are important, but a rigorous acclimatization schedule is the key. Guides shepherd their clients to successively higher camps, and then back down to base so their bodies can recover. After a month on the mountain, climbers are sufficiently acclimatized to attempt the summit. At higher altitudes, hypoxia can be so severe as to create hallucinations and lead to disastrous lapses of judgment. The standard Everest route deliberately minimizes the time spent above 25,000 feet, the so-called Death Zone, where there is only about one-third the level of oxygen of sea level air. At these heights, climbers tire quickly, become disoriented, and take in so little oxygen that their bodies begin to literally shut down.

Although experienced Himalayan climbers frequently summit Everest without supplemental oxygen, all commercial expeditions use it. Each oxygen cylinder weighs about six pounds and holds up to 12 hours of oxygen, depending upon the flow setting. Oxygen is delivered by means of a bulky rubber mask that almost covers your entire face and makes some climbers claustrophobic. In addition to enhancing performance while you are awake, using oxygen at higher elevations will improve your sleep quality so you recover faster.

Surprisingly, climbers do not have to be world-class athletes to tackle Everest. You do, however, have to be well-conditioned to survive the rigors of the climb. Guides recommend a vigorous cardiovascular program of running or bicycling for at least an hour a day in preparation for the attempt. Depending on your initial fitness level, it could take from six months to over a year before you are ready. Long hikes with a pack will also improve endurance. Indoor training can include stair climbing and weight lifting to increase upper body strength. One especially useful attribute is good balance—critical for getting through the diabolically tricky Icefall at the foot of the mountain.

Everest climbers do not need to be highly experienced in mountaineering. The standard route presents only modest technical challenges, though there are places where rock and ice climbing skills are required. Skills required on Everest include climbing with crampons, using the ice axe, belaying another climber, performing a crevasse rescue, and stopping your fall. Some guides include pre-expedition clinics where they review climbing techniques used on Everest.

Although guides can coach you on basic ice climbing techniques, they would prefer not to have to. If you have not climbed before, do yourself (and everybody else) a favor and enroll at a basic mountaineering school. There are many schools across the country—inquire with your local outfitter or climbing club. Mountain schools vary from weekend field trips to three-week expeditions. Costs vary from $100 to over $3,000. If you have climbed in the past but are a little rusty, your guide may offer a refresher course.

One of the best ways to prepare for Everest without leaving the United States is to climb the highest mountain in North America, Mount McKinley in Denali National Park, Alaska. At 20,320 feet, McKinley's air is thin enough and the temperatures cold enough to give you a real feel for high-altitude climbing. For a challenge at lower altitude, little-known Mount Hunter (14,570 feet) in Denali will give you great technical climbing experience. There are numerous other climbs that provide technical challenges throughout the United States, Canada, and Europe. But a paucity of tall mountains limits the altitude exposure one can obtain without going overseas. South America offers a number of confidence-builders, like Argentina's Aconcagua (22,835 feet), the tallest mountain outside of Asia. Cho Oyu, 20 miles west of Everest, is the world's sixth-highest mountain, and is probably the ideal warm-up for the Big 'E'. Cho Oyu is both the most popular and the easiest 8,000-meter peak to climb. Still, at 26,906 feet, Cho Oyu offers comparable high altitude and brutal weather conditions to Everest.

The best way to get to Kathmandu is to fly into Bangkok, Thailand. En route from Bangkok you will be able to see some of the spectacular Himalayan Mountains, including Everest. You can recognize the great mountain by its signature: a perpetual comet-tail of snow whipped off the top of the mountain by the jet stream.

When Hillary first climbed Everest, the trip to Base Camp took a month on foot with numerous river crossings that left the adventurers covered with bloodsucking leeches. The trip has since been shortened by three weeks with a helicopter or airplane ride from Kathmandu to the village of Lukla. From Lukla, your team will hike to Namche, where a bazaar presents the last chance to buy supplies. The next village on the trek, Thyangboche, is the home of a historic monastery near the foot of Ama Dablam, one of the most impressive Himalayan peaks. On the way to Base, you will likely stop in Lobuche, a squalid village that, at 16,200 feet, is one of the highest inhabited places in the world. Although the walk in from Lukla to Base Camp can be covered in under a week, guides slow down the trek to enhance acclimatization. After seven to 10 days, you arrive at Everest Base Camp (17,500 feet).

Base Camp is located in a boulder-filled moraine. Like a little quonset city, it consists of dozens of colorful tents strung with Buddhist prayer flags to protect their occupants. Base Camp is equipped with basic medical facilities, a camp doctor, tons of provisions, climbing gear, communications equipment, and support personnel. Through satellite telephone connections, climbers can send and receive e-mail and receive calls from anywhere in the world. During the peak of the season, there are scores of people at Base Camp.

The Khumbu Icefall is the most terrifying part of the climb. The Icefall, at the upper reaches of the Khumbu glacier, lies between Base Camp and Camp I. The Icefall consists of an enormous river of ice chunks called *seracs* that can be as large as a house. Gravity pulls the ice steadily downward about four feet per day, making the Icefall extremely dangerous because a large serac can topple over without warning. Each season, a new route through the Icefall is established and maintained by Sherpas from one of the expeditions. To prepare the path, the Sherpas install dozens of aluminum ladders across gaping crevasses (some of which are hundreds of feet deep) and string ropes along the entire route for safety. The only way to minimize the danger is to start out by 4 a.m. and scramble through the Icefall before the sun warms up the ice. With the light of a headlamp, you must thread your way through the course in the dark, and gingerly walk over rickety ladders (sometimes up to 20 lashed together) that span the black crevasses underfoot, to hopefully finish by 7 a.m. If you are to make the summit and return alive, you will have to make at least eight trips through this devilish course.

Camp I (at 19,500 feet), at the top of the Icefall, is a resting point after clearing the treacherous glacier. For the first time since arriving, you will be able to clearly see the peak of Everest, which is not visible from Base Camp. Camp II, sometimes called Advance Base Camp, is a mini version of the Base Camp. At 21,000 feet, it is the launching pad for higher elevations and is well-stocked with provisions, gear, and medicine. Climbers generally make two trips through the Icefall before moving up to Camp II. The route from Camp II to Camp III follows what is known as the Western Cwm (pronounced "koom") up the face of Lhotse, which abuts Everest on the east. Camp III (at 23,500 feet) is considered the most dangerous camp on the mountain because it is totally exposed to wind and avalanches on Lhotse. Camp IV is the highest camp at 26,300 feet and is pitched on a miserable barren plateau called the South Col. On the east end of the Col is a 7,000-foot drop into Tibet; on the west, a 4,000 foot fall down to the Western Cwm. At Camp IV and above, oxygen is a virtual necessity. Sleeping is difficult and normal tasks like tying your shoelaces are a struggle. In

1996, Camp IV was the site where eight people died after being caught in a snowstorm near the summit. You cannot stay here. It's up or down.

Summit bids usually start around midnight. This early start-time allows climbers to reach the peak and get back to Camp IV before extreme hypoxia or frostbite sets in and makes the descent treacherous. Guides establish rigid turnaround times to get climbers back to safety if they haven't made the summit for whatever reason. Climbers move up the Southeast Ridge to the South Summit, a tiny dome with a view of the last 335 feet to the top. Next, you and your fellow climbers will be strung along an exposed knife-like ridge, where winds can reach 100 miles per hour. Just to keep things interesting, there is an 8,000-foot drop to the bottom of the Southwest Face on the left, and a 10,000-foot drop down the Kangshung Face on the right. At the top of the ridge is the famous Hillary Step, a 40-foot vertical climb up a chimney of rock. From here it is only 250 feet to the summit. At the top of the world you will find surveying equipment, old oxygen bottles, prayer flags, and various oblations. The easy part is over. Now you just have to get back down.

How to calculate your fortune

A rough estimate can made of when your money will double by dividing the percentage annual return on your portfolio into 70. Stocks have historically averaged inflation-adjusted returns of about 7 percent. Thus if your portfolio consists solely of equities, it should double in 10 years (70 divided by 7). An all-bond portfolio typically yields closer to 5 percent, doubling in 14 years. If inflation remains as low as it is today, real returns could increase a couple of percentage points, but don't look for them to return to the late 1990s, when equities yielded over 15 percent after inflation.

If you would rather be the hare than the turtle, see "How to become a day trader."

How to pack for a business trip

Follow these simple instructions and you will be a well-organized, efficient road warrior.

Checking your bag, as any frequent flier will tell you, is asking for trouble. Although according to the United States Department of Transportation, the odds are about 1 in 100 your bag will be lost, carousel waits can be interminable. Unless you have a lot of time to kill at your destination or are packing for over a week's travel, take a carry-on bag. If you will be working on the airplane, bring a second bag or soft briefcase for your files, laptop, reading materials, and other goodies.

The main carry-on bag is a matter of personal choice. If you have broad shoulders or frequently race through airports to catch planes, the ubiquitous garment bag is good for trips of two or more days. Roller bags relieve the strain from your shoulders and are immensely popular with frequent fliers (take a look at what the flight crew is carrying). Roomy canvas or leather duffels are useful because they can be crushed and jammed into small spaces.

The second bag, which will be stowed under the seat in front you, should contain anything you could want during the flight. Here are some handy things to put in it: cell phone, pens, pen refills, stamps, return address labels, miniature stapler, paper clips of all sizes, and a penlight. Another neat gizmo is a paper cutter with a ceramic nib (available from Levenger, (800) 544-0880, *www.levenger.com*) for trimming articles out of magazines and newspapers. For personal comfort, foam earplugs are essential, should you wind up next to a screaming infant. You can buy them at any drugstore and they come with a little storage case. If you have even mild allergies, carry antihistamines and decongestants—airplanes can be like flying petri dishes of mold and bacteria. Some travelers also like to bring bottled water and snacks in case they get stuck on the tarmac. And never fly without a flight guide. Thanks to online competition, the cost of these paperback flight schedules is now under $100 per year—well worth it if your flight gets canceled because you can see your other options immediately.

The pros are in two camps on packing: bundling and rolling. Bundling involves carefully wrapping everything into a big ball, with bulky items like shoes or books in the middle. The ball should have durable materials on the inside and the easy-to-wrinkle items on the outside. The idea behind bundling is to immobilize clothing, thus preventing wrinkles. The obvious drawback, however, is that you have take the whole thing apart to unpack and vice-versa. Rolling everything up is highly economical space-wise, if a bit of a chore. Rolling does not work well on pressed garments like dress shirts and trousers; either plan to get out the iron, or get a roomier bag. Plain-old folding works fine for casual clothes, but forget about it for business. Like the man in the movie *The Graduate* said, the secret is *plastics*. Save the polyethylene sheets from the dry cleaners and encase all your pressed clothes in them before bundling, rolling, or folding. Some people even go nuts putting their socks in one zip-lock bag and their underwear in another.

Don't get obsessed with making lists of what to take. There is nothing wrong with lists, mind you, but for a business trip they are overkill. Instead, mentally dress yourself each day and put the items in the bag as you go. Keep your ancillary items, like toiletries and humidors, in a certain area, fully stocked and ready to go.

Certain clothes are versatile enough to lighten your load. All women know about the little black dress. The equivalent for men is the blue blazer, which can be both dressy and casual depending upon the pants and shoes paired with it. Actor and inveterate traveler George Hamilton has taken the idea to new heights by carrying a dark suit and three sets of buttons that let him wear it as a suit, blazer or dinner jacket, depending upon the occasion. Lightweight travel raincoats are great if you're not sure what kind of weather you'll find at your destination. They fold up into tiny little packages and wrinkles fall out in a hot shower. Best of all, travel raincoats weigh much less than even a small umbrella.

A small roll of duct tape has many travel uses, including fixing a hole in your sock. A Swiss Army knife is great for opening beer bottles in your hotel room and trimming threads off your suit, although you won't be able to put it in your carry-on luggage. If you are going to a conference or carrying many files, be sure to bring a blank overnight express courier's waybill with your firm's account number printed on it. Ship all that superfluous paper back to the office rather than lugging it home. You probably won't work on it on the flight home anyway.

How to crash a black-tie party

People seem to have a perverse respect for party crashers. The more brash and audacious the attempt, the better. Stories about uninvited guests cutting in on the dance floor with starlets are legendary. Although crashing is not an entirely riskless enterprise, at a black-tie party (besides the Oscars) most unwelcome visitors are simply booted. It's fun. Besides, you could save yourself about $200.

First, you need to do your homework. Who went last year? Where is it this year? Which entrances will be used? What is the security like? Look up the prior year's newspaper society pages to get a sense for some of the guest names. Then cruise by and take a look the day of the party. Make careful note of the entrances and exits, including service areas. Generally speaking, the bigger the party, the more sophisticated the security.

While party-crashing is easier than it looks, gaining entrance to a respectable event does require a healthy dose of *chutzpah*. Here are some tactics that have been known to work.

Do the Rich Little

Impersonation is the most brazen approach to party crashing. Armed with one of the guest names from last year, you simply walk up to the entrance and casually announce that you are "Mr. Big Giver." If the door person knows Mr. Big Giver, you are sunk. If not, you are in. (If there is a reasonable chance of detection, you may want to try Mr. Medium Giver instead.)

The obvious downside to this approach is that if Mr. Big (or Medium) Giver has already checked in or is not on the list, then you are probably headed home—unless you can talk your way in. A virtuoso crasher in New York repeatedly gained entry to parties by claiming to be the son of socialite Dianne Von Furstenberg. It was reported in the *New York Observer* that once, when a doorman who knew that the real Alex Von Furstenberg was out of town confronted him, the quick-thinking poseur reportedly shot back that people often mistook him for Ms. Furstenberg's son, but that *his* name was spelled *First*-enberg.

Name-drop with a vengeance

Another relatively high-risk, but effective tactic is to throw big names around. For example, "Oh, I must be on the list, Ms. Party Coordinator said she would be certain to give you my name," or "I'm Mr. Fatcat's son-in-law." If you can read upside down, try to get a peek at the list, "There I am, Mr. Noshow." Talking fast is essential. If you time it right, the door personnel may let you in just to keep from holding up the line.

Blend in with the scenery

Another effective means of gaining admittance is to blend right in. Be careful how you go about it, though. Do not linger on the periphery of a party waiting for an opportunity. Security personnel are trained to look for malingerers who try this exact approach. A better way is to arrive near the main entrance and stride purposefully up to the door. If things get really hopping, you may just slide by. Some gatecrashers even add the over-the-top theatrics of hiring photographers to pretend they are *paparazzi* photographing a celebrity. As you arrive, photographers pop out of the bushes and start firing electronic flashes. The crowd is likely to be mystified, but the doormen may be too, and that's the idea.

Expert crashers also suggest coming mid-way through the party. There is a chance the door people have moved inside, or stopped paying attention as some guests have come and gone already. If questioned, you can say you went to get something out of your car, make a phone call, etc.

Smoke if you got 'em

One of the most effective techniques is available to smokers. In our nonsmoking society, even big donors have to stand outside in the cold to take a drag. Come by after the party has started and locate the smokers' area outside. Slide as gracefully as you can into the group with a cigarette in your mouth and strike up a conversation with a fellow smoker. When your "friend" heads back in, just follow. As you slip by the security guard, say something like, "Enjoy the party. See you later."

Keep them entertained

You could also emulate an intrepid fellow in Boston in his 60s who famously crashes only the best parties in town. Although notorious on the Brahmin social party circuit, the guy is rarely ejected, apparently because he provides a valuable service by dancing with all the ladies. Clubfooted husbands gladly turn their wives over to the crashing hoofer for a few twirls to spare them the embarrassment.

How to make great chili

Whether you make your chili the regular way, with kidney beans and bits of onion and tomatoes, or Texas-style, with only meat and gravy, there are a few tricks to making truly great chili.

Always start with lean beef (90 percent lean), browned and well-drained. Add a can of beef broth to strengthen the flavor of the gravy. The base of most chilis is tomato sauce. If you like it a little sweeter and more mellow, use a can of tomato soup instead. Dice up onions very finely. For non-Texas chili, use canned kidney beans in the ratio of one 15-ounce can of beans per two pounds raw meat.

For heat and flavor the pros use dried spices, including lots of chili powder, cayenne pepper, onion powder, and garlic powder. But the secret ingredient is *cumin*, which is found to varying degrees in most winning chili cook-off recipes. Exotic-smelling cumin comes from the seeds of an aromatic plant grown in Egypt and Syria. Use one tablespoon per pound of meat. Here's another secret: Because dried spices weaken after cooking, expert chefs add a second, smaller dose towards the end of cooking for additional flavor.

Simmer the brew between two and two-and-a-half hours on low heat in a covered pot, or until all the liquid is cooked off. Serve with cornbread and cold beer.

How to improve your memory

The modern brain is one overtaxed machine. For thousands of years, human brains didn't have to store more than about 50 names, a song or two, and perhaps a little scripture. Compare that with today—we've got phone numbers, fax numbers, pager numbers, PINs, batting averages, instructions for resetting the VCR, and keeping count of Elizabeth Taylor's husbands (eight...or is it nine?). Human memory peaks at age 25, falls off 20 percent by age 50, and is only 50 percent effective by age 80. Losing your car keys is one thing, but when you forget where you left your children, it's time to think about memory enhancement.

How memory works

The average brain has 100 billion cells called neurons that communicate through electrochemical signals. Memories are complex arrays of neurons "talking" to one another by sending and receiving electrochemical impulses, drawing information from all over the brain. The hippocampus is the brain's switchboard, connecting the attributes of memory found in different sensory cortexes (auditory, visual, olfactory, etc.).

The greater the number of senses associated with a particular memory, the more powerful it is. Next to scents, visual memories are the most acute; some people write down everything they want to remember so they will have a picture of the words in their head. Do not believe all this stuff about photographic memory—it's a myth. Besides, even superb visual recall is not necessarily indicative of high intelligence.

Short-term memory is used for immediate tasks, like dialing phone numbers. Long-term memory is for permanent storage of important information (like birthdays and anniversaries). Although it becomes increasingly harder to access with age, the stuff you put into long-term memory tends to stay there. People forget 60 percent of what they learn within three years (which explains the return of gas-guzzlers, bell-bottoms, and the minting of still another one-dollar coin), yet over the next 50 years only another 5 percent is lost. Like a house with decrepit wiring, older peoples' memories flicker when the electrical impulses between neurons weaken. The erosion of memory is exacerbated by the gradual loss of brain cells and the reduced efficiency of those that remain. Some memory deterioration, however, is attributed to people just getting lazy about using their brains when they get older.

Drugs

Medical technology is at a loss where much of memory is concerned. Although some progress has been made with certain neurotransmitter-affecting drugs, like donepezil, piracetam, and tacrine on Alzheimer's patients, proven off-the-shelf cures for basic absentmindedness are scarce. For lack of anything better, doctors have begun prescribing massive doses of vitamins C and E for their antioxidants, which are believed to prevent the formation of cell-killing free radicals in the brain.

Natural memory enhancers

Herbs and spices are pretty much worthless, too. Ginkgo biloba (extract of the Chinese ginkgo tree), vinpocetine (an extract of periwinkle seeds), and Panax ginseng are popular nutritional supplements. Of the three, only ginkgo biloba, which contains antioxidants and is believed to enhance blood flow to the brain, had any effect on memory in clinical trials—and it was modest at best.

Some researchers endorse daily doses of the supplement phosphatidylserine (PS) as a pep pill for the brain. The supplement is thought to improve memory by rejuvenating brain cell membranes to allow information to travel between neurons more easily. Research has shown significant improvement in subjects' abilities to remember names, as well as cognitive abilities. Thomas H. Crook III, Ph.D., founder of Psychologix (a medical research firm) and author of *The Memory Cure*, concluded PS prevented up to 12 years of memory decline in test patients over age 50. Phosphatidylserine is widely available in nutrition and drug stores as a pill or capsule, and is also available in chewable form under the ridiculous brand name Brain Gum.

If you are a Ravi Shankar maven, you may want to try Ayurvedic medicine, a 5,000-year-old healing system from India. Among other things, Ayurvedic doctors believe that dripping hot oil on the forehead will improve blood circulation and therefore, memory. (Do not try this at home!)

Brain aerobics

Memory Centers of America (225 E. 64th St, New York, (212) 616-6484), offers a $1,200 program featuring a battery of computer-based tests, psychological analysis, and memory-boosting exercises to help get that flabby grey matter into shape.

Popeye food

Researchers at Human Nutrition Research Center on Aging at Tufts University have determined that two cups of raw spinach or one cup of fresh blueberries a day keep cobwebs out of the old attic. Although scientists are not sure why, they believe the flavonoids (antioxidants) contained in spinach and blueberries lessen the natural damage to brain tissue as people get older.

Some memory tips

Try a few of these little helpers and see if you can remember where you set down the cordless phone.

- *Concentrate.* The older you get, the longer you need to store something so you can remember it. If you need to remember something for more than a few minutes, concentrate on it for at least 10 seconds to send it into archival brain storage. In addition, some physicians believe large daily doses (more than 500 milligrams) of the nutrient acetylcarnitine (available at nutrition stores) can improve attention spans and stave off age-related memory loss.
- *Take note of what your read.* Skim things first, then reread them in their entirety. Underline important phrases and words. Sum up chapters and arguments after you read them. Take a short break every half hour to refresh your mind.
- *Tie words to images.* It doesn't really matter if the image is a little weird or the connection is convoluted as long as it works in your own pumpkin head.
- *Break down long numbers.* Convert long numbers into a series of short clumps of numbers that you can remember, like your area code, street address, old football number, etc.

- *Use mnemonics.* The colors of the light spectrum are ordered ROY G. BIV. In Chicago, the Great Lakes streets run south in the order S-H-E-O (Superior, Huron, Erie, Ontario).

- *Gesticulate.* Some medical researchers actually believe waving your arms in the air can help you remember what was on the tip of your tongue—which must mean Italians are the most unforgetful people on the planet.

- *Get organized.* Well-organized people have an easier time recalling information; a tidy mind is easier to search than a cluttered one.

- *Stimulate the grey stuff.* Read a newspaper, do a crossword puzzle, or prove Fermat's last theorem—anything but park yourself in front the tube.

- *Use the two-step name program.* Studies show that nearly half of people over age 50 can't remember names a mere hour after they have been introduced. If you are perpetually bumping into old what's-her-name at cocktail parties, try this technique. First, after you have been introduced, immediately use the person's name in a statement, "Deborah, I was just telling Fred here what a great portrait that is..." Second, burn the name into your long-term memory by making up a goofy image that you associate with the name. Ms. Reynolds is wearing a suit made of aluminum foil; Mr. Remington is a crack shot with a pistol, and so on. Believe it or not, it works.

How to solve the problem of public schools

Three million parents can't be wrong.

If your local public schools are the pits and you cannot afford to shell out for a private education, home schooling may be the answer. There are an estimated 1.5 million students receiving home educations, and the number is believed to be growing about 10 percent annually. Supporters say home schooled children are more motivated, self-confident, and well-rounded than their public school counterparts. They do better on standardized tests too: A 1999 University of Maryland analysis of over 12,000 cases showed home-schooled students scored between the 70th and 80th percentile nationally.

The home schooling movement, started by educational reformer John Holt in the 1970s, is based upon his idea that children learn individually, not in groups. Proponents say very bright children especially profit from home schooling because it enables them to learn their lessons at an accelerated pace and move on to other subjects. The benefit from home schooling increases the longer the child is taught at home. By eighth grade, students home schooled since kindergarten score as well as high school seniors on achievement tests.

Although home schooling is frequently associated with conservative Christians, parental motives are not necessarily religious. Some parents believe they can provide a better education at home. Others just want to spend more time with their children. An overriding theme, however, is that unwholesome behavior flourishes at schools. Home schooling is used by many parents to impart their children with a greater sense of morals and ethics—more *Leave it to Beaver* and less *Married with Children*.

Home schooling is legal throughout the United States, although the state laws governing it vary tremendously. A handful of states require no notification or monitoring of any kind, while others require a mountain of paperwork. More typical state laws require parents to notify authorities of their intent to home school, submit a lesson plan, and file periodic reports on their children's education. Some states also require standardized testing of home school students. But no state requires parents to have teaching certificates. You can review your state's laws at the Home School Legal Defense Association Website, *www.hslda.org*.

Like the name implies, children are taught by parents in their own homes. School hours are whenever mom (or dad) says they are. Limited distractions (no fire drills or milk fights in the cafeteria) mean the school day can end hours before the public schools let out. Parents establish the curricula and purchase textbooks, either from specialty home school publishers or from standard textbook purveyors. Online courses are also available (sample lesson: "Sloths are very strange mammals"). Numerous free resources are available through home schooling organizations and the public library. Educational materials can cost over $1,600 per year, but most parents spend $600 or less.

Arguably one of the greatest benefits of home schooling is that you can accomplish what a decade of educational reform could not—wipe out 50 years of bad educational ideas and replace them with the basics. No more "new" math, "creative" spelling, or revisionist history.

Some home school parents advocate natural learning, or so-called unschooling. No formalized lessons or homework, just casual tutelage from a grown-up. "The world is your classroom"—a kid's dream. Supporters claim natural learning is more interesting for children and therefore holds their attention longer. But even among ardent home schoolers natural learning is controversial. One man's unschooling is another man's truancy.

Experts caution that for home schooling to work, parents must commit themselves to educating their children and not get caught up in being free spirits. Besides having infectious enthusiasm for schoolwork, you have to be highly disciplined. Home schooling is a major time commitment that only increases with the number of children you have. In desperation, some time-cramped parents have concocted lessons for road trips and called them "carschooling." Sure. Twenty questions, name the capitals, "Billy keeps touching me!" "I have to go to the bathroom... ." Sounds like a rich educational experience.

From an economic standpoint, the obvious drawback to home schooling is somebody has to stay home with the juvenescent wonders. And that somebody—usually mom—is not likely to find time to earn a living; over three-fourths of home school mothers do not work.

Critics say the biggest problem with home schooling is the lack of social opportunity, that isolated students will have trouble interacting with others as adults due to their sheltered existence. Hogwash, counter home school advocates. The average home-schooled student has numerous outside interests and activities. In many areas, a well-established network of home-schooled families offers ample social opportunities for children. Home school children also have more time for socializing because they watch a lot less television.

There is ample evidence that colleges take home schoolers seriously. Every Ivy League school has admitted home-schooled students. Although they lack grades and class ranks, their higher test scores, superlative essays, and impactful letters of recommendation are well received. Furthermore, greater freedom to engage in extracurricular activities improves home schoolers' "portfolios" so they appear more well-rounded than other applicants. Some parents try to have it both ways by home schooling their children from kindergarten through eighth grade, then enrolling them in the local high school.

Before you get too serious about home schooling, though, you need to answer this threshold question: Do you really want to see your little darlings 16 hours a day?

How to cure tennis elbow

Acupuncture is claimed to help cure musculoskeletal disorders, asthma, and migraines, reduce dental pain, and lessen menstrual cramps. Studies have even demonstrated acupuncture's efficacy in curing drug addiction. It is estimated that over 1 million Americans go in to be needled each year.

A 2,000-year-old staple of Chinese medicine, acupuncture is the practice of sticking hair-thin needles into precise points on the body—of which there are hundreds—to eliminate specific pains. Although not necessarily licensed as physicians, accredited American acupuncturists train for a minimum of 1,750 hours, and must pass an exam on the various point locations.

Treatments typically consist of a series of painless 20-minute sessions of being stuck in funny places like the bottom of your foot or your ear. Sessions generally cost around $100, and most healthcare insurers will pay for at least part of your treatment.

No one is sure how acupuncture works. Some medical experts believe it affects the central nervous system by disrupting pain signals. Others believe acupuncture triggers the release of endorphins that temporarily mask pain. Skeptics say it's all rubbish, that acupuncture is just a great big placebo effect wrapped up in oriental mysticism.

But if you've tried everything else, it may be the best hundred bucks you've ever spent. To find a qualified acupuncturist, contact the American Academy of Medical Acupuncture at (800) 521-2262; *www. medicalacupuncture.org.*

How to get an audience to pipe down

It is a sorry sign of our uncivil times that symphony performances are constantly punctuated by audience noise. A veritable orchestra-full of instruments are employed by the rude: rustling papers, jangling bracelets, wristwatch alarms, and the bane of all concert artists—coughing.

Here are some methods that have proven effective on the great triumvirate of audience vulgarity, including coughing, talking, and cell phones.

Coughing

New Yorkers and Chicagoans have long been notoriously bad audiences, but even sedate Londoners now feel the need to wheeze. Coughing at concerts has gotten so bad in recent years that conductors have tried all sorts of things. Pre-performance lectures, free cough drops, icy stares from the podium, and long pauses between movements to allow the infirmed to whoop away have all been employed to little effect. It is clearly time for some new approaches.

Kurt Masur, the former music director of the New York Philharmonic, recently came up with a solution that worked. During the serene third movement of the Shostakovich Fifth Symphony, the hacking got so bad that the maestro simply stopped the orchestra and walked offstage—to applause from the audience. He returned two minutes later to finish the symphony... without interruption.

Probably the most elegant solution ever devised was by the great composer and pianist, Sergei Rachmaninoff, in 1931. He played his *Corelli Variations* in accordance with the politeness of his audience. When the coughing increased, he skipped to the next variation. At one concert the coughing was so bad Rachmaninoff played only 10 of the 20 variations. His all-time record was 18, set in (of all places) New York.

Talking

Chin-wagging during performances appears to have gotten worse recently, but is really a very old problem. If so inclined, conductors can easily dispatch the problem with a stern message from the podium. Over 100 years ago, Theodore Thomas, the founder of the Chicago Symphony Orchestra, chastised a Washington, D.C. audience for talking, saying, "I shall stop if you do not. We do not play music as an accompaniment for people to talk to." While performing one of his pieces, 19th-century composer

Franz Liszt curtly stopped playing after noticing his patron, Emperor Alexander of Russia was talking. "When the King speaks, everyone else should be silent," Liszt explained.

Cell phones

Cell phones have become the bane of concert performers everywhere. Some halls insist that people check their phones and pagers at the door, but many patrons ignore the request, leading to the jarring cell phone *obligato*. Recently performers have begun to strike back in an effort to embarrass the scofflaws. After an abashed audience member let a cell phone keep ringing during a performance of *The Scarlet Pimpernel* in New York, actor Douglas Sills turned towards the phone's owner and asked, "Don't you think it's probably for you?"[1]

Violence also works. At a theater performance in St. Louis, audience members used their programs to whomp a woman in front of them whose cell phone had gone off. John Corcoran, a writer for the *Los Angeles Times*, sarcastically suggested a system called THUGS, short for Telephonic Harmony Ushers Guaranteeing Security: "When a cellular phone or beeper goes off, the THUGS politely and unobtrusively fling the offending lout from the concert hall for a complimentary thrashing outside."[2]

Canada had the best solution of all—jamming. In 2001, Industry Canada seriously considered allowing private companies to put up jamming umbrellas around their properties to create cell-phone-free zones. It concluded, however, that jammers could potentially interfere with emergency communications, so the move was rejected. In 1999, the United States Federal Communications Commission killed a similar proposal and appears unlikely to consider it. Mark our words, though, the day will come...

If you can't beat 'em, join 'em. Golan Levin, a composer and software engineer with a master's from M.I.T., recently premiered his original composition "Dialtones: A Telesymphony," in which 200 cell phones held by audience members chime at predetermined moments, with a crescendo ending of 60 phones ringing at once.

[1] *USA Today*, July 28, 1999, p. 1D.
[2] *Los Angeles Times*, May 1, 2000, p. 3.

How to beat the odds in Vegas

It is axiomatic that there is no table game at any casino in Las Vegas, Atlantic City, or anywhere else for that matter, where the odds are in the player's favor. Table payouts range from pure suckers' bets, like numbers in roulette, to slightly unfavorable, like the pass line in craps. But there is one game, as many experienced gamblers know, where the highly observant player can tilt the odds in his favor and cash in handsomely—blackjack (a.k.a. 21).

Ever since mathematics professor Edward O. Thorp first publicized a workable system for card counting in 1962, casino pit bosses have gotten heartburn from gamblers raking it in at the blackjack tables. Teams of system players have been known to take hundreds of thousands of dollars in a single night. Variations of Thorp's original system have proliferated, but they all employ the same principles of card counting, betting, and basic play. You may not break the bank in Las Vegas, but by learning and using a card counting system you can make your trips to the desert pay for themselves and more.

The object of blackjack is to draw cards to get as close to 21 as possible without going over. Face cards are worth 10. Aces count as either one or 11. Hands that include an ace are known as "soft" hands, and hands that do not are "hard." The dealer must hit 16 and stand on 17. Blackjacks pay 3 to 2, or 1 1/2 times the bet. (The differential payout on blackjacks enables card counting systems to work. Another element at work is that the dealer, who draws under fixed rules, is more likely to bust when there is a surplus of face cards in the deck.)

The way card counting works is this: The player's position relative to the dealer becomes stronger the more high cards are remaining in the shoe; by varying the amount of the bet to reflect whether the deck is favorable or unfavorable, the player can nudge the returns in his favor.

Using mathematical probabilities, Thorp and others established what is known as "basic strategy," a set of rules for when to hit, stand, split pairs, double down, and take insurance, based upon the dealer's up card. (Basic strategy is so ubiquitous that friendly dealers will even teach you if you don't know it.) There are only a few inviolable rules. Always stand on 19, 20 or 21. Never split pairs of fours or tens. Always split pairs of eights or aces. Insurance is almost always a sucker's bet; never take it unless the running card count is +3 or more (discussed later). All of the other rules change based upon what the dealer shows.

Here is a basic strategy grid. Failure to memorize these rules cold will doom even a flawless card counter.

Basic Strategy for Soft Hands

You Hold

Dealer Shows		2	3	4	5	6	7	8	9	10	A
	A, 2	hit	hit	hit	dbl	dbl	hit	hit	hit	hit	hit
	A, 3	hit	hit	hit	dbl	dbl	hit	hit	hit	hit	hit
	A, 4	hit	hit	dbl	dbl	dbl	hit	hit	hit	hit	hit
	A, 5	hit	hit	dbl	dbl	dbl	hit	hit	hit	hit	hit
	A, 6	hit	dbl	dbl	dbl	dbl	hit	hit	hit	hit	hit
	A, 7	stand	dbl	dbl	dbl	dbl	stand	stand	hit	hit	hit
	A, 8	stand	stand	stand	stand	stand	stand	stand	stand	stand	stand
	A, 9	stand	stand	stand	stand	stand	stand	stand	stand	stand	stand
	A, 10	stand	stand	stand	stand	stand	stand	stand	stand	stand	stand

Basic Strategy for Hard Hands

You Hold

Dealer Shows	2	3	4	5	6	7	8	9	10	A
5	hit	hit	hit	hit	hit	hit	hit	hit	hit	hit
6	hit	hit	hit	hit	hit	hit	hit	hit	hit	hit
7	hit	hit	hit	hit	hit	hit	hit	hit	hit	hit
8	hit	hit	hit	hit	hit	hit	hit	hit	hit	hit
9	hit	dbl	dbl	dbl	dbl	hit	hit	hit	hit	hit
10	stand	dbl	dbl	dbl	dbl	stand	stand	hit	hit	hit
11	dbl	dbl	dbl	dbl	dbl	dbl	dbl	dbl	dbl	stand
12	hit	hit	stand	stand	stand	hit	hit	hit	hit	hit
13	stand	stand	stand	stand	stand	hit	hit	hit	hit	hit
14	stand	stand	stand	stand	stand	hit	hit	hit	hit	hit
15	stand	stand	stand	stand	stand	hit	hit	hit	hit	hit
16	stand	stand	stand	stand	stand	hit	hit	hit	hit	hit
17	stand	stand	stand	stand	stand	stand	stand	stand	stand	stand
18	stand	stand	stand	stand	stand	stand	stand	stand	stand	stand
19	stand	stand	stand	stand	stand	stand	stand	stand	stand	stand
20	stand	stand	stand	stand	stand	stand	stand	stand	stand	stand
21	stand	stand	stand	stand	stand	stand	stand	stand	stand	stand

Basic Strategy for Pairs

You Hold

Pair of	2	3	4	5	6	7	8	9	10	A
deuces	hit	hit	split	split	split	split	hit	hit	hit	hit
threes	hit	hit	split	split	split	split	hit	hit	hit	hit
fours	hit	hit	hit	hit	hit	hit	hit	hit	hit	hit
fives	dbl	dbl	dbl	dbl	dbl	dbl	dbl	dbl	hit	hit
sixes	split	split	split	split	split	hit	hit	hit	hit	hit
sevens	split	split	split	split	split	split	stand	hit	hit	hit
eights	split	split	split	split	split	split	split	split	split	split
nines	split	split	split	split	split	stand	split	split	stand	stand
tens	stand	stand	stand	stand	stand	stand	stand	stand	stand	stand
aces	split	split	split	split	split	split	split	split	split	split

(left margin label: **Dealer Shows**)

A player with a good grasp of basic strategy can bring the odds down to almost even. Applying card counting techniques gives the player a typical advantage over the House of 0.5 percent to 2.5 percent. Card counting *does* require intense concentration (the more decks in the shoe and the more players, the harder it is), but does not require exceptional math skills.

The simplest and most effective card counting method, developed by Ken Fuchs and Olaf Vancura, is called the Knock-Out system. Counts under the Knock-Out system are as follows: Cards from deuce through seven count as +1; eights and nines are zero; tens, face cards, and aces count as -1. If you do not see a card, it is not counted (unseen cards are randomly distributed and have no statistical impact on your winnings). The initial count varies with the number of decks in the shoe. For one deck, the initial count is zero. Each time a card appears—either in your hand, a fellow player's hand, or the dealer's hand—it is added to the count. (Practice counting decks rapidly at home; if the count does not equal +4 at the end of the deck you made a mistake.) The system handles multiple decks the same way, the only difference is the initial count. For a two-deck shoe, you start with an initial count of -4; for three decks, -8; four decks is -12, and so-on, up to an eight-deck shoe, which is -28.

The running count is your betting cue. When the running count is higher, the remaining cards in the deck are richer in tens and aces and hence favor the player. When the deck is favorable you increase your bet and when it is unfavorable you decrease it. *The deck is always considered favorable when the count goes to +2.* Basic strategy can be enhanced by card counting to improve your advantage still further. The variance between the normal bet and the favorable situations bet magnifies your advantage, but it also has two other implications. First, counting systems rely upon narrow odds over many hands to produce winnings; the more you bet, the more capital you need to stay in business before the inevitable advantage materializes. Second, the greater the variance, the more you look like a card counter to the dealer. You should never exceed five times your original bet, no matter what the count.

It would be gross negligence to avoid discussing the casino's views on card counting. Here's how badly the odds are stacked against players: If someone starts winning "excessively," the casino can throw the player out on *suspicion* of cheating. (Editorial comment: Card counting is not cheating in the "According to Hoyle" sense. Card counters beat the casino by using their brains and mathematics *while still playing by the House rules*.) Don't pity the casinos. Even after taking into account the numerous system players, the average Las Vegas casino keeps $14 of every $100 wagered at its blackjack tables.

The fewer the players at the table, the easier it is to keep track of the count. Seek out an empty table and if it gets too crowded, move. The best way to disguise that you are counting cards is to bet erratically at the beginning of each shoe, when the odds are close to 50-50. Learn not to move your lips when you count by practicing in front of a mirror. A pair of tinted glasses or a good Foster Brooks routine may also help you avoid detection. Casinos can, and do, eject card counters. Worse, they broadcast your computerized visage to the other casinos in town so you will be met by a thick-necked welcoming committee when you arrive. Still, unless you bet insane amounts or have a sustained lucky streak, as a newly minted card counter your winnings are not likely to be noticed. Even better, by wagering lots of money you will probably get your entire stay "comped."

How to hit out of a water hazard

Arguably the most heroic-looking shot in golf is from a ball lying in a water hazard. The ostensible purpose of hitting out is to avoid the one-stroke penalty. But to some players it is a macho challenge too tantalizing to pass up. Ironically, French pro Jean Van de Velde's only intelligent move during his meltdown on the last hole of 1999 British Open was to decide *not* to try to hit out of the water (although Van de Velde was so tempted that he rolled up his pants and stomped into the water barefoot before thinking better of it).

Experts warn against even attempting the shot. As Jack Nicklaus says in his classic instruction book *Lesson Tee*, "My best advice on playing a ball from water is don't, especially if it's completely submerged." Frankly, you should never try the shot unless *at least half* of the ball peeks above the water line and it is not imbedded in the bank or stuck in the weeds.

If you still feel like demonstrating your foolhardiness after these caveats, at least take our advice. Play the shot as if the ball were a "fried egg" in a sand trap. Unless the banks and bottom are really slippery, take off your shoes and socks. (Playing with wet shoes is a good way to develop blisters.) Get yourself lined up and dig your feet into the streambed so you don't slide around. Use an 8- or 9-iron, which will penetrate the water easier than a wedge. Remember not to touch the banks or the water with the club, which would constitute illegal grounding and cost you a stroke. Take a compact swing at the ball with the clubface slightly closed, aiming two inches behind the ball, and pray that it gets out. Make sure you have a dry towel handy. You'll need it.

How to obtain a title of nobility

"When I want a peerage, I shall buy it like an honest man."

—Lord Northcliffe

Yearning to get into a club that is just a little *too* selective to have you? Tired of always getting the table next to the kitchen? For an immodest sum of money you can attach an impressive title of nobility to your name guaranteed to get you better service at the dry cleaners.

There is now a thriving industry dedicated to recycling old British titles. Through the efforts of numerous title merchants and enterprising English solicitors terming themselves "peerage lawyers," a cornucopia of desirable titles can be purchased through the mail—from the Lordship of the Manor of Brimpton to the Marquis of Removille.

In England, all royal titles are hereditary, and all peerages bestowed upon living persons can come from only one source: (you guessed it) the Queen. Even if you found a knight or a lord who wanted to part with his title, it could not be done. If the title is hereditary it is non-transferable, and if it is a "life peerage" it does not survive the holder's death.

However, there are scores of perfectly legitimate *feudal* titles still kicking around. Feudal baronies were first bestowed upon lords of the manor who supported King William I following the Norman Conquest in 1066. Through writs of the crown over the years, various additional titles and associated lands were granted to the king's supporters in exchange for their fealty. Although feudalism was abolished throughout Europe by the 17th century, feudal lords retained their titles and property and passed them on to their heirs. The hierarchy of feudal titles is as follows:

Duke/Duchess
Marquess
Earl
Viscount
Baron, or Baron of X
Lord/Lady of the Manor

Sadly, English aristocrats don't get as much mileage out of ancient titles as they used to. In Tony Blair's England, no one really gives a fig if your ancestor was the Earl of Coventry. And medieval castles are difficult to maintain, especially after forking over 40 percent of your inheritance to the British government. What's a poor earl to do? Sell the title, of course.

The Titles market

There are at least a half-dozen reputable resellers of feudal titles, and probably at least twice as many more disreputable ones. These outfits generally hold a sizable inventory of more common titles, ranging in price from $5,000 to $30,000, depending upon the peerage.

Entry-level honors are *seated titles*, called lordships or baronies *of the manor* because they were originally attached to a piece of land. Lordships of the manor are widely available and priced at a comparatively reasonable $2,000 to $20,000. However, if you have visions of puttering around the grounds of your country estate, sipping Pimm's and eating strawberries, we have bad news: Almost all of the properties have been detached from the titles and sold. No house, no horseback riding. All you get is a lousy piece of paper.

If you acquire a seated title but still have trouble getting upgraded to first class, maybe you should think bigger. For discriminating social climbers, more prestigious viscountcies and baronies are available, starting at about $30,000. Marquistrates and dukedoms—the rarest of titles—will set you back at least $100,000. A small price to pay, really, when you consider the instant status you gain.

British snobs sniff that *purchased* titles won't cut any ice in England. (Seated titleholders, in fact, are not nobles, only *gentry*.) And while they may be right, who cares? The average American is not concerned with such picayune details as the finer points of feudal law. On this side of The Pond, anybody with a lord, baron, or viscount in front of his name is *royalty*...no matter how inconsequential he may actually be.

Rehabilitating titles

No need to find a down-on-his-luck nobleman to obtain a title. If you have European ancestry, title rehabilitation may be feasible. It works like this: For a small fee, a thousand bucks or so, a peerage attorney inspects your family tree for long-lost noble ancestors whose titles you can claim. Suppose it turns out your great-great-great-grandfather's second cousin twice removed was the Baron of Slaphappy, who died without heirs. *Bingo!* You send the peerage attorney, say, $25,000, and he files a few papers and sends you a certificate identifying you as the rightful heir and *new* Baron of Slaphappy. Capitalism at its finest.

To get you started on your quest to acquire greatness, here are a few purveyors of noble titles and title rehabilitation services:

Burke's Titles

For 175 years, British nobles have turned to the venerable *Burke's Peerage* when they needed to know who's who. In keeping up with the times, Burke's has diversified into such unlofty areas as title sales and rehabilitation. Burke's specializes in Scottish and French baronies that come with a piece of land (typically one-half to five acres). Burke's seems to be a bit on the pricey side, but there is compensation: Your name gets listed in the official *Burke's Peerage* directory—handy if some twirp questions your bonafides.

Manorial Auctioneers

Although it sounds like the Sotheby's of noble titles, Manorial Auctioneers is more of a broker than an auction house. Manorial Auctioneers principally deals in lordships of the manor and feudal baronies, which are offered through a published catalog. Each title is described and accompanied by family history, lineage, coats of arms, etc. Titles are sold on a first-come, first-served basis. Buyers pay a 10 percent premium to the sale price.

British Feudal Investments Ltd.

BFI handles a wide range of titles, including English lordships of the manor, baronies, viscountcies, Scottish lairdships, as well as feudal titles gathering dust in France and Germany. BFI has also gotten into Eastern European titles of nobility in the wake of the fall of communism. BFI, like Burke's, also searches for vacant titles that can be rehabilitated and claimed by a shirttail relative. Best of all, BFI publishes a monthly report on the state of your investment entitled "BFI Feudal Titles Market Index" (the Dow Jones, it ain't).

English Titles Co.

English Titles purveys British seated titles on the cheap. Their list price is $1,600, which also covers a tiny square of land somewhere that you can call your own. They even offer titles of your own choosing on "as yet, unnamed areas of land." Yes, you *can* be the Lord of Benny Hill.

Nobilitat Regalia

Nobilitat Regalia caters to the aspiring noble on a budget. Prices range from $100 for a knight and $500 for a viscount of the Barony of Clermont. Apparently, St. Michel de Clermont was a tiny fiefdom of the Latin Empire of Constantinople founded during the 4th Crusade in 1232 A.D. Nobilitat Regalia keeps costs down by enlisting their very own *fons honorum* (font of honor), The Prince Douglas, St. Michel de Clermont. His Excellency The Prince can issue titles until his pen runs dry.

There's just one stipulation: The Prince will only grant honors to those who assure him of their good character and dedication to the ideals of chivalry (saving damsels in distress, that sort of thing). The Prince requests you write him a letter in care of his personal secretary, Count Sean Borelia ("Lord Sean"), and tell him why you are worthy of his graces (they ask that you keep it short since His Excellency gets a lot of mail). Assuming you pass His Excellency's stringent standards and your check clears, you will receive a calligraphic scroll signed by The Prince and, naturally, suitable for framing. Nobilitat suggests that before you tack it up on the wall, you have a reduced-size copy of it made for carrying in your wallet or attachment to your resume. Nobilitat Regalia also sells nifty medals, sashes, and other titular decorations for wearing to formal occasions (or job interviews).

General caveat: There are a number of unsavory operators marketing various titles as a means of avoiding the Internal Revenue Service. These groups frequently operate from offshore locations in Bermuda, Panama, and Belize, where assets are difficult for U.S. agencies to get at. Do not fall for these scams. As an American citizen, you are still liable for your taxes, whether you are the Duke of Frankincense or not.

Acting like nobility

Once you have obtained your title, you need to bear several things in mind if you wish to be properly assimilated into the upper reaches of society. First, royals and nobles feel very secure about their positions; they don't need to impress people with mere *things*. As critic Nancy Mitford said in *A Talent to Annoy*, "In England, if you are a duchess you don't need to be well dressed—it would be thought quite eccentric." Second, do not affect a phony British accent. Just say your father was in the Foreign Office and you were born and reared in the States. Do, however, sprinkle in a few British words for spice, such as, *toffs* (dandies), *loo* (toilet) and *chin-chin!* (bottoms up!). Third, it is far better to be discretely introduced by a friend as nobility—never announce yourself as "Lord So-and-So"—people will be more apt to treat you with the respect you so richly deserve.

How to resurrect a dead philosophy

Follow the lead of the master of "New Journalism," Tom Wolfe, who knows that the path to classical learning runs straight through popular culture. Wolfe's 1998 best-selling novel, *A Man in Full,* features an anti-hero named Conrad Hensley who endures a Job-like trial of one undeserved indignity after another. After nearly going off the deep end, Hensley discovers the answers to his problems in the teachings of ancient Stoic philosopher Epictetus.

A Man in Full, which sold over 1.5 million copies in its first year, had the unintended consequence of starting a boomlet in Stoicism at colleges around the country. Shortly after its release, bookstores ran out of works by noted Stoics like Epictetus, Seneca, and Marcus Aurelius. Professors began offering courses on Stoicism and listed *A Man in Full* as required reading. Four years after the book's introduction, students are still eager to learn who these Stoic guys were and why all the hubbub over a 1,900-year-old philosophy that died out with the Roman Empire.

Now if Wolfe will just write a book featuring existentialism, philosophy majors everywhere will have jobs.

How to cure bad breath

As comedian Johnny Dark used to say in an impersonation of a tactless Charles Bronson doing a breath mint ad, "What the hell did you do...swallow your socks?"

If people at work keep coming over and offering you Altoids, maybe you should heed the message. To test your breath, sit quietly and breathe through your nose for three to four minutes. Cup your hands over your mouth and nose and exhale. What do you smell? If it is noxious and sulfuric, you've definitely got a social problem.

Bad breath may be an intensely private matter, but it has dire consequences for those around the offender. It can break up marriages and ruin careers. Most people who have it probably are not even aware of their stinky oral emissions. Still, just take a look at the array of gums, mints, toothpastes, and mouthwashes at the drugstore, and you can be assured *somebody* is aware of it. Unfortunately for the afflicted, most of these products are just so much gargle-and-spit. They work for a few minutes and dissipate. Yet there are plenty of effective, inexpensive ways to put your social life back on track.

First, a brief explanation of halitosis. Oral odor has two types of causes. The overwhelming majority of bad breath is caused by anaerobic bacteria in the mouth, nasal, or lung passages. While unpleasant, bad breath is not usually symptomatic of a serious illness. Instead, it is the result of microbes that live in your mouth and multiply each day. Less frequently, bad breath signifies a serious systemic disorder, such as diabetes, liver disease, sinus infection, or bronchitis. If you have ulcers, frequent heartburn, or stomachaches accompanied by bad breath, the root cause could be the stomach bacteria *Helicobacter pylori*, which can be treated with antibiotics. In cases of systemic disorders, halitosis is created by sulfurous chemicals building up the bloodstream and being exhaled through the lungs.

While mouth odor may be caused by eating pungent foods, it is more likely caused by bacteria accumulating below the gum line, on the back of the tongue, or on food particles stuck between your teeth. Everyone experiences "morning breath," which is a build-up of bacteria in your mouth during sleep, when salivation stops. Gargling with mouthwash is unnecessary. After you have something to drink or eat to get the saliva going again, morning breath will go away. If your bad breath recurs during the day, though, you need to do something about the little buggers colonizing your mouth. Here are some solutions.

Brush and floss your teeth

Just like the dentist always said, frequent brushing and daily flossing will help maintain good oral health, not to mention fresh breath. Caution: If your gums bleed frequently during flossing, you may have gingivitis or periodontal disease—both of which can produce vile breath and demand treatment by a dentist or periodontist.

Brush and scrape your tongue

Your tongue is like a deep-pile carpet, covered with tiny cavities that harbor bacteria with bad intentions. Brush your tongue with your toothbrush at the same time you brush your teeth. If you still have noxious breath, use a tongue scraper. These devices are made of thin plastic or rubber and are dragged over the surface of the tongue to dig the bacteria out. You also can use the edge of a spoon. Be careful not to gag.

Cure your cold

Postnasal drip leaves a thick mucous in the back of the mouth and throat that is rich with sulfuric proteins—it stinks. (This phlegmy blanket also gives bacteria a place to hide from mouthwashes.) If you are experiencing postnasal drip, take decongestants and antihistamines—and blow your nose.

Keep it wet

After reaching age 25, people secrete less saliva than before. A dry mouth means less oxygen and bacterial production, which means...well, you already know. To increase salivary production, drink a lot of water or chew gum.

Change your diet

Everyone knows garlic and raw onions can cause bad breath, but not in the way people think. They are absorbed into the bloodstream through the stomach and exhaled through the lungs—a good reason why the odor lingers for so long and why mints do no good. Proteins in dairy products increase production of sulfurous gases in the mouth. Acids in coffee can also enhance microbe growth, leading to the antisocial morning condition, "coffee breath." Don't worry though, both milk and coffee breath can be washed away with a glass of water.

Rinse your mouth out

Although Listerine is claimed to improve breath quality for over eight hours, some clinicians maintain its true usefulness is 15 minutes at most. Still, swishing and gargling reaches areas the toothbrush cannot, making mouthwashes significantly better than brushing alone. Far better than garden-variety drugstore mouthwash is *chlorhexidine (a.k.a.* Peridex and PerioGard), a fast-acting, prescription-only disinfectant used to treat gum disease. Unlike weaker solutions, chlorhexidine kills bacteria for an extended period. One drawback, however, is that chlorhexidine may stain teeth and cosmetic fillings. An alternative solution, *chlorine dioxide,* may also be used. Chlorine dioxide works by neutralizing hydrogen sulfide gases in the back of the mouth. It is available in a mouthwash, toothpaste, or spray and is sold over the Internet under the brand name CloSYS II. Chlorine dioxide is best used in three steps, first by brushing with the toothpaste, then swishing the rinse around, and finally with a good scraping of the tongue.

Visit the clinic

Breath clinics diagnose patients with a halimeter, a device that measures how disgusting one's breath is based upon bacteria counts. Sinus or throat problems are referred to specialists. Clinics employ multiple weapons in the bad-breath battle, including scraping, strong disinfectants, and daily home applications of rinsing solutions. Each clinic claims to have its own proprietary system for defeating halitosis. An initial visit to a clinic can cost up to $150 per day (some clinics offer multiple-day sessions). Home breath maintenance kits generally cost about $25 for a one-month supply.

Try a home remedy

If you have tried everything else and still can't get your coworkers to go to lunch with you, try a home remedy. Allspice is not just an ingredient in pumpkin pie, but is supposedly a powerful antibacterial agent and breath cleanser. Folk doctors say the best way to apply it is to rub a little of the essential oil (found in nutrition stores) on your finger and run it along your gums and tongue. Ground-up allspice may be substituted (mixed 1 teaspoon to 1 cup of warm water), although it is not as powerful as the oil form. Others suggest drinking peppermint tea. You could also try chewing on fresh parsley, which contains breath-freshening chlorophyll. If all else fails, make home-brewed mouthwash from one part ground cinnamon to eight parts 100-proof vodka. Put the mixture in a bottle and shake it each day. Strain out the cinnamon after two weeks. Take a swig, gargle, rinse, spit, and repeat. For your money, though, you would be better off just buying a bottle of schnapps and taking a swig.

How to eat with chopsticks

In America, using chopsticks in an oriental restaurant is considered good taste (though somewhat silly in a Thai restaurant—they don't use chopsticks in Thailand). Chopsticks are not hard to master. Simply grip them as you would a pencil, holding one between the knuckle of the thumb and ring finger, and the other between the tip of the thumb and the tip of the forefinger. Move the upper chopstick up and down to grab food and hold the lower one still. Do not apply too much pressure or the chopsticks will slip and the item will squirt out. Never poke at your food either, as it is considered bad form. Sticky rice will cling to chopsticks just fine.

In a Japanese restaurant, soup is eaten by bringing an individual bowl to your mouth. Reverse the sticks (fat ends forward) when diving into a communal bowl to fill your plate. In a Chinese restaurant, spoons are used for both tasks. Japanese chopsticks are tapered to a point, while Chinese chopsticks are rounded. Mercifully, sushi may be eaten with the fingers.

When properly used, chopsticks demonstrate a suave sophistication. Klutzy attempts at impaling your food, however, have the opposite effect. Judith Martin ("Miss Manners") cautions ersatz connoisseurs who use chopsticks when in the Far East. As Miss Manners aptly put it in one of her columns, "tourists attempting a difficult foreign custom should cultivate a look of appealing stupidity that will give their mistakes a sort of childish charm."

How to do a swan dive
into an empty pool

The master of the high dive is—without a doubt—George Shaheen. In the summer of 1999, Shaheen had the sort of high-octane job that merits a stippled portrait in *The Wall Street Journal*; he was the chief executive officer of Andersen Consulting (now called Accenture), the largest, most prestigious information technology consulting firm in the world. At 55, Shaheen was a 30-year veteran earning $4 million a year with 65,000 people working for him. Shaheen's 10-year run at the top was an immensely successful period when the company grew from $1.1 billion to $8 billion in revenues. Andersen Consulting was in the midst of getting its legal separation from the accounting firm Arthur Andersen, which was widely expected to be followed by an IPO that would be highly lucrative for the partners. All he really had to do was sit tight for a couple of years and wait for his gilded parachute to open.

Then some wired-in Silicon Valley venture capitalists with more money than God came calling to pitch a new concept in online grocery retailing called Webvan. With the right business model, blue-chip backers, and a strong management team, Webvan had it all. Except for one thing: a star-quality CEO to succeed its aging founder and visionary, Louis Borders. At first Shaheen wasn't interested. But in the end, it was an offer he could not pass up. Shaheen left behind not only his $4 million salary, but also the estimated $50 million he would have received when Andersen Consulting went public (as Accenture in September 2001).

On September 21, 1999, virtually on the eve of its initial public offering, Webvan announced Shaheen was joining the company as CEO with a compensation package that included options to buy 15 million shares of stock at $8 per share. Webvan thus had all the earmarks of a winner—tons of business press, Internet buzz, impeccable timing, and an Old Economy CEO who lent the whole thing *gravitas*. After the IPO was priced at $15 and closed the first day at $24.88, Shaheen's options were worth $253 million. If the stock price reached $75 a share, he would be a billionaire on paper.

Alas, paper profits are aptly named, and Internet grocery stores turn out to have margins even lower than regular grocery stores. Webvan floundered as it rapidly expanded into one unprofitable market after another. On April 13, 2001, 18 months after taking the job, with the stock trading at less than a dollar, Shaheen resigned. As part of his retirement package,

Shaheen was to receive $375,000 per year for the rest of his life. On July 9, 2001, Webvan—which raised and burned through the staggering sum of $800 million in two years and never made a nickel—filed for Chapter 11 bankruptcy protection. Shaheen may not even get his retirement pay. He is now one of the largest unsecured creditors of Webvan.

How to find Blackbeard's treasure

Edward Teach, commonly known as the ruthless pirate Blackbeard, was killed on November 22, 1718 after he and his fellow brigands were ambushed by British ships at Ocracoke Inlet, North Carolina. They made sure he was good and dead; Teach received at least 25 sword wounds and five gunshots at the hands of his killer, Lt. Robert Maynard, who had been secretly commissioned by Virginia's governor, Alexander Spotswood, to locate and kill the notorious villain. The famous pirate's head was cut off and displayed in the bowsprit of Maynard's man-of-war. Upon return, it was delivered to Gov. Spotswood as proof.

During the preceding two years, Teach terrorized vessels along the coasts of the Carolinas and Virginia, conducting murderous raids on poorly defended merchant ships. Teach cultivated a Mephistophelean appearance with a thick black beard and a long waxed mustache. To make his devil-like appurtenance complete, Teach shoved canon fuses into his beard and beneath his hat and lighted them before going into battle. His face ablaze, Blackbeard frightened many sailors into immediate surrender. Teach was estimated to have captured some 40 ships containing tons of merchandise, rum, and treasure.

To Spotswood's disgust, Teach was given safe harbor in the colony of North Carolina by Gov. Charles Eden. Some believe that Eden chose to ignore the pirate's larcenous activities because they generated income for merchants in the state who resold his stolen goods for handsome profits. More likely, Eden himself directly profited from the relationship. Whatever his reason for settling in North Carolina, it is known for certain that Teach had residences at one time or another in Edenton, Elizabeth City, Ocracoke, and Bath.

Not long before his brutal death, Teach is believed to have ditched some of his loot in North Carolina. Evidently, Blackbeard refused to even tell his wife the location, reputedly saying only, "Nobody knows but miself and the Devil, and may the longest liver take all!"

One legend has it that Blackbeard buried a huge wooden treasure chest at the foot of a tree on Ocracoke Island in 1717. Teach was said to have marked the tree's trunk with his sword so he could find the treasure later, dubbing it "The Money Tree." Some people believe that the tree was found during the 20th century. The tree was supposedly spotted by a couple of treasure hunters who then sought the assistance of a local fisherman to help dig it up. The three men determined the area around the tree was too dense with roots and the tree would have to be pulled up with heavy equipment. According to the story, when the two treasure hunters returned later to unearth their treasure, they found the enormous tree yanked out of the ground and no treasure in sight. Meanwhile, the fisherman who had "helped" them had vanished. Something about this tale seems just too poetic to be true. So if you visit Ocracoke, keep a sharp eye out for massive 300-year-old oaks and cypress trees with peculiar markings on them.

Perhaps the most intriguing possible cache is in the Pamlico River near Blackbeard's former home in Bath. According to published stories, during the 1930s, two fishermen became entangled in an underwater obstruction that turned out to be the wooden roof of a crudely made brick vault. (It has been reported that Teach kept such a vault lashed to the deck of his pirate ship, *Queen Anne's Revenge*. Speculation is that Teach tossed the vault overboard to keep his pursuers from finding it.) Inside the vault, which lay in shallow water, were three iron kettles. Each kettle was said to contain 200 gold coins dating to the early 1700s.

According to the 1956 guide *Shipwrecks, Skin Divers, and Sunken Gold* by treasure hunter Dave Horner, the fishermen emptied the pots and buried the coins at a "small landing place where there was a sandy beach surrounded with bleached cypress knees." The burial spot was indicated to be "twenty or thirty yards from the bank of the river." The two men evidently agreed to come back and get it sometime later. Legend has it that after one of the fishermen died or went to prison, the other sought to reclaim the booty. Unfortunately for the hapless fellow, floodwaters had uprooted trees and destroyed landmarks, making it impossible to locate the burial spot.

Provided the story is true, the treasure is probably still there. If you want to take a crack at finding it, get yourself a metal detector and search the area near Bath where the Pamlico Inlet meets the Pamlico River channel. Your search should extend well inland, as the river may have changed course significantly over the past 70 years. The cypress trees may or may not have been washed away. If you go in the summer, be sure to take along super-strength insect repellent; the mosquitoes are so large they have their own airstrips.

If you don't have any luck with a metal detector, the supernatural may be of assistance. According to W. C. Jameson's book, *Buried Treasures of the South*, the headless ghost of Blackbeard has been spotted carrying a lantern on the beaches of Ocracoke Island. It is said that the spot where he sets down the lantern illuminates the location of buried treasure.

How to avoid hitting a moose

If you have taken our advice and elected to do your autobahning in a remote western state like Alaska or Montana, you should be aware that danger is potentially lurking around every curve and even on the shoulders of the road up ahead. No, not police—moose.

This is no joke. According to the Alaska Department of Fish and Game, 72 percent of Anchorage residents have been in a car that swerved or braked for a moose; 11 percent have been in a car that hit one. Alaskan motorists even warn one another with hazard lights if a moose is nearby.

A fully grown bull moose weighs up to 1,800 pounds, stands over six feet tall, and can quickly bring a speeding car to a dead stop. If a collision on the highway with a much smaller white-tailed deer can flip over a car, imagine what hitting a moose would do. Needless to say, neither you nor the moose would be in very good shape afterwards. If you know a little about moose behavior, however, you may be able to avoid hitting one.

Most accidents occur between dusk and dawn, because moose are more active at night and people have a hard time seeing them in the darkness. Unlike deer, which are light colored and whose eyes reflect headlights well, moose are dark brown to black, and their eyes reflect light poorly.

During the warmer months, moose like to reside near a lake or stream, which provides them with aquatic plants to eat and relief from insects. Although bulls are content to remain in the forest feeding on trees during summer, in the fall mating season, bulls will follow the scent of a cow moose for miles. During the winter, moose often cluster on the shoulders of highways foraging for vegetation. Moose also are known to walk along the highways so they can lick the winter's accumulated road salt. But a particularly dangerous time for drivers is the spring, when adult moose hoof it out of their winter lairs to find a new habitat. At the same time, yearlings leave their mothers for good and make tracks to find their own apartments. The sum is a lot of moose roaming around in the spring, showing up in peoples' backyards, and wandering all over the roads.

Almost half of the moose killed by vehicles are calves. Motorists often spot a cow moose crossing the road but fail to pick up the calf following behind its mother. Younger moose are particularly hazardous to motorists because they have not gotten used to cars and can panic and run into traffic instead of away from it.

To prevent a collision in moose country, always pay attention to both sides of the road, including the shoulders. It's also a good idea to turn on your high beams and lower your driving speed at night. Watch out for moose near lakes and rivers. If you see one, especially a cow (no antlers), look for another right behind. Moose are nearsighted; never assume one sees you or will stay put. Pass slowly by the moose so you will have time to stop if it bolts. And be sure to heed those MOOSE X-ING signs.

How to avoid inheriting the Earth

Benjamin Franklin said, "Blessed is he that expects nothing, for he shall never be disappointed."

Memo to the current generation: Stand by for disappointment. In a 2000 poll taken by the college recruiting firm JobTrak.com, a majority of college students and recent graduates surveyed expected to make their first million by age 40.

How to remove a tattoo

If you spend time in a tattoo parlor, you will learn several things. First, tattooing is now completely mainstream. Everybody gets tattoos, and many are hidden is some pretty strange places—and not necessarily visible on the beach. They are available in every color and can be remarkably large and intricate. Tattooing is a lot more high-tech and sanitary than it used to be, although it still hurts. For all of these reasons, tattooing is booming. Statisticians are not even sure how many people have tattoos, but estimates for adolescents range from 10 to 16 percent of the population. These teenagers will grow up some day, and when they do, they will confront another statistic: 58 percent of campus recruiters preferred candidates without visible body art, according to online labor exchange Vault.com.

Tattooing has been practiced off and on for 4,000 years. Ritualistic tattoos have been found on ancient Egyptian mummies. The Romans used tattoos to identify domestic slaves and criminals. Sometime later, Asiatics applied tattoos to their faces to protect themselves from evil spirits. Since then, the popularity of tattoos has risen and fallen many times, as they have gone from chic body art to symbols of nefariousness and promiscuity, and back.

Tattooing's chief asset, permanence, is also its chief liability. There are few sentiments one would wish to convey for a lifetime, as so many drunken sailors have come to appreciate. The more professional and recent the tattoo, the harder it is to remove. Older, cruder methods did not inject ink as deeply under the skin. In addition, tattoos that have been in the body for a while have usually faded a bit. Plus, the vibrant colors used today are harder to eliminate than basic black or blue. One option is to have an old ugly tattoo artfully turned into a new one instead of getting rid of it.

In the old days, tattoos were sanded off using a technique called salabrasion, where a salt solution was scrubbed into anesthetized skin until the area turned bloody. A more recent version is called dermabrasion, in which the skin is frozen and then peeled off. Surgical removal has also been used to basically replace the tattoo with a scar, or a skin graft for larger tattoos. Besides being generally unpleasant and painful, each of these techniques causes disfigurement. In the 1980s, a new CO_2 laser became available, although it did such a good job, it not only vaporized the tattoo, it vaporized the skin as well.

Fortunately, medical science has advanced considerably. The latest removal technology is the "Q-switched" laser, which uses bursts of thermal energy measured in billionths of a second. The shortness of the light bursts emitted by the laser enable it to attack the tattoo without damaging the skin. The new laser's pulses chemically change the tattoo pigment (chromophor) and scatter the tiny particles into the epidermis. Eventually the particles come to rest at the body's graveyard of ill-advised body art—the lymph nodes. Tattoos are gradually lightened over time to give the skin time to recover between treatments. Like everything else in healthcare, laser tattoo removal is not cheap. One session can cost from $100 to $500. A small tattoo may take one visit every other month for a year. A full-body tattoo (known as a "suit") could take a decade to erase.

There are complications as well. The laser output must be the complement of the color of the tattoo, for example, a red laser eliminates green ink. Unfortunately, modern tattoo artists often mix pigments to create a whole spectrum of colors. Because the equipment is so expensive, doctors cannot always match the laser to the tattoo. Also, certain colors are difficult to erase, especially red, orange, yellow, green, and white. Laser treatments on lighter colors may sometimes leave ghostly traces of the image, while cosmetic tattoos can react with the laser and actually become darker rather than lighter. And as rule, light-skinned people with tattoos usually have better success with removal.

Most states' medical associations have information on tattoo removal. You can also look in the Yellow Pages under dermatologists, plastic surgeons, and in larger cities, tattoo removal. Avoid small clinics; the larger the operation and more equipment they have, the more likely they will be to match the colors in your tattoos. If you have a larger piece of body art, try to find someplace close because you will be going back many times.

Incredibly, some people have their tattoos removed just so they have a clear place to get another one.

How to tell if a president is any good

As former United States Rep. James P. Johnson said during a House Agricultural Committee meeting, regarding the attempted assassination of President Gerald R. Ford by Lynette ("Squeaky") Fromme in 1975, "Mr. Chairman, I think the record should show that for the first time since McKinley, we have a Republican president worth shooting, and I think that's a good sign."

How to prevent jet lag

Anyone who has ever taken the red-eye from New York to Los Angeles knows that lethargic feeling that washes over you after 20 hours awake and a couple of drinks as you gamely try to make conversation at dinner. The feeling intensifies until you begin to babble incoherently and your host wonders if you are on some kind of medication. Mercifully, dinner ends just as you are about to go nose-down into your creme brulee. You stumble back to your hotel room, grateful your body will receive an extra three hours' sleep. You slog through the rest of the trip and start to feel fine by the time you leave. Yet when you return home you can't get to sleep and wake up tired and grouchy.

Transcontinental travel is even worse. Besides causing fatigue, major jet lag impairs your memory, disrupts cognitive processes, and interferes with motor functions. Some researchers even believe it shrinks your brain. If long-distance air travel is on your docket, get acquainted with some ways to prevent jet lag.

Jet lag is caused by rapid crossings of time zones that discombobulate your circadian clock. Symptoms include lethargy, fatigue, mental fogginess, disorientation, headaches, and moodiness, (in short, just about everything associated with getting old except constipation and thinning hair). Jet lag has been blamed for accidents, faulty negotiations, and poor athletic performance. Champion diver Greg Louganis cited jet lag as the reason why he bonked his head on the diving platform at the 1988 Olympics in Seoul.

Symptoms of jet lag are exacerbated by traveling in a sealed metal tube filled with stale air. Due to cabin pressurization, the humidity on an airplane is typically very low (less than 10 percent), and after a couple of hours you will start to dry out. Drink plenty of liquids, especially water, and stay away from those little bottles of Drambuie they ply you with on overseas flights. Alcohol is the last thing you should put in a dehydrated body. Indigestible food served at bizarre hours (like dinner at midnight followed by "breakfast" at 3 a.m.), is no real benefit either. Your body will thank you if you have a light meal before the flight and pass up the junk they serve you on the plane.

Besides eating ahead of time, you may want to alter what you eat as well. Researchers believe that food is used by the body to set its internal clock. Dr. Charles F. Ehret, senior scientist emeritus of the Argonne National Laboratory, spent 40 years developing a scientific four-day diet that he claims comes close to eliminating jet lag. (Ehret now offers a customized jet lag prevention program based upon his research at Argonne through his company, StopJetLag Travel Service.) Follow this closely now: The first day of the diet calls for a high-protein breakfast and lunch, followed by a high-carbohydrate dinner and dessert; the second day, you are supposed to get by on soups, salads, fruits, and fruit juice; the third day is a repeat of the first; the fourth day is a repeat of the second. You can only have caffeine between 3 and 5 p.m. on days one, two, and three, and cannot have caffeine until the evening on the fourth day. Got it? (We're not sure if this diet really cures jet lag, but you will probably lose a couple of pounds.)

Maybe more important than split personality eating is adjusting your mealtimes. Eating at odd times can cause gastrointestinal misery—not a pleasant experience in a coach seat for 12 hours. A recent University of Virginia study found the liver is highly important to regulating the internal clock in rats. Although it has not yet been proven, it is thought that changing your mealtimes before traveling would "phase-shift" your liver more quickly and help avoid symptoms of jet lag.

If there is anything like a magic pill for jet lag, it is the coenzyme NADH (nicotinamide adenine dinucleotide hydrogen). Available over the counter as a nutritional supplement called ENADAlert, NADH is believed to allow brain and central nervous system cells to produce more energy. Research done by Gary Kay, Ph.D., clinical associate professor of neurology and neuropsychology at Georgetown University School of Medicine, revealed NADH taken upon landing significantly mitigated the effects of jet lag from long flights.

Experts suggest you try to sleep on the plane. But in a coach middle seat...good luck. Some somnolent few sleep right through, though most sleep fitfully, if at all. Bring an extra pair of thick socks to keep the blood moving through your feet. Earplugs and pricey, Walkman-like "noise cancellation devices" are lifesavers if your seatmates happen to be small children. If you have a daytime flight, black eyeshades may come in handy. With diligence, you can put yourself on the time zone where you will be staying by steadily adjusting your sleep habits the week prior to departure. Researchers also suggest taking supplemental doses of the brain hormone melatonin starting five days before a long flight to help reset your clock and improve your sleep. Even better, combine melatonin with a modified sleep schedule. (See "How to get a good night's sleep" if nothing seems to work.)

Part of adjusting is psychological. You can start to mentally adjust the moment you board the plane by resetting your watch to the destination time zone. More important, researchers say, is your exposure to light. (Ever notice casinos are always dark and have no clocks?) If you really want to be scientific about it, you can hasten your adjustment by precisely limiting exposure to sunlight after you land at your destination. Medical Services for Travellers Abroad offers a free light exposure calculator at *www.masta.org* that calculates how much light you should have based upon your particular trip. An even more recondite technique has people strapping flashlights to the back of their knees, where photoreceptors supposedly take in light and help adjust the body's clock.

Even if sunlight avoidance is truly effective, how many people want to spend precious days in a foreign city like vampires, holed up in hotel rooms adjusting their circadian rhythms? Perhaps the simplest way to lick jet lag is to pick the right flight. Veteran fliers will tell you if you are flying west to east on a short business trip, leave the night before so you arrive in the morning. Catch a quick shower; take a short nap; hook up an intravenous coffee drip; and go directly to your meetings without sleeping. You should make it through the day okay, although you will probably feel like death warmed over by 8 or 9 p.m. All-nighters may be fine for a one-or two-day trip, but an accumulated sleep deficit can wreck a longer journey. For a lengthier west-to-east trip (like New York to London), leave early in the morning so you arrive at night. Sleep as much as you can and try to get up on local time. The next day, force yourself to stay up until your normal bedtime so you will adjust faster. Going east to west is far easier on the way out because you will get additional sleep time when you arrive. Follow the directions above for the trip back home.

How to get elected to the Senate

Why fiddle around running for city council if your real ambition is to be a United States senator? Getting elected to the Senate is easier than you might think. Incumbents are remarkably beatable. These days voters are suspicious of career politicians, especially senators. Seats in the Senate turn over three times more frequently than seats in the House of Representatives. Although still uncommon, skillful amateurs entering politics for the first time have had success winning election to the Senate, including entrepreneurs, athletes, surgeons, and actors.

Who should run?

Based upon an analysis of the current and previous Senate bodies, certain traits have been shown to enhance electability. Complete the following checklist to see if you have the stuff to be elected.

Male. (Add 10 points)

It may not be politically correct, but with the exceptions of the Northeast and the West Coast, the Senate is the province of men. Although there has been a lot of talk about women in the Senate during the past decade, there are still only 14 out of 100.

Age 50 or younger. (If not, deduct 15 points)

Although the average age in the Senate is 59, statistics compiled by political scientist Joseph A. Schlesinger show your chances of winning the Senate as your first elected office past age 50 are low. When you get past age 60, forget it.

Married. (Add 10 points)

A startling 88 percent of senators are married. As to whether they are happy or not, one can only speculate. We note, however, that extramarital hanky-panky has brought down more than one sitting senator.

Military veteran. (Add 10 points; decorated veterans add 15 points)

Of the current senators, 36 are veterans. Serving in uniform, especially during wartime, quickly answers any questions about your patriotism. Decorated war heroes are disproportionately represented in the Senate and include Daniel Inouye, John Kerry, Chuck Hagel, and John McCain.

Churchgoer. (Atheists deduct 10 points)

The census takers will not ask about it, but voters want to know. Roman Catholics do well in most parts of the country. Naturally, there are some exceptions. Baptists and Methodists run best in the South. Jews do well in California and the Northeast. And don't even think of running for the Senate from Utah unless you're a Mormon. If you are not sure what you are, consider joining the Episcopal Church. There are 10 times as many Episcopalians in the Senate as there are in the United States population at large.

Well-known businessman, entertainer, or professional athlete. (Add 15 points)

Senators John Glenn, Bill Bradley, Jesse Helms, Hillary Rodham-Clinton, Jon Corzine, and Bill Frist all had no previous political experience before running for the Senate. Being famous helps these days when an appalling percentage of voters cannot even name their governor, let alone their two United States senators. The advantages of celebrity are pronounced in large states like California and New York where media costs are exorbitant. While no guarantee of success, notoriety means you have the luxury of spending time and money articulating your message rather than identifying yourself.

Tough as nails. (If not, deduct 15 points)

Senate campaigns are long, tedious, exhausting, and often unpleasant (especially the groveling for money part). You and your family will be subjected to scrutiny rivaled only by certain medical procedures. A hardy constitution and mental fortitude are essential.

Attorney. (Add 5 points)

A real plus for an aspiring lawmaker is a law degree: Over half of all senators are attorneys. Some even practiced law before going into politics.

Master in the art of blather. (Add 5 points)

Rhetorical flourishes are a lost skill, but flapdoodle sells. *Baltimore Sun* political writer Frank Kent put it best, "Probably the most important single accomplishment for the politically ambitious is the fine art of seeming to say something without doing so."

Independently wealthy. (Add 25 points)

The Senate isn't called the "Millionaire's Club" for nothing. The average successful Senate race now costs about $5 million and the cost has increased by 8 percent on average during each of the past five election cycles. Self-financed campaigns have become more popular lately, accounting for 44 percent of the dollars spent during 2000 Senate races.

(If your score totals 50 or more points keep reading.)

Before you put yourself through the trial of running for public office, stop and consider if you really want the job. Being a senator carries a lot of responsibility: making laws, approving presidential appointments, ratifying treaties, attending countless state dinners and sounding off on Sunday morning talk shows. Far less glamorous is constituent service and the near-constant preoccupation with campaign fund-raising. Then there is the equally distasteful abandonment of your principles in order to get elected. Of course there are worse occupations—like being a congressman.

When to run

If you're patient, you can run when conditions are most favorable. The best times are when there are vacancies, a freshman is standing for re-election or the incumbent has been tainted by a scandal.

- *Run for an open seat.* Incumbency is so powerful that even formidable challengers are often reluctant to oppose a sitting senator. Nearly 60 percent of current senators were elected when incumbents were retiring. The problem for an amateur Senate candidate is that open races attract the strongest, best-financed candidates from both parties, and therefore your chances of winning may still be poor. If you can't run for an open seat then try to...

- *Run against a freshman incumbent.* The Senate, with its strong belief in the seniority system, seldom gives a first-term senator an opportunity to get much done. Take advantage of the freshman's inexperience and run against him when his only sponsored legislation is the Boll Weevil Eradication Act. Next time around, with plum committee positions, he may be impossible to beat. But if both incumbents are veterans then your best option is to wait and...

- *Run when the incumbent is vulnerable.* Out of 18 variables affecting Senate races analyzed by David T. Canon in his book on amateur politicians, *Actors, Athletes, and Astronauts,* the single-biggest swing factor is political scandal, which improves the likelihood of success by a whopping 13 percent. Also, presidential scandals usually rub off on incumbents of the same party, as was the case in 1974 in the first elections after Watergate when Republican candidates were crushed.

How to get started

The modern Senate campaign requires a lot of people. Among the important senior advisers necessary are a communications director, chief strategist, marketing director, and campaign finance committee chairman. At the junior level, possibly the most important people on your staff are the campaign coordinators. They do the long, hard work of traveling all over the state, meeting with local and county officials, and setting up your grass roots network. You also will need numerous paid staffers to help organize and manage your campaign, put out press releases, set up fundraisers, and coordinate campaign events.

Here is a summary of major campaign expenses.

- *Advertising.* The largest single campaign expenditure in any modern campaign is advertising. The more media markets, the more expensive it is; in large states, media purchases can easily run over $15,000 per day. Slick campaign spots produced by professional advertising agencies are not cheap. Figure a minimum of $150,000 per month.

- *Direct mail.* What good are your supporters if you can't ask them for money? Sure, it's obnoxious to repeatedly hit the same people up for donations, but direct mail works and is more efficient than $1,000-a-plate dinners. Add $50,000 a month.
- *Campaign staff.* For a truly professional campaign, big-ticket outside experts (advertising people, pollsters, and media consultants) are a must. Yet aside from senior advisers, whose annual salaries run well into the six figures apiece, campaign staff comes fairly cheap. You can hire recent college graduates hungry for experience for a pittance. You also will need numerous volunteers for any number of menial tasks like answering phones, doing data entry, and passing out leaflets. Campaign staff is a bargain at $75,000 per month.
- *Incidentals.* Office space, telephones, travel, and other miscellaneous expenses (catering, yard signs, bumper stickers, buttons, silly hats) all add up. Tack on another $125,000 per month.

Total budget: $400,000 per month in an average-sized state and up to 10 times that amount in a large one. Now you just need to figure out how to pay for it.

How to finance your campaign

- *Spend your personal fortune.* The easiest way to be worth $100 million is to start with $150 million and run for the Senate. Just ask Jon Corzine, who blew (or invested, if you prefer) a record $63 million—almost all of it his own money—in his 2000 New Jersey Senate race. Corzine, the former co-chairman of Goldman Sachs, outspent his challenger, Congressman Gary Franks, by 10-to-1. Personal fortunes launched the Senate careers of Herb Kohl (department stores), Peter Fitzgerald (law), Mark Dayton (department stores), and Jay Rockefeller (great-grandfather's dimes). Voters don't seem to mind rich candidates because they presume anyone who can buy an election is beyond the reach of moneyed special interests.

  Spending a ton of your own cash, however, won't overcome an inept campaign. In the 1994 California Senate race, Republican challenger Michael Huffington outspent his opponent, Democrat Diane Feinstein, by 2-to-1, but still managed to lose in a GOP landslide year.
- *Spend somebody else's money.* The traditional way of raising money is to get a firm grip on the money tree and shake the

living daylights out of it. The $42 million Hillary Clinton raised and spent of other peoples' money in her successful 2000 race against Rick Lazio, who himself raised and spent $39 million of other peoples' money, pretty much says it all.

It takes a lot of individual donations to finance a campaign. Federal law limits ordinary citizens to contributions of $2,000 each. To raise money faster, you may also want to find some political action committees (PACs) that favor your candidacy. PACs can contribute $5,000 per candidate during each election and can finance or run advertisements on your behalf. P.S. Don't forget that if you get elected, your contributors might want something in return.

Before raising any money you will have to form a campaign finance committee and appoint a treasurer and board of directors. Paperwork must be filed with the Federal Election Committee (see *www.fec.gov* for filing information).

How to get on the ballot

To get on the primary ballot, you must submit signed petitions of registered voters with your state election commission. There are very strict requirements on what must be filed, and failure to adhere to them could get you thrown off the ballot. Contact your state election commission or party organization for the requirements.

How to win the primary

As a newcomer, winning the party primary is difficult. Incumbents are rarely dumped, and even an open primary race is tough. Unless you have been recruited by the state and national party apparatchiks, you are liable to find roadblocks to your candidacy around every curve. Still, because primary turnout is typically low, challengers who cultivate an energized base of voters can pull off upsets. The keys to winning the primary, like all elections, are simple: (1) get your message out, (2) identify your supporters, (3) make sure they vote.

In the primary, a sharp, consistent message is essential to distinguish yourself. If your name recognition is poor, you need to start earlier than other candidates just to be a player. Buckets of money help. Stunts, like walking all over the state, can be effective at generating name-awareness. State fairs, parades, and other feel-good events are other inexpensive ways of getting noticed. Though debates generally help challengers, voters have a tendency to ignore them in the primary.

Donations, election petitions, campaign event sign-up sheets, and even sneaky telephone polling are some of the ways used to identify supporters.

Once identified, supporters should be put into a computerized database to so you can hit them up for money. (Sophisticated campaign software is available to manage solicitations, track fund-raising, and prepare state and federal election filings.) More importantly, these people become your identified base. It is critical they get out and vote on Election Day.

One of the biggest problems you must overcome is voters' inclination to ignore primary elections until the last minute. If your funds are limited, be sure to harbor plenty of cash for a big media blitz in the weeks prior to the primary. And without the party's machine, you will need lots of volunteers to work the phones just before the election to encourage people to go to the polls.

How to win the general election

The general election is a whole new ballgame. The reward for defeating your party's favorite is an automatic boost in the general election: When you're the new sheriff in town, people sit up and take notice. Unlike the primary race, you can count on strong support from your party's national senatorial election committee, especially if you defeat an incumbent (nothing like the fear of losing a safe seat to get the dollars flowing from Washington).

If you are running for an open seat, you may want to soften your primary image a bit. The traditional course is to tack right or left during the primary then back towards the political center in the general. Your opponent will try to brand you as an extremist for things you said during the primary. Fortunately, two can play this game. The key is to cling tenaciously to the middle and never get ruffled. In most states, running as a moderate improves your chances significantly. Even if you stink as a campaigner, with enough money, paid consultants, and strong party backing, you should be able to run a credible race.

But if you are running against an incumbent senator, more drastic measures are required. The best approach is usually to take the low road. Contrary to widespread reports, Americans have not tired of mudslinging. If done well, in fact, negative campaigning is extremely effective. According to a 2001 study published in the *Journal of Politics,* negative campaigning actually tends to *increase* turnout in all but the dirtiest campaigns. Sneering, attack-dog ads are especially effective against scandal-plagued opponents. Warning: While incumbents prefer to be senatorial and act like personal insults are beneath them, they can let it fly with the best of 'em if threatened. And their fat campaign piggybanks will give them a pretty big advantage in airtime.

How to get blood from a stone

Answer: Get a really good advertising agency. Now in its 22nd year, the ubiquitous two-word ad campaign for Absolut vodka has proven so durable that it may never end.

In 1979, management of Swedish Wine and Spirits Corporation, the former state-run liquor monopoly of Sweden, came to the United States desperate to crack the vodka market but without a clue how to do it. A year later they had one of the most famous advertising slogans in the world and a redesigned bottle that, if hung upside down, would look right at home in a hospital. The original creative agency, N. W. Ayer, came up with the famous slogan. They knew immediately they had an inexhaustible supply of ad ideas. According to *Absolut Book* by Richard W. Lewis, the man who thought it up, Jerry Siano, exclaimed to the Swedes "Absolutely *anything!*"

TBWA Advertising replaced Ayer before the campaign got started, and was responsible for both the original spotlighted bottle ads and the later series of not-so-subliminal Absolut bottle images in familiar places. *Advertising Age* magazine recently ranked TBWA's Absolut campaign the seventh-greatest advertising campaign of the 20th century. As the editors noted, "It was a neat trick for a product that is by law and by its very nature a flavorless commodity."

While critically acclaimed, some would argue the campaign ceased being clever and started being absolut-ly monotonous about 20 years ago. Still, there is no denying the result. Absolut went from a nothing brand, selling 10,000 cases in 1979 to the third-largest premium spirit in the world, selling 7.3 million cases by 2000.

Now, after over 800-odd ads, we still await the ABSOLUT END.

How to stop solicitors

Ever get to your door and hear the phone ringing, scramble to find your keys, drop all of your things, sprint down the hall and pick up the receiver, flushed and out of breath, only to hear "This is Tony, calling from your long-distance phone company with a special offer..."?

Don't get mad, get expunged.

The federal Telephone Consumer Protection Act restricts telemarketers from calling before 8 a.m. or after 9 p.m. Callers must identify themselves, the firm they represent, the purpose of the call, and provide you an address and phone number for their company. You can verbally ask telemarketers to put you on their "do not call list," which they are obligated to do without further effort on your part. If the firm subsequently calls more frequently than once a year, you can sue them under the TCPA and collect $500 (up to $1,500 if they willfully disregard your request to be left alone). You might eventually make some money, but there is an easier way.

For $20, Private Citizen, Inc. will add you to its directory of 4,000 fellow citizens who are sick of telemarketers. The *Private Citizen Directory*, sent to over 1,500 telemarketing firms across the country, threatens a $500 fee and, if necessary, a lawsuit to collect it, for each telephone solicitation its members receive. For most telemarketers the threat is enough to get you off their list. Even so, Private Citizen claims its members have collected over $1 million in the past five years from firms that failed to heed their demand to cease and desist. Contact Private Citizen at P.O. Box 233, Naperville, Ill. 60566, (630) 393-2370, *http://privatecitizen.com*.

If you get repeatedly called by stockbrokers, particularly those with a smooth New York rap working from a "boiler room," there is a simple way to get rid of them. Tell them you would love to chat, but are employed by a broker-dealer (such as Merrill Lynch). This tactic will quickly brush off even aggressive callers because by law, employees of brokerage firms must have their accounts where they work (so their employers can monitor potential insider trading), or receive written permission (rarely granted) to have them somewhere else. If brokers still keep pestering you, contact the Securities and Exchange Commission at (202) 942-7040.

If your mailbox sags under the weight of all those catalogs around Christmastime, there is a fix for that as well. For $10, Private Citizen will send your name to the largest junk mail and "list sales" firms in the country and say "Enough!" While Private Citizen will not get them all, your mailbox should be noticeably emptier within a couple of months. Be patient. Names that are sold tend to travel like a contagious virus from one list to the next. To do it yourself and save the ten bucks, write to the Mail Preference Service (MPS) of the Direct Marketing Association, P.O. Box 643, Carmel, NY 10512. The MPS maintains a master list of names of people who do not wish to be solicited by the mail. Once a quarter, an updated list is made available to members of the association, so it takes up to three months before you see a drop-off in junk mail.

Credit bureaus routinely sell your financial data to card issuers, a cozy little business arrangement at the root of those relentless offers for new credit cards, flight insurance, and other unnecessary financial services. You can stop the insanity with one phone call to the credit bureaus at (888) 5-OPTOUT.

Whether you use Private Citizen or write to the MPS, inevitably some junk mail will still get through. For these exceptions, write each company individually and ask for your name to be placed in the "suppress" file. If some mailers still don't get the message, you have one more arrow in your quiver. Go to your local post office and request Form 1500. This form was designed to stop illicit catalogs, but consumers have used it successfully to end all types of junk mail. Fill out the form, attach the objectionable piece of mail, and return it. By law, the offending party must stop sending you mail within 30 days. As for "saturation" mailings sent to every address in a given area and marked "RESIDENT," you are out of luck. The United States Postal Service will not stop such bulk mail. Install a large wastebasket next to your mailbox.

Your digital mailbox can fill up with garbage too. Junk e-mails, or "spam," can be reduced by using the e-Mail Preference Service of the DMA. Fill out the online form at *www.e-mps.org*—it's good for a year. Never respond to spam—it just encourages more. You can get rid of those annoying banner ads by going to *www.doubleclick.com/optout*.

As for all those magazines jamming your snail-mailbox, if you didn't want them, why did you subscribe in the first place?

How to avoid gridlock

Quick, in what category is Atlanta the national leader?
A. Debutante balls.
B. Streets beginning with the word "peach."
C. CEOs named "Ted."
D. Consumption of cobbler.
E. Highway congestion.

Answer: B, of course. There are 32 street names starting with the word "peach" in Atlanta. If you said E, you may be surprised that Atlanta is only the fifth-worst congested city in the country.

Los Angeles leads by a mile in total highway delays, at a staggering annual 792 million hours, costing motorists $2.1 billion in fuel alone, according to the Texas Transportation Institute's "Annual Mobility Report." On a per-person basis, L.A. also leads, at 62 hours in delays, followed by San Francisco (41 hours), Dallas (37), Houston (36), and Denver and Washington D.C. (35). The rest of the worst are Seattle (34), Atlanta, Miami and San Jose (33). New York, which is No. 2 in total delays owing to its large population, ranks only 21st in delay hours per person due to its heavy reliance on mass transit.

Gridlock can creep as well as crawl. There are a lot of otherwise attractive cities that are now, or soon will be, major motoring messes. Large cities with the fastest-growing highway congestion are San Antonio, Atlanta, Minneapolis, Austin, Denver, and Charlotte. (Special mention also goes to Washington, Chicago, and "Big Dig" Boston for having the most crowded surface streets.) Medium-sized cities getting worse are Austin, Charlotte, Hartford, Connecticut and Providence, Rhode Island. Colorado Springs, Colorado, and Eugene, Oregon are distinguished as the only small cities to make the list of the top 30 worsening metro areas.

The fastest-moving large cities with pleasant weather most of the year are New Orleans, Norfolk, Virgina, and San Antonio. The weather is worse, but the Rust Belt offers some good commuting deals in Pittsburgh, Kansas City, Cleveland, Columbus, Ohio and St. Louis. If you don't mind bitter-cold winters and 100 inches of snow per year, upstate New York has a number of promising places to live, including Rochester, Albany and— the speediest large city in the United States—Buffalo. Medium-sized cities with minimal delays include Richmond, Virginia, Tulsa, Oklahoma, Omaha, Nebraska, and Salt Lake City. (Unfortunately, Salt Lake City is not building new roads to keep pace with population growth and is getting worse.) For smaller cities, just about anywhere in Texas and the Pacific Northwest are good bets. Cities that combine the shortest commute times with the cheapest housing are, in order of size, Philadelphia, Buffalo, El Paso, and Corpus Christi, Texas. The worst of both are San Francisco, Seattle, Austin, and Colorado Springs.

If you just get completely sick of it all, consider Alaska. It has 29 people for each rural highway mile, versus the national average of 45. The highways aren't very crowded either; one-third of Alaska's citizens live so far away from roads that they get around by snowmobile, airplane, or boat. Yet Alaska is deceptively close to major cities in the Northern Hemisphere by air because of its latitude near the top of the globe. Anchorage, for example, is only a seven-hour flight to Tokyo, New York, and London. Thanks to its tremendous oil revenues, Alaska has no income tax and actually pays each resident an annual dividend ($1,541 in 2002). Sure, winters are dark and miserable, but you can play golf at midnight during July, when the average daily high in Anchorage is 65 degrees and the average low is 52. Although you won't have to worry too much about traffic tie-ups, be careful of the roadside wildlife. (See "How to Avoid Hitting a Moose.")

How to correct your credit report

Every American with a credit card, mortgage, or even a utility bill is being monitored by a credit reporting agency. If you haven't looked at your credit report in the past six months, it's high time you did. Not only are credit reports used by lenders to make credit decisions, but, in a dubious extrapolation of their usefulness, credit reports are used to assess the moral fiber of jobseekers and set insurance rates. Orwell would have loved them.

Under the Fair Credit Reporting Act, all consumers can see their credit reports for a fee of $8. (The report is free if you have recently been denied credit, insurance, or employment, or have spotted inaccuracies or fraud during the past 60 days.) Reports vary by vendor, but each one contains a list of your current overdue payables, recent late payments, and principal amounts due on mortgages, credit cards, auto loans, etc. A number of accounts may be omitted because not all credit card issuers submit information to credit reporting agencies. There are three titans in the credit reporting industry: Equifax (800) 685-1111, Experian (888) 397-3742, and TransUnion (800) 888-4213. Take the time to order your credit report from each vendor.

Carefully review the information on each report. Besides the amounts, pay close attention to the names and addresses that show up—they may reveal identity theft. For example, your name might be attached to an account with an address where you have never lived. Or there may be merging errors, where the credit bureau has crossed your information with a database containing information from someone else. If you suspect somebody has stolen your ID, you need to take action immediately (see "How to prevent identity theft"). You should also identify dormant or closed accounts, which should be expunged from your file.

If you find an error, notify the credit reporting agency in writing. (Phoning the agency's hotline does not create an adequate paper trail.) Clearly describe which items on the report are inaccurate. Be factual and enclose photocopies of documents supporting your corrections. There is no need to be threatening...yet. Send the letter by certified mail, return receipt requested. By law the agency must investigate any items you call to their attention within 30 business days. The agency also is obligated to forward your complaint to the source of the flawed information, usually a bank. Should the information provider be unable to verify the disputed data, it must be deleted from your file. Errors must be quickly corrected, sent on to the other credit bureaus and, at your request, to anyone who got a copy of your report during the past six months.

If you don't get satisfaction, send a follow-up letter. It that doesn't work, then it's time to play hardball. Contact the Federal Trade Commission, Bureau of Consumer Protection, CRC-240, Washington, D.C. 20580, (877) 382-4537, and explain the problem. Because credit bureaus and lenders try to avoid entanglements with the FTC, you should get prompt action.

In the worst case, where you dispute something but simply cannot get it corrected, you are allowed to insert an explanation of up to 100 words in your file. Make the statement factual yet reassuring. For example, if one creditor was especially nasty you might suggest the reader evaluate your credit based upon all your other accounts. Don't go off and proclaim a jihad against a creditor—prospective lenders will not be impressed.

Credit report errors produce a ripple effect. Fair, Isaac & Co., a financial software developer, crunches data from credit bureaus to estimate the likelihood of a consumer defaulting on a debt. The Fair, Isaac system produces consumer credit ratings, known as "FICO" scores, that are scaled from 300-850 points (725 is the average). Not only are FICO scores used by 75 percent of all credit card companies and mortgage lenders to make credit decisions, but they also can determine what rate you will pay. According to Fair, Isaac, your bill payment history is given the heaviest weighting and accounts for 35 percent of your FICO score. If your credit report is screwed up, your ability to get a loan may be impaired. Take a peek at your credit score by ordering it online for $12.95 at *www.myfico.com.*

If you were turned down for credit before repairing your records, there is a little-known method of gaining a second bite at a loan. You can ask the loan officer to do a "rapid re-score," which will update your FICO score for recent activity in your finances. Re-scoring can be beneficial if you recently corrected errors in your accounts, paid off large overdue debts, or had credit problems that are now ancient history. (Charge-offs disappear from your record after seven years, bankruptcies after 10.) Beware of negotiated deals to partially repay your debts. From a FICO standpoint, semi-deadbeats and bankruptcy filers are considered equally bad risks.

How to ace an interview

Interviewing for a job is easy if you understand it is an entirely superficial act. Many candidates are rejected because they bare their souls, express their doubts, or otherwise make a verbal hash of things. The interviewer is not your psychiatrist. Interviewers are only interested in the answers to two questions: (1) Can you do the work?, and (2) Will you fit in with the organization? Here's how to ace these two questions and get hired.

Preparation

It is imperative to do your homework on the company. Being prepared will significantly enhance your confidence during the interview. Thoroughly review the company's Website, research the company on the Internet, and pull up news stories. If you are interviewing with a public company, pull up SEC filings (*www.sec.gov*) or telephone its investor relations department and ask for an investor kit. Pay particular attention to the chairman's letter in the annual report, which often reveals a lot about the way management views the company. When the conversation reverses with the throat-clearing, "Do you have any questions for *me*?" you will be ready.

During your research, try to ascertain something about the firm's culture. If corporate hierarchy, internal buzzwords, and acronyms pepper their descriptions, you are probably dealing with an inward-looking organization. These organizations tend to be large, uncreative, and rigid in their analysis of candidates. It is important to always put things in their terms. Make a list of questions about corporate initiatives: "How is Quality 2002 important to your operating division?" "What is the profile of this group within the overall organization?" and so on. To get hired by one of these firms, you have to emphasize how similar you are to everyone else. At the same time, you have to hammer home the value you bring to the operating unit.

Externally focused organizations are generally leaner and more bottom line-oriented. They tend to describe things in terms of market opportunities and growth. They like employees who are self-starters and burning with intensity. These firms also want to know what your incremental value is, but are less concerned about whether you fit the mold. They are looking for aggressiveness, creativity, and extreme dedication to goals. You need to demonstrate passion and problem-solving abilities to get hired by a firm like this.

Some firms, particularly larger ones, have elements of both inwardness and market orientation. As the interviewee, you need to figure out what drives the organization so you can play that up. But do not overlook the interviewer, who may disagree with the company line. Successful candidates establish repeated congruence with both the interviewer and the organization. Look for every opportunity to do so during the interview.

First interview

First interviews are used as initial screens to vet candidates who look good on paper. From the candidate's perspective, the objective of the first interview is simply to leave a favorable impression and be invited back for the next round. Avoid scheduling interviews on Mondays and Fridays, when people are too distracted to concentrate. Attempt to get an interview time when your body functions well. This may not always be possible, but it never hurts to ask. The end of the day is always bad.

Everyone has heard the clichés about first impressions, and in interviews, they largely hold true. Although some people don't mind if you dress casually for an interview, those who do will reject you instantly. Men should play it safe and wear a dark suit, white shirt and conservative tie. Shoes should be highly polished and jackets buttoned. Women should wear a dark suit and white or cream blouse and coordinated shoes. Scarves and tasteful, simple jewelry are acceptable. Both sexes should go easy on the cologne. Your suitcoat should remain on unless the interviewer invites you to remove it. If you are unsure about your ability to dress well for an interview, see John T. Molloy's indispensable guide, *New Dress for Success.*

Eat a little something before the meeting—it will keep your stomach from gurgling. Be sure to arrive on time. If you are unfamiliar with the address, leave extra time to get there. If you arrive early, take a walk around the block. Showing up ahead of schedule is just as bad as being late—both imply that your time is more valuable than the interviewer's. If you get sweaty palms, visit the rest room and run your hands under warm water. Some interview guides say never to accept anything to drink at an interview. This is malarkey. If you are running low on caffeine, take a cup of coffee. It will help your brain react more quickly to questions. If you get nervous and swallow a lot, ask for a glass of water. If possible, ask the interviewer's assistant discretely before the interview starts. Order lightly if your interview is over a meal—if all is going well you will be too busy talking to eat.

Bring a briefcase with extra copies of your resume in it. Whether you wait in the reception area or are ushered into the interview room upon your arrival, ignore the invitation to make yourself comfortable. Instead— this is important—*always stand* while you wait. Look out the window, or pace back and forth if necessary, but do not sit. When the interviewer arrives, she will know you mean business and are full of energy. Look the interviewer straight in the eye, smile and say, "Ms. Jones? It's a pleasure to meet you!" If you have already spoken on the phone say, "Good to *finally* meet you!" Do not sweat this moment—it's not Lee and Grant at Appomattox—just don't let some pointless remark about the weather or traffic be the first thing out of your mouth.

Some experts suggest using a technique called "mirroring" that involves subtly aligning your body with your interviewer's. The idea is to create a subconscious sense of affinity between you and the person across the table. At best this technique is modestly helpful, and if you get caught you will be branded a buffoon. A simpler approach is to follow George Washington's advice and keep both feet on the floor and your hands in your lap. If this seems too stiff or unnatural to you, cross your legs, but be sure to sit upright. Keep your hands away from your face. If you have a choice as to where to sit at a rectangular table, sit at the end. This way, your interviewer will not face you directly, which is a psychologically confrontational position.

Questions at first interviews tend to center around basic background information. Interviewers generally use your resume as a discussion tool, so be prepared to explain it backwards and forwards. (Keep in mind many interviewers have not even looked at your resume before you arrive.) Study it carefully and try to put yourself in a stranger's shoes, looking at it for the first time. Gaps in employment history leap out, but so do demotions and questionable career changes.

There is, naturally, a very good explanation for everything. Think of yourself as a candidate for office (which you are, really). Be humble, but try to put everything in a positive light. If you were young and stupid, admit it, although not precisely in those words. Demotions or lateral moves are new "opportunities" and "challenges." What looks like a capricious move to an interviewer, is to you a smartly calculated step to take your career in a new, more interesting direction. But never get into an argument with the interviewer. Confrontation does not get you points for boldness, it sends you to the elevator bank for arrogance.

Some jerks may fire off questions like, "What did you do today?" or "Why are you here?" Such questions are designed to catch you off-guard. Don't let them ruffle you. If you get a stress-inducing question, particularly one that is off-the-wall, pause and reflect a moment before answering. Try not to ramble; the interviewer is not interested in your answer anyway but, rather, to see how you handle yourself. Unless the interviewer is a total sadist, the vast majority of the time you will only get one of these questions.

If you are qualified and excited about the position, there is no excuse for blowing the first interview. Answer questions straightforwardly and succinctly. Use active verbs as much as possible. Avoid extended discourses into your personal history. The more you talk, the more likely you are to make a mistake. Consciously try to move towards the interviewer's temperament. If she is dour and serious, do not try to make any jokes. If she is friendly and humorous, lighten it up a bit, but avoid letting yourself become too informal.

You need to have well-prepared questions for the interviewer too. Although some questions will develop during the interview, you should have at least two general questions ready ahead of time. Q & A is a two-way street; do not be afraid to ask penetrating questions of the interviewer to assess whether you even want the job. For example,"What would your expectations of me be if I was hired?" A backdoor way of finding out how to portray yourself is to ask, "What are the distinguishing characteristics of others who have been successful in this position?" When you are done asking questions, shut up. The pregnant pause will indicate to the interviewer that she can go back to work, which in most cases is exactly what she wants to do. Thank the interviewer for her time, and say you look forward to hearing from her. Although it is not necessary to write a thank-you letter, it does set you apart. For extra credit, slip an interesting article pertaining to the company's industry in the envelope.

As a general rule, do not call to follow up until at least one week has passed, but do not wait more than two weeks. Put a second call in two days later if you do not hear back. Then wait a week before calling again. Do not get discouraged. No news is no news. Unless instructed otherwise, phone the person with whom you met. Avoid human resources personnel if possible. They are gatekeepers and can only prevent you from being hired. Many candidates are afraid of calling for fear of irritating someone and blowing their chances. Ironically just the opposite is likely to happen— they will forget about you. Phoning demonstrates interest and distinguishes you for your initiative. Do it.

Second interview

At the second interview, you will likely meet with a larger cast than before. Depending upon the organization, it could be assembled from a cross-section of departments and could include superiors, peers, or subordinates. You may meet with the hiring manager at the beginning or the end of the interviews, but probably not for long. The classic second interview is the one where a consensus is formed by those who have input in hiring decisions. Its purpose is to make sure everyone favors your candidacy.

More probing questions usually come up at the second interview. "What would you say is your greatest weakness?" is a classic. There is only one acceptable way to answer the question—you must always turn your weakness into a positive. Always qualify your self-appraisals. For example, "I work my subordinates very hard, but I try to appreciate their needs, too"; or "Sometimes I get very excited about a project and lose focus on my personal life," etc. (the more martyrdom the better!). Interviewers know better than to expect straight answers to these questions. That is why good interrogators do not ask them, but use other methods to suss you out.

Be respectful of juniors. Bear in mind it is an awkward task to interview someone who could turn out to be your boss, and juniors may come across as timid at first. If you are interviewing for a science, engineering, or finance position, subordinates may do the heavy-lifting to determine if you are technically competent. Try to answer all their questions fully and treat them like equals. Oftentimes their opinions count more than those of the senior people you meet.

A common mistake candidates make in multiple-person interviews is running out of questions. Keep repeating your best, most insightful questions for each interviewer. Just because somebody else answered it already does not make it off-limits. Also, you may get very different answers to the same question, which will further dimensionalize your knowledge. By the end of the day your questions should reflect a significantly deeper understanding of the organization and not sound like they were written down the night before. A far worse mistake is speaking ill of your former boss or firm. Even if your boss was a louse, try to be diplomatic. Talking down your old firm just cheapens your experience. Save your criticism for some other time, preferably over cocktails.

In the second interview, the firm is still trying to get a handle on your capabilities. Hard skills, like knowing how to program in Visual Basic, are easy to demonstrate. It is the "soft" skills that are both so valuable and so difficult to convey. A successful interviewee constantly links experience with qualifications. Ticking off projects with which you have been involved is very effective. Don't overdo it. Remember Dan Quayle in the 1988 vice presidential debates?

Third interview

If you make it to the third round in most organizations you are in the running for the job. At this stage you have been qualified for the position. What they are really trying to discern is whether you will work and play well with others. Hiring managers will try to make sure you see everyone who has a say in the hiring decision. (Firms hate rescinding offers almost as much as they hate hiring the wrong person.) If your sponsor within the organization has set you up properly, your candidacy should have so much momentum that you are almost a presumptive hire. Later-round interviewers often sense this and go easy on you, if for no other reason than you could be a colleague soon. If you get the same questions again, give the same answers—they worked before. Resist the temptation to elaborate unless you really blew one. By the end of the interview, you should be able to visualize yourself working there. Subsequent interviews, if any, are hopefully just a formality to getting an offer.

Occasionally, though, an interviewer who is opposed to your candidacy will appear on the interview schedule. Interviewers predisposed to be negative usually have a problem besides you. It could be they were left out of the loop, dislike your prospective boss, or are just insecure and threatened by your presence. Defuse their hostility by being highly deferential and emphasize what a team player you are. Smile. A little Dale Carnegie goes a long way.

You should follow up immediately after the interviews. If you get strung along, try not to be dispirited. Make a habit of phoning the hiring manager once a week to check in. If the hiring process suddenly stalls there could be a problem. Sometimes the firm is bringing in another candidate. In other cases, the hiring manager has gotten ahead of the organization and is waiting for the green light to hire. Be patient, not all companies are butter-smooth at hiring.

If all systems are go, they will probably ask you to fill out paperwork or provide references. The names you give them should be "ringers" who have agreed to serve as references; there should be no chance any of them will say something negative about you. Although they will be checked, do not assume *your* references will be relied upon for making the hiring decision. In many cases, unless you are fresh out of school, your prospective employer will check you out on the sly to get an unbiased perspective. If you irked somebody at a prior job, you could get rejected and never know why. To a certain extent, there is nothing you can do to prevent such backstabbing. One countermeasure is to preemptively strike by contacting former colleagues and ask them to put in a kind word for you if contacted. Even real turkeys will usually help if you ask. After all, it's no real effort on their part.

Another method occasionally used to evaluate candidates is the personality test, administered by a psychologist. Do not fear...these things are really hokey and, if you are clever, you can figure out what kind of person the firm would like you to be and answer the questions accordingly. Also, credit reports may be pulled to see if you have deadbeat tendencies (if yours is in bad shape, or you think it might be, see "How to correct your credit report"). Recent grads should be mindful not to exaggerate grades— transcripts are easily obtainable.

Should you get to the offer stage, remember: If you don't ask, you won't get. Profitable firms did not get that way by always offering the maximum they could pay. Be honest about your salary requirements, but don't insult them with an outrageous number. Once you come to terms, get the offer in writing. In no case should you feel pressured into accepting. (So-called exploding offers that expire in a few days are degrading and should not be tolerated by experienced hires.) If the offer letter is not to your liking, explain why and request changes. You may be surprised that economic factors are easier for big firms to negotiate than non-economic ones. The reverse is generally true for smaller firms, where a higher quality of life and stock options can make up for lower salaries.

Sometimes plain old luck is the key. We are reminded of the true story of a fellow coming out of college with outstanding grades. He went through on-campus interviews and several on-site interviews with a major bank, was offered a position, and accepted. After he had been on the job a few weeks, his supervisor informed him that, due to a clerical error, they had hired the wrong person by mistake. The good news was that he was doing so well he could keep his job.

How to get admitted to Augusta National

Well, you certainly don't *ask*. You may as well paint your face green and chain yourself to the gates for all the good it would do. In fact, you cannot apply for membership at the Augusta National Golf Club ("The National," to members)—it applies to you.

Or at least that is how we understand it. Like everything else at the storied home of the Masters Tournament, membership policies are entombed in mystery. (So seriously is secrecy taken that even corporate titans are scared to death of speaking to the press for fear of being booted out.) Still, some things are known. There are 300 members and a waiting list about as long. Jack Welch, George Schultz, Sandy Weill, and Arnold Palmer are members. Bill Clinton and Gerald Ford are not. And, in case you haven't been keeping up with the news, women are not allowed. At least not yet.

Given what *has* leaked out, here are the qualifications for membership into golf's Mecca: You (1) run a major company (Fortune 100 preferred); (2) comport yourself as a gentlemen at all times, or at least while you are on the golf course; (3) had nothing to do with the Clinton administration or Monica Lewinsky; (4) are a pretty fair, or at least *serious*, golfer; and—this is the key—(5) are known and liked by somebody down there. If you can only know one member, make it Hootie Johnson, an executive with BankAmerica from Columbia, South Carolina. He's the chairman of the club and exercises final discretion over all membership decisions.

If you meet all these qualifications, don't ruin it by making inquiries. Being chummy with the members is one thing, but pandering is considered unseemly. Bill Gates (a mediocre but avid golfer) has reportedly been pressing his good friend, fellow billionaire and National member, Warren Buffett, to get him in—without success.* Power is everything at Augusta and it trumps even money.

Memberships come out in the fall. If you are lucky enough to be admitted to the National you will start getting a bill in October. The initiation fee is $25,000, which may sound steep, but is a lot lower than many lesser clubs. Monthly dues are a reasonable $100, although the season only lasts from October through May due to the ghastly humidity and heat of central Georgia that make summer play unbearable.

For those prone to tantrums, expulsion of members is also handled without fanfare: If your bill stops coming, you have been kicked out.

*Published reports claim Gates was admitted recently, though the club won't confirm them.

How to avoid being hit by lightning

Americans don't get too worked up about getting struck by lightning. It occurs so randomly and so seldom that precautionary measures seem unnecessary. The odds are awfully long: Your lifetime chance of being struck by lightning is one in 607,000. Lightning can even be survived if it misses your spinal column and heart. (Roy "Dooms" Sullivan, a United States National Park Service ranger, was struck seven times between 1942 and 1977, burning holes in his hat, setting his hair afire, and burning his eyebrows off, among other things—and lived.)

Still, you are far more likely to die from a lightning bolt than being poisoned, accidentally shot, or drowning. We have tamper-resistant packaging, firearms instruction courses and swimming lessons, but nothing for lightning. According to the National Severe Storms Laboratory, there are about 20 million cloud-to-ground lightning strikes per year in the continental United States. Why chance it?

Cloud-to-ground lightning occurs when water vapor becomes separated into positive and negative charges within a cumulonimbus cloud. Positive charges are carried to the top of the cloud by warm air, while negative charges drift to the bottom of the cloud. The attraction between the positively charged ground below and the negatively charged particles inside the cloud creates lightning. The stroke moves downward towards the ground in 50-yard steps until it makes solid contact with something and completes the circuit. Brilliant flashes result from a strong positive charge shooting back up the lightning channel to the cloud. When conditions are right, another flash will be sent back down the channel. (It is entirely possible for lightning to strike in the same place twice.) The downward and upward strokes take less than a second. Lightning can attain temperatures of 60,000 degrees; thunder is caused by air in the lightning channel becoming superheated and exploding.

Many lightning casualties occur at the beginning of a storm before it starts raining. Look for large, very tall, anvil-shaped formations that are the signature of cumulonimbus clouds; electrical charges can develop as soon as five minutes after a cloud is formed. Lightning also is deceptively dangerous at the end of a storm, when the rain has stopped and people venture out from shelter, even though flashes may still be occurring periodically.

Thunderstorms most frequently occur during the afternoon, when the atmosphere is unstable. In coastal areas, there is often lightning after midnight and again at sunrise, due to sea breezes. Lightning is strongest during the summer months, picking up in May and tailing off in September.

Lightning seeks the path of least electrical resistance to the ground. It is therefore attracted to good conductors of electricity, especially metal. During a storm, avoid standing near fences, railroad tracks, and tall freestanding objects such as trees, telephone poles, and electrical stations. Two outdoor sports are particularly dangerous in the vicinity of a thunderstorm: golf and fishing. A golfer wearing metal spikes and holding a club in his hands is, as Arnold Palmer says, "a perfect lightning rod." Ask pro Lee Trevino. He was hit by lightning during the 1975 Western Open, permanently damaging his lower back. (Trevino offered this advice when confronting lightning: "In case of a thunderstorm, stand in the middle of the fairway and hold up a one-iron. Not even God can hit a one-iron.")

Holding a fishing rod surrounded by water is not too smart, either. If you are caught in a boat in the middle of a lake, set down your rod and hightail it out of there.

At 60 percent water, the human body is also a pretty good conductor of electricity. It is important to never be the tallest object during a thunderstorm. If you are caught in an open field and can't find shelter, crouch down in a depression and remain there until the storm passes. Dive into a shrub if you can. Cover your ears—hearing loss from thunder is the most common injury from lightning. You are relatively safe if you are in a car, which acts as a shield and conducts the charge to the ground. Roll up the windows and don't touch anything metal. Airplanes are also theoretically safe in a thunderstorm, although flying through one is not a pleasant experience. Avoid sheltering in tents or buildings with metal roofs, like garages and storage sheds. The safest shelter is a well-constructed building that contains electrical conduit and pipes, which act as a ground.

It can even be dangerous inside during a storm. Avoid using the telephone, which is not well-grounded, should lightning strike a telephone line outside. Current surges can be caused by lightning hitting outside power poles and wires, so avoid using electrical appliances (including televisions) during a thunderstorm as well.

The most deadly state in the country for lightning is Florida, due to its unstable moist air and Floridians' enthusiasm for outdoor activities. Adjusted for population, the other most dangerous states are Colorado, North Carolina, Tennessee, and Georgia. The Midwest, Southeast, South, and Gulf Coast are the most dangerous regions. The West, Northwest, and New England are the safest. For reasons not fully understood, large urban areas receive more lightning strikes than rural areas.

To detect how far away lightning is, count the number of seconds from seeing the flash to hearing the thunder and divide by five to obtain the distance in miles. If you are six miles or less from the lightning, take shelter immediately. (Lightning clusters can be up to six miles wide.) If you cannot hear the thunder, the storm is probably 10 miles or more away.

How to travel in style

As Eric Roberts, playing the indebted loser Paulie in *The Pope of Greenwich Village*, said, success isn't how much money you have, "it's knowing how to spend it." The same could be said of modern travel. The superwealthy can afford the Concorde, but only the super-classy would choose to travel in a way that celebrates not speed, but leisure. The greatest way to express how non-*parvenu* you are is to travel by train. And the most civilized train in existence is the Orient Express.

The Orient Express has endured as a symbol of Victorian-era elegance since it began service at the end of the 19th century. Its founder, French entrepreneur Georges Nagelmackers, first got the idea for a pan-European luxury train when he toured the United States in 1865 and saw President Lincoln's lavish funeral car, built by George Pullman.

The original Orient Express began operations on October 4, 1883 and was an immediate success. The train prospered and sprouted branches all over Europe. From the 1880s to the 1930s, the Orient Express was the pan-European conveyance of choice for kings, diplomats, smugglers, wealthy adulterers, and businessmen. By the First World War, the Orient Express was serving Paris, Nice, Zurich, Innsbruck, Salzburg, Venice, Rome, Belgrade, Athens, Bucharest, Constantinople, and St. Petersburg. After the war, the victorious Allies decreed in the Treaty of Versailles that the train—now called the Simplon Orient Express—would run daily from Calais and Paris to Istanbul, completely skirting the territories of former enemies Germany, Austria, and Hungary.

Numerous kings rode the train, including Leopold II of Belgium, and English monarchs George VI and Edwards VII and VIII. (After he abdicated, Edward the Prince of Wales traveled incognito back to France aboard the Orient Express to marry the woman for whom he gave up the throne, Miss Wallis Simpson.) Ferdinand I of Bulgaria and his son the future King Boris, were train buffs who did not ride the train: They *drove* it, often with frightening effect on their fellow passengers. Once, trying to make up lost time, Boris ordered the fireman to stoke the engine so much that a draft entered the cab and set the poor man afire, killing him. Boris paid no mind to the accident and triumphantly delivered the train into the station on time as the passengers sat aghast.

In 1920, French president Paul Deschanel somehow fell off the train on the way to Lyon and lost his shoes. He found his way to a village, where he ran around barefoot, excitedly claiming to be the president of France, prompting the retort from the townspeople, *"Oui...et je suis Napoleon!"*

(The villagers ultimately decided it was really him when they noticed he had exceptionally clean feet.) After he was picked up and word got out, Deschanel's misadventures became a running joke in Paris. He endured four months of public ridicule before resigning from office.

Other notables to ride the train included Harry Houdini, Aga Khan, Marlene Dietrich, Arturo Toscanini, Maurice Chevalier, and its most notorious rider (executed for spying), Margaretha Gertrud Zelle *a.k.a.* Mata Hari. And where else could you find the founder of the Boy Scouts, Robert Baden-Powell, disguised as a butterfly collector, sneaking off the train to do reconnaissance of military installations as an English spy?

Four thousand cars were built for the Orient Express, but one had a singular role in world history. On November 11, 1918, Car No. 2419 was the site of Germany's humiliating forced signing of the armistice to end The Great War. On June 22, 1940, Hitler had the car hauled to the exact place where it stood previously and dictated surrender terms to France. The car was blown up by the Nazis in 1944 to keep it from being captured by Allied troops.

Following the Second World War, the train's fortunes began to decline. The airplane began to replace the luxury train as the mode of transportation for the wealthy. At the same time, it became increasingly difficult to maintain high service when rolling through Communist Eastern Europe. As the Iron Curtain went up for the Soviets, it began to go down for the proud Orient Express. The old Orient Express had its last run in 1977. Things had gotten so bad one historian called it "euthanasia."

The train's rebirth began when the president of Sea Containers Ltd., James Sherwood, bought a pair of Orient Express cars at a Sotheby's auction. He began adding to his collection and restoring them to immaculate condition, eventually spending £16 million on acquisition and refurbishment. The 17 blue-and-gold 1920s-vintage cars drip with Jazz Age beauty, with sleek lines, mahogany paneling richly laden with marquetry and polished brass fixtures. In 1982, Sherwood's new train, the *Venice-Simplon Orient Express,* began European service.

The new VSOE strives to duplicate the white-glove service of the original train, including the legendary resourcefulness and quiet efficiency of the conductors—called train managers—who still work exhausting 36-hour shifts and catnap in tiny compartments when things slow down. Train managers typically speak at least three languages (French, English, and Italian) fluently. (During the train's heyday, managers could also speak at least four others passably, German, Serbo-Croat, Bulgarian, and Turkish.)

Each traveler is assigned a cabin steward who looks after your every need. He delivers your morning breakfast and newspaper, wakes you for dinner, gets you a seltzer water and fluffs up your pillows. He even takes care of your passport. All you need to do is press a little button on the wall of your cabin and the steward will magically appear...24 hours a day!

Orient Express French chefs are renowned for their ability to hatch up world-class cuisine in dinky kitchens. Table d'hôte meals are included in the fare, although a la carte service is also available for extra charge. Continental breakfast and afternoon tea are served in your compartment. Lunches and six-course dinners are served in the train's three dining cars on tables set with white linen tablecloths, fine china, French silverware, and heavy crystal. The elegantly prepared haute cuisine is offered alongside a well-paired wine list. Formal attire is encouraged at dinner, although a coat and tie are all that is required for gentlemen (about half of the diners turn out in black-tie). During the day, casual attire is acceptable but jeans are verboten. As they say, "You can never be overdressed on the Venice Simplon-Orient Express."

The compartments *are* small; a standard, double-occupancy sleeper is about 6' x 5'. Seats are converted into snug double bunk beds by the bellman each night. There is only a small amount of luggage space, comparable to that of the airlines' overhead bins. Single compartments have wash basins with hot and cold water and an individually controlled radiator for heat. There is one big drawback—no showers. (The VSOE cars date to the 1920s, and the first cars with showers were made in the 1930s.) Another drawback is that toilets are shared, with one at each end of the sleeping car. If you need to stretch your legs, there is the Bar Car, a snug, inviting lounge with a full bar and baby grand piano shoehorned in.

The standard route from London to Paris to Venice takes two days. Since there is no Eurotunnel rail connection, travelers chug down from London to Folkestone aboard a VSOE British Pullman train. From Folkestone, the English Channel crossing is made via the EuroTunnel aboard a bus-like conveyance mounted atop a freight car. Across the Atlantic, passengers board the train at Calais for Paris. From Paris, it is a scenic one-day trip across the Alps, with intermediate stops in Switzerland, Austria, and Italy, before finally arriving at Santa Lucia station in Venice.

The VSOE does not have what you would call a regular schedule. Its runs are dictated by the season and schedules of connecting trains. The standard route (London-Paris-Venice) is the closest to having a predictable timetable. From March through November, it departs from London on Thursdays and Sundays and returns on Wednesdays and Saturdays.

Approximately twice a month, there are additional routes from Venice to Rome and back, featuring a morning stop and walking tour of Florence.

In keeping with the spirit of the original train, the VSOE offers a once-a-year trip across the Bosporous to the glittering, minaret-peaked Islamic city of Istanbul. On the way, you can disembark near Bucharest to visit the bizarre Peles Castle, for which the inaugural train detoured four hours to be received by the King of Romania. Special trains also run to Lucerne, Prague, Salzburg, Vienna, and Frankfurt. The longer, nonstandard routes include hotel stays at major European cities and include time for sightseeing on foot.

If the Far East is your destination, the fully air-conditioned Eastern & Orient Express offers runs through Thailand, Singapore, and Bali, with boat connections to Burma. The company also operates the Great South Pacific Express along the eastern coast of Australia, from Sidney to Brisbane and Cairns. Prices and schedules vary.

The VSOE operates from March through November. Round-trip fare from London to Venice in a shared double cabin is $2,885 per person. It is possible to purchase one-way tickets and individual legs on most of the routes as well. For information about the Venice-Simplon Orient Express, the Eastern & Orient Express, or the Great South Pacific Express, contact Abercrombie & Kent at (800) 524-2420.

For those more in search of scenery than Old World luxury, there is a train called the American Orient Express that operates in North America. Train buffs know that many railroad lines span gorges and mountain ranges far away from highways, and that even pokey Amtrak trains offer some of the most spectacular vistas on the continent. The American Orient Express, too, has scenery in spades. But, unlike Amtrak, the AOE does not represent travel for the masses. Like its European namesake, the American Orient Express is one of the last refined trains in existence.

The AOE (no affiliation with the VSOE) was put into service in the mid-1990s as the rail-child of American businessman Henry Hillman, Jr., CEO of Oregon Rail Corp. The AOE's 15 cars were originally manufactured during the 1940s and 1950s and used on some of the most famous American passenger routes, such as the "Capitol Limited." (A second train is expected to come on line in the summer of 2002.) Like its European cousin, the American train's cars have been meticulously restored to their original condition. Although its compartments are a bit plainer that those of the VSOE, the more modern train has the edge in one key area: plumbing. Even the AOE's smallest compartments (7' x 6') have their own toilets. In addition, everyone has shower access. Travelers in the smallest classes of compartments share shower facilities at the end of the car. Larger, more expensive compartments have private showers.

The AOE experience is quite different from the VSOE. There is a lot of stuff to see in America and the operators are determined you will see it. The train typically runs for a day and stops for overnight lodging at a hotel. Travelers spend the day sightseeing via a bus tour and reboard in the evening, bound for the next destination. In true American-style self-improvement, the tours feature lectures by academics on subjects like North American Indian tribes, geology, and the Civil War. (If this stuff bores you, you're in good company; many travelers skip the tours and while away the hours on the train.)

Americans are the quintessential loungers, and the AOE knows it. Trains have two club cars and one 1940s-vintage Vista dome car, which is a lounge car with a Plexiglas dome over a second-story platform that permits 360-degree viewing of the scenery. The three cars, which together can accommodate three-fourths of the passengers at once, are hubs of social activity.

Travelers take breakfast, lunch, and dinner in the dining cars. Dinner caters to hearty American appetites, with five substantial courses gracefully served on fine china. Menus include several basic items and additional regional fare, based upon where the train is at the time. The food is a sort of inventive American fare popular with recent graduates of domestic cooking schools. In contrast to the Venice-Simplon train, there is no dress code for dinner on the American Orient Express.

The American Orient Express does not run a regular schedule at all, although each route is repeated at least once a season. Its most frequent route, "The Great Transcontinental Rail Journey," only runs four times a year. What it lacks in frequency, though, it makes up for in variety. The AOE's current schedule features eight different historical routes covering an impressive amount of territory: the Rocky Mountains, parts of Canada, the Pacific Northwest, the Southwest and western Mexico, and every coastal southern state. Each of the current trips last between eight and 11 days. All but one of the routes originate and terminate in different cities, necessitating one-way air travel connections (the AOE offers special rates on flights). It is also possible to purchase round-trip train tickets.

Fares vary by route, but basic Pullman car accommodations (double bunk beds) for a seven-day trip start at about $2,600 per person, double-occupancy. Larger cabins cost a fair amount more. Contact the American Orient Express at (800) 320-4206.

How to drink like Hemingway

"I was very hungry and the meal was good and I drank a bottle of Capri and a bottle of St. Estephe and a bottle of Chianti and a bottle of grappa."

—from the 1993 International Imitation Hemingway Competition

Though he denied being a habitual drinker, Ernest Hemingway was awfully fond of a good drink. It showed in his writing—his characters consumed an incredible quantity and array of liquor. For example, in *The Sun Also Rises* the following drinks are consumed by the narrator, Jake Barnes: 32 glasses of wine, 10 coffees, eight beers, seven unnamed liqueurs, five whiskey and sodas, four brandies, three martinis, three champagnes, two vieux marcs, and two cognacs (one to get rid of the beer taste). He also imbibes one Pernod, one hot rum punch, a vermouth, one anise liqueur, a glass of port and, for good measure, one lemon juice with shaved ice. Barnes drinks no water during the entire novel.

Doubtless Hemingway wrote from his own considerable experience with the bottle, which began at the age of 15. But Papa's own tastes were a bit more prosaic than Jake Barnes's. Standbys included Spanish, Italian, and French wines, scotch with lime, rum drinks, and arid martinis. Bourbon and soda (sometimes water) was possibly Hemingway's favorite drink, which he drank while counting the number of words he wrote each afternoon after he finished working.

Unlike many famous writers, Hemingway claimed never to drink while he was writing. He did, however, attest to the restorative powers of alcohol. As he once put it, "When you work hard all day with your head and know you must work again the next day what else can change your ideas and make them run on a different plane like whisky?" Maybe a nice bottle of St. Estephe '82?

How to make great grilled chicken

Forget about all those goofy grilling products sold through infomercials or by former heavyweight boxing champions. An inexpensive, foolproof way to make great-tasting chicken on the grill is to use that ubiquitous symbol of modern civilization found at every campsite—the beer can. Filled with spices and placed on the grill under a chicken, a beer can creates a tiny, barley-and-hops steam bath that results in richly seasoned, moist, and tender meat like you've never had.

Beer-can chicken (sometimes called "drunken chicken" or "chicken-on-a-throne") is a snap to make and virtually impossible to burn. You need either a charcoal or gas grill with a high enough dome or lid that it will clear a chicken on top of a beer can (about eight inches). Most standard-sized grills will work, but mini-grills will not. You can easily do two or three chickens at once on a good-sized grill. Here's how:

1. Get yourself a fresh 3 1/2- to 4-pound broiler chicken. Wash it well and pat dry with paper towels. Apply a spice rub (use your own favorite rub or see the recipe below) by lifting up the skin and thoroughly rubbing the spices into the meat until well-covered. Massage the rub mixture into the outer skin as well. Finally, liberally apply rub to the large inner cavity of the bird. Cover the chicken in plastic wrap and put it in the refrigerator for one hour.

2. Prepare the grill for the indirect method of cooking, in which the fire is hottest on the side opposite the meat. Soak two cups of wood chips in water for an hour, then drain. If you are using a Weber-type grill, make two good-sized piles of coals—do not skimp—on either side of the bottom of the

grill, avoiding the middle. Light the charcoal. After the flames have died down, drop the wood chips directly onto the hot coals. If you are using a gas grill, fire up one burner on high and the other on low. Place the wood chips in the smoker box or wrap them loosely in aluminum foil and set them between one of the burners and the protective grate.

3. Drink down about one-third of a 12-ounce beer (any kind will do—even Schlitz). To the partially-filled can, add one tablespoon of the rub mixture. Park the chicken's cavity on top of the beer can and stretch out the legs to provide a tripod-like support and keep the bird from falling over. (If you have a high grill lid, you can cook a large roaster chicken on a 16-ounce "tall boy" can.)

4. When the grill is hot, set up the enthroned chicken in the middle of the rack, away from the hottest section of the fire (properly assembled, the chicken will look like a headless man sitting on a bar stool). If you have a thermometer, the grill should register about 350 degrees. Cover and cook the chicken about 1 1/2 hours. Add more coals as necessary to keep the fire hot. If you have a temperature probe, insert the device into the fattest part of the thigh, and remove the bird when it registers 170 degrees.

5. For tangier flavor, barbecue sauce may be brushed on near the end of cooking. When the chicken is done, discard the beer can, carve, and eat. Serves four.

Anita's Chicken Rub
3 Tbs. sugar
3 Tbs. salt
1 Tbs. paprika
1 tsp. garlic powder
1 tsp. onion powder
1/2 tsp. black pepper
1/4 tsp. red pepper
Pinch of oregano

Mix ingredients well. Apply to chicken before cooking as directed.

How to learn to fly fish

They still talk about "The Movie" (as it is sometimes referred to) at fly fishing schools around the country, even though it came out a decade ago. Spectacular Western scenery, an engaging plot, and graceful casting by Brad Pitt's angling stand-in, made fly fishing too attractive to resist. Old hands aren't sure whether to bless it or curse it, but *A River Runs Through It* permanently changed the state of fly fishing in the United States. Since the film came out, seems like everybody wants to pull on a pair of waders and go stand in a stream. So if you aren't serious about learning to fly fish, skip this chapter and save some water for the rest of us.

Banish those impressions that only weather-beaten, craggy-faced old outdoorsmen can fly fish. Fly fishing is mostly a science, and science can be taught. Experience plays a role, but trout are actually very dependable in their habits, and streams change little from year to year. A good fly fisherman can walk up to just about any stream, figure out what the fish are eating, tie on the appropriate fly, and catch a fish. A mediocre angler can sometimes get the right fly on, but has no idea how to fish it. Proper education and proper equipment are essential. (If you just want to take in the scenery, stand in the water, and look sporting, skip to the Equipment section.)

Self-teaching

If you are a go-it-alone type, it is quite possible to teach yourself to fly fish. Casting is the most important skill; like the swing in golf, the cast is everything. It is not tremendously difficult, but requires an all-forearm-and-no-wrist motion that is alien to golfers, spin fishermen, and softball players. For starters, practice the basic motion in front of a mirror using just the butt section of the rod. After you have mastered the arm motion, venture out to your lawn or the park. Don't be surprised by a few teenage wisecracks—just tell them you're fishing for land sharks. Watching casting videos helps.

An easier way to learn casting is to hire a personal tutor. Professional casting instructors—typically fishing guides making some money on the side—charge anywhere from $25 to $75 an hour for lessons. Your local outfitter should be able to give you names of some good casting instructors in your area. The other fundamentals of fly fishing—trout behavior, insect etymology, stream reading, and equipment usage—can all be learned from books, videos, and experience.

Fishing school

If you've tried fly fishing on your own but still catch more tree branches than fish, consider enrolling in the Orvis School. For about $400 tuition, Orvis Schools compress the science of fly fishing into two-and-a-half days. If you consider that some people spend a lifetime fly-fishing and never quite master it, a complete overview in under three days is a bit much to ask. Still, Orvis Schools do an excellent job preparing the novice for what to do on the stream.

Considerable attention is paid to casting—and rightly so. Orvis instructors work with students on basic form, using videotape and on-site at small ponds stocked with gullible rainbow trout. Even hopelessly uncoordinated students have the hang of it after a couple of days. Classroom instruction is also given in stream reading, knot tying, line control, proper catch-and-release techniques, and naturally, bugs: mayflies, caddisflies, and—the prime rib of the trout world—stoneflies. Fly tying is not taught at the Orvis School, but can be readily learned through books, classes, and practice.

The value of a fly fishing school is obvious when it comes to basic tactics that can only be presented on the water. Streamside tactics such as how to approach a rising trout, where to stand, how to present the fly, and how to keep your feet quiet are included. Proper fishing etiquette—often absent in unschooled anglers, much to the chagrin of neighboring fishermen—is also presented. Orvis fly fishing schools are offered from spring through fall at several locations across the United States, including the main school in Manchester, Vermont near the legendary Battenkill River. Call (800) 815-5900 for more information.

Equipment

Fly fishing has maintained its reputation as a leisure pursuit of the wealthy partly because of the substantial investment required to get started. Besides skiing and golf, there aren't many sports that require so much equipment. Thankfully for fly fishing addicts, collecting equipment is almost as fun as fishing and can be done in mid-January.

First, you need a good fly rod. The perfect all-around rod to start with is a 5-weight, 9-foot, medium-fast action stick, which works for trout fishing just about anywhere. Plan to spend from $250 to $500. Almost all good rods today are made of graphite or a carbon-fiber composite. If you have the dough, traditional bamboo rods ($1,000 and up) offer a light, supple feel, but you will cry all the harder if you lose it or smash the tip in the car door. High quality rod makers include Orvis, Sage, Reddington, and Scott. You also will need a reel matched to the rod. Orvis and a host of smaller manufacturers make them. A good reel costs from $100 to $250. Have the shop wind it up with high-visibility, weight-forward floating line (another $50 or so). For convenience, buy a second spool to hold a different type of line.

Most fly fishing is done while standing in the middle of the stream. A decent pair of waders is a must, but you need not pay top dollar. Waders come in waterproof nylon and neoprene (like skin diving suits). Breathable nylon is suitable for summer months, but spring and fall require neoprene, a considerably warmer material. Waders come with or without boots. Stockingfoot waders are the more versatile because they give you multiple boot choices. Boots should have felt soles, which grip best on slippery, algae-covered rocks. Avoid hip boots entirely; they are only suitable for dinky streams, and better for carrying water than repelling it. Boots and waders should run about $200 to $300 for nylon and $300 to $400 for neoprene.

You will need too many other things to list them all here, but two major items merit a mention: the vest and sunglasses. Vests are wearable tackle boxes. Get a good one and make sure it fits comfortably. High-quality polarized sunglasses are essential if you want a fighting chance of seeing (and catching) a trout. If you wear glasses or contacts, your local optician will custom grind polarized glass to your prescription. Good polarized sunglasses run anywhere from $75 to $250 a pair.

To fill up your vest, see your local outfitters and tell them what you are doing. When you are all through you will have a head-to-toe ensemble that costs over $1,000, including the rod and reel. One tip: Keep all the hangy things (scissors, nippers, thermometers, etc.) descending from clips on your vest to a minimum. These metal gadgets reflect light—advertising your presence to trout—and get in the way of tying knots. Besides, they make you look like a geek.

How to prevent identity theft

"Who steals my purse steals trash...But he that filches from me my good name robs me of that which not enriches him and makes me poor indeed."
—Iago, Act III, William Shakespeare's *Othello*

A biblical adage says it's better to lose your money than your reputation. But it is surely worse to lose both your money *and* your reputation—which can happen with frightening speed if your identity falls into the wrong hands. Authorities believe between 500,000 and 750,000 Americans are victims of identity theft each year, and by one estimate the crime is growing 40 percent per year. Armed with just your name and Social Security number, a thief may as well have blueprints to your house and the combination to your wall safe.

There are numerous methods of appropriating someone's private information. While identity theft is considered the white-collar crime *du jour*, many of the thieves' methods are decidedly blue-collar—like dumpster-diving for credit card receipts, mail theft, and purse-snatching. Crooks can also gather an appalling amount of facts about you via the Internet to supplement pilfered information. (If you don't believe it, take a look at the Website *www.docusearch.com*.)

With your vital information, impostors open bank accounts and take out new credit cards in your name. Thieves then go around passing bad checks and charge the new credit cards up to the limit. Some impudent scoundrels will not only run up debts, but actually file for bankruptcy under your name! According to the Privacy Rights Clearinghouse, victims spend an average of 175 hours and $800 to clear their names.

Here are some ways to foil the would-be identity thief:

- The key to the modern castle is the Social Security number, which is heavily used by many institutions, especially managed healthcare companies, as a personal identity number. Put your Social Security card in a safe deposit box—don't carry it in your wallet (don't have your Social Security number printed on your checks either).
- Shred all credit card statements, pre-approved offers, loan statements, tax files, old checks, and bank statements before tossing them so that all the dumpster-diver gets from you is rotten bananas and smelly old tuna salad. Treat your Social Security number-rich healthcare information the same way. Compact paper shredders have gotten ridiculously cheap,

with some even going for less than $20—and they are well worth it.

- If your monthly credit card statement is late in coming, contact the issuer immediately. While probably just the good ol' post office, you shouldn't chance it. Credit card fraud is by far the most common use of stolen identities.

- Review your credit reports at least once a year to make sure nothing fishy is going on. Pay particular attention to the section that lists which firms have obtained copies of your report; bogus requests from people posing as landlords or employers are often used to gain access to personal information (see "How to correct your credit report").

- Get to know your postman; many thieves either steal mail outright or file a change of address form to have your mail sent where they can snatch it.

- Get yourself off the list for pre-approved credit offers, which contain information useful to ID thieves (see "How to stop solicitors").

- Don't give out personal information over the phone unless you initiate the transaction.

- When ordering merchandise over the Internet, never type in your Social Security number, and be cautious about entering credit card numbers at unknown Websites. For additional security, take out a second e-mail address for all your e-commerce transactions, (Microsoft Hotmail and Yahoo! both offer them for free).

- Your computer can be easily hacked into if you have a continuous high-speed Internet connection, like a direct subscriber line or cable. Get a router and put up a software firewall, like Zone Alarm, to prevent a hacker from sneaking onto your computer and snagging private information.

- Underage college students beware: Fake IDs available over the Internet are often fronts for identity theft rings.

- Travelers Property Casualty Corp., Farmers Insurance Group, and Chubb Group each offer identity theft insurance as add-on coverage to existing homeowners' policies in most states for a small additional premium. Travelers and PromiseMark Insurance also offer separate identity theft insurance policies in certain states for around $100 or less annually. Victims are covered for expenses incurred in sorting out the nightmare, including lost wages and legal fees.

If your identity is stolen, contact the FTC's Identity Theft Hotline and Clearinghouse at (877) IDTHEFT and the Social Security Agency's fraud hotline at (800) 269-0271. Then contact the major credit bureaus and ask them to insert a "fraud alert" in your file to prevent any additional accounts from being opened in your name. Cancel any stolen credit cards. As a last resort, you can get new Social Security and driver's license numbers assigned.

Do not delay. Under the federal Fair Credit Billing Act your liability is limited to $50 if you promptly report stolen credit cards (although Visa and MasterCard have voluntarily waived the time requirement for reporting them stolen). Federal laws also limit your liability if ATM cards are used fraudulently, provided you immediately contact the issuing bank. State laws generally protect consumers from check fraud. Even though it is a tremendous hassle, you should go to the local police and file a theft report. It could prove immensely useful later if you get bound up in red tape trying to clear your name.

How to compete at altitude

Even at 6,000 feet in elevation there is far less oxygen available to the lungs than at sea level. If you are a flatlander who suddenly gets the urge to, say, run the Pike's Peak Ascent race in Colorado, you have two choices.

The optimal method of competing at altitude is to exercise at higher elevations for at least three weeks. After just one day, your body will start to produce more oxygen-carrying red blood cells to compensate for the thin air. After about four weeks, you will be back to normal, athletically speaking. Plus, all those red blood cells will make you feel superhuman when you go home.

If you can't live at altitude for a month, the second-best alternative is to arrive as close as possible to the start of the event. This approach is used by professional football teams playing at Mile High Stadium in Denver. During the first 24 hours at higher elevation, your body will partly compensate for the thinner air by breathing deeper and more rapidly. Taking acetazolamide (available with prescription) may help prevent altitude sickness.

For what it's worth, some geniuses have determined that living in the mountains but *training near sea level* produces the best fitness. If you can figure out how to do that, contact the U.S. Olympic Training Center in Colorado Springs, Colorado as soon as possible.

How to watch the Tour de France

The Super Bowl is not the greatest spectacle in sports—not even close. That honor belongs to the greatest bicycle race in the world, the Tour de France. For three weeks each July, *Le Tour* captivates not only all of France, but bicycle racing enthusiasts throughout Europe and the United States. Sadly for CBS Sports, which has been covering the event for two decades, Americans still just don't get too aroused by the Tour.

Well, if the Americas Cup can get people to stay up until 3 a.m. to watch Dennis Conner at the helm in 12-meter yachting—a sport about as exciting as watching water drain out of a bathtub—why not the Tour? The viewing hours are better and the action is exciting. If you have passed it by for years in favor of the Greater Milwaukee Open or reruns of *This Old House*, give it a look. You may just like it. Here are some pointers:

The race

"Gruelling" does not begin to describe it. The race lasts around 21 days and covers over 2,000 miles. There is generally one stage per day of 100 to 150 miles in length, lasting up to six hours. The Tour snakes its way around France over a different route each year, alternating between a clockwise and counterclockwise direction. Roughly half of the race is in the mountains. The rider with the lowest cumulative time upon completion of the Tour is the winner. All other riders are listed by how far behind the leader they are.

There are only three constants with respect to the route: (1) it always goes through the Pyrenees near Spain; (2) it always goes through the Alps, usually near Switzerland; and (3) it always finishes in Paris. In a sort of EU solidarity, the route increasingly goes through other European countries. In 1998, the Tour started in Ireland (no, riders didn't pedal through the Eurotunnel; they came by ferry). In recent years it also has had stages in the Netherlands, Switzerland, and Spain.

Even though there is exhaustive live TV coverage, scads of French turn out by the roadside to watch it in person (one-third of the population in a typical year). Sometimes their national passions become a bit overheated, particularly where foreigners—who regularly take a pounding in the French sporting press—are concerned. In 1975, a French spectator punched the great Belgian cyclist Eddy Merckx in the stomach as he neared the top of a difficult climb in hot pursuit of his French rival Bernard Thevenet. Although Merckx kept riding, the assault had its intended effect: He went on to finish second to Thevenet and never got his record sixth Tour victory.

The racers

Race organizers decide the size of the field based upon how many good teams there are. Teams are invited to participate based upon their pre-Tour performance and other factors. The trend is towards more teams with fewer riders per team. In 2002, there were 21 teams with nine riders apiece. Each team generally has one star, who is highly paid and is the anointed team leader at the beginning of the race. The physical fitness of these guys is off the charts. They train at least 11 months a year, routinely logging 150 miles a day. Team leaders must be immensely strong in both climbing and time trialing to have a shot at winning the Tour. Recent champions Bernard Hinault, Greg Lemond, Miguel Indurain, Jan Ulrich, and Lance Armstrong were all dominant time trialists and expert climbers.

CBS spends so much time slobbering over the leaders, one might assume bicycle racing is just an individual sport of stars with team members for window dressing. Not true. Teams are vital to the success of the leader. They usually contain a couple of climbing specialists and five or six all-purpose riders. Everyone except the team leader is known as an *equipier* (teammate). These extremely hard-working professional racers are, compared with second stringers in the NFL, ridiculously underpaid (good ones might make $100,000 a year). Equipiers are expected to do whatever is necessary to support their leader. If a leader crashes and needs a wheel or a bike, the equipier will give him his. The lowest level equipiers are known as *domestiques* and do things like fetch water bottles and rainjackets from the team car.

Popular imagination is fueled by the idea of a "Cinderella Tour," where an equipier finds himself in a breakaway and somehow manages to hold on and win the race. In practice this almost never happens. The last time was in 1983, when Laurent Fignon, a lieutenant to five-time Tour winner Bernard Hinault on the powerful Renault team, became de facto team leader after Hinault unexpectedly pulled out just before the race started. Fignon, riding in his first Tour de France, seized the overall lead in the mountains and rode an inspired race for the next five days to win. (He proved it wasn't a fluke by winning—this time as Renault's designated team leader—the very next year.)

Support

Each team is supported by two team cars equipped with mechanics, doctors, and team directors (coaches). Team cars follow behind the racers in cars bristling with spare wheels and bikes. Cars also carry water, food, extra clothing, and first aid. Team leaders use tiny two-way radios to talk to directors about strategy and what other riders are up to. Except during time trials, riders eat on the road. At periodic feeding stations, racers receive food (mostly fruits and starches) and water from team assistants who hand it up to them in sacks called *musettes*. If the race is moving too fast to eat, they sling the bags over their shoulders and keep going. Riders eat and drink a lot on the bike. When nature calls, pastures are available, but riders often just go by the side of the road in front of hundreds of spectators. (Thankfully the French are blasé about *le pee-pee*.)

Prologue

With much fanfare, riders assemble for the Prologue, a short time trial that establishes who will wear the race leader's *maillot jaune* (yellow jersey) on the first stage. The prior year's winner wears the yellow jersey during the Prologue and wears race No. 1. During the Prologue, racers use aero-dynamic bikes, rubberized suits, disk wheels, and teardrop helmets to mini-mize wind resistance and shave seconds off their time.

Early stages

The early stages are designed to be lazy rides (well, lazy by Tour stan-dards) through picturesque fields and little villages lucky enough to be put on the route. During the first week, the race is on flat or rolling terrain, which leads to bunching of the field. When the group is together, it can move incredibly fast, reaching over 40 miles per hour on level ground. At these speeds, it is difficult for individual riders to break away from the field. Occasionally, however, with effective blocking by teammates in the *peloton* (main pack), a small group can get clear and end the day with a huge lead on the field. In the law of the pack, these breakaways are only permitted if the group contains no team leaders: Equipiers are allowed to have their day in the sun, or in this case, the yellow jersey—everyone knows it won't last (though accidental race leaders sometimes find inspiration in the jersey and doggedly hang on for a week or more). The press always gets excited about breakaways in these early stages, but they rarely have any bearing on the race, which doesn't really start until the Tour reaches the mountains.

On the flat stages, if no break occurs, the whole screaming mass will whiz into some little town for the finish—an elbow-throwing, hip-checking sprint. This is the time for sprinters—who tend to be taller, heavier, and ill-suited to the mountains—to shine. Because riders bunched together are all awarded the same time and because mass sprints can be dangerous, team leaders hang towards the back. The prize for the best sprinter is the *maillot verte* (green jersey).

Individual time trials

The French call the time trial *le prix de la verite* (the race of truth). The individual time trial is a race solely against the clock. Racers start out from a gate at predetermined intervals. Riders start in reverse order, with the last-place rider going first. Courses vary widely in hilliness and length. For flat time trials, riders wear the streamlined outfits seen in the Prologue. For mountain courses, where air resistance is less important than comfort, racers wear a skin suit and ride a normal bike. Regardless of the route, time trials are incredibly taxing and require extraordinary conditioning. There are usually two individual time trials during the Tour, one during the first week and one during the last week, although organizers have a cruel penchant for inserting an alpine time trial in the middle of the mountain stages.

Team time trial

The team time trial is an amazing exhibition; the entire team rides together, hunkered down and hammering, one in front of the other, wheels about six inches apart. The leader rotates constantly, in a bike version of an Indian run, so there is always a fresh pair of legs at the front. After taking a pull breaking the wind, the previous leader drops to the back and recovers. The pressure to keep up is intense; slow riders, sometimes even team leaders, may be left behind. (The first five or six riders get the same time; the others get their actual times.) There is normally one team time trial, which occurs during the first or second week. Though interesting to watch, team time trials seldom change the overall standings much.

Mountain stages

After the rolling hills of wine country the Tour gets serious. From the very first day in the mountains, the race has a different complexion. The peloton cracks apart and spreads out for miles. Mountain stages are the best places to view the race if you want to see it in person. If you go, select a spot near the summit of a tough climb (the race map will indicate the climb ratings). You should get there very early and will probably have to walk a considerable distance to get a good vantage point. (Many people even camp out days before the race arrives.) Bring a picnic, wine, and some colored chalk so you can write good wishes on the road for your favorite cyclist.

In contrast to the flat stages, in the mountains, race favorites ride near the front to make sure nobody gets away. A solo breakaway can be sustained much more easily on a climb. Pocket-sized climbing specialists can pedal away as if the rest of the field is standing still—without even getting off their seats. The tall and big-boned have it tough here, often out of their saddles, furiously tossing their bikes side-to-side to keep up their momentum. For the team leaders, this is where climbing equipiers are worth their weight in gold. They ride alongside the leader, give assistance, and help chase down breakaways.

Climbs are rated on a scale of one to four plus another level they just call *hors categorie* (beyond category). To fully appreciate the steepness of these climbs, you would need to try to ride up them yourself. You can get a sense for them, though, in the Rocky Mountains. If you have spent any time in Colorado, most mountain roads there have a gradient of 5 percent, a rise of five feet for every 100 feet traveled. By comparison, Alpine climbs typically have a 7 to 8 percent grade, while the Pyrenees have 8 to 9 percent.

Imagine peddling up a winding hill as steep as any you have ever driven for over an hour, then descending at 60 miles per hour around hairpin turns, then doing it again, *three more times*. The toll on the human body and spirit is severe. Interviewed about his experience for *Winning Bicycle Racing Illustrated*, Jonathan Boyer—the first American to finish the tour and a climbing specialist—said if someone pulled up next to him during a mountain stage with a shotgun he would beg him to pull the trigger. We don't *think* he was serious.

In counterclockwise years, the Tour hits the Pyrenees first and the Alps second. The Pyrenees section is known for short, very steep climbs. One of the most famous is the Col du Aubisque, where, in an awesome display of his dominance, Eddy Merckx went on an 80-mile solo breakaway during the 1969 Tour. When the stage ended, the second-place finisher was eight minutes back and the race was over. Mount Ventoux is another famous Pyrenees climb. In 1967, Ventoux was forever memorialized when British racer and reigning world champion Tom Simpson collapsed and died in 95-degree heat near the summit after taking amphetamines to make up for a lost night's sleep. His last words were "Put me back on my bike."

After a travel or rest day following the Pyrenean climbs, the Tour reaches the Alps. The old adage is that while the Tour may not be won in the Alps, it is usually lost there. Probably no Alpine ascent has been the scene of more meltdowns than the stupendously difficult climb to the ski station at the top of L'Alpe D'Huez. A traditional mountaintop finish in the Tour, the hors categorie climb is eight miles long, with 21 switchbacks and an average gradient of 9 percent. In a typical year, over 300,000 spectators will line the road up L'Alpe D'Huez, cheering and spraying water on their favorites. The best climber in the Tour wears the red-and-white polka dot jersey and bears the title "king of the mountains." By the end of the mountain stages, the race is usually decided.

On to Paris

The headlong progression toward Paris picks up speed as it wends through wine country for four days. This section mirrors the first week, with little in the way of hills to break up the field. There is typically a time trial inserted into the last week to make things interesting. Despite the build-up as the last chance for challengers to catch the leader, the time trial usually just affirms the standings. But not always.

The greatest race in Tour history was a time trial that finished on the Champs-Elysées in Paris in 1989. American Greg Lemond, in second place, needed to make up 50 seconds on race leader and French favorite Laurent Fignon in a short, flat time trial through the streets of Paris—too short, really, for Lemond to have a prayer. But, at each time check...*C'est impossible!*...Fignon's lead kept dwindling. As his team director screamed at him to go faster, Fignon, riding behind Lemond, pedaled furiously to hang on to his slender lead. At the finish line Fignon collapsed. Moments later he broke down in tears upon learning that after 87 hours and 38 minutes of racing he had lost the Tour...*by eight seconds*. Lemond, who had nearly died after losing four pints of blood in a hunting accident two years before, capped off his return to racing by winning the cycling World Championship two months later and *Sports Illustrated's* "Sportsman of the Year" award. While you may never see another race so close, if the course features a closing time trial in Paris, you will not want to miss it.

Most years, instead of a time trial, there is a road stage that ends in Paris. When the peloton arrives, fans cheer and wave national flags as the racers do several laps past the Arc de Triomphe and down the Champs-Elysées in one of the most photographed scenes in sport. On the second to last lap, riders start jockeying for position. The finish is always a wild sprint, meaningless to the standings but still hair-raising. Teams try to set up their designated sprinter near the finish line by "leading out"—blocking the wind and allowing him to draft and save energy. Even on a wide road, 150 bikes going by is tight, but in a mass-sprint with riders weaving all over the road, it's downright chaotic. Near the finish line, everybody is out of the saddle, their bikes madly pitching from side to side. At the line, sprinters lunge their front wheels forward in hopes of nosing out the victory. The winner gets his picture in the paper, but the yellow jersey goes home with the real champion, freewheeling across the line at the back of the pack.

How to get rid of tailgaters

If another car is on your bumper and refuses to back off, use this technique from defensive driving school: *gradually* ease off on the accelerator. Upon realizing you are going *even slower*, practically all tailgaters will get frustrated and decide to go around.

Just watch out for flying milkshakes and other objects ejected from the car as it zips by.

How to avoid jury duty

"The probability of your receiving a jury duty summons in the mail is directly proportional to the degree to which you are looking forward to your vacation."
—Dan Dustin, author of a book about jury duty

Since the ordeal of fire and water was replaced by the jury in 1215, laypersons have had an important role in determining guilt or innocence of the accused. Unfortunately, those poor souls selected for jury service face an ordeal of their own. Endless questioning by attorneys hoping to stack the jury in their favor can mean hours, even days, of sitting around waiting. Not only that, but complicated trials can go on for months. What's more, serving as a juror in a criminal case presents the unnerving prospect of publicizing your name and address to a violent felon. Frankly, unless you are itching to see our legal process close up, you may want to think about leaving jury duty to someone else.

Because of a quaint notion that jurors should judge the accused by an inbred community standard, juries are always drawn from the local area where the case is tried. The federal Jury Selection and Service Act of 1968 requires that voter rolls be the primary means of obtaining prospective jurors. Many jurisdictions supplement voter rolls with driver's licenses and state welfare lists. These lists are used to create a pool of jurors called a "panel" from which 12-person trial juries are drawn. Panels can be quite large, with dozens of prospective jurors available for service.

A really simple way to keep yourself from being summoned for jury duty is not to register to vote or drive a car. Assuming you don't want to completely drop out of society, though, you will eventually face the summons. Attached to the summons will be a questionnaire (age, physical status, occupation, criminal record, etc.) used to eliminate candidates who cannot serve. Courts generally excuse people with serious physical disabilities. Although less common, some courts also excuse people deemed to hold "vital" occupations—and the definition can be pretty broad: mothers of small children, doctors, nurses, firefighters, police officers, schoolteachers, ministers, rabbis, and owners of small businesses. Ex-cons are also disqualified. This practice, however, is being restricted by many jurisdictions to compel more people to serve.

If you wind up on the panel, fear not. You will have another chance to get out of jury duty during the jury selection, or the *voir dire* (truth speaks) phase of the trial. During voir dire, both defense attorneys and prosecutors question prospective jurors in hopes of ferreting out prejudicial views or beliefs detrimental to their side. Modern legal experts believe—and after the O. J. Simpson trial who would doubt them—that the verdict can be substantially influenced by the voir dire. (Some weaselly attorneys even shape their questioning in order to subtly influence jurors' opinions before the trial even starts. F. Lee Bailey co-authored a manual describing how to do it.)

Prospective jurors may be rejected by either side in *peremptory challenges* without any explanation. Attorneys use peremptory challenges to keep people off the jury whom they fear would be averse to their side. Peremptory challenges offer the greatest potential for dismissal from the panel (on average, one-third of all panel members are dismissed this way). Each side is given a limited number of peremptory challenges, ranging from three in civil cases, up to 15 in capital cases.

A little courtroom theory: Both sides consider naive jurors ideal. Second best are those with an open mind. The worst are opinionated know-it-alls, commonly known as jackasses. While you should never lie during questioning (you could spend even more time in court for that), there is no law against expressing your obnoxious beliefs: It could earn you a peremptory challenge. Careful! Transparent attempts to get booted will earn you a lecture in the judge's chambers.

There is another perfectly agreeable way out. If you happen to be an expert in a key subject relevant to the case (or can act like one), you will probably be challenged, because (more courtroom theory) attorneys worry that experts cannot be as easily molded by their arguments during the trial. Such actions give validity to the words of British legal scholar Glanville Williams, who described the jury as "twelve men of average ignorance."

If the attorneys run out of peremptory challenges, your last chance for dismissal is a *challenge for cause*. These challenges must be based upon demonstrable prejudice rather than a hunch and agreed to by the judge. Challenges for cause are granted stingily by judges to keep from "busting the panel," or running out of jurors. Only particularly strident opinions will get you dismissed for cause, like being a conscientious objector to the death penalty in a capital case.

How to choose a Christmas tree

For most people, the Currier & Ives tradition of whacking down your own tree from the woods is as distant a notion as roasting your own chestnuts or seeing Santa Claus smoking a pipe. Instead, there is the obligatory post-Thanksgiving trek to some vacant lot filled with scrawny, brittle trees cut who-knows-when. By the 26th of December, the tree has worn out its welcome. Its aroma is gone, needles start dropping, and the arid branches festooned with lights are a serious fire hazard. Then comes the day that everyone dreads, the day to take down the tree—The Grumpiest Day of the Year—when you have to vacuum about a half a million needles out of the carpet. What kind of Christmas tradition is that?

Of course, you could buy a plastic tree, but they look tacky and the aroma of vinyl doesn't exactly conjure up visions of sugarplum fairies. Instead, buy a real one and follow a few simple tips to insure it doesn't turn into a heap of needles soon after you bring it home.

The best way to secure a tree is to find a tree farm. You look over the inventory during the early fall and tag the tree you want, which will be cut when you return later. If driving to a tree farm is impractical, the ubiquitous vacant lot sellers will do in a pinch. Most tree varieties they carry are hardy, although the condition of the trees may be atrocious. In large cities, some of the inventory will have been cut as early as October.

To test a tree's dryness, bend its needles at several locations. They should spring back if the tree is fresh. If it's dry, they will break or fail to return to shape. Another dryness test is to grab the tip of a branch in your hand and gingerly pull it toward you. A fresh tree will not leave a pile of needles in your hand. Still another method is the "thump test." Lift up the tree by the trunk and thump it on the ground a couple of times. A stale tree will rain down green needles (brown ones fall out normally).

The choice of a tree is largely aesthetic. There is little difference in needle retention among Christmas tree varieties. About the only commercially available trees to worry about are spruces, which have a nasty habit of dropping their sharp needles if they get too warm or dry. If you must have a spruce, make sure it's been freshly cut.

When you get the tree home, cut about an inch off the bottom before putting it in the stand. A fresh cut allows the stem to absorb water more effectively. Initially, the tree may consume a gallon of water and will require up to two quarts a day after that. Never allow the stand to dry out, which can permit sap to form and harden on the bottom, damaging the tree's ability to absorb moisture. (If it does dry out, you can restore the tree by sawing off the bottom again.)

As for taking down the tree, spreading out plastic sheets is helpful. One other recent development has made post-Christmas cleanup easier— the drop in popularity of shag carpeting.

How to lose weight without dieting or breaking a sweat

Researchers at the Mayo Clinic in Rochester, Minnesota have determined that chewing gum increases your metabolic rate by 19 percent and burns 11 calories an hour. If you chew sugarless gum constantly during your waking hours, after one year you will have lost 11 pounds.

How to fake it at a bullfight

The average *gringo* thinks of the bullfight as a barbaric spectacle that one watches with a mix of curiosity and horror, like two scorpions in a jar. There is a lot to a bullfight, but you will have to witness dozens before you will be able to distinguish good from bad. The best way to learn more is to read Hemingway's 1932 classic, *Death in the Afternoon*, still the best guide to understanding the bullfight ever written.

Real *aficionados* are not reticent about voicing their displeasure at a bad *corrida*, and some of their descriptions of the participants would make a New York hockey fan blush. If you are planning to see a real bullfight in Mexico or Spain, you may find the following vocabulary words handy:

Buscando guerra: Itching for a fight. A bull that races into the ring and immediately attacks anything in sight is buscando guerra (literally "looking for war").

Cojones: Testicles. Brave bullfighters have big ones. Never say *criadillas*—that refers to the bull's equipment, considered a delicacy by many Spaniards.

Hijo de puta: Son of a harlot. Used to describe a bullfighter not performing in a brave or dignified manner.

Manso: Cowardly. Can refer to either the man or the bull.

Ole!: What you say when a bullfighter is on a roll. The equivalent of "bravo" at the opera.

Que se vaya!: Get out and stay out! Shouted at a bullfighter who fails to please the aficionados.

Toro bravo: Brave bull. Too seldom matched up with a good bullfighter. The ideal of every bullfight is a brave bull with a brave and artistic torero. If the crowd seems disappointed but you are not sure why, just use this all-purpose, inscrutable phrase: *Cuando hay toros no hay toreros y cuando hay toreros no hay toros.* (When there are bulls there are no toreros and when there are toreros there are no bulls.) Or, as we say in America, "Whaddya gonna do?"

How to conduct like Toscanini

"There are two rules for an orchestra: start together and finish together. The public doesn't give a damn what goes on in between."

—Sir Thomas Beecham

Max Rudolph, a famous music teacher and author of the seminal treatise *The Grammar of Conducting*, said the best way to learn conducting is by doing it. News flash: You can take Rudolph's advice even if you can't read a note of music. About all you need is a stereo and a baton (chopsticks and wooden spoons also work) to begin impersonating your favorite maestro.

Besides starting and stopping the orchestra, symphony conductors must do five things: beat time, control the volume, shape phrases, mark accents, and cue various instruments. Between hand gestures and facial expressions, all of these things can be conveyed. Aspiring conductors spend many years in training just to learn the fundamentals of conducting. Thankfully, no such schooling is required to conduct your imaginary orchestra, which will miraculously keep on playing with mechanical precision whether you flub a note or not. (If you become unsynchronized, you can even scold the players for failing to obey your commands.)

First, you need to start with the controls—the hands. If you want to look like a proper conductor, order yourself a real baton, which come in 10-, 12- and 14-inch lengths. You can get batons at your local music store, or by mail order for about $10 (available from the Brook Mays Music Company, (800) 637-8966). Hold the baton by loosely pinching the base of the stick between your thumb and forefinger; the handle should be buried in the palm of your hand. Always keep the tip of the baton pointed slightly up and try not to get too "wristy" with it. The baton should only be waved in a "strike zone" extending from your eyes to the base of your sternum.

Right hand

The right hand holds the baton, which is used primarily to beat time, establish the tempo, and, to a lesser extent, emphasize phrases and change the volume. To the untrained eye, conductors constantly do the same thing: wave a stick up and down to the beat. Actually, the stick is waved in a pattern that carefully corresponds to the meter of the music.

Here are the time-beating patterns. The easiest beat is the *one pattern*, a simple up-and-down motion, rarely used except for very fast music. The *two pattern* is more common; its motion is a Nike-looking "swoosh" with a little more verticality. The first beat is the J-downstroke and the second beat is the hook that returns you to the top (Figure 1).

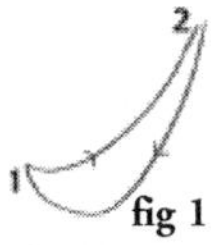

fig 1

fig 2

Music in "three" is beat using the *three pattern*, which is a right triangle with a curved hypotenuse (Figure 2), where each point is a beat. Classical music is widely composed in four. The *four pattern* moves down, over to the left, crosses back to the right, then back up to the top (Figure 3). There are *five* and *six patterns* as well, but they are seldom used and too complicated to learn. Practice inscribing the pattern in the air with the tip of the baton.

fig 3

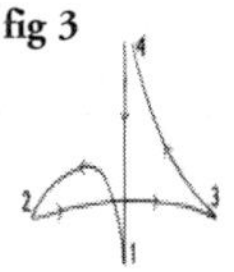

If you are a musician and know the meter of the piece, then you know how to beat time. And if you don't know the meter of the piece? You fake it, of course. Start with the four pattern. If you can't keep up, switch to the three, and so on. Even the fastest music can be beat to with the one pattern.

The *staccato* stroke is very sharp and angular with a noticeable, but slight, pause between notes. Using the wrist, snap the baton smartly from one beat to the next. Practice to get the pause between the beats just right. In contrast, *legato* notes are smooth and rounded, with no discernible pause between each beat. Hold the baton more loosely and put some lilt into the motion. Think mellow thoughts. Close your eyes and imagine yourself in front of the Vienna Philharmonic.

Left hand

The left hand is used for volume control, cueing, accentuation, and as a mirror of the right hand. Volume control with the left is simple. Turn your palm up and hold it steady in front of your chest to indicate loud; turn it down and hold it to indicate soft. Variations between soft and loud are indicated by the angle of the hand. *Pianissimo* (very soft) is a downward palm almost parallel to the floor. An upward palm at 45 degrees or so is *fortissimo* (very loud). Dynamic levels in between (piano, mezzo piano, mezzo forte, and forte) are indicated in a similar fashion.

To execute a *crescendo*, pretend you are holding a grapefruit in your left hand, extend your arm and raise it steadily to eye level. For a *decrescendo*, reverse the motion with a cupped palm facing downward. To indicate a slight drop in volume, hold up your left hand (Check, please!) for just a moment and let it drop. Like the right hand, the left is not supposed to descend below the sternum or extend above eye level. Even so, sensitive conductors have been known to scrunch their whole bodies down when the music gets really quiet and stand on their tiptoes during climaxes.

Coordination

To really look like a conductor, you have to coordinate your left with your right. As the music gets quieter, the baton stroke should become more compact and can be executed mostly with the wrists. When the music gets louder, put your forearm into it and make the stroke more exaggerated. Strive to keep your left hand moving in the same vertical plane as the baton. Legato phrasing can be emphasized with a vast sweeping motion of your left hand. Your hands should never cross, although when mirroring they should almost touch at your sternum. In spite of the late Leonard Bernstein's near-hysterical contortions on the podium, conductors are supposed to keep their lower bodies still and their feet together. Practicing in front of a mirror is the best way to perfect your patterns, tempo, and phrasing.

Cueing

One of the most difficult aspects of conducting to fake is cueing. Because major symphony orchestras are so well-trained, most cues only require the conductor to make eye contact with the musicians. But there is nothing like a dramatic cue to demonstrate you know a piece cold. Just before a soloist or instrument section is supposed to come in, lift your left hand and give them the finger. The index finger, that is. To start a chorus, look up and raise your left hand like you are acknowledging someone. Return to the music after cueing. Anything more is showboating!

Starting

As Beecham pointed out, starting the orchestra together is an essential skill, but an impossible task when conducting to a recording. Just start out as soon as you can find the beat.

Stopping

One of the few chances for embarrassment while "air-conducting" is in stopping the orchestra. Anticipation is critical, so you need to know the resting places by heart. For a note that is held and then cut off, the simplest gesture is to make a counterclockwise "loop-de-loop" with a snap of your right wrist. If you are ending a movement, bring the baton to a dead stop. If you just want a pause, let the baton drift back up to start the next note.

At the end of a piece, there are more dramatic ways to stop the orchestra. For a piece that fades into silence, like Mahler's *Das Lied Van Der Erde*, just gradually lower both hands. The baton should barely be moving by the very end. At the last note, allow your arms to drop to your sides and hang there limply as though you are exhausted (and after a Mahler, you probably are). For a rousing finale, pull out all the stops. As the dynamism of the piece increases towards the end, widen out your strike zone and exaggerate every gesture. If the music ends on a big note that is held, hammer down the last beat, smartly raise the baton above your head and hold it there until the music stops. For a piece with a more complicated ending, vigorously beat time, flailing madly with the baton. For a really big finish, like Mahler's First Symphony, leave your feet on the last note (some conductors fall off the podium and hurt themselves doing this). Cutoffs are normally executed with both hands, so get your left up in the air and gesture wildly at the end.

Refining your technique

Attending symphony concerts is a good way to pick up some of the nuances of conducting. Sit as close to the stage as possible. The first few rows (usually inexpensive seats) will give you a great view of the conductor's socks and possibly a sore neck, but you can see all the action on the podium. Even better is a behind-the-stage seat, common in Europe but found in only a few American halls. A less expensive way to study the habits of famous conductors is by watching the cable television Arts Channel.

The Japanese, who invented karaoke and routinely gather by the thousands in baseball stadiums to sing "Ode to Joy" in German, married their passions for classical music and gadgets in a computer program called Magicbaton. This "virtual conducting" software made by PFU Limited allows users to conduct an orchestra using a mouse instead of a baton. It includes built-in recordings of classical titles that can be altered by the virtual conductor, saved, and played back.

If you get really ambitious, there is an abundance of literature on conducting available at libraries and music schools. Advice ranges from the simple, like Richard Wagner's famous insight regarding Beethoven's Ninth Symphony to "find the melody in every bar"; to the pretentious, actual line from a conducting textbook by William J. Finn entitled *The Conductor Raises His Baton*: "Obviously the sonorousness of this interpolated period must be most sedulously restrained." But who really cares what some gasbag musicologist says. It's your orchestra—conduct it the way you want.

The ultimate amateur conductor is Gilbert Kaplan, a man so taken with Mahler's Symphony No. 2 ("Resurrection") that he resolved to conduct it in front of a live orchestra. A self-made millionaire, Kaplan had the means to make his Walter Mitty fantasy a Plimptonesque reality. Tutored by a recent graduate of the Julliard School nine hours a day for seven months, Kaplan, who initially could not read music, learned the intricacies of Mahler's sublime work. To further his training, Kaplan hired the American Symphony orchestra and chorus for a full private rehearsal. The next year, Kaplan's first public concert of the work at Carnegie Hall was met with surprising critical acclaim. Since then, he has conducted the Mahler Second—still the only piece in his repertoire—with nearly 50 orchestras around the world. Kaplan's recording with the London Symphony Orchestra is the top-selling Mahler record of all-time.

Even if you never conduct a live orchestra, keeping your baton handy is a good way to stay in shape. Strenuous conducting can raise the heart rate as high as 195 beats per minute, and conductors are renowned for their fitness and longevity. Do yourself a favor, though, and save the really spastic conducting for short pieces. Longtime Boston Symphony maestro Seizi Ozawa once offered his advice to a beginning conductor who had an exuberant style, "If you go like *this*, end of symphony you need ambulance."

How to fly a jet fighter without joining the armed services

Have you ever daydreamed about piloting a jet fighter? Imagined yourself at the controls, pinned to your seat by the intense G-forces, afterburners glowing as you hit the throttle to go supersonic, the blood-curdling engine roar and vapor trail left behind the only evidence of your existence?

Well, daydream no more. Thanks to the implosion of the Soviet Union, the desperate financial straits of its former military contractors, and several enterprising American tour companies (see Additional Resources), the copilot's seat of a Russian-made fighter aircraft is for rent. For prices ranging from $6,500 to $38,500, an abject novice can fly an advanced MiG or Sukhoi under the supervision of a Russian civilian test pilot. (If you are on a budget, for as little as $900 you can fly a Czech-built L-39 trainer on an a la carte basis.) Besides cash, you only need to be in decent health and have average coordination. Wimps, however, need not apply.

Although the flights only last about 40 minutes each, they offer a lifetime's worth of cocktail party stories. And they are definitely *flights*, not *rides*: Unless you chicken out or the pilot is concerned about your abilities, you will actually fly the plane—often for over half the flight. Pilots typically demonstrate a maneuver, like a roll, and then ask you to repeat it. (In a favorite tactic to induce you to take the stick, the pilot, who sits in front of you, will raise his hands up and say "Your plane!") If you would rather just sit there and be mesmerized, that's okay too. The pilot will be very pleased to show you a few stomach-churning maneuvers. Should things get to be too much for you, he will bring you down.

Flights take off year-round from Zhukovsky Air Base outside Moscow, a joint commercial and military airport similar to Edwards Air Force Base in California. Some firms also offer flights from other Russian and Ukrainian airbases. The fighters used are owned by the Russian government. The host Russian pilots are all former top military fliers who now test experimental aircraft with the Gromov Flight Research Institute based at Zhukovsky. Unlike America, in Russia many test pilots are well-known as national heroes or aerial acrobats. They all speak enough English to get by in a cockpit ("You no get sick, okay?").

No flying experience is necessary and there are only minimal physical requirements. Some firms may require you to get a physical and a letter from your doctor stating you are in reasonably good health before booking the trip (a current pilot's license also works). Others may require you to pedal an exercise bicycle while hooked up to a heart monitor. Naturally, you also will need a valid passport and a visa to enter Russia. Visitors to Zhukovsky require a security clearance—arranged by the tour operator—to gain entry to the base.

Most packages include multiple rides for the price, starting with a ride or two in the subsonic L-39 trainer to learn basic maneuvers, and additional rides in the second warbird of your choice. Generally, prices are based upon the type of aircraft you choose. Options include a state-of-the-art Russian spy plane, the MiG-25 "Foxbat," and the super-maneuverable Su-27/30 "Flanker" jet fighters. Because a supersonic ride could be a once-in-a-lifetime experience, you may be tempted to get the most expensive package. Most people find, however, that a middle-of-the-road fighter like a MiG-29 is more than enough airplane for them.

As guest copilot, you wear a helmet with built-in oxygen flow, sun shade, and communications equipment. You also wear a pressurized "G-suit" that inflates to help prevent blood from pooling in your lower body during the flight and causing a loss of vision or consciousness. Military pilots routinely pull two to four G-forces during normal training. Most pilots lose consciousness at about five-and-a-half sustained Gs. In actual MiG rides, amateurs have withstood over seven Gs for a few seconds without blacking out.

Dual controls on each airplane theoretically prevent a maniac from putting the plane into an unrecoverable position. The instructors are highly experienced and the planes (some of them from the Vietnam War era), are supposedly well-maintained. But in a military jet, the potential for a crash always exists. So, just in case, you will be trained how to eject from the aircraft before you climb into it.

A typical ride features a variety of standard maneuvers, including loops, rolls, tight turns, climbs, and dives. Yes, sonic booms are included too; all of the MiGs and Sukhois used are capable of breaking the sound barrier. Pilots also take client requests for certain maneuvers. The "hammerhead," which starts with a slow-speed, vertical climb, and ends with a rapid, bladder-emptying dive, is particularly popular. Eat lightly before flying: A big meal is a surefire way to upchuck your way through $10,000.

Another popular maneuver is the "tailslide," an air show stunt where the pilot orients the plane with the nose pointing straight up and allows the plane's airspeed to drop until it stalls. Warning lights come on, the cockpit fills with smoke, and the plane starts to wobble and fall tail-first. After a few heart-stopping moments, the pilot reverses the slide. If you have ridden the scariest roller coasters and still not had the bejeezus scared out of you, this should do it.

In the ultra-expensive MiG-25 flight, you may not pull as many Gs in spectacular maneuvers, but there is significant compensation: You will fly at nearly three times the speed of sound, see the curvature of the Earth, and experience the singular sensation of black space above you in the middle of the afternoon. The view is pretty incredible as well. At a MiG-25's typical flying altitude (80,000 feet-plus), the visible horizon is over 700 miles wide.

Perhaps the ultimate move to experience is the "cobra," a formerly secret move so hairy that even the Russian hotshots don't like doing it. The cobra, which can only be performed in the super-agile MiG-29 and Su-27/30 fighters (and a handful of American-made fighters), is a dogfight maneuver invented by Soviet pilots to get an enemy off their tails. The cobra starts with the plane flying level at fairly slow airspeed. The pilot pulls sharply back on the stick until the aircraft is pointing straight up, nose at one o'clock. Then, instead of doing a loop, the pilot sharply pushes the nose back down, causing the plane to appear to pop up and shoot backward, like a striking cobra. In a combat situation the bandit would then be in front and, without a doubt, dead meat.

How to vex the terminally pleasant

Ever tire of total strangers wishing you well?

Employ the curmudgeon's response of social critic Paul Fussell in his book *Class*. When the cashier says "Have a nice day!" respond with "Thank you, but I have other plans."

How to cure a mid-life crisis

We all know the signs: the realization you're halfway dead and don't have much to show for it; obsession with your physical appearance; compulsive checking of ages in the obituary section; perennial grouchiness at home; a powerful urge to quit your job and open a Dunkin Donuts franchise. Although researchers differ on whether the "mid-life crisis" even exists, there is no doubt that many people, especially men, begin acting strangely between the ages of 40 and 50.

Cures teem. There are transcendental meditation classes, Outward Bound adventures, and lots of self-help books for those who feel the mid-life malaise is strictly an internal affair. We, however, subscribe to the concept that there is no better—or more American—way out of your crisis than a nice acquisition. Here are some presents to yourself that give effective relief.

BMW Z4 Roadster

A snappy convertible is the quintessential mid-life crisis toy. With more power than before, BMW's new Z4 ragtop comes with a 2.5-liter, 184-horsepower engine, classic styling, manual or automatic transmission, and handles like a dream. Enough space in the trunk to hold a couple of suitcases. Very practical for getting to weekend retreats with Robert Bly. Not enough car? Try the 3.0-liter version, with 225 horses and hair-parting acceleration of zero to 60 in 5.9 seconds (2.5-liter: $33,795; 3.0-liter: $40,945; at your BMW dealer).

T-Rex

If you still wish you had kept your old go-cart, the T-Rex is the perfect toy for you. A three-wheeler that looks like a miniature Indy race car, the T-Rex has howling power and acceleration to rival a Ferrari. What's more, it seats two and is street-legal, though there are a lot of ways to break the law in this thing. T-Rex is made by Campagna, of Quebec, Canada ($39,000). For a dealer near you, phone (845) 883-7910, or visit *www.go-t-rex.com*.

Redline 1300 Revolt snowmobile

If you are stuck in the Great White North or just want to act like a kid without causing an accident, this rocket sled is the thing. The Redline 1300 Revolt, however, is not your father's snowmobile. With a 225-horsepower, liquid-cooled, three-cylinder engine, the Revolt is one serious arctic toy. Hemorrhoid sufferers will appreciate the advanced suspension system that keeps bouncing to a minimum, even over rough terrain. Be careful of half-frozen ponds and low-hanging power lines (around $13,000). To find your local dealer, go to *www.redlinesnowmobiles.com*.

Powerski Jetboard

Stoke it, baby! Aging surfers can go the young punks one better with this motorized surfboard by Powerski. Propelled by a two-stroke engine and controlled with a handgrip, the Jetboard will reach speeds of 40 miles per hour on smooth water. A carefully designed hull puts the center of gravity under your feet so you can carve radical turns at high speeds ($5,995-$6,995) at *www.powerski.com*, (949) 369-3920.

Harley-Davidson FXSTD Softail Deuce

It is no longer a secret that most Harley buyers only wear leather on the weekends. Despite (or perhaps because of) their deafening roar and primitive suspension system, Harleys remain the favorite of Hell's Angels and weekend road warriors alike. The Softail Deuce is a lot of bike at 645 pounds, with an 88-cubic-inch, twin cam engine, five-speed transmission, and dual over-under shotgun exhaust pipes. There are also tons of color options so your bike will stand out in a crowd with other mid-lifers ($17,180 at your local Harley-Davidson dealer).

Home tanning machine

What do Britney Spears, Bob Dole, and George Hamilton have in common? They all have a permanent tan, and you can have one too—even in the middle of winter—without going to those unsanitary tanning salons. The Garda Sun Proline 32 tanning bed boasts 32 energy-efficient, 100-watt lamps for a golden body and three 400-watt lamps for a fast facial. Built-in digital timer to prevent overcooking (about $7,000 at *www.directleisure.com*).

Nose job

Nothing like a new nose from which to look down at the world. Craving a Jimmy Stewart? Maybe a Martha Stewart? Even a Thomas Jefferson is available. Rhinoplasty can make a world of difference in one's life—ask Michael Jackson. See *www.plasticsurgery.org* for a list of surgeons approved by the American Board of Plastic Surgery ($3,000 to $5,000).

How to cut an onion without crying

"Onions can make even heirs and widows weep."

—Benjamin Franklin

Americans eat an average of 18 pounds of onions per year—and that's a lot of crying. Onions probably cause more tears than divorces, lost cats, and soap operas combined.

The reason for the root vegetable's malevolent streak is the amino acid sulfoxides that reside in the onion's cells. When you cut into an onion, tiny sulfoxide particles float into the air and produce sulfenic acid (a mild form of sulfuric acid), which reacts with the water in your eyes. The irritated cornea sends out a distress signal and tears are the result. The key, therefore, is to keep the irritating fumes away from your eyes.

There are a least 10 ways to do it, including heating the onion in the microwave for a minute before cutting it, chilling the onion in the refrigerator first, cutting the onion under running water, and this odd one: holding a piece of bread in your mouth while chopping, which, curiously, works. Then there's the cheater's way: putting the onion in the Cuisinart.

How to improve your public speaking

"There is but one pleasure in life equal to that of being called on to make an after-dinner speech, and that is not being called on to make one."

—Charles Dudley Warner

Horrified by the prospect of getting up in front of a group of people and making a speech? Tremble at the sight of a microphone? Stop falling all over your tongue; there is a group for people just like you.

Toastmasters International has helped over 3 million people work up their nerves and deliver speeches with confidence since 1924. Toastmasters Clubs meet once a week for an hour. Members deliver prepared and impromptu speeches and are given constructive criticism by their peers on how to improve (rotten fruits and vegetables are very seldom thrown).

There are 180,000 Toastmasters members in 70 countries, including 130,000 in the United States. New members have to pay a $16 fee. Dues are $36 a year. To locate the club nearest you, call (800) 9WE-SPEAK or log on to *www.toastmasters.org*.

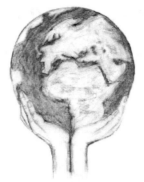

How to save the Earth

For those who believe we should rid the world of nuclear weapons and bury the plans for building them, we have just one word for you: Asteroids.

You might not believe it, judging by our relatively protected interstellar existence, but the Earth lives in a dangerous neighborhood. The local thugs are meteors, asteroids, and comets. Millions of these near-Earth objects (NEOs) constantly swirl around our planet. Some of them occasionally wind up on a path heading straight for us. Thankfully, the vast majority are bowling ball-sized or smaller, and burn up harmlessly once they enter Earth's atmosphere. But there are thousands of larger objects out there on Earth-crossing orbits that threaten our very existence.

Because of the almost incomprehensible speed at which they travel (50,000-80,000 miles per hour), an asteroid a mere one kilometer (six-tenths of a mile) in diameter would explode with a force millions of times more powerful than the atomic bomb at Hiroshima, causing unimaginable world-wide destruction. Such an asteroid striking land would eject huge amounts of dirt and rock into the upper atmosphere that would return to Earth as flaming meteors a short time later, starting fires all over the globe. The dust and ash kicked up would be so dense it would block out sunlight for months or even years, leading to global crop failures and mass starvation. An asteroid landing in the ocean would be even worse. Enormous tsunamis caused by the impact would fan out and travel for thousands of miles, burying coastal cities across the globe in waves hundreds of feet high. Some scientists estimate over 1 billion people would be killed. Don't bother stockpiling canned goods and bottled water: No place on Earth would be safe.

Geological evidence shows the Earth has been nailed by large asteroids numerous times before. Scientists now widely believe the extinction of the dinosaurs 65 million years ago was caused by a mammoth (10-mile-wide) asteroid that slammed into the Yucatan Peninsula of Mexico and left a 150-mile wide crater as its calling card. As recently as 1908 a 60-meter-wide NEO landed in Tunguska, Siberia, scorching a thousand-square-mile area. Nearly 100 years later, the damage is still plainly visible.

The Earth *will* definitely be hit with a big one again. The question is when. Scientists believe an asteroid the size of the one in Siberia pelts the Earth somewhere between once a century and once a millenium. Terrifying to be sure, but it wouldn't endanger mankind. The real threat comes from the *really big* rocks—the 1,000 or so asteroids with diameters greater than one kilometer—that scientists believe are large enough to cause a global catastrophe. These larger asteroids very rarely strike Earth. According to David Morrison of NASA's Ames Research Center, the odds of a catastrophic impact during an average lifetime are about one in 20,000. Still, you are more likely to be killed by an asteroid than die in an airplane crash or win the lottery. And given the dire consequences of a large NEO striking Earth, it seems worthwhile to do something. But what?

First, we need to figure out where these orbiting death threats are. Congress has charged NASA to identify 90 percent of the one-kilometer and larger near-Earth asteroids by the year 2008. Despite a puny budget of about $3.5 million annually for asteroid research, thus far approximately 600, or 60 percent, have been found. NASA supports several independent teams of skywatchers doing the tedious work, although with more funding for large telescopes the search could be accelerated. The need to get moving was made clear in June 2002 when asteroid 2002 MN snuck up on us and zipped by a mere 75,000 miles away—about one-fifth the distance to the moon—and was not detected until three days later. It was the second-closest shave ever recorded.

Okay, suppose we discover a large asteroid on a collision course with Earth. What then? Fortunately, as science fiction writer Arthur C. Clarke pointed out, unlike the dinosaurs, humans have a space program. There are two basic ways to eliminate an asteroid bound for Earth: (1) blow it up or (2) nudge it into a new orbit. Option one has one major problem: The blast would likely fragment the asteroid into numerous smaller, but still-deadly pieces, what physicist Paul Davies likened to turning "a bullet into buckshot." Nudging the asteroid is the better option.

The idea is to create minute changes in the asteroid's speed that would, over a long time period, throw it off course by hundreds of thousands of miles. Astrophysicists differ about how much of an adjustment to the asteroid's velocity would be necessary, but in simple terms, the more time we have, the less force required to divert it. If a killer asteroid is spotted sufficiently far in advance, say about 20 years, we would have a number of feasible solutions.

Scientists theorize a "mass driver"—part digging machine, part catapult—is one option. The device would be landed on the asteroid and, using solar energy, continuously strip mine the surface of the asteroid and fling the matter into space at high velocity. As the catapulted material left the surface, it would create an equal and opposite reaction on the asteroid, nudging it in the other direction. The biggest problem is there is about 1 billion tons of matter in a one-kilometer asteroid. With our present technology, a mass driver would take many decades to remove enough material to alter the asteroid's course—probably too long for us endangered earthlings.

Another idea is to use a giant mirror coupled with a smaller, secondary mirror that would catch the sun's rays and train them on the asteroid. Theoretically, the beam would create enough heat to vaporize rock from the surface of the asteroid and propel it the same way the mass driver would. Sounds good in theory, but we would need a mirror about the size of eight football stadiums.

Still another proposed solution is to hitch a solar sail to the asteroid and use solar radiation to blow the asteroid off course. Unfortunately, solar sails suffer from their own technical problems. A sail large enough to move a one-kilometer asteroid would be enormous and unwieldy. Astronauts would have to fasten it to the asteroid and unfurl the thing in deep space. Moreover, even if they got the sail deployed, it might not survive the ride on a spinning asteroid going 70,000 miles per hour.

If you had to bet your life on it (and we may have to), there is only one solution: nukes. Thomas Ahrens and Alan Harris of the California Institute of Technology, who have extensively analyzed the issue, have calculated relatively small (100 kiloton) nuclear warheads are powerful enough to do the job. Ignore Hollywood; rather than directly impacting the asteroid, the preferred method would be a "standoff" explosion about 1,300 feet above the surface. Such an explosion would drench the asteroid in radiation, causing the superheated surface layer to fly off and act like a rocket motor, propelling the asteroid into another orbit. Ahrens and Harris believe a properly calibrated blast could leave the asteroid largely intact.

Even this fairly straightforward solution stretches the bounds of our current technology. We would need precision guidance and communications systems to zero in on our target, a comparative speck in the solar system millions of miles away. In addition, we would need to develop or adapt existing booster rockets powerful enough to put nuclear missiles into orbit. Or carry them up on the Space Shuttle, which would require numerous safeguards to ensure we wouldn't accidentally blow ourselves up. Still, given enough time, brainpower, and money, these issues could be overcome.

If we had only a limited advance warning of an impending asteroid attack—years rather than decades—we would need much larger nukes. A physicist at Los Alamos Nuclear Laboratory, Johndale Solem, has calculated a series of standoff explosions using Cold War-era, 4-megaton nuclear warheads would yield enough firepower to move the asteroid without fragmenting it, provided we had at least five months until impact. The obvious drawback is that if it didn't work there might not be time for a second attempt. Talk about pressure.

Even more depressing for Chicken Little is the threat of comets. These giant "dirty snowballs" are many times larger than asteroids and move twice as fast. Their devastating force was vividly displayed when comet Shoemaker-Levy 9 crashed into Jupiter in 1994 in a celestial fireworks display that left scars bigger than the Earth. Long-period comets, whose orbits take over 200 years to complete, pose the greatest threat because most are not tracked by astronomers. If a comet is coming our way from the outer reaches of the solar system, we probably won't discover it until it's too late.

Keep your fingers crossed. And tell your congressman to keep voting for NASA funding.

How to turn a mountain back into a molehill

Thirty miles off the southern coast of Sicily in the Mediterranean Sea lies Graham's Shoal, a modest chunk of basalt about 20 feet underwater. After recent volcanic activity, the shoal threatens to peek its head above water and become an island. When this happens, it will no doubt fire up a 170-year-old international dispute over who owns it—Great Britain, Sicily, or France.

Prince Carlo Di Bourbon, a descendant of the last king of Naples, is not leaving anything to chance. After geologists reported the shoal was creeping near the surface, the Prince motored out to the shoal and planted a plaque and Sicilian flag on it, just in case.

Serious business, this is. The last time Graham's Shoal became Graham's *Island*, in 1831, England, France, and Naples (a separate country ruled by the Bourbons at the time) each successively claimed it was theirs. Navy ships from all three nations prepared for war to decide which country possessed the tiny isle. Alas, five months later, conflict was averted.

The island sank.

How to get rid of all those frequent flyer miles

"Winning a free ticket for flying 25,000 miles is like getting a free trip to the dentist with each root canal."

—Anonymous frequent flyer

If you are like many frequent flyers, about the last "gift" you need from the airlines is a free ticket. More legroom, fewer lies, a decent bag of peanuts, yes. Extra ticket, no. Even if you can make use of a free flight, the mileage programs have so many blackouts and restrictions that it can be difficult to use up your miles faster than you accumulate them. If you think there ought to be a way to monetize your hard-earned miles, there is—with a catch, of course.

Mileage brokers stand ready to buy your miles (or sell you some, if you prefer) for cash. The going rate is two cents a mile. Active brokers include Mileagebrokers.com and Award Traveler (*www. awardtraveler.com*). Here's how it works: You contact the broker with the amount of miles you want to sell and how much you want for them. They keep your information on file until a customer indicates they want to travel on the airline where you have your miles. The broker works out price and other details with the buyer, then contacts you with the buyer's name and flight information. You book the ticket yourself, listing the buyer as the passenger and pay for it with your miles. When your ticket arrives, you overnight it to the broker C.O.D. The whole thing is nonrefundable and non-cancelable. Expedient and tidy.

The catch is that the airlines hate bartering. After all, they created the mileage programs' rules precisely so they could control both supply *and* demand for miles. And when some wise guy violates the tenets of their carefully constructed fantasy economies, well, they get a little testy. All of the major airlines except Southwest (they say it's not a problem) claim they are feverishly policing ticket brokerage using analytical software. (A common tripwire is a frequent flyer obtaining first-class international award tickets for someone with a different last name or who originates from somewhere else.) If the buyer gets caught and can't talk his way out of it, the airline will make him pay full freight to get home. You, on the other hand, can lose some or all of the miles in your account. Cash today or miles tomorrow. You choose.

P.S. To those of you with a lot of miles on US Airways, for 10 million miles you can travel to space. If you would prefer to pay cash, see "How to travel to space."

How to live to 100

"By the time a man gets well into the seventies his continued existence is a mere miracle."

—Robert Louis Stevenson, "Crabbed Age and Youth"

Living to age 100 is not as far-fetched as it used to be. Although in 1800 there were likely no centenarians in the world, today there are an estimated 70,000 in the U.S. alone. Hallmark now offers six different birthday cards for people turning 100. By the time the Love Generation becomes the Metamucil Generation around the middle of the century, there will be over 1 million really old hippies toddling around America.

Sharply lower infant mortality, better nutrition, improved medical care, and elimination of widespread diseases vastly extended the average American's life span, from 47 to 77 years, during the 20th century. But medical technology can only do so much. Illnesses, injuries, and plain old bad luck will end the lives of 99 out of 100 people born today before they reach the century mark. And scientists estimate that even if all cancers were eliminated, average human life expectancy would grow by only two years.

Yet living to 100 still fascinates people. Researchers have observed and interviewed thousands of centenarians in hopes of uncovering the secrets of reaching the century mark. Here are the latest theories they have sallied forth.

The It's All-in-the-Genes Theory

Researchers have found the main reason centenarians live so long is because (*duh!*) they stay out of the hospital. Out of 1,127 hundred-year-olds interviewed by the Social Security Administration, only one heart attack or stroke was reported before age 75. When disease does eventually strike these hardy few it is often after age 100, suggesting centenarians are simply born with superior constitutions.

Scientists believe there is a single gene on chromosome-4, dubbed "Indy" (I'm not dead yet), that controls how long human cells can live. Evidence suggests Indy genes of people from long-lived families are programmed so their bodies age more slowly and are less susceptible to age-related illnesses. Of course, genes don't drink, bungee-jump, or ride a motorcycle without a helmet. In fact, only about 30 percent longevity is due to genetics, according to a landmark 1993 study of 600 Danish twins.

Your genes may give you a shot at reaching 100, but there are a lot of ways to blow it. Smoking, for example. The odds of living to 100 go from remote to astronomically long if you smoke. Sure, there are exceptional cases of very old smokers. Jean Calment, the oldest-lived person in the world (age 122), did not stop smoking until age 118. Bear in mind, though, the first "Marlboro Man" died of lung cancer at 51.

The Flat Abs Theory

Some researchers believe old age is largely a function of a healthy diet and vigorous exercise. Aerobic activity is widely praised for its salutary effect on the ticker. Yet being active when you are young is not good enough. You have to keep it up even after your knees start to creak. When you get too old to jog or play tennis, take up activities that are easy on the old bones and joints, like swimming and resistance training. Plain old hard work is another good source of exercise. Many 100-year-olds still chop wood, tend gardens, and spank their great-grandchildren to stay active.

Diets are more controversial. Some researchers hypothesize that the diets of certain Asian and Mediterranean peoples—lots of fish, and fresh fruits and vegetables—are responsible for their long lives in comparison with junk food-eating Americans. If only it were that simple. It turns out American centenarians share practically nothing in common where diet is concerned, especially in terms of fat and calories. (One centenarian attributed his longevity to eating a lot of fatty pork.) There is one unmistakable common denominator though: *moderation*—no bingeing, no crash diets. Centenarians have very stable body weights throughout their lives. And virtually no one makes it to 100 overweight.

The Healthy Brain Theory

This theory says taut stomach muscles and a trim waistline are irrelevant if your brain goes soft. Alzheimer's disease strikes one out of every two people by the age of 85. Brain researchers believe Alzheimer's is less likely to take root in an active mind. Continuing to learn new things will help you maintain mental acuity into old age (see "How to improve your memory").

Furthermore, scientists believe nasty little molecules in your brain called *free radicals* steal electrons from other cells in your brain, eventually causing a breakdown in its ability to function. Physicians recommend daily doses of vitamin E, which contains antioxidants that help combat free radicals. (Fruit flies have been shown to live up to 20 percent longer when receiving antioxidants.) Though the research is still incomplete, studies suggest that women can significantly reduce their chances of getting Alzheimer's disease if they take estrogen supplements after menopause.

The Mellow Out Theory

Geriatric researchers say centenarians have one resoundingly strong trait in common: a shockproof system for coping with life's stressful events. The single-most important personality trait identified in the New England Centenarian Study was an exceptionally low level of neuroticism. Overreactions to stress cause the production of catecholamines (such as adrenaline). Sustained high levels of catecholamines weaken your body's immune system. A sunny, even mischievous, demeanor helps; George Cook, who at 108 was England's oldest dirty old man, reportedly grabbed the nurses' bottoms each morning when they came to wake him up.

Happiness at work makes a big difference too. A Duke University study of 268 elderly volunteers conducted over a 24-year period found work satisfaction to be the second-highest predictor of longevity for men (good physical condition was first). Working for a jerk creates stress, frustration, and inevitable conflict. Stress is correlated with higher incidences of heart attacks and lower survival rates after major surgery. Better to quit that job you hate and do something you really enjoy.

The Umbrella Drinks and Coconuts Theory

The people living on the tropical island of Okinawa have the longest life spans and count more centenarians per capita than any other country. Some claim their longevity is due to their wholesome diets, mental well-being, and ritualized regular exercise. But the real reason is obvious: With average temperatures of 73 degrees, you would stick around a while longer too.

The Fountain (Test Tube?) of Youth Theory

As the human body ages, its cells continuously divide. Telomeres, located at the ends of each chromosome, get shorter with each division. Scientists have found that when the enzyme telomerase is added to cells in a test tube, telomere shrinking stops. Latter-day Ponce de Leons theorize that some day a telomerase elixir could be taken to slow aging dramatically, perhaps even extending human life spans beyond the theoretical limit of 125 years.

Researchers say there is still a lot to learn about longevity. Fifty-year longitudinal studies have been proposed, under which 50-year-olds would be followed to age 100. The only problem is finding enough 30-year-old researchers who will outlive their subjects.

How to run a democracy

"You've got to work things out in the cloakroom, and when you've got them worked out, you can debate a little before you vote."

—Lyndon Baines Johnson, former master of the Senate

How to win a basketball game when your team is down by two with the ball and 30 seconds remaining

Most coaches would try to hold for the last shot and hope to tie the game with a two-point field goal to take it into overtime.

But, if your team shoots, say, 45 percent from the field and 35 percent from behind the three-point-line (about average for a decent squad), that is the wrong strategy. The probability of winning is the sequential probability of making the two-point field goal (45 percent) times the probability of winning in overtime (arguably 50 percent), or about 23 percent—less than one in four. (Forget about winning it on the free-throw line: The opposing team is unlikely to foul when the worst that can happen if the shot goes in is overtime.)

Even if your team shoots poorly from behind the arc, the better strategy is to go for the win by putting up a three-pointer as time runs out, which improves the odds to 35 percent.

How to select a single malt scotch

"There is no such thing as a bad whisky. Some whiskies just happen to be better than others."

—William Faulkner

If you've graduated from beer but fuzzy navels and "chocolate" martinis just aren't your taste, maybe you should try scotch—*single malt scotch whisky* to be precise.

No adult beverage has more variety and sophistication than scotch, including wine. Trouble is, to most people scotch means *blended* scotch. Now blends won't hurt you, at least not the better ones like Johnnie Walker Black Label and Chivas Regal. And even run-of-the-mill blends can be choked down if you drown them in ice and water. But to really appreciate the stuff Gaelic-speaking Scots called *uisgebeatha* (water of life), you've got to have a wee dram of single malt.

Scotch whisky is the authentic beverage made in Scotland: Nothing made in the United States, Ireland, Canada, or Japan can carry that label. Malt whisky is made entirely from malted barley that is dried over peat or charcoal fires then fermented with yeast and distilled in onion-shaped "pot stills." For it to be a single malt, only whisky from a single distillery can be used (although different vintages may be combined, or "vatted"). The spirit is then put in casks to age (whisky does not mature in the bottle). It goes into the cask at about 70 percent alcohol by volume. About two percent of the alcohol evaporates each year, which distillers wistfully call the "angel's share." Whiskies are bottled at around 40 percent to 50 percent alcohol.

By law, whisky has to be aged for at least three years, though in practice most are aged eight years or more. Standard bottlings for single malts are aged 10 to 12 years; special vintages are aged from 18 to over 50 years. In general, the longer a whisky ages the mellower it is and the better it tastes. This is not always true though; some whiskies hit their peak as teenagers and any further aging is useless or even detrimental. Furthermore, a young whisky from a good house is better than an ancient whisky from a bad house.

The cask imparts over half of the flavor of whisky. Aging was originally done exclusively in sherry casks because the Scots, being thrifty, could get them cheaply from the sherry-swilling English. Today most distilleries use casks from American bourbon distilleries that impart less flavor and color to the spirit. One notable exception is Macallan, which only uses Spanish oak casks pre-filled with sherry.

Tell a stillman that all of the work is done by the cask, and you'll have one mad Scot on your hands. The essence of the whisky, he'll say, is from the "new spirit"—the alcohol drawn off in the distilling process. The new spirit is affected by the water, how the barley is dried, the shape of still, the conditions in the warehouse, and other mysterious factors that even master distillers can't completely fathom. Geography is perhaps the most often noted but least understood influence on whiskies. There are four whisky-producing regions in Scotland: the Lowlands, the Highlands, Campbeltown, and Islay. Each region has different waters, peats, microclimates and whisky-making styles that give the whisky a recognizable character.

Acquiring the taste

The range of flavors, aromas, and textures among the hundreds of different bottlings is immense. Single malts start at about $20 a bottle and can run into the thousands. Before you invest $200 in an astringent Laphroaig 30-year-old, do the following:

(1) Get into a contemplative mood; (2) Go to a bar that offers a broad selection of single malts; (3) Sample one from each region, starting with the mildest scotches and working your way up to the strong stuff. Here's a rundown of what to try.

- *The Lowlands.* Lowland scotches are the most approachable of single malts. Their soft feel and mild flavor are easy to like. Lowlands malts are known for their citrus, grassy, and sweet flavors and exceptional softness. A nice glass of Auchentoshan or Glenkinchie is a good place to start. Old bottlings of Rosebank (now closed) are even better.

- *The Highlands.* Next, move on to the Highlands, whose whiskies are still agreeable but more interesting. Speyside, a vast region of Highlands distilleries near the River Spey, is home to over half the world's scotchmakers. Speyside malts are known for their smoothness, drinkability, and sweet, rich flavors. Start with a lighter Speyside, like Glenfiddich or Glenlivet. Then try a richer, darker malt from outside Speyside, like Balvenie or Highland Park. If you've got the money, return to Speyside for the Macallan 18-year-old— the gold standard among Highlands malts—which costs around $85 a bottle retail ($12 to $15 a glass most places). Too much? Try the Macallan 15-year-old, which is almost as good and much cheaper. There are dozens of other delicious examples, and some whisky drinkers' taste buds never leave Speyside. However, there is more out there for the adventurous.

- *Campbeltown.* Campbeltown's signature taste, as represented by its leading distillery, Springbank, is a subtle blend of salt air, toffee, fruits and hot spice. Its 10-year-old flagship malt is an excellent choice for a developing palate, and combines five or six distinct flavors with an icy-hot, syrupy finish. Not for beginners, but oh so warming on a cold evening.
- *Islay.* If you are a Starbucks coffee drinker, smoke maduro cigars, or you favor imported ale over watery American beer, you need to try Islay ("*eye*-luh") malts. The Islay flavor is peaty, smoky, floral, redolent of salt air and iodine; you can taste the sea (some wags would say you can taste the sea-*weed*). Try the Bowmore Darkest; Laphroaig ("la-froyg") 10-year-old; Caol Ila ("cull-*eela*"); or the most powerful peaty mouthful of them all, Lagavulin 16-year-old. If you can get beyond the idea you are swallowing medicine and Epsom salts, you'll be hooked for life.

Drinking it. Here are nine steps to properly consume your carefully chosen single malt.

Step 1: Get the right glass.

Save the lowball glasses for your bourbon-drinking friends. Scotch tasters favor a tulip-shaped glass for nosing and swirling, like the Riedel crystal single malt glass or sherry copita (both under $15), though a brandy snifter works in a pinch. The glass does make a difference and the cost is nothing compared to the expensive whiskey you are about to serve.

Step 2: Pour it neat.

No ice, no water, and certainly no soda. Pour about one to one-and-a-half ounces at a time; any more and it will spill when you swirl it.

Step 3: Aerate it.

Swirl it around the glass like wine connoisseurs do. The liquor has been in the bottle for a while and casked for a lot longer than that. A little oxygen gets the aromas going.

Step 4: Nose it.

Stick your snout into the glass. Turn from one nostril to the next (take a decongestant if you're stuffed up). Keep your mouth ajar—deep breathing of strong whiskey with a closed mouth will make all your words come out in Gaelic.

Step 5: Add water.

Dilution is more art than science. Diehards add just a splash, though you may want to add more. Tap water is okay if it doesn't reek of chlorine, otherwise use bottled water. The water combines with the whiskey to let the bouquet out. (Didn't think scotch had a bouquet, did you?)

Step 6: Nose again.

Swirl the water around and nose the glass again. There are hundreds of identifiable aromas in malt whisky—far more, in fact, than any other beverage. Try to identify as many as you can (vanilla, flowers, sherry, cough syrup, old feet, etc.).

Step 7: Taste it.

Finally...take a sip—never *gulp*. For the full taste experience, let it roll back on your tongue. Don't swallow. Instead, "chew" the whiskey for five or six seconds, then gradually let it slide down your throat.

Step 8: Chase it.

Some whisky mavens like a chaser of ginger ale or club soda. Others like to eat crackers between drinks. For really old malts, taking a bite of chocolate between sips can enhance the flavor. Whatever you choose, be sure to also drink plenty of water; neat scotch will dehydrate you fast and give you a vicious headache later.

Step 9: Smell it again and take another taste.

Repeat until satisfied or the bottle is empty, whichever comes first.

Don't blame us if you never go back to Cutty Sark.

How to run with the bulls

Proof that stupidity knows no national boundary can be found every July at the Festival of San Fermin in Pamplona, Spain, where thousands of drunken tourists from all over the globe (and a large contingent of locals) try to outrun six of the world's fastest, most dangerous animals in a lurid spectacle known as the "Running of the Bulls."

The Running, or *encierro*, has been going on since 1591, but Ernest Hemingway's 1926 novel, *The Sun Also Rises,* brought it international notoriety. Ostensibly the encierro is a means of conveying fighting bulls from their holding pens to the bullring so they may be fought each evening. In reality it is one of the only government-sanctioned activities in which the possibility of being injured or killed is the main attraction. Some runners get so nervous they literally pee their pants.

From the corral at the church of Santo Domingo through the narrow, cobblestoned streets of Pamplona to the *Plaza de Toros* (bullring), six 1,200-pound bulls and eight to 10 herding steers gallop through a crowd of 3,000 lunatics bent on proving their bravery by risking death at horn's point. *Cornadas* (horn wounds) are common, but getting trampled is also a real possibility. The event is so dangerous that ambulances and medical technicians are posted on every block. Depending upon the mood of the bulls (and the crowd), from a handful to over a dozen runners are injured during each morning's run. Although thanks to the skill of the local surgeons, only 13 people have died since they started keeping track in 1924 (the last one was an American, killed in 1995).

The "race" starts at 8 a.m. sharp each day of the festival, which lasts from July 7 to July 17. No registration is necessary and anybody over age 18 can run. You enter the route, which is barricaded off to everyone except runners, through official entrances at Plaza Del Ayuntamiento (town hall) and Plaza Consistorial. Do not hop over the fence; Pamplona police take a dim view of that practice. Get there early to get yourself positioned; the doors are closed at 7:30 a.m.

Basque locals deck themselves out in the traditional runner's uniform of starched white trousers, white shirt, red *panuelo* (kerchief) around the neck and red *faja* (sash) tied around the waist. Huge crowds mass behind the barricades and assemble on balconies to watch the carnage. The encierro is also carried live on television. A rocket sounds when the bulls are released their pens. Moments later a second rocket signals that all the animals have left the corral and are in the street. A third rocket signals the bulls have reached the bullring. The fourth and final rocket indicates all the bulls are safely penned up at the ring. The total distance is 850 yards and takes about three minutes to complete.

Pamplona can be reached by car or bus from Madrid (about 200 miles). You would be wise to book your hotel room a year in advance; during the festival, all the rooms are sold out and many tourists are forced to sleep in the park because they didn't make reservations.

If you must run with the bulls, here are some tips for returning home with all your vital organs:

- Wear shoes that will give you good traction. Skip the run if it rains: wet cobblestones are slick as glass. If you happen to fall in front of a bull, stay down, cover your head and remain motionless; bulls have a tendency to jump over obstacles.

- Start running when you hear the second rocket go off. Unless you are a matador, never stand still in the middle of the street waiting for the bulls to go by (surprisingly, a lot of people do). Fighting bulls will attack anything that gets in their way.

- Never try to outrun a bull. It is impossible (bulls can briefly outrun a horse) and a good way to get a firsthand look at the local infirmary. Instead, do what the experienced locals do. Walk the route ahead of time to look for possible escape areas, especially a doorway to duck into, a gap in the fence to slip through, or a window grate to hang from. When the bulls draw near, make yourself scarce.

- Ignore Satchel Paige's advice. Something *is* gaining on you: six half-tons of anger on the hoof. Look back frequently and be sure you know where the bulls are. Once they overtake you, do not try to keep pace with them. Drop back a little bit in case one of the bulls gets turned around in the confusion and starts charging backwards—a common reason people get gored.

- Never touch a bull or attempt to get its attention. (For example, do not wave your arms and shout "Yo Bull!") Bulls that get separated from the pack are especially dangerous.

- Watch out for the other runners, many of whom have fortified themselves with something other than orange juice for breakfast. Avoid running on the weekends when the crowds are thickest (and drunkest). The other runners can be as dangerous as the bulls.

- Newcomers should avoid the stretch of Santo Domingo street leading into Plaza Del Ayuntamiento, which offers no protective fence to dive over. The sharp right-hand turn where Mercaderes street turns into Estafeta is also dangerous because the bulls often lose their footing and smash into runners as they take the turn. And avoid the last section, from the Telefonica building to the Plaza de Toros, which is often crowded with novice runners.

- The most crazed runners station themselves about 100 yards from the corral at the top of the Santo Domingo hill. Just as the bulls start the uphill climb, these nuts dash down the hill *toward* the bulls until they are almost upon them, then do a U-turn and run away, ditching at the last moment to escape. Needless to say, this activity is not advised.

- Get a good night's rest the night before and, of course, don't drink before running. If you can run with the bulls sober, you are braver than most of the people in the race.

How to become a Scrabble master

Professor Kingsfield: V-A-V-A-S-O-R.
Hart: Vavasor? I've never heard of Vavasor!
Professor Kingsfield: If you had studied Middle English, you would.
        —from the "Scrabble" episode of the PBS series *Paper Chase*

There is a vast difference between an occasional Scrabbler, derisively referred to by Scrabble devotees as a "living room player," and an expert. If you are among the millions of people who enjoy Scrabble because you find it a good opportunity to show off your vocabulary without sounding like William F. Buckley, Jr., you will be saddened to learn you are reading at the first-grade level compared with top players, who know such words as AI, BIS, CALX, DISME, EOSINE and FITCHEE. There are over 100,000 words in the *Official Scrabble Players Dictionary* that governs hobbyist play. American clubs and tournaments use an uncensored dictionary with another 200 or so words. International tournaments allow another 25,000 words. The amount of time it takes to memorize all these words is absurd.

It's no accident that a large percentage of champion Scrabble players don't hold steady jobs.

Unless you are unusually gifted, becoming a competitive Scrabble player is just about a full-time occupation. So if you happen to be independently wealthy, retired, unemployed, or doing hard time, you can become a Scrabble expert too. Here's how to get started.

Get over weird words

If you want to be really good at Scrabble, you have to accept the belief that words like EH (...Eh?), AGA (as in Aga Khan) and SENITI (a monetary unit of Tonga) are real words. If you fancy yourself a learned reader, you may be shocked to find onomatopoeic words like ARF ("woof!") are perfectly legal. Well, now hear this: If it has eight letters or fewer and is listed in the *Official Scrabble Players Dictionary*, it's a word—no matter what your fifth-grade English teacher told you. (The generally accepted source for longer words is *Merriam-Webster's Collegiate Dictionary*.)

Learn the twos

Perhaps the largest category of preposterous words is two-letter words. There are 96 of them. For the most part, the twos are surprisingly commonplace: musical scales—DO, RE, MI, FA, SO...; prepositions—TO, ON, OF, AT; expressions—HM (as in "I'm thinking..."), UM, OH. It seems, however, that to make the game more playable, dubious words were imported by the mouthful: AA (Hawaiian for "rough lava"), AE (Gaelic for "one"), NA (Scottish for "no") and OY (Yiddish for "ouch"). Whatever. If you want to get good at Scrabble, you have to learn all this nonsense. Knowing the short words will help you to rack up points by seeing parallel plays, where you form two or more words at once along two axes. According to the National Scrabble Association, learning the twos will increase your scoring by an average of 30 to 40 points per game.

Learn the Qs

Perhaps it goes without saying, but a stand-alone "Q" is the least valuable letter you can have on your rack. Get rid of Qs as fast as possible. Don't hang onto a Q in hopes of nabbing a "U" and creating a QUEENLY Q-word. Q without U? Yep. Actually, there are 21 Q-words without a U (for example, QAT, QANAT, FAQ IR, SUQ and—believe it or not, typists—QWERTY.) Memorize them, and your game will take another leap forward.

Learn the threes and fours

What next? The threes, of course. There are nearly 1,000 of them, with such gems as ADZ (wood-shaping tool), OOT (Canadian for "Scram!") and ULU (Eskimo knife). Most threes can be formed by adding a letter to one of the twos, making the two-letter words doubly versatile. Only two of the two-letter words cannot be converted into something (MY, XU). The short words containing J, Q, X and Z are particularly useful to know since they are high-scoring and can get you out of a jam.

There are around 1,200 fours. Unfortunately for those of you with a salty bent, most of the four-letter expletives have been deleted from the *Official Scrabble Players Dictionary*, although they are permitted in tournament play.

You can become a very good Scrabble player just by learning the short words. According to lexicographer Mike Baron, the twos, threes, and fours together, which account for only 5 percent of the dictionary, account for 75 percent of the words played in an average game and contribute almost half of the total score. But knowledge of the longer words is what separates the hacks from the pros. Longer words contain more points, and can span two premium squares (like double word or triple letter) for whopper scores. And the killer: emptying your rack of tiles, playing seven letters at a time—called a bingo—earns you a 50-point bonus. Repeated bingos are the key to winning Scrabble.

Learn the stems

The fastest way to generate more bingos is to learn the six-letter stems that generate multiple seven-letter words. Statistically, the most useful of them are SATINE, SATIRE and SANTER. There are approximately 200 useful six-letter stems. After you memorize those, in your spare time you can learn the seven-letter bingos. You may need to quit your day job, though: There are 21,734 of them.

Move the tiles

Rearrange the tiles constantly to help find more bingos. Look for common prefixes and suffixes and then set them off to the side. This practice will enhance your ability to form words because you can concentrate on fewer letters.

Practice anagramming

Shuffling the tiles on your rack will help you see more bingos, although shuffling them in your head is much faster. Anagramming is a skill possessed by all top Scrabble players. Mathematicians, musicians, and linguists are often natural anagrammers. With practice, you can teach your brain to do it, rearranging the letters until a new word falls out. Anagramming workbooks, computer programs, and flash cards will help make this task easier. Scrabble pros also use mnemonic devices and word association tricks to store and retrieve all this jabberwocky.

Manage your rack

Rack management is a key element of creating bingos. According to the National Scrabble Association, the most valuable letters (after the blank) are, in order, S, E, X, Z, R, A, H, N. The least valuable are Q, V, U, W, G, B, F, O, P. Try to get rid of high-value, problem letters as quickly as possible. If possible, save S, E, R, D, and Y to use as "hooks" on the front or back of other words on the board (example: READ becomes READY). And be sure to look one turn ahead: It's often preferable to put down a lower-scoring word if it leaves you with a better rack for the next turn.

The ideal ratio to maintain is four consonants to three vowels. In general, the only duplicate letters worth keeping are E and O. Retain useful prefixes such as OUT, RE, UN and PRE and suffixes such as ING, IER and EST. If you draw an unplayable rack, like UUQVVKZ, you are probably better off passing a turn and exchanging your rack for all new letters. In some cases, you are better off passing just to exchange three or four letters to clean up your rack.

Game tactics

Once you have memorized the twos, threes, fours, bingo stems, and a few thousand new 5-, 6-, and 7-letter words, you will be ready to try some game tactics.

- *Use hooks.* Hooks are words placed before or after other words to make new ones (B+ROOM = BROOM). The most common hook letter is the S, though every letter is a potential hook. For example, 16 new words can be created by adding 15 different letters to ALE. Knowing the hooks will open up opportunities on the board.

- *Track the letters.* Top players keep track of the letters that have been played so they know what combinations are left in the bag and their opponent's rack. Tracking sheets (legal in tournament play) contain a list of all the letters in the bag at the start of the game, which are crossed off as they are played. Letter tracking is especially valuable at the end of the game. For example, if you know the last letter in the bag is a Q, you may be better off passing your turn and making your opponent draw it.

- *Copy down your rack.* Write down all the tiles on your rack on each turn. After the game, you can analyze your play to see how many words you missed.

- *Play phonies.* Illegitimate words are perfectly legal in Scrabble unless they are challenged. If a word is challenged and turns out to be good, however, the challenger loses a turn. If you are playing a weaker opponent, try playing a phony early in the game. If it goes unchallenged, you have a green light to continue making mischief. On the other hand, if you get caught, your opponent may become suspicious enough to challenge perfectly good words, so you can win both ways.

- *Control the board.* Scrabble game boards are either "open" or "closed," depending upon how tightly spaced the words are. If you are leading in the game, you can limit your opponent's ability to catch up by playing shorter words, or by packing words more densely onto the game board. Conversely, if you are behind, you create more opportunities to lay down bingos and other high-scoring words by leaving the board more open. Be particularly careful about laying down easy-to-hook words next to bonus squares.

- *Jawbone.* Tournament players sometimes resort to the Scrabble equivalent of rattling ice while someone is putting: talking while your opponent is thinking, also known as "coffeehousing." Try humming "The Candy Man" to really get your opponent's goat.

In the end, no matter how many tactics you learn, to be a master Scrabble player you have to learn the words. Scrabble zealots often tote around notebooks filled with words to study. Others carry flash cards to test their anagramming ability. (For example, INSTEAD has four anagrams: DESTAIN, DETAINS, SAINTED and STAINED.) Canadian music professor Joel Wapnick, a former world champion, has memorized over 16,000 bingos. There's proof it can be done: Wall Street Journal sports reporter Stefan Fatsis, during just three years of competitive Scrabble, went from a ranking of about 2,000th to 180th in the country.

To get your competitive Scrabble career started, join the National Scrabble Association (annual dues: $18), P.O. Box 700, 403 Front Street, Greenport, NY 11944, (631) 477-0033, *www.scrabble-assoc.com*. The NSA sanctions tournaments, oversees more than 200 Scrabble clubs, and publishes the Scrabble News. It also maintains official ratings on each player (similar to those in chess), which range from 500 to over 2,000. Players with ratings over 1,800 are considered experts.

If you aspire to play in international tournaments, you will have to learn the British sourcebook, *Official Scrabble Words*, which contains words like VOZHD (supreme leader of Russia), Brian Cappelletto's play in the 2001 World Scrabble Championship finals. For a Scrabble champ it's just another DARG. In Scottish that means day's work.

How to prevent mosquito bites

Ants may be more common visitors to a picnic, but mosquitoes are surely more annoying guests—and dangerous too. Besides the irritation of mosquito bites, the pesky buggers can transmit all sorts of deadly diseases, including malaria, yellow fever, and the latest scourge to hit the United States, West Nile Virus. The good news is properly used repellents will prevent over 95 percent of mosquito bites.

A little mosquito entomology

There are nearly 3,000 different species of mosquitoes (about 150 in North America). Only female mosquitoes bite. Females draw blood to produce eggs, which they lay in standing water. Eggs can also lay dormant in soil for up to four years, waiting for a good rain to activate them. Within two to three days, the eggs hatch into larvae. About a week later the larvae morph into pupae, from which adult mosquitoes emerge a few days later by popping out of their pupal skins and flying off. Oils, larvicides, and detergents sprayed into mosquito breeding water are of some value, but a simpler, more effective means of abatement is to dump over containers of standing water. Birdbaths, kiddie pools, and junkyards full of old tires are especially popular nurseries for the little blighters.

Most species are active at dusk and dawn, but some bite right through the day. Mosquitoes are nearsighted. Targets are identified by movement and dark colors (tip: wear light clothing to make yourself harder to spot). After they get within 100 feet, mosquitoes locate their targets using tiny sensory receptors on their antennae that detect exhaled carbon dioxide and lactic acid. The skeeters then fly towards their targets, seeking out a telltale halo of warm, moist air surrounding the body—the sign of a living being. Mosquitoes then use their chemoreceptors to plop down on the involuntary blood donor. Although scientists have spent a lot of time trying to figure out why some people taste better, about all they have determined is that mosquitoes are finicky connoisseurs of human sweat.

Forget about frying 'em

Research has shown that bug zappers, including models marketed as mosquito killers, are worthless against mosquitoes, which favor carbon dioxide over fluorescent light. A 1996 study published in *Entomology News* found that fewer than one percent of the insects killed by bug zappers are biting insects.

Bats eat them, just not enough

The creepy bat has made a resurgence in recent years, as bat conservation groups have extolled its insectivorous nature as good for mankind. True, some bats are voracious mosquito eaters, but many others would rather dine on moths and mayflies. There are simply too many mosquitoes for bats to eat them all. Even a large, guano-producing bat colony in your backyard will not rid your barbecue of mosquitoes.

Purple martins also have been promoted as mosquito eliminators by (surprise!) companies that sell purple martin houses. The problem is that purple martins feed during the day when most mosquitoes are lying low, and aren't particularly fond of mosquitoes to begin with.

How repellents work

Think of your body as an airport and exposed flesh as the runway. What repellents do is make the runway invisible: Mosquitoes come in for a final approach and suddenly fog is covering their landing strip. Thus for repellents to work they must completely cover any exposed skin. Leaving a six-inch strip of skin free is like turning on the landing lights and inviting mosquitoes down for a Bloody Mary in the Admiral's Club.

The most powerful insect repellent available is N,N-diethyl-3-methylbenzamide, commonly known as DEET, available in various formulations (including aerosols, pump sprays, lotions, and gels). It is available in concentrations ranging from 5 percent up to 100 percent, but research has shown that it's effectiveness tends to plateau at about 50 percent strength. Depending upon the species of mosquito it's used against, 35-percent DEET can reach 12 hours of effectiveness. Dr. Mark Fradin, a dermatologist who has extensively studied mosquito repellents, suggests using 10-percent to 35-percent DEET for general use, and 50-percent DEET for jungle-like conditions.

The United States military's standard insect repellent is a time-release formula of 35 percent DEET produced by 3M and sold under the brand name Ultrathon. It can be purchased from SCS Limited, (800) 749-8425, or online from Travel Medicine, *www.travmed.com*. Over-the-counter products containing DEET in higher strengths include Off! Deep Woods for Sportsmen (100% concentration); Muskol Ultra 6 Hours (40%); Off! Deep Woods (23.8%); BugOut (15%); and Cutter Unscented (10%).

DEET is remarkably safe when properly used. It has been used by hundreds of millions of people worldwide for over 40 years, with only a handful of adverse cases. Still, follow the directions carefully and never spray the stuff into your face or eyes. One cautionary note: The American Academy of Pediatrics recommends a maximum concentration of 10 percent DEET for young children.

DEET can be applied to clothing and is safe on natural fibers and nylon. On the minus side, it can damage rayons and other synthetic fabrics, melt plastic eyeglass frames and destroy plastic watch crystals. DEET also tends to break down at higher temperatures and can be sweated off or washed off in the rain.

Accept no substitutes

In a clinical study by Dr. Fradin and John F. Day, Ph.D. published in the *New England Journal of Medicine*, none of the various essential oils marketed as insect repellents, including citronella, lemon eucalyptus, and soybean oil offered protection longer than two hours. The effectiveness of citronella candles is particularly overhyped. In a field trial in Canada, citronella candles were shown to reduce biting by 40 percent—good for shooing the mosquitoes to the next picnic, but not an effective shield without repellent. Wristbands impregnated with citronella may be considered stylish in some quarters, but they do nothing to prevent mosquito bites. Also, forget about Avon's Skin-So-Soft Bug Guard, marketed as a combination skin lotion and repellent; it might make your skin supple as a baby's bottom, yet Fradin's study showed it will only save you from mosquitoes for about 10 minutes. (Avon disputes Fradin's findings and claims Skin-So-Soft Bug Guard Plus IR3535 was proven effective for up to three hours in field tests submitted to the Environmental Protection Agency.)

Serious skeeter protection

If you're the sort of person who prefers the belt-and-suspenders approach, or are planning a trip to the North Woods, carry permethrin. Made from crushed chrysanthemums, permethrin is a powerful knockdown agent that kills mosquitoes and other annoying insects on contact. In a field experiment conducted in Alaska, one group used 35-percent DEET and permethrin-treated clothing and another group had no protection. The first group was virtually unbitten, while the unfortunate second group received an average of 1,200 bites per hour!

Unlike repellents, permethrin is used to treat clothing, mosquito netting or tents, and should never be applied to the skin. It is odorless, non-staining, and remains potent even after two washings (tents need only be treated once a year). Clothes sprayed with permethrin should be allowed to dry before they are worn. Permethrin is available commercially as Repel

Permanone in a 0.5% solution and from Fite Bite in a 35% concentrate form that is diluted with water.

Chemical sprays give you the heebies? See below for what to do when you get bitten.

Bites swell up and itch because of the body's reaction to the mosquito's saliva injected under the skin when blood is drawn. Drugstore remedies like corticosteroid ointments and calamine lotion offer post-bite relief, while over-the-counter antihistamines have been shown to reduce swelling when taken prophylactically. If you are particularly sensitive, ebastine has been shown in clinical trials to provide effective relief (available by prescription as Ebastel).

Some folks in mosquito country have decided that to itch is divine. The Great Texas Mosquito Festival is held each year during the last weekend in July in the town of Clute. Among its many activities is a mosquito calling contest. First prize is a mosquito trophy made out of a spark plug, ball bearings, and horseshoe nails.

How to choose a fast food

Would you like extra-tallow fries with that double-fat greaseburger? How about a supersize high fructose corn syrup "McSlurry" shake? A no-calorie prebagged garden salad straight from the distributor with creamy garlic "diet devastator" dressing? No? Well, could we interest you in a plain baked potato?

Now you're talking.

Hoo boy! Waistline watchers beware: It's a diet minefield out there in the land of fast food. Americans love their fat, sweets, and salt and hate skimpy portions. And the kindly folks at McDonald's, Burger King, Popeye's and the other fast food chains will gladly ensure you get what you want, though not necessarily what you need.

We needn't recite the ills of an unbalanced diet here, and those of you succumbing to the latest diet fad are, at least temporarily, beyond hope. But the rest of you sensible eaters could profit from a little truth-in-eating.

Plain hamburgers (either broiled or fried on a griddle) are actually pretty lean and much better for you than any kind of burger with bacon or cheese. Likewise, unbreaded skinless chicken sandwiches are much lower in fat and calories than fried chicken patties, tenders, or nuggets. Naturally, french fries absorb a lot of oil too, but their sodium content is surprisingly low since only a small amount of salt actually sticks to the fries. (The real sodium killers are processed meats like ham, sausage, and bacon.)

Don't overlook the beverages either, especially those swimming pool-sized fountain drinks; each extra-large 42-ounce soda contains 500 calories. Shakes are a slight improvement over sodas; a small vanilla milkshake is a low-fat alternative to a side order of onion rings or fries. A Wendy's 12-ounce Frosty has 330 calories and only eight grams of fat. Only don't make a habit of it if you plan on keeping your natural teeth: Each one contains 11 teaspoons of sugar.

As a general dictum, the best-tasting stuff is awful for you and the bland things are only recommended by do-gooder nutritionists who obviously never tried the McLean sandwich. The three most healthful menu items in most fast food restaurants are baked potatoes, salads (with low-cal dressing), and hamburger buns.

But let's not be all fog and drizzle here. If you look hard enough, you'll find that fast doesn't necessarily equal bad. The menus have gotten too large for us to survey everything, but here is a brief tour of that great American invention, fast food.

McDonald's

If you grew up saying "two-all-beef-patties-special-sauce-lettuce-cheese-pickles-onions-on-a-sesame-seed-bun," (thank you, DDB Needham) you may still think of McDonald's as the primal source for hot junk food. But the ubiquitous Golden Arches have gotten considerably slimmer over the years. No longer are the fries cooked in beef tallow (purists say they don't taste as good either), apple pies are baked, salads are on the menu everywhere, and at certain McDonald's we've even seen carrot sticks and celery. In fact, some new menu items are almost, well...nutritious. *Sacre bleu!* Still, dieticians need not fear losing their favorite nemesis; in 2001, some McDonald's stores added bratwurst to their menus.

If taste is no object

McDonald's "breakthrough" product from 1991, the McLean Deluxe, was a marketing disaster. McDonald's apparently learned its lesson and is restricting vegetables to salads. The calorie- and fat-conscious consumer could do worse than Micky D's salads. They are all benign, low in fat and calories, if a bit on the bland side. Steer clear of honey mustard, ranch, and Caesar dressings, which each contain more fat than a small order of french fries. Fat-free vinaigrette is the waist-watcher's best call.

Better than you thought

The plain old McDonald's hamburger is relatively low in fat (nine grams) and only has 255 calories. A little small for a big appetite? Have two—you get the same amount of calories as a Quarter Pounder with Cheese and about one-third less fat.

You knew it was bad for you

Okay, the Big Mac does have a certain consumer appeal, especially with 300-pound offensive linemen. But why stop there? McDonald's is starting an aggressive national marketing campaign for the Big Mac's chubby brother, the Big N' Tasty. One Big N' Tasty with Cheese sports an eye-popping 590 calories (over half from fat), a big dose of salt, and 95 milligrams of cholesterol (equal to half an egg).

But not this bad

The Spanish Omelet Bagel is a whale of a way to start your day. It packs 690 calories, 38 grams of fat (14 of which are saturated), 1,570 milligrams of sodium (equivalent to four Super Size orders of french fries) and 275 milligrams of cholesterol (a whole day's supply). Though it's called a breakfast item, this stomach brick should get you through lunch, too.

Wendy's

"Where's the beef?" Where it always was: stuck in between two buns, dripping meat juice on your chin. But it's a good question nowadays at Wendy's, which has steadily moved into more adventuresome and beef-less menu items, like the big-selling Mandarin Chicken Salad. Wendy's diverse menu offers a wide range of salutary options, and a few that could make Fat Albert blanch.

If taste is no object

A plain baked potato, loaded with potassium and vitamin C, delivers a virtually fat-free lunch. Go ahead a put a little margarine on it—you'll still only have seven grams of fat and the same amount of calories as a small hamburger. But don't fall off the wagon by piling on the sour cream.

Better than you thought

Wendy's large chili weighs in at three-quarters of a pound and offers a filling lunch at 310 calories. Yet it's low in fat (only 10 grams) and high in fiber, thanks to the kidney beans. Saltines are a good meal extender at 25 calories a pack with virtually no fat.

You knew it was bad for you

The Big Bacon Classic is definitely big, comprising a quarter-pound hamburger, bacon, cheese, and fixin's. But the only thing classic about this sandwich is its bell-ringing amount of calories (570), not to mention fat (29 grams), cholesterol (100 milligrams), and sodium (1,460 milligrams).

But not this bad

The real gutbuster on the Wendy's menu isn't a sandwich, it's the potato-jacketed caloric bomb known as the Chili & Cheese Baked Potato. With twice the calories (630) of a plain baked potato and double the fat (24 grams) of even a potato with margarine and sour cream, this spud has been adulterated almost beyond recognition.

Kentucky Fried Chicken

In his book *Big Secrets*, William Poundstone claimed KFC's formula for batter containing "11 secret herbs and spices" is nothing more than salt, black pepper, flour, and monosodium glutamate. *Mon dieux!* The good Colonel Sanders turned millions of people into MSG junkies? We're not buying it—fat junkies, maybe.

MSG or not, the dangers of fried food have been well-known for decades, as Satchel Paige said in his biography in 1953, "Avoid fried meats, which angry up the blood." Well the Colonel is long gone, but his finger-lickin' fried chicken is still with us, working its magic on a new generation of arteries. KFC may be the most unreconstructed of all the big fast food purveyors, but at least it's consistent. And if you hunt around you can even find some menu items that won't raise your blood pressure.

If taste is no object

Mashed potatoes and gravy are a good choice in most fast food places that offer them. They are relatively high in nutrients and low in calories and fat—even with gravy poured on top. The taste, however, sometimes leaves a little to be desired. Even Colonel Sanders didn't care for KFC's mashed potatoes, once pronouncing them "sludge" and saying the gravy had begun to "look and taste like wallpaper paste," These remarks, uttered after the Colonel had sold his company, triggered a libel suit in Kentucky court that was later dismissed as groundless. (Whether his comment was unfair to wallpaper paste did not come up.) Still, if you can choke them down, KFC's mashed potatoes will only cost you 120 calories and six grams of fat.

Better than you thought

The Tender Roast sandwich (without sauce) is a satisfying mouthful at 270 calories, but only has 5 grams of fat and is relatively low in cholesterol. It even tastes pretty good.

You knew it was bad for you

Anything given away by taverns to entice people to drink more beer is hard to take seriously as a restaurant item. Take spicy chicken wings, for example. The KFC version, called Hot Wings, is a scrawny, six-piece appetizer weighing about as much as one chicken breast. But Hot Wings are so greasy they pack in 471 calories (63 percent from fat). Each order supplies half your daily allowance of both fat (33 grams) and cholesterol (150 milligrams). For goodnessake don't dunk them in ranch dressing.

But not this bad

The lowly pot pie may not be on the menu at Cordon Bleu, but it's supposed to be comfort food that's good for you—you know: chicken, flour, carrots, peas, onions. We're not sure how they did it, but KFC managed to make a pot pie that is 50 percent fat. The Chunky Chicken Pot Pie weighs as much as two hockey pucks and offers up a mean 770 calories, 42 grams of fat (13 grams of saturated fat), and 2,160 milligrams of sodium.

Taco Bell

What can we say about the chain that made Mexican food synonymous with bad tacos? *"Yo quiero Taco Bell?" Necesito Maalox!*

If taste is no object

The Soft Taco with Chicken is low in calories (190), fat (7 grams), and cholesterol (35 milligrams). To us, though, the rubbery chicken tastes like a soft-shell wiper blade.

Better than you thought

The Bean Burrito and Fiesta Burrito are the best calls on the menu, with slightly under 400 calories and 12 to 15 grams of fat apiece. Of course, it's the musical fruit that we have to thank for that.

You knew it was bad for you

Who is kidding whom about these taco "salads"? Okay, you can poke around and find a few tomatoes and some lettuce. But mostly what you'll find is a deep-fried taco shell and greasy ground beef. At a whopping 850 calories, one Taco Bell salad is equivalent to eating four tacos. Order it without the shell and you peel off 450 calories and 30 grams of fat.

But not this bad

This one is not even close. Taco Bell's pound-and-a-half, 1,320-calorie Mucho Grande Nachos are simply too mucho. If you can polish off an order of the cheesy nachos, congratulations: You have just consumed over a day's worth of fat (82 grams), saturated fat (25 grams) and sodium (2,670 milligrams). Can you say arteriosclerosis in Spanish?

Burger King

Customers have been having it their way at Burger King since 1954. According to the company's Website, there are 1,537 different ways to order a Whopper. Care to guess how many ways are low in fat?

If taste is no object

Like McDonald's, Burger King's salads are safe to eat if you opt for low-cal dressing. But unlike McDonald's, Burger King still thinks it can inoculate itself against hamburger bashers with a vegetable burger. BK's Veggie Burger scores predictably low in fat and cholesterol yet still has enough calories (330) to fill you up—that is, if you can get one of these things down.

Better than you thought

The broiled Chicken Whopper Jr. packs in a satisfying 350 calories, offset by only 14 grams of fat. Hold the mayo and you'll shave off 80 calories and over half the fat.

You knew it was bad for you

The eggy, gooey Croissan'wich with Sausage, Egg, & Cheese sounds as gross as it is: 520 calories, 39 grams of fat (14 saturated), 210 milligrams of cholesterol and 1,090 milligrams of sodium. Ask for a side order of arterial stents.

But not this bad

When you say "Double Whopper with cheese" you've said a mouthful. This sandwich has more fat (76 grams) than two orders of King-size fries, more saturated fat (30 grams) than four Egg'wiches with Egg & Cheese, and the same amount of calories (1,150) as two Bacon Double Cheeseburgers. (Burp!)

Cinnabon

People love Cinnabon. Cinnabon's sticky buns are huge, decadent, and covered in cream cheese frosting. The chain expects to sell its billionth cinnamon roll by 2004, about the time stretch pants will be making a big rebound.

If taste is no object

If you stumble into a Cinnabon "with a face as white as death," as Larry Groce put it in "Junk Food Junkie," you're really stuck. The smell is intoxicating, everything tastes good, and nothing is low in calories or fat. So try our four-step program: (1) Order one Minibon (the smallest roll on the menu); (2) Cut it in half; (3) Take a bite of each half; (4) Throw both halves away.

Better than you thought

CinnabonStix, introduced in 2000, were actually the first "hand-held" Cinnabon product. (Is it a cell phone or is it food?) While not exactly nutritious, the other items on the Cinnabon menu are so fattening that the CinnabonStix's 346 calories and 11 grams of fat actually qualify as reasonable.

You knew it was bad for you

Cinnabon's signature roll is so rotund it could double as a shot put. At half a pound, the Cinnabon is a sugar and fat intestinal exploder that yields 670 calories and 34 grams of fat, more of both than a Pizza Hut Personal Pan Supreme pizza.

But not this bad

The Caramel Pecanbon was recently named "Food Porn" by the Center for Science in the Public Interest—and for good reason. This gooey dieter's nightmare has 900 calories and 41 grams of fat. Help your cardiologist make his boat payments by ordering one today.

How to remove a fishhook

It's not as tough as it looks. If the barb is visible, simply snip it off with wire cutters and back out the hook.

The advance-and-cut method is used for fishhooks that are in really deep. In this method, the barb of the hook is pushed forward (further in) until it sticks out the other side. The barb of the hook is then snipped off with wire cutters and the hook is backed out. Because of the additional tissue damage and pain it causes, this method is best left to a trained physician using an anesthetic. We don't recommend non-physicians trying it. However, if the barb of the hook is stuck in the skin superficially, the safest, quickest, and most painless removal method is the string-yank technique. This method has been successfully used for years by both emergency room physicians and fishermen at streamside. Caution: Do not use this method if you have hooked any part of your face, head, or neck.

Here are step-by-step instructions to unhook yourself:

1. Cut off the fishing line from the hook.
2. Get a shoelace, piece of fly line, or thin rope about three feet long.
3. Form a slipknot at the end of the line and position the loop of the knot around the bend of the hook. Pull it just snug enough so it doesn't slip off the bend.
4. If you have protective eyeglasses or goggles, put them on.
5. Mash down on the eye of the hook as hard as you can using your thumb.
6. While maintaining downward pressure on the hook eye, use your other hand to jerk the line sharply in the opposite direction of the barb. Turn your head away to avoid getting hooked in the face.
7. The hook should pop out from the wound the same way it went in.
8. Dress the wound using an antibiotic and bandage.
9. If you haven't had a tetanus shot in the past five years or can't remember when your last one was, go get one as soon as possible.
10. Invent a story about how a large fish drove the hook into your skin, to save yourself from embarrassment.

How to avoid catching a cold

Sorry, there is still no cure, but medical research has shed some light on how the common cold is spread. After reading this, you may never think of shaking hands in the same way again.

For centuries, colds were thought to be caused by mean winds. It wasn't until World War I that modern scientists began to question the notion of whether chills cause colds. Researchers have since spent 80 years and traveled as far as the North Pole in search of answers. And despite the mounds of scientific evidence they have gathered, folk prescriptions still predominate.

The Myths

Your mother may not like it, but her advice was probably wrong. Here are some of the myths researchers have exposed.

- *Being chilled to the bone will make you catch a cold.* Although going out without a hat in the middle of winter may be stupid, it won't make you any more likely to catch a cold. Large-scale experiments were conducted in England and Chicago during the 1950s and 1960s in which people were made to stand around practically naked and wet in a chilly room. After they were thoroughly miserable, the subjects were nasally injected with cold virus. Control groups kept nice and toasty were also injected. Guess what? About the same number of each group caught colds.

- *Cold viruses are more active during the winter months.* In fact, although the cold season runs from September through April, cold viruses are active year-round. The reason people catch colds more readily during the winter is because they spend more time indoors with other people who are infected.

- *You can develop immunity to colds.* The common cold is caused by a number of virus families (principally rhinovirus) that comprise over 200 individual viruses. While you can develop temporary immunity to certain cold viruses after suffering through them, it is impossible to develop immunity to them all.

- *Colds can be prevented or treated with antibiotics.* Antibiotics only work on bacteria, not viruses. Overprescription of antibiotics has become a serious health concern.

- *Massive doses of vitamin C will stave off a cold.* Few medical theories have been subject to more scrutiny than Linus Pauling's famous 1971 claim that vitamin C was a preventive for the common cold. Thirty years and hundreds of clinical studies later, the evidence suggests vitamin C, even in massive doses of up to 3,000 milligrams a day, does nothing to prevent a cold. Some clinical trials have shown the symptoms of a cold can be lessened by taking large doses of vitamin C after you feel a cold coming on, though researchers disagree about this. Sorry, Linus.

- *Zinc will prevent a cold and lessen its symptoms.* Nope, afraid not, although zinc tablets do make everything you eat taste like pocket change.

- *You can catch a cold by kissing.* Research has shown that exchanging spit with a cold sufferer won't infect you unless you manage to somehow get it up your nose.

- *Colds are spread primarily through the air.* Extensive clinical tests by Jack M. Gwaltney, M.D. (a.k.a. "Dr. Cold.") and his colleagues at the University of Virginia School of Medicine in Charlottesville have proven conclusively that virus is spread primarily through direct contact with the hands. Although it is possible to be infected through coughs and sneezes, the main method of cold transmission is filthy paws.

How to (Mostly) Avoid a Cold

Follow the advice below and you may be able to keep from catching the average three to six colds a year most adults get.

- Wash your hands frequently. Use ordinary soap and scrub thoroughly (it's the rubbing motion that gets the virus off, not the soap). Research has shown cold viruses can live for hours on nonporous surfaces like countertops. Drinking fountains, turnstiles, keyboards, and telephones are all bug transfer stations. Avoid shaking hands with people who have colds. And keep your mitts out of those office candy jars.

- Keep your hands away from your eyes and nose. Hidden observation studies show people rub their eyes and pick their noses with surprising frequency. Cold virus works by getting into the upper reaches of your nasal cavity. Virus can get in from the top, by sliding down the tear ducts in the corners of your eyes, or from the bottom, with a helpful boost from a finger. If you're a picker, at least wash your hands before. Come to think of it, wash your hands after, too.

- Use disposable tissues instead of handkerchiefs. The trouble with hankies is that you use them a couple of times and they get wet. Next time you draw your handkerchief out of your pocket guess what's on your hands? Yuck! Do the rest of us a favor and use a Kleenex instead.

- Wash towels frequently. Although cold viruses have a short life if allowed to dry out on a cloth surface, they find moist towels a comfortable place to live and a perfect hiding place to infect the next victim.
- Don't fly if you can avoid it. Flying on a commercial airplane, especially on a long-haul flight, has another bonus besides cramped seats and long delays—colds. Researchers at the University of California-San Francisco found that one out of five passengers reported developing a cold within one week after flying.
- Drink red wine. Several studies have found links between moderate drinking of alcoholic beverages and cold protection. A recent study in the *American Journal of Epidemiology* concluded people who drank an average of two or more glasses of red wine a day were less likely to be infected by the common cold than teetotalers or beer or spirits drinkers.
- Stay away from babies and small children with runny noses. Need we say more?

When the inevitable occurs

In lieu of a cure, scientific studies have been conducted to determine which treatments are most effective. A team of University of Virginia researchers led by Dr. Gwaltney recently reported in the *Journal of Infectious Diseases* that the combined treatment of intranasal interferon, chlorpheniramine (an antihistamine), and a non-steroidal anti-inflammatory (ibuprofen, naproxen), taken during the early stages of illness, significantly reduced the severity of major cold symptoms.

Gwaltney and other physicians say to avoid multisymptom cold relievers and take medication specifically for your symptoms. Gwaltney's own remedy: As soon as you sense a cold coming on, start taking ibuprofen to cut down on aches and coughing, and a first-generation antihistamine (the kind that makes you drowsy, such as Chlor-Trimeton, Dimetapp, Tavist) to reduce sneezing and runny nose. Gwaltney's research indicates newer, non-sedating antihistamines like Claritin and Allegra are not as effective on cold symptoms as the older kind.

Remember, if you treat a cold, it will last a week. If you don't, it will last seven days—any longer and you should see your doctor: You probably have the flu.

How to permanently cure a slice

"Lay off for a few weeks and then quit for good."

—Sam Snead

How to tell if you are getting fat

America has become a nation of chunky monkeys. According to the Surgeon General's office, over 60 percent of the adult population is now overweight and obesity may soon surpass smoking as the leading cause of preventable death in this country. In one of his last public statements prior to leaving office, former Surgeon General David Satcher called on Americans to eat sensibly, avoid diet fads, and get off their duffs. "This is probably the most sedentary generation of people in the history of the world," he proclaimed.

Et tu, Brutus? Are your love handles becoming a bit too...handy? Saddlebags bigger than your handbags? Because muscle weighs more than fat, the bathroom scale can only tell you so much. To find out for sure if you've joined the ranks of the porky, you need to find out your body fat percentage.

Physicians and many health clubs can evaluate your body fat using precise measuring techniques, such as underwater weighing and air displacement analysis. For most people, though, simple skinfold calipers are plenty accurate (to within 4 percent). Plus, even high-quality calipers are relatively inexpensive (about $100), and can be used without embarrassment in the privacy of your home.

Skinfold calipers are used by clamping onto a chunk of skin just above your hipbone. The thickness reading is converted into body fat percentage by using a simple table. For adult males a range between 9 percent and 18 percent is generally considered normal; for females the range is 18 percent to 24 percent. The old "pinch-an-inch" rule is actually way off. One inch of skinfold between the calipers equates to over 20 percent body fat in an adult male and over 30 percent body fat in an adult female.

You can order a set of calipers from Accu-Measure, in Englewood, Colorado, (800) 866-2727, *www.accumeasurefitness.com*.

If you just want to get an idea of whether you are overweight or not, there is a simple calculation called the Body Mass Index, or BMI. The BMI was developed by the National Institutes of Health as a quick way to tell people they need to cut out the Chubby Hubby.

Here it is:

1. Multiply your weight in pounds by 703.
2. Square your height in inches.
3. Divide (1) by (2) to get your BMI.

Government guidelines are as follows:

	BMI Score
Underweight:	Less than 18.5
Normal weight:	18.5 - 24.9
Overweight:	25.0 - 29.9
Obese:	30.0 - 39.9
Extremely obese:	Greater than 40

Now that you know how to calculate it, what you do with this valuable information is entirely your business.

How to get rid of a fruitcake

Of course, the time-honored method for ridding yourself of that dreaded 5-pound holiday confection is to pass it on to someone else, more or less uneaten. There is, however, another way that is far more satisfying: violent disintegration.

If you plan to be in the vicinity of Colorado Springs during the month of January, be sure to bring along your Aunt Mabel's homemade doorstop for the annual Manitou Springs Great Fruitcake Toss. During this exciting event, contestants toss, hurl, launch, and drive (as in with a driver...Fore!) fruitcakes for distance. Fruitcakes must be made from flour, fruit, and nuts and may not contain inedible ingredients (as to whether the cake itself is edible, that's another story). If you forget your fruitcake or it gets eaten by rodents on the way, you can "rent" one for 50 cents.

If you are a mechanical engineer or spent quality time in a fraternity house, you may want to consider the launch competition. In the launch, competitors use homemade human-powered devices, ranging from medieval-style catapults to water balloon slingshots, to bombard greater Manitou Springs with stale fruitcake.

The contest is held in Memorial Park, near City Hall, on the first week-end following New Year's. Admission is free. Be sure to park at least a block away. Last year's winning toss was over 300 feet.

How to become a billionaire

"Rise early. Work late. Strike oil."

—J. Paul Getty

How to train a basset hound

One doesn't so much train a basset hound as influence it. Bassets do not (reliably) fetch, do tricks, or even walk in a straight line. Their low centers of gravity, deceptive strength, and willful attitudes can make bassets a handful on a walk. But do not mistake a basset's stubbornness for stupidity. Like all scent hounds, bassets simply have their own agenda. Most of the time they follow their noses, though they are occasionally tempted to go see other dogs, play, or just do nothing. Bassets are highly analytical creatures. They constantly weigh their various options and select the one offering them maximum enjoyment. It may turn out after careful review, for example, that laying down on the sidewalk during the middle of a walk is the best option. Such unpredictable behavior, which is hard-wired into the basset's DNA, makes the basset hound a very poor choice for people with limited patience. On the other hand, bassets are mild-tempered, gentle with children, affectionate, and utterly hilarious.

Bassets love to forage for leftovers. This is the natural outcome of breeding generations of bassets who are unaware they are supposed to sniff out rabbits for a living. Unless you take your dog hunting regularly, it's a good bet he believes the walk is the hunt and the prey is a half-eaten ham sandwich or a stray Oreo. This curse is also the blessing that makes life with a basset bearable. Pay close attention and we will now reveal the secret to training a basset hound.

Ready. Okay, here it is...

Food.

Come? Food.

Sit? Food.

Heel? Food.

Housebreaking? Food—and use a crate, too.

Chewing? Tape old carpeting around your furniture legs and hide your slippers. Sorry.

The particular food is up to you, but we recommend cheddar Goldfish, peanuts, croutons, saltines, raisins, and cereal. If you are out of human food, dog biscuits will work, though not as well. Food should be awarded whenever your dog does what he's supposed to. Be consistent or you'll send mixed signals (and invite perpetual begging). Don't give your dog a treat just because "he looks like he needs one" (he always needs one, and bassets actually practice that woebegone expression while you're out—they're slyer than you think). Plus, fat bassets have back problems and shortened life spans.

Always use positive reinforcement. Never hit a basset hound. A short, firm scolding "No!" for misbehavior will accomplish far more than corporal punishment. Reward the good behavior and ignore the bad. Soon enough your basset will be putty in your hands.

Just don't run out of cheddar Goldfish.

How to listen in on the CIA

You might think that in this era of wireless e-mail something as trailing edge as shortwave radio would be left out of the spook's field pack, alongside the Minox spy camera and the self-destructing tape recorder. Not so. Although the CIA, NSA, and various covert ops divisions of the United States military have surely upgraded to better gadgets than these, shortwave radio is still widely used by United States and foreign intelligence agencies to communicate with agents in the field. It's inexpensive, portable, reliable, and can be heard around the globe. In all likelihood, even as you read this, somewhere in the world an intelligence agent is secretly transmitting an enigmatic sequence of numbers into the ionosphere.

According to insiders, these numeric transmissions are jotted down by recipients who pick up the signals at preordained times. They are then decoded into important messages ("The Eagle has landed." "Meet me at 0800 hours." "Your dry cleaning is ready") using what is known as a one-time pad, with a different code for each day. Because the code is used only once, it is impossible for counterspies to break. Some CIA agents reportedly eat the pages when they're finished with them (high in fiber and low in fat).

Although the Agency and its overseas cousins, MI6, the Mossad, and others will not even confirm these stations exist, there are plenty of short-wave hobbyists with tape recordings to prove otherwise. Some begin with tones, whistles, Atencion! or Achtung! Others play the beginning of a popu-lar melody. Most numbers stations use a female voice. Avid shortwave listen-ers, known as DXers, have even nicknamed the announcers (Bulgarian Betty, Sexy Lady, Russian Man, etc.). Numbers are typically read in blocks of five, sometimes with a pause between the third and fourth digit.

Shortwave being an equal opportunity medium, anyone with a set can listen. If you need a new hobby, buy yourself a shortwave radio with a good tuner and a strong antenna. You don't need to spend a fortune. Even an inexpensive shortwave radio (less than $200) will do the job. Numbers stations can be located by methodically tuning outside the normal com-mercial bands. North American listeners will find more numbers stations on the air during the evening hours.

In addition, DXers have carefully compiled lists of numbers stations' frequencies, transmission dates, times, and educated guesses about who is doing the broadcasting. For an exhaustive listing of numbers stations by time of broadcast (always given in Greenwich Mean Time) see *www.spynumbers.com*. If you have no luck getting a numbers station to come in or don't want to buy a shortwave set, go to *http://home.freeuk.com/spook007/* to listen to sample recordings.

Of course, without a decoder pad, these numbers are just gibberish. Even with one they may turn out to be gibberish, too, a sort of Hardy Boys caper for adults. Only the spies know...and they're not telling.

How to allocate your assets

"A stockbroker is someone who keeps investing your money until it's gone."
—Woody Allen

Stop investing for your stockbroker's retirement and start investing for yours. Armed with the basics of asset allocation, chances are your investment decisions will turn out better than your broker's. Plus, you'll sleep better knowing that a 29-year-old "financial consultant" isn't holding your retirement in the palm of his hand.

Modern portfolio theory was first asserted in 1952 by Nobel Prize winner Harry Markowitz, who posited that investment risk could be minimized by holding stocks that tended to move in opposite directions. Later research found that by adding bonds and cash in the right proportions, an investment portfolio will produce smoother returns with less risk over the long run than a randomly assembled one. Here's how to do it.

Stocks

The bedrock of every portfolio is common stock. Since World War II, stocks, have earned about 8 percent more than bonds. Although bear markets will pop up every now and then, over the long haul you will be much better off with an equity-stuffed portfolio.

Statistics show you need a minimum of 20 stocks for a well-diversified portfolio. But if all 20 are in technology, you may as well fly down to Las Vegas and put all your money on red. The key is to get a cross-section of industrial, consumer, technology, transportation, retail, financial, energy, real estate, and utility stocks. Healthcare, utilities, and consumer staples all tend to weather recessions well. Cyclicals, like automakers, airlines, and retailers, suffer during recessions but make up for it when times are good. Financials, energy stocks, and real estate investment trusts (REITs) are driven by other factors, such as interest rates and oil prices, and hence are useful for balancing cyclicals. You also need a blend of large-, medium-, and small-cap stocks to militate against Wall Street's narrow attention span, which is seldom able to focus on more than one size company at a time.

Investing in foreign stocks is a mostly overlooked diversification play. American stocks are easier to get information on, understand, and trade. But international equities offer good diversification with mitigated risk due to the stabilizing effect of exchange rates. Statistics show that devoting as little as 25 percent of your equity portfolio to international stocks will lower overall risk without appreciably affecting returns. Many foreign companies trade over the counter with ADRs (American Depositary Receipts), and some are jointly listed on the New York Stock Exchange and overseas exchanges. If you don't want to go to the trouble of looking them up, buy an international mutual fund or two. Be leery of developing markets like China, Russia, and Latin America, where investors have already been burned a few times.

Probably the best way to ensure that your stocks do well over the long haul is to buy them when they are undervalued. Easier said than done, but there are good barometers. Price-to-earnings (P/E) ratio is one. If the stock's P/E is much higher than its industry peers, chances are it is not undervalued and is, at best, fairly valued. Look for quality companies selling at relatively low P/Es for transient reasons (economic cycles, short-term earnings concerns, etc.). If you start out with an expensive stock, there is a greater chance it will fail to meet the market's expectations. Don't bet your whole retirement on a biotech start-up.

Another useful measure is the P/E to earnings growth, or PEG ratio, which compares the relative price to the earnings growth you are getting. The PEG ratio is good for apples-to-apples comparisons of expensive stocks with cheap ones. For example, if Oracle sells for 50 times next year's earnings and long-term earnings growth projections are 25 percent, it trades for a PEG of 50/25 = 2.0. Compare that with IBM trading at, say, 30 times forward earnings and long-term growth estimates of 10 percent, for a PEG of 30/10 = 3.0. On that basis, the nominally more expensive Oracle, selling for 50 times earnings, is cheaper than IBM selling at 30 times. You can get forward earnings estimates and long-term growth projections at the Zacks investor Website, *http://my.zacks.com*.

One other nugget of wisdom: Never confuse asset allocation with stock picking. Make reasoned choices and stick with them. Do not try to time the market; pros have been trying to for decades and failing. Frequent trading jacks up commissions, ruins your returns, and accomplishes little else.

Equity mutual funds

After diligently trying to assemble a diversified portfolio with individual stocks, you may say, "the hell with it," and do what millions of other investors have done—buy a mutual fund. In theory, most professional fund managers should be able to at least beat the overall market. But according to the Schwab Center for Investment Research, during the 10-year period that ended in 2000, fewer than one-third of United States large-cap funds consistently outperformed the S&P 500. Still, mutual funds offer an efficient, low-cost way of diversifying your portfolio and, in some cases, improving your returns. They simplify record-keeping and cut down on the amount of stocks you have to follow. Check out a fund rating service, like Morningstar.com or Barron's, to decipher which funds are worth holding.

There are two devilish aspects to mutual funds that can chew up perfectly respectable returns. Load is a sales commission, generally from 3 percent to 8 percent, on a mutual fund that goes to the brokerage firm that sold it. It is paid up front by the buyer. What do you get in return? Nothing. In fact, according to Morningstar, load funds significantly underperform no-load funds on average. With thousands of no-load funds to choose from, if you buy a load fund you must really love your broker.

Management fees, however, are not optional. They are charged by every fund to cover the high salaries paid to portfolio managers for trying to beat the S&P 500 each year. You would expect that really hot funds charge more and poor performers charge less, but it isn't necessarily so. Just like load charges, management fees reduce your returns. If you are indifferent between two funds, take the one with lower fees, which are disclosed in the prospectus.

If you would rather bet on the whole market, there are dozens of index funds to choose from. But why pay management fees to an index fund? Instead, bypass mutual funds altogether and purchase SPYders, the American Stock Exchange's units of the S&P 500. They trade just like stock, are liquid as water, and can be purchased in small increments.

Now that you have diversified your equity holdings, here's the bad news: Even if you construct a perfectly diversified equity portfolio, you will still bear systematic risk—the risk the stock market will tank. In order to diversify market risk, you have to buy bonds.

Bonds

Like gin and tonic, stocks and bonds mix well together. Fundamental finance theory says if you can borrow money more cheaply than the expected return on stocks, you will do so and put the proceeds into stocks. The reality is not so neat. When interest rates are falling, investors furiously sell bonds and buy stocks, inevitably bidding up stock prices to unsustainable levels and depressing bonds. Investors sober up, bonds begin to look attractive relative to stocks, and the cycle reverses. This absurdly reliable pattern makes bonds an ideal diversification tool. In fact, empirical data by Schwab shows that by adding bonds to your portfolio, you reduce overall volatility but give up little in total returns.

Bond prices always move in the opposite direction of interest rates. If rates increase, bonds you own will decline in value. So in a low-interest rate environment, should you own bonds if rates may go up? The simple answer is yes, because (A) you cannot predict interest rate moves—even if you study Alan Greenspan's Delphic utterances like a Talmudic scholar; (B) to a certain extent, the price already reflects the market's perception of future interest rates; and (C) perhaps most importantly, the yield (coupon) is your hedge against price volatility.

If you hold a bond to maturity and the issuer does not default, you receive the return printed on the bond. It is only when you sell before maturity that you have to worry about what interest rates do. This brings up another maxim: The longer term the bond, the more the price volatility and the higher the yield (and vice-versa). If you think you might sell your bonds soon, buy short-term maturities. You will suffer a little in yield, but sleep better if interest rates go haywire.

Like equities, bonds come in lots of flavors: long-term, short-term, municipal, junk, government, etc. Each issuer is assigned a rating by one of the major rating agencies (S&P, Moody's and Fitch) based upon a complicated set of financial data and qualitative interpretations by underpaid, overworked wonks. Very few issuers are AAA-rated by S&P; those that are the next best thing to holding Treasuries. Single- and double-A-rated companies should be considered safe, although who knows what could happen 10 years from now (look at once-proud AT&T). By comparing yields on bonds with the same rating, you can spot values. Careful, though. While rating agencies sometimes get it wrong, the market seldom does. Cheap bonds are usually cheap for a reason. Here is an overview of the three main types of bonds.

- **Guvvies.** Government bonds are safest, and their low yields reflect it. Treasury bonds and notes have maturities ranging from 10 to 30 years, in minimum denominations of $1,000. You can buy them direct at *www.publicdebt.treas.gov* or through a mutual fund. If you want the security of Treasuries but are paranoid about inflation eating up your returns, Treasury inflation-protected securities (TIPs) continually adjust both interest and principal for inflation.

- **Munies.** Because most municipal bonds are exempt from federal and state income taxes, they are one of the best legal tax shelters around. High-quality munies are very safe and also carry low yields. Lower-quality munies issued by thousands of taxing entities have a wide range of risk and yields. Avoid stuff you have never heard of. (Who wants to get stuck holding paper for the Pewaukee Municipal Airport authority?)

- **Corporates.** Corporate bonds are divided into investment-grade and high-yield, or "junk" bonds. Unless you have an appetite for risk, avoid junk bonds (rated by S&P "BB" or lower). While some may be issued by strong companies with good fundamentals that got the shaft from the rating agency, it's just as probable they are junky companies. When it comes to bonds, stick with large, liquid issuers; illiquid bonds issued by small companies usually trade at a discount. Better yet, buy a corporate bond fund, which, besides offering better liquidity, will give you better diversification of default risk.

Cash

In the quest for higher returns, do not overlook plain old savings. America's pathetically low savings rate (2 percent of disposable income) means little cushion when the market turns sour. Most checking and brokerage accounts offer daily sweeps of unused cash into interest-earning investments. The trouble is that the typical investment vehicle is a money-market mutual fund with very low returns. Better than putting it in your mattress, but not a very sound retirement plan.

While one-year CDs are a terrible deal right now, earning less than the rate of inflation, longer-term CDs offer better, if still feeble, yields. If you think you will need the money in the next year, leave it in a money-market account. But if you won't need it for several years, divide your cash into CDs with different maturities, say three, four, and five years. Thus, if rates rise, your rollovers will capture some of the benefit, yet if they fall, you won't bear total refinancing risk. Shop around; some of the best deals are at banks you never heard of. *The New York Times* business section and the *Wall Street Journal* list banks offering attractive CD yields.

Dividing the pie

Your age, employment status, and tolerance for risk are the three factors that drive where you put your hard-earned dinero. The longer you have until retirement and the greater your appetite for risk, the more heavily invested in stocks you should be. There may be a dozen boom-bust cycles in your lifetime, but trying to figure out where you are in one is folly, and the only way to guarantee catching the updrifts is to be invested.

As a rule of thumb, if you are under 40, your portfolio should consist of 70 percent stocks, 25 percent bonds, and 5 percent cash. (Caution: Just because you have a lot of time is no reason to sink all your money into the latest investment fad. Remember, pigs get fat, and hogs get slaughtered!)

When you reach middle age (sigh), your portfolio should be about 60 percent stocks, 35 percent bonds, and 5 percent cash. As you near retirement, investments should gradually swing towards fixed-income securities, with 50 percent stocks, 40 percent bonds (with a mix of short, medium, and long maturities), and 10 percent cash.

Once you stop working, you need to make sure your investments and pension income provide enough for you to live on without selling assets, especially in the event of major illness. The preponderance of your investments should be in bonds and cash. But don't dump all your stocks right away. You still have a few years (maybe more than you think—see "How to live to 100"). Instead, move towards higher-quality common and preferred equities that pay dividends. To really fine-tune your asset mix, click on the asset allocation tools at *www.finportfolio.com* or at Fidelity's *www.401k.com*.

On other thing: You may be wise to ignore your stockbroker's advice on asset allocation. Merrill Lynch & Co.'s chief U.S. strategist, Richard Bernstein, has found Wall Street's average equity allocation is valuable only as a contrary indicator. When the consensus of Wall Street investment gurus is to put 61 percent or more in stocks, a bear market is coming; less than 50 percent in stocks means it's time to buy. For what it's worth, at last check, the consensus was 68 percent stocks.

No matter what your mix of stocks, bonds, and cash you have, you will benefit by holding your portfolio in a company-sponsored 401(k), or a self-employment retirement account (Keogh or Roth). A 1996 study published in the *Financial Analysts Journal* found that, because of the significant tax advantages, an investor using an IRA could expect to earn 2.5 percentage points more return at retirement than one who used a standard brokerage account. This advantage was even more pronounced for investors whose tax rate was lower at retirement.

The 401(k) is a no-brainer. Put in the maximum contribution (now $3,000) and take full advantage of company matches. Likewise, if you qualify for a Keogh or Roth, put in the maximum contribution each year. One caution about 401(k) accounts: If you borrow from your 401(k), you have to pay tax on the withdrawal (20 percent) as well as a penalty tax of 10 percent. If you are young and have few liquid assets outside your retirement account, set up a separate rainy-day account to cover short-term emergencies so you won't have to borrow.

Be careful of employee stock purchase plans. As the Enron Corporation. collapse demonstrated, loading up on your own company's stock is not always such a good idea. Just because you work there does not mean the stock will go up. Furthermore, holding a big chunk of company stock increases your overall risk tremendously because your livelihood is already tied to the company. For every Microsoft, where secretaries retire as millionaires, there are hundreds of companies that earn mediocre returns, and a few that go bankrupt.

It merits mentioning gold here, in case someone thinks we overlooked precious metals as an investment category. Gold (like silver and other precious metals) has traditionally been viewed as a hedge against inflation, presumably because paper money can be devalued, but a Kruggerand is still a Kruggerand. A workable theory, perhaps, but it hasn't held water since Jimmy Carter left office. Gold's chief sponsors are known as "Gold Bugs," an odd mix of government conspiracy theorists, doomsayers, survivalists, and other kooks. Gold Bugs believe the end of the world is nigh, hyperinflation will lead to worldwide panic, then...Ta-da!...gold will replace the dollar as the world's favorite currency. Since gold's last rally in 1983, the Bugs have spent most of their time explaining why gold's ascension is just around the corner. It's a lonely job, but somebody has to do it.

Just for the record, $1,000 invested in the S&P 500 in 1980 would now be worth $17,498. The same $1,000 invested in gold would be worth $689. Remember, when it comes to investing, being early is the same thing as being wrong.

Additional Resources

How to travel to space

As of this writing, there is just one firm offering trips to space: Space Adventures, Arlington, Virginia., (888) 85-SPACE, *www.space adventures.com*. If you lack 100 Gs but are dying to send your ashes into space, contact Celestis Inc., Houston, Texas, (713) 522-7282, *www.celestis.com*. To keep up with the latest developments in consumer space travel, see the Website *www.spacefuture.com*.

How to join Mensa

To take the pre-test, register to be tested by Mensa, or to submit a standardized intelligence test, contact American Mensa at 1229 Corporate Drive West, Arlington, TX, 76006, (800) 66-MENSA, *www.us.mensa.org*. Additional sample test questions and mind exercises can be found on American Mensa's Website and on the Mensa international Website (*www.mensa.org*). If you are a puzzle or word game freak, check out *Match Wits with Mensa Omnibus* by Marvin Grosswirth, Abbie Salny, and Allan Stillson (Perseus Publishing, 1999).

How to try your own case

Most libraries have a reference section dedicated to do-it-yourself lawsuits, divorces, etc. A great book to start with in your quest to personally see justice done is *Represent Yourself in Court* by Paul Bergman and Sara Berman-Barrett (Nolo Press, 2001). If you are looking for a legal coach and can't find one, consider joining the Legal Club of America, at *www.legalclub.com*. The Legal Club lists attorneys who offer discounted attorney services to club members, all of whom must be rated "BV" or higher in the Martindale-Hubbell directory.

How to decode Wall Street

The easiest way to learn more about what equity research analysts are saying (or *not* saying) is to read the *Wall Street Journal* and *Barron's*. Analysts' prevarications are a hot topic right now and will continue to be until crusading officials decide they have bigger fish to fry. The *Journal* publishes an annual ranking of estimate accuracy that is of some value in evaluating analysts, although the annual "All-American" list in the October edition of *Institutional Investor* is the Michelin Guide of research.

How to hire a contractor

Sadly, we have found few books on hiring a contractor that are worth the money, because most go on *ad nauseum* about esoteric construction issues. One book we can recommend is *How to Hire a Home Improvement Contractor Without Getting Chiseled* by Tom Philbin (St. Martin's Griffin, 1996). If you are unable to find a reputable contractor, contact the National Association of the Remodeling Industry, a not-for-profit trade association, at 780 Lee Street, Suite 200, Des Plaines, IL., 60016, (800) 611-6274, *www.nari.org*. If you have doubts about a contractor, phone your local Better Business Bureau office.

How to get rid of the budget surplus

The late Senator William Proxmire (D-Wisconsin) got many yucks out his famous "Golden Fleece" awards that went to the most egregious wastes of taxpayer money from 1975 to 1988. "My own favorite was the study to find out whether sunfish that drink tequila are more aggressive than sunfish who drink gin," Senator Proxmire reportedly told *The Atlanta Journal and Constitution* in 1985. Happily, the Fleece was revived by Taxpayers for Common Sense in 2000 and may be viewed at *www.taxpayer.net*, along with Proxmire's oldies-but-goodies.

How to take the cure

We have not found an adequate reference book for European spas, though most European spas have Websites in English. If you can find a copy, Alev Lytle Croutier's *Taking the Waters: Spirit, Art, Sensuality* (Abbeville Press, 1992) is interesting. You can also pick up the advertising-laden *Spa Finder* magazine at your local newsstand.

How to get a good night's sleep

For general information about how to nod off (and why you *should*), go to the National Sleep Foundation's Website, *www.sleepfoundation.org*. The latest in sleep disorder research can be found at the National Institutes Health National Center on Sleep Disorders Research, at *www.nhlbi.nih.gov/about/ncsdr/*. You can contact the NCSDR at (301) 435-0199, or write them at Two Rockledge Centre, Suite 10038, 6701. Rockledge Drive MSC 7920, Bethesda, MD 20892-7920. If you are looking for a sleep clinic, contact the American Academy of Sleep Medicine at One Westchester Corporate Center, Suite 920, Westchester, IL, (708) 492-0930, *www.aasmnet.org*.

How to become a movie star

Extras are made, not born. If you want to be in a movie, it's essential to get into as many extras casting databases as possible. Central Casting, 220 South Flower Street, Burbank, CA., 91502, (818) 562-2755, *www.ep-services.com*, is the biggest extras casting agency in the world; its sister organization, Cenex (same address and telephone number), handles nonunion extras. And you can sign up at the Websites *moviex.com*, *moviextras.com*, *actioncasting.com,* and *extrascasting.com*, among others. Casting firms usually have open calls at certain times during the week when acting hopefuls are invited to come in and register in person. Also, keep an eye out for ads in your local newspaper announcing casting calls in your area.

How to get your hair back

The best resource for information about all types of hair treatments, including fake hair, is the Website *www.regrowth.com*. It does a particularly good job covering emerging treatments and tracking them even before clinical experiments are underway. Another resource to try, especially if you are considering replacement surgery, is the American Hair Loss Council, *www.ahlc.org*.

How to buy a used car

Before you buy a lemon, check it out at one of the vehicle history Websites, *www.carfax.com* or *www.autocheck.com*. Car values can be found in Kelley's *Consumer Edition Blue Book* ($9.95 retail), available in most bookstores or on its website, *www.kbb.com*.

How to get a patent

An overview of patents and the patenting process can be found in *Nolo's Patents for Beginners* by David Pressman and Richard Stim (Nolo Press, 2000). There are lots of good Websites for patent information, like *www.patentcafe.com*. For invention promoter scam information, see *www.inventorfraud.com*, the website of the National Inventor Fraud Center. For the patent process, filing requirements and doing online patent research, see the U.S. Patent & Trademark Office Website, *www.uspto.gov*.

How to become a day trader

The books *How to Get Started in Electronic Day Trading* by David S. Nassar, and *Electronic Day Traders' Secrets* by Marc Friedfertig and George West (both published by McGraw-Hill in 1999), are loaded with useful information, though the strategies they recommend may not prove as productive as they were during the tech stock craze. If you really want to learn to day trade, first take a course from a local day trading firm. On the other hand, if you want to talk yourself out of day trading, see the SEC's special report on day trading at *www.sec.gov/news/studies/daytrading.htm*.

Some large DAT firms are listed below:

- Bright Trading, (800) 249-7488, *www.stocktrading.com*.
- Cybertrader, (888) 76-CYBER, *www.cybertrader.com*.
- Datek Online   , (888) U2-DATEK, *www.datek.com*.
- Momentum Securities, (800) 706-4493,
  www. trademomentum.com.
- MB Trading, (866) 628-3001, *www.mbtrading.com*.
- Sutton Online, (800) 339-2778, *www.suttononline.com*.

How to dodge speeding tickets

The reference materials on avoiding speeding citations are unsurprisingly weak. James M. Eagan's *A Speeder's Guide to Avoiding Tickets* (Avon Books, 1999) has some good driving tips. *Beat the cops* by Alex Carroll (AceCo Publishers, 1998) also contains suggestions for contesting traffic tickets in court. The National Motorists Association Website, *www.speedtrap.org*, contains lists of speedtraps compiled by motorists, an indexed listing of state traffic laws and news stories. The Website *www.radartest.com* offers performance reviews of various models of radar detectors, as well as a discussion of how radar works.

How to photograph an active volcano

Information about Hawaii Volcanoes National Park can be found on the National Park Service's website at *www.nps.gov/havo/*. For the latest information about volcanic eruptions, see *http://hvo.wr.usgs.gov*, maintained by the United States Geological Survey. A good primer on taking pictures from the air is *Aerial Photography: Professional Techniques and Commercial Applications* by Lloyd Harvey (Amphoto, 1990). It's out of print, but used copies may be available at Amazon.com.

How to drive like Richard Petty

Driving classes are held throughout the year. Although some driving schools operate from just one location, the larger schools offer classes at tracks across the country. Here is contact information for selected driving schools:

- BMW High Performance Driving School, (888) 345-4269.
- Bob Bondurant School of High Performance Driving, (800) 842-RACE.
- Fast Track High Performance Driving School, (704) 455-1700.
- Porsche Driving Experience, (888) 204-7474.
- Richard Petty Driving Experience, (800) BE-PETTY.
- Skip Barber Racing School, (800) 221-1131.
- Track Time Driving School, (734) 428-2700.

How to go public

Most IPO books stink. They identify the steps in the process, but fail to capture the sturm und drang of the thing. An inside, if a bit naive, view of what it's like can be found in *Going Public*, the story of tech highflyer MIPS Computer Systems' IPO, by Michael S. Malone (HarperCollins, 1991—out of print). Market conditions and even SEC regs are constantly changing. We suggest contacting a few investment bankers, who will have the most current information and share it with you for no charge. See *www.ipo.com* for news about what deals are getting done.

How to avoid an audit

In the fall of 2002, the IRS kicked off a new round of random audits designed to update its database and improve its Discriminate Information Function. As a result, the tripwires used by the IRS to kick out returns for examination are likely to change somewhat for upcoming tax years. *Kiplinger's Personal Finance Magazine* is an excellent source to keep up with the taxman's tactics. And don't overlook the Beast That Ate Kansas City's Website, which is surprisingly helpful: *www.irs.ustreas.gov*.

How to climb Mount Everest

There is a mountain of information about Mount Everest, much of it found in the memoirs of professional climbers. Among these, we recommend Sir Edmund Hillary's classic *Nothing Venture, Nothing Win* (McCann & Geogheagan, 1975). The bestseller *Into Thin Air* by Jon Krakauer (Villard Books, 1997) is a thrilling first-person account of the 1996 disaster that will give even the most gung-ho climber pause. The Internet is loaded with high-quality Websites on mountain climbing, probably the best of which is *www.mountainzone.com*, which contains video clips, daily dispatches from climbers on the mountain, and a searchable archive of previous expeditions. Considering having a go at the Big "E" yourself? Here is a list of some established Everest guiding organizations based in the United States:

- Adventures International, (800) 247-1263, *www.adventuresintl.com*.
- Alpine Ascents International, (206) 378-1927, *www.alpineascents.com*.
- Earth Treks, (800) CLIMB UP, *www.earthtreksclimbing.com*.
- Mountain-Link Expeditions, (800) 408-8949, *www.mountain-link.com*.
- Mountain Madness, (206) 937-8389, *www.mountainmadness. com*.
- Ultimate Ascents (303) 443-2076, *www.ultimateascents.com*.

How to pack for a business trip

For more advice on traveling light and smart, see *How to Pack*, by Laurel Cardone (Fodor's Travel Publications, 1997). Noise cancellation headphones are available from Bose Corporation, (800) 600-2073 (*www.bose.com*)

How to make great chili

Chili champs usually guard their recipes like plans for a nuclear weapon, though a few have been generously placed in the public domain. Check out the Website of the International Chili Society, *www.chilicookoff*, which contains award-winning recipes, contest information, etc. You may also find *The Magic of the Chilli* (Palmerston & Reed, 2000) by Christine Toney interesting. It contains a history of chili in the Midwest, numerous recipes, competition cooking tips, and answers one of the most burning topics of the day: why "chili" should have two Ls.

How to improve your memory

Before we forget, there are a couple of books we can recommend. *Use It or Lose It!: How to Keep Your Brain Fit as It Ages* (Allen D. Bragdon Publishers, 2000) by Allen D. Bragdon and David Gamon is now available as an e-book at *www.addall.com*. Thomas H. Crook, III and Brenda D. Adderly lay out an interesting, if not airtight, case for taking PS supplements in *The Memory Cure* (Pocket Books, 2000).

How to solve the problem of public schools

Two good places to start if you are considering home schooling are the National Home Education Research Institute, *www.nheri.org*, and the Home School Legal Defense Association, *www.hslda.org*. You will find many books available on home schooling at bookstores and the library.

How to beat the odds in Vegas

If you get serious about card counting, Edward O. Thorp's classic *Beat the Dealer* (Vintage Books, 1966) is a must-read. For more information about the Knock-out System, pick up a copy of *Knock-out Blackjack* by Olaf Vancura and Ken Fuchs (Huntington Press, 1998). If you want to try out a new strategy or have an unnatural attachment to statistics, see the Blackjack Data Repository at *www.bjstats.com*.

How to obtain a title of nobility

It's a good idea to consult with a British peerage attorney before purchasing any title. All reputable title houses will be glad to provide you a list of solicitors who specialize in titles. If you become a Lord or Lady of the Manor, there are about 1,500 other mail-order nobles to hobnob with.

Contact the Manorial Society of Great Britain at 104 Kennington Road, London, U.K., SE11 6RE, or phone 011-44-171-735-6633.

Contact information for purchasing titles:

- Burkes Peerage, 011-44-1-903-506-440, *www.burkestitles.com.*
- Manorial Auctioneers, 011-44-207-735-6633, *www.msgb.co.uk.*
- British Feudal Investments, 011-44-207-419-5011, *www.nobletitles.com.*
- English Titles, 011-44-207-681-2811, *www.english-titles.co.uk.*
- Nobilitat Regalia, P.O. Box 1944, Victoria, BC, Canada V8W 3A8, *www.themarketplacedirect.com/peerageconfirmed.*

How to resurrect a dead philosophy

We highly recommend Tom Wolfe's novel *A Man in Full* (Farrar, Straus, and Giroux, 1998). For a good introduction to Stoic philosophy, we suggest *The Stoic philosophy of Seneca*, Moses Hadas, translator (W.W. Norton, 1968); and Marcus Aurelius's *Meditations*, A.S.L. Farquharson and R.B. Rutherford, translators (Oxford University Press, 1998).

How to cure bad breath

A number of clinics in the United States specialize in malodorous mouths. The ambiguous-sounding Richter Center in Philadelphia, which opened in 1992, claims to be the first dental clinic of its kind (215) 545-8600. Others include:

- The California Breath Clinic: Los Angeles, (310) 556-5600; San Francisco, (800) 973-7374.
- The Bay Area Breath Clinic, Tampa, Florida, (813) 251-1442
- SUNY-Buffalo School of Dental Medicine Breath Disorders Clinic, Buffalo, N.Y., (716) 832-9835.

Peridex and Periogard are brand names for chlorhexidine, which is only available with a doctor's prescription. Chlorine dioxide, sold as CloSYS II, is widely available through mail order and the Internet.

See *www.dental-mart.com*, or call (877) 363-9876.

How to find Blackbeard's treasure

For more reading about Blackbeard's supposed buried treasure, look in your library for *Shipwrecks, Skin Divers, and Sunken Gold* by Dave Horner (Dodd, Mead & Company, 1965—out of print), and W.C. Jameson's *Buried Treasures of the South: Legends of Lost, Buried, and Forgotten Treasures, from Tidewater Virginia to Coastal Carolina to Cajun Louisiana* (August House, 1992). If you are planning a trip to Blackbeard's old stomping grounds, see the Website *www.northcarolina.com/stories/ocracoke.html.*

How to prevent jet lag

For more information about Charles Ehret's customized jet lag prevention program contact StopJetLag Travel Service, 12672 Skyline Boulevard, Woodside, CA 94062, (650) 851-4484, *www.stopjetlag.com*. The nutritional supplement NADH is sold under the brand name ENADAlert, which is available at most health and nutrition stores and directly from the manufacturer, Menuco Corporation, at (800) 636-8261.

How to get elected to the Senate

The best analysis of novices running for higher office we have found is *Actors, Athletes, and Astronauts: Political amateurs in the United States* (University of Chicago Press, 1990) by political scientist David T. Canon. For a close analysis of Senate and House elections see *The Almanac of American Politics* (National Journal Group, 2001) by Michael Barone, which also includes Charlie Cook's handicapping of every Congressional race.

How to get blood from a stone

If you can't get enough of those ads, check out *www.absolutad.org*, which maintains an extensive archive of Absolut advertisements. If you enjoy behind-the-scenes books, read Richard W. Lewis' *Absolut Book: The Absolut Vodka advertising story* (Charles Tuttle Co., 1996).

How to stop solicitors

If you can't stop the junk mail and telephone calls, try writing the major list rental firms and asking to have your name removed from their lists:

- Metromail, List Maintenance, 901 West Bond, Lincoln, NE 68521

- R.L. Polk & Co., List Compilation, 6400 Monroe Boulevard, Taylor, Mich. 48180-1814.
- Database America, Compilation Department, 100 Paragon Drive, Montvale, N.J. 07645-4591.
- Donnelley Marketing, Database Operations, 416 S. Bell Avenue, Ames, Iowa 50010-3502.

Also see the Federal Consumer Information Center, Pueblo, Colo., which has some good information about eliminating cold callers on its Website, at *www.pueblo.gsa.gov*.

How to avoid gridlock

The Texas Transportation Institute's "Urban Mobility Report" ranks metro area congestion in over a dozen different ways. A free copy of the report in PDF form is available from the Institute's Website at *http:// mobility.tamu.edu*.

How to correct your credit report

Check out the Fair, Issac Website (*www.myfico.com*) for tips on improving your FICO score. But if you have really big credit problems, get a copy of *The Complete Guide to Credit Repair* (Adams Media, 2001) by Bill Kelly, Jr. To get a copy of your credit report by mail write to the following addresses.

- Equifax, PO Box 740241, Atlanta, GA 30374-0241.
- Experian, PO Box 949, Allen, TX 75013.
- Trans Union, 760 West Sproul Road, PO Box 390, Springfield, PA 19064

How to ace an interview

There are dozens of interview books available at every decent bookstore. The most helpful interview book we have found is *Jeff Allen's Best Win the Job* (John Wiley & Sons, 1990) by Jeffrey G. Allen. Another decent resource is *The Perfect Interview: How to Get the Job You Really Want* (Amacom, 1991) by John Drake. Recent graduates may also want to take a look at the Website *www.vault.com* for more tips. For sartorial advice, consult John T. Molloy's *New Dress for Success* (Warner, 1987, revised).

How to get admitted to Augusta National

Although they won't help you get in, *The Masters: Golf, Money and Power in Augusta, Georgia* by Curt Sampson (Villard Books, 1998); and *Augusta* by Steve Eubanks (Rutledge Hill Press, 1997) are entertaining looks at the most hallowed fairways in golf and those who created them.

How to avoid being hit by lightning

For more information about lightning safety, go to the National Oceanic and Atmospheric Administration Website *www.lightningsafety.noaa.gov*.

How to travel in style

If you enjoy history, read about the Orient Express's madcap maiden run, its heyday, and the many infamous characters who rode it in the tremendously engaging *Orient Express: The Life and Times of the World's Most Famous Train* by E.H. Cookridge (Harper & Row, 1980). Also see *Luxury Trains from the Orient Express to the TGV* by George Behrend (Vendome Press, 1982).

How to make great grilled chicken

Want more recipes? Pick up the book *Beer-can Chicken: And 74 other offbeat recipes for the grill* by barbecue impresario Steven Raichlen, (Workman, 2002). Warning—some of them are pretty weird.

How to learn to fly fish

For reading at night when you get off the stream, we strongly suggest *The Orvis Fly-Fishing Guide* by Tom Rosenbauer (Lyons & Burford, 1984), and the timeless *Matching the Hatch* by Ernest G. Schwiebert, Jr. (Stoeger Publishing, 1955). For more titles, request a catalog from Abenaki Publishers at (802) 447-1518, or pick up a copy of *American Angler* magazine at the bookstore. Good casting videos include "The Essence of Fly Casting" by Mel Krieger and "The Dynamics of Fly Casting" by Joan Wulff. Visit *www.flyfishingvideos.com* for a vast selection.

How to prevent identity theft

For free information online, download the pamphlet "When bad things happen to your good name" from the federal government's I.D.

theft Website, *www.consumer.gov/idtheft/*. And see *www.privacyrights.org* for tips on privacy protection. To read more about how identity theft is perpetrated and ways to prevent it, pick up *Identity Theft: How to protect your most valuable asset* by Robert J. Hammond, Jr. (Career Press, 2002).

How to watch the Tour de France

To follow the Tour online, see *www.velonews.com* or *http://velocity1.sportsline.com*. For less timely but more in-depth coverage, get a copy of *Cycle Sport* magazine at your local newsstand. For the real deal in French, visit the Tour's official Website at *www.letour.fr* or pick up the French sports daily *L'Equipe*. For a detailed look at the world's greatest bicycle race, read Samuel Abt's *Breakaway: On the road with the Tour de France* (Random House, 1985).

How to avoid jury duty

An interesting analysis of our jury system can be found in *Judging the Jury* by Valerie P. Hans, et al (Perseus Books, 2001).

How to choose a Christmas tree

More than you ever wanted to know about Christmas trees can be found at the National Christmas Tree Association website, *www.realchristmastrees.org*.

How to conduct like Toscanini

If you really get into doing Toscanini impersonations, you may want to check out a conducting book from your local library. We suggest *Basic Techniques of Conducting* by Kenneth H. Phillips, and for more on conducting theory, *The Compleat Conductor* by Gunther Schuller, (both Oxford University Press, 1997).

For an online presentation of basic conducting technique, see the Melbourne Symphony Orchestra's Website at *www.mso.com.au/edu/*.

How to fly a jet fighter without joining the armed services

Contact information for leading American firms offering MiG flights is listed:

- Military Adventures, (678) 907-8265, *www.flymigs.com.*
- Incredible Adventures, (941) 346-2603, *www.incredible-adventures.com.*
- Space Adventures, (888) 85-SPACE, *www.spaceadventures.com.*

How to vex the terminally pleasant

For more of Paul Fussell's irreverent observations, we highly recommend *Class: A guide through the American status system* (Touchstone/Simon & Schuster, 1992).

How to save the Earth

Fascination with asteroids comes and goes in the popular press, though most news stories are superficial. If you want to really understand the threat and what can be done about it, read *Rogue Asteroids and Doomsday Comets: The search for the million megaton menace that threatens life on Earth* by Duncan Steel (Wiley, 1995). For additional reading, see *Cosmic Impact* by John Keith Davies (St. Martin's Press, 1986). There are also many excellent Websites that track asteroids and comets. See NASA's Near-Earth Objects program Website at *http://neo.jpl.nasa.gov* and the Spaceguard Foundation's U.S. homepage at http://*cfa-www.harvard.edu/ ~marsden/SGF/*, which has links to other sites.

How to live to 100

An interesting analysis of 169 centenarians' longevity can be found in *Living to 100* by Thomas T. Perls, M.D. and Margery H. Silver (Basic Books, 1999). A compilation and analysis of the Social Security Administration's interviews of over 1,100 centenarians is contained in *Living to 100* by Osborn Segerberg, Jr. (Charles Scribner's Sons, 1982). *The Longevity Strategy* by David Mahoney and Richard Restak (Wiley, 1998) argues that mental fitness is essential to physical longevity.

How to select a single malt scotch

The bible of single malts is Michael Jackson's (no, not that Michael Jackson) indispensable *Complete Guide to Single Malt Scotch* (Running Press, 1999). It contains every single malt commonly available with helpful tasting notes. For more on the history of scotch, look for *The Whiskies of Scotland* by R.J.S. McDowall (New Amsterdam, revised 1987). To keep up with whisky developments, pick up a copy of *Malt Advocate* magazine at your newsstand. Thirsty for more interesting drams? Join The Scotch Malt Whisky Society, whose members get access to limited bottlings of rare whiskies. Contact the Society at 4604 N. Hiatus Road, Sunrise, FL 33351, (800) 990-1991.

How to run with the bulls

Two Websites are worth reviewing before you go: *www.sanfermin.com* (has video clips of the run) and *www.pamplona.net/engl/tourism/ encierro.html.*

How to become a Scrabble master

For basic Scrabble theory, word lists, and tips, pick up the essential *Everything Scrabble* by Joe Edley and John D. Williams, Jr. (Simon & Schuster, 2001) at your local bookstore. Free downloads of LeXpert word generation software are available online at *www.carolravi.com/ LeXpert/.* If you want to get really good, try to find a copy of Joel Wapnick's *The Champion's Strategy for Winning at Scrabble*, (Stein & Day, 1989—out of print). For an inside look at the world of competitive Scrabble, with enough characters to rival the bar scene in Star Wars, read Stefan Fatsis' *Word Freak* (Houghton Mifflin, 2001). There are numerous Websites with Scrabble tips. See the Electronic Scrabble Club's site: *http://members. ozemail.com.au/~aspa/.*

How to prevent mosquito bites

If you want to learn more about mosquitoes see *www.mosquito.org*, the Website of the American Mosquito Control Association. Repel Permanone may be ordered online from *www.drugstore.com*. Fite Bite is available from Travelrede Travel Outfitters, (888) 535-6052, *www.travelrede.com*. For information about the Great Texas Mosquito Festival in Clute, Texas (55 miles southeast of Houston), phone (800) 371-2971, *www.mosquitofestival.com.*

How to choose a fast food

Fast food menus change rapidly. The most up-to-date nutritional information can be found on the restaurants' Websites: *mcdonalds.com, wendys.com, kfc.com, tacobell.com,* and *burgerking.com* (Cinnabon is apparently too embarrassed to publish nutritional stats). For other chains, see *www.dietriot.com*. The Center for Science in the Public Interest also publishes studies and gives awards to the worst fast foods at *www.cspinet.org*.

How to avoid catching a cold

See *www.commoncold.org*, which is maintained by leading cold experts, Drs. Jack M. Gwaltney and Frederick G. Hayden, at the University of Virginia School of Medicine. For more on the history of medical research into what causes colds, read *In Cold Pursuit* by J. Barnard Gilmore (Stoddart Publishing, 1998).

How to get rid of a fruitcake

The Great Manitou Springs Fruitcake Toss is held the first weekend after New Year's Day. Phone the Manitou Springs Chamber of Commerce at (800) 624-2567, or log onto their Website at *www.manitousprings.org*, for more information.

How to train a basset hound

Every owner of an obstreperous basset will enjoy Diane Morgan's hilarious book, *The Basset Hound Owner's Survival Guide* (Howell/Macmillan, 1998).

How to listen in on the CIA

A good selection of shortwave radios and equipment can be purchased from Universal Radio, Inc., 6830 American Parkway, Reynoldsburg, OH 43068-4113, (800) 431-3939, *www.universal-radio.com*. "The Conet Project," a collection of 150 numbers stations recordings spanning 20 years on four CDs can be ordered by writing to Irdial-Discs, PO Box 424, London SW3 5DY.

How to allocate your assets

Reading the *Wall Street Journal* every day is the best advice we can give to any investor. A highly approachable and witty book about the market is Burton Malkiel's *A Random Walk Down Wall Street* (W.W. Norton, 1999). For some good old-fashioned investing advice, see Benjamin Graham's *The Intelligent Investor* (Harper & Row, 1973) and Warren Buffet's folksy but sage letters to shareholders on the Berkshire-Hathaway Website at *www.berkshirehathaway.com/letters/letters.html*. Some useful financial websites include *www.bloomberg.com*, *http://my.zacks.com*, and *www.morningstar.com*.

Index